In Defense of Home

Random Survival Book 6

Ray Wenck
Glory Days Press
Columbus, Ohio

Ray Wenck

Glory Days Press
Columbus, Ohio

Publisher's Note: This is a work of fiction. Names, characters, places, and incidents are a product of the author's imagination. Locales and public names are sometimes used for atmospheric purposes. Any resemblance to actual people, living or dead, or to businesses, companies, events, institutions, or locales is completely coincidental.

Book Layout © 2016 BookDesignTemplates.com

Random Survival Book 6/ Ray Wenck. -- 1st ed.
ISBN 978-1-7360350-3-0

Dedication

This story is dedicated to all those who, during a pandemic, chose to do the right things for the betterment and safety of those around them. It is also dedicated to those who went that extra distance to spread cheer and love during these difficult times.

Acknowledgments

I am often asked what it is like to write apocalyptic stories in the time of a pandemic, especially since the catastrophic event in the story is also a pandemic. It does bring up interesting correlations. Although the virus in my story was fast-acting and didn't give scientists a chance to react and develop a vaccine, it does have one thing in common. It is changing.

I have stated before that my belief and fear is not that we will succumb to a massive global nuclear event but that we will come up against a virus that morphs faster than we can to keep it in check. We are now seeing variations of the original strain pop up around the world. Though it makes for great suspenseful fiction, the reality is terrifying.

Do I believe this will be the virus that brings us to our knees? No, but it certainly has made us more aware of the possibility. It has also taught us to be more prepared for whatever may come next.

I wish to thank all of those wonderful and dedicated people on the front lines of this war. I pray for your health and your strength.

Book six in the Random Survival series brings to a conclusion the storyline that was introduced in A Journey to Normal. Where it goes from here, well, I don't even know. Thanks for your support.

I'd like to thank Steve Wilhelm for another fine job of the editing and Mibil art for their cover design.

Until next time, read all you want, I'll write more.

Ray Wenck

CHAPTER ONE

Britta watched from the cover of a small copse of trees just off State Route Two as three military trucks passed heading west. They looked like HMMWV M1165 variants that someone had adapted in their garage. Each had a Browning fifty caliber machine gun mounted to the platform. They now possessed two of the same vehicles back at the town. She knew where the vehicles came from and who was on board. The medical facility was sending out a team, but for what purpose and why such a large force. Was there an imminent threat approaching, or were they out hunting for new guinea pigs to experiment on?

She glanced back at her team. The three women each had vantage points and their weapons ready should the need arise. She met Maretha's expressionless eyes. They offered nothing. The other two, Alishia and Mariah, equally as trained but less skilled than Maretha, were as calm.

The light armored trucks moved down the road. She waited for them to be nothing more than dots on the horizon before giving the command to rise. With a head motion, Britta sent Alishia to the point and Mariah to rear guard. Maretha moved next to her matching her steps.

"Thoughts?" Britta asked.

They were a full minute in coming. Britta waited patiently, knowing her friend and most trusted ally was giving the question the time it merited. "It's a larger team than they usually send out for daily patrols. They are heading west.

Although our normal search zone was east, we know there is an encampment of about thirty people a few miles west."

"You think that's their target?'

"I do not know. They have been there for a while now, and the military has never bothered with them before."

"They might have good reason now. They need test subjects for their new vaccine."

Maretha pondered the statement.

They had been on the road for more than an hour since being exiled from the town she had helped build. As much as she tried not to, she harbored resentment over her fate, both toward the council and her friend and co-founder, Iso. She understood it was politics, but the eviction had hurt. Maretha, Alishia, and Mariah had not been included in that verdict. They thought the decision unfair and decided to travel with her rather than stay with people who did not appreciate or support them. Britta argued against their coming but, in truth, was happy for the company.

"Didn't your new male friend say his camp was to the west?"

Britta frowned at the use of 'male friend' but did not comment. Instead, she focused on what Mark had told her about his community. It was large and to the west about seventy miles. They'd traveled perhaps four. Not that they were heading there, even though she'd been invited, or at least that's what she told herself.

But as she walked, she started to fit pieces together. Dr. Ohtanda did not appear to be a person unused to getting her way. She did not want to let Mark and his daughter, Becca, go. Would she send a team out to recapture them? Of course, she would.

Britta swung her gaze toward Maretha. Without a word, the other woman nodded. "Let's hurry to the barricade," Britta said. "If the trucks stopped there, we'll observe and decide what to do. If they passed through—" she didn't have to finish.

"We'll need transport if we are to get there in time to warn them," Maretha said.

They broke into a jog. Fifteen minutes later, the barricade across Route Two became visible. They slowed and veered off the road to approach unobserved. The barrier was made up of cars and trucks and had walls built up on both sides, allowing the people who lived there to walk across the vehicles' tops like they were ramparts. In the center, two vans were being maneuvered back into place, having been moved to allow the military convoy through. They could just make out the form of the rear truck as it continued to head west.

"Guess we know where they're going now," Maretha said.

Though there was no proof and thousands of places they could be going, Britta had a nagging and unshakeable feeling Maretha was right.

They turned and moved north, almost to the Lake Erie shoreline, to avoid contact with the barricade people. Then they resumed a western heading until they were far enough away to return to the road. Once there, Britta sent her team in search of a vehicle that might still contain some of its precious fuel. That task took longer than her patience allowed but was finally resolved when Mariah cried out, "Here. I've got one."

Mariah had the steering column apart by the time they reached her. It was a skill she taught her entire team. Even though the use of vehicles was forbidden because they were noisy and drew too much attention, she wanted everyone to be able to hotwire a car in case of an emergency. A minute later, the engine turned over and they were driving at high speed.

"Careful we don't get too close to the convoy," Britta said.

Maretha rummaged through the glove box. "No map. How do we find an alternate route?"

No one had the answer.

Mariah said, "What about the turnpike?"

"Do you know how to get there?" asked Alishia.

"It's someplace to our left."

Britta said, "Make the turn at the next main road. Hopefully, there's a ramp. Look for signs that say 80. They'll be in blue."

"Do you know where you're going?" Maretha asked.

"Mark said it was about fifteen miles west of the city. The turnpike should go right past it. If the convoy stays on Route Two and we can get to the turnpike, we should arrive well before they do."

Alishia pointed. "There's the sign for 80."

Mariah made the turn. Four miles later, they found the turnpike ramp. Long-abandoned vehicles crowded the road. Many had been gone through by scavengers, leaving the doors open and the path more restricted. Several times Alishia got out and closed doors so they could continue. Each time they did, Britta and Maretha kept their weapons pointed out the windows in case of an ambush.

Progress was much slower than anticipated, but Britta still felt they were ahead of the convoy. As they picked up speed, she sat back and relaxed. Twenty minutes later, they spotted the city's skyline in the distance to the north. They were getting close. "Let me know when you reach fifteen miles past the city," she said to Mariah.

The city came and passed. Two minutes later, the car sputtered and cruised to a stop, out of gas.

CHAPTER TWO

Early the first morning after his return, Mark realized how difficult things had been, both physically and mentally. His muscles ached, his body bruised, and his mind was unwilling to shut down, allowing him the rest he so desperately needed. In the end, he got up from the couch he now slept on, glanced at the closed door of the bedroom he once shared with Lynn and went into the kitchen. He collected the makings for coffee, trying to be as quiet as possible so as not to disturb the other members of the household. He then eased himself out the rear door.

He set the mug, filter, and coffee on the table and walked to the outdoor water pump. They had running water in the house thanks to a windmill they'd constructed several months back, but it made too much noise. The mineral water from the well would work fine.

He added a small amount of wood to the smallest of the three fire pits, set the kindling ablaze, and placed the battered well-used pot on the grill set over the pit. Then Mark sat back on the picnic bench and stared off into the starlit sky.

So much had happened since what he'd learned was a bio-engineered disease had been released to wreak havoc and death across the country. It was still unknown whether the release had been accidental or a purposeful attack. They might never know the entire truth, but at this point, it didn't matter. What did matter was the knowledge obtained from Dr. Ohtanda. The virus was still inside everyone and may be morphing into a new, deadlier strain if that was even possible. The thought was mind-numbing.

He looked around at the dark shapes and envisioned all they had accomplished. What did it all matter if they were all going to die again anyway? His memories roamed, first landing on the horrible doctor who had a hand in creating such a deadly and efficient killer. He should have killed her when he had the chance. Blood boiling, he felt his breathing change and worked to relax. To do that, he changed to different memories, but they were all so intertwined. It was difficult to find one that didn't make him angry.

His daughter, Becca, had been used as a lab rat and had been injected with the virus by Ohtanda. It had been a trial to test her new serum, with no guarantees of success, but so far, she'd been unaffected. She could have died. The thought stuck in his throat. It took a moment to swallow the lump. He glanced impatiently at the coffee pot.

Mark turned his head searching for something more positive to focus on, landing on the new brick constructions at the end of the long row of picnic tables. Caleb, Lynn's creative and hard-working son, had come up with the idea of building brick ovens for baking. He had two of them built, each with two levels inside, allowing a lot of bread baked at once. He'd been gone so long it looked like both were now completed.

So far, they'd been lucky finding food items in houses and stores that hadn't been scooped up by other survivors or had gone bad. Those times were fading fast, and plans had to be made to continue feeding the ever-growing population. Their stores were dwindling more quickly than they were being replenished.

Elijah's group had built three greenhouses and planted a variety of vegetables and herbs, but most wouldn't be ready for months if they grew at all. It was mid-October now, and the air was beginning to chill. Mark had to make sure each of the buildings could be heated in some way or they'd freeze to death.

That thought increased the stress he already felt. His brain needed a break. He leaned forward to grab the coffee pot, stopping inches from contact. He had nothing to hold the hot pot handle with. Annoyed at his lack of foresight, he rose and crept back into the house, returning with a potholder. He snatched up the pot and set it on the table. The heat was already bleeding through the thin material. He placed coffee into a filter, held it over the cup, and dribbled steaming water over the top. Not the most efficient way of making coffee, but he hadn't been sure how much he would drink.

He set the sodden filter down and embraced the mug. The heat absorbed into his hands and made him more aware of the chill in the air. A quick shiver passed through him as he sat back and blew across the rim.

Another new addition was the massive structure Elijah's people were erecting on the corner lot across the street. It was a large open floor plan with a surrounding upper balcony that could sleep at least forty people. When Mark left to find help for Becca, the building was in the final planning stage. Since then, a foundation had been poured, and the four framed walls had been lifted. They were moving fast, but with the threat of winter on the horizon, they had the incentive to get it done.

They were fortunate to have a member of the community who had experience mixing and pouring cement. They were lucky to be able to draw on the knowledge of so many different professionals. That was one of the great things about this community: everyone was willing to help. When you had all day and so many helping hands, a lot could get accomplished. He'd have to step in and help today. It would feel good to do something less aggressive for a change.

He stared off into the darkness. He was startled awake.

"Have you been out here all night?"

The sun was on the horizon. The coffee was cold, but at least it hadn't spilled. He looked around, still in sleep-induced confusion. Caryn set an armful of cooking utensils on the table. The tall, attractive woman had taken on the duties of head cook and did a marvelous job keeping everyone fed and using every scrap of food.

"Oh, uh, hi," he said. "Guess I have been."

"Weren't you cold?"

"If I was, it didn't prevent me from falling asleep."

She went about getting her cooking stations prepared. "You all right?"

"Yeah. Yeah. I'm fine. Just had trouble sleeping. Guess I needed to be in the fresh air. Last thing I remember, I was sipping a hot mug of coffee. Then," he shrugged.

"Sorry I woke you. I'm just not used to anyone beating me out here in the morning."

"No problem. It'll take me a day or two to get back in a routine." He stood and stretched. "What can I do to help?"

Caryn said, "Can you start a fire in the two brick ovens?"

"Sure."

"Thanks."

He gathered wood from the pile and placed them inside the firebox. Doors opened behind him and two teenage girls, Rachel and Alyssa, came out carrying various food items. Right behind them was Lynn. She didn't notice him at first, giving him the chance to absorb her presence and warm his heart.

She reached the bottom of the steps wearing a smile that beamed. "Good morning, Caryn."

"Good morning, everyone," Caryn said.

Then Lynn saw him. The smile faded, and her step faltered. Just for a second, but it was there and he noticed. She forced a smile to return and greeted him. "Morning, Mark."

He smiled, "Morning, Lynn."

She set the items she carried on the table and went to where Caryn was tending the fire. Mark watched her with an ever-sinking heart, then noise across the street drew his attention. Elijah's camp was stirring. It gave him his escape from the awkwardness. Without a word, he headed across the street.

As bodies crept from their tents or makeshift abodes, Mark examined the new building. It was good work. Not that he was an expert, but he could see it was well put together. He squatted and drew his hand across the freshly poured cement. It was dry and hard. Then, an idea struck and he stood, scanning the grounds. He spied one of the men he knew had a hand in the construction and approached. "Hey, Bill."

"Oh, good morning, Mark."

"You did good work here."

"Thanks. Can I count on you for some help today? We've got a lot to do if we're going to get it buttoned up before the bad weather hits."

"You bet. I'll be here. Hey, where can I find Milo?"

Bill chuckled. "Milo tends to sleep in. Give him about a half-hour. He'll be along."

Mark smiled. "Sure. I'll go grab some coffee and join you later."

He turned and walked back to the house. He poured coffee and helped set the table. A steady flow of people arrived over the next twenty minutes as the meal was cooked and plated.

At the breakfast table, he enjoyed warm biscuits, eggs, and fried potatoes. He had a conversation with Lincoln and got caught up on what was going on with the community. He tried to avoid glancing down the rows of tables at Lynn, who sat at the far end, but that was a losing battle. He missed her. Wished things were different but resigned himself to the fact they were over.

The group that ate each meal together daily had grown to over forty. Add Elijah's group of nearly thirty, plus the offsite members, and their community was close to a hundred members. A lot had changed in the few months since the disease ravaged humanity. Those early days they had eight people staying at the house. Now they were out of room. Hence, the reason for the expanded structure being built across the street. But even that only had room for perhaps ten additional people over what they already had. True, the Viking-style open lodge might be adjusted to fit in others, but no one wanted to be crowded.

Depending on how well this first one went up, Mark wondered about finding another suitable building lot. The land diagonally across from the farmhouse would work but had a lot of trees that needed clearing before that was feasible. Still, it was a thought. If not now, in the spring.

"Hey, Mark."

He was snapped from his thoughts by a large man with a bald head and a permanent smile.

"I heard you were looking for me."

"Hi, Milo. Yes, I was, but you didn't have to come over. I'd have found you."

"No problem."

"You want something to eat or some coffee?"

"No, I just had a bite. I'm not much of a morning person. Whatcha need?"

"It'd be better if I showed you."

"Okay. Lead on."

Mark stood, drained the last drops of his coffee, and walked toward the barn. Milo stepped in beside him. "Not that I want to create extra work for anyone . . ."

"Let me guess. You want something built."

Mark laughed. "Yeah. Sorry."

Milo laughed. "That's the problem with being good at what you do. Everyone wants you."

"Job security."

"Yeah, right."

He opened the door on the barn and stepped inside, leaving the door open for the sunlight. By necessity, the barn had been converted into a medical facility. Over the past few months, they'd had a tremendous need for it, but in the end, it was still a barn and needed updates to be more efficient and germ-free.

"You've seen our medical facility, right?"

"Yeah, but I've never been in here." He stepped back and knocked on the wooden door.

"Doc does a great job. She's saved many lives here, but despite what we've done to make it work, it still has dirt floors throughout much of it. We've been fortunate so far no one has come down with any serious infections but what I'd like to do is pour concrete floors. We hand-mixed and poured the portion used for operating but never got to the rest. You can see it wasn't such a great job. Is this something that can be done?"

Milo walked around the space, then drew back the curtains that divided the various rooms. "Yeah, it can be done, but you've got people in here. They'll have to be moved, or this area will have to be sectioned off and the cement wheelbarrowed in. It'd be a lot easier if I could back the truck in as far as possible and pour. The spaces will have to be framed, plus we'll need a lot of hands spreading and leveling, but it can be done."

"Great. What time frame are we looking at?"

"As you can see, we still have a lot of work to do across the street. Once we get the outside buttoned up and roofed, I can break away, but that has to be the priority."

"Understood. I'm not trying to undermine that project. When I saw the foundation you poured, the idea came to me. What's the projection on getting the exterior completed?"

"End of the week. Might be sooner, depending on available bodies to get the work done."

"Okay. If you would sketch out how you want it prepared and I can have that ready."

"I can do that. I'll go get my pad and have it for you in about fifteen minutes."

"Thanks, Milo. I appreciate this. I'm sure Doc and her staff will as well."

CHAPTER THREE

"Sir, we're about twenty miles out," Corporal Diaz said.

Captain Ben Childs nodded. They were getting close. "Let me know when we've reached the three-mile mark."

"Yes, Sir."

They were a long way from the protection of the facility and the hundred trained men stationed there. Well, less now—a lot less. Another reason he was glad he was the one assigned for this duty. He was looking forward to some payback for all those killed when this Mark character opened fired on men he'd gotten to know over the past six months.

They'd moved into the facility a month before the outbreak occurred. Childs still wondered about the timing of that move. It had to have been planned, as if someone already knew the pandemic was going to happen. But that meant someone high up the chain of command knew. He'd never asked and knew better not to, but the thought had occurred to him that the virus that killed so many had been deliberately released. But if that were true, and they were sent there in advance of the outbreak, that meant his own country had set the disease loose. Didn't it?

There were rumors, of course, that a foreign government had attacked America. Because of our intelligence operations around the world, we caught wind of the plot and began taking steps to ensure someone survived. It was only speculation, but it was thought their facility was one of a hundred other secret bases set up to find a cure for the disease and combat any foreign invasion or local mobs.

He may never know the entire truth, but at this point, he was thankful to be alive and for the opportunity to serve his country. With this mission, he would be able to wipe out what he saw as a terrorist organization.

"Sir," Private Cash said, "We're at the three-mile mark you requested."

"Thank you, Private." He reached through the opening to the truck's cab and tapped the man in the passenger seat. "Pull over at the first place that offers some security. Get far enough off the road so we're not seen."

"Yes, Sir."

Two minutes later, the convoy of trucks stopped and Childs climbed out. He stretched and examined the surroundings. The driver stopped behind a farm with several outbuildings. Corporal Urban exited and stood next to him.

"Deploy the men, Corporal. Make sure we're secure here."

"Yes, Sir." He left to see to the task.

"Private Cash, give me details."

"Sir, we are two point eight miles from the location. It is in a southwestern direction from here. Using the street grids, if we traveled two miles down the road and turned left on Parish Street, it will take us there."

"I don't want to go straight there. We need to approach unobserved and reconnoiter."

"If we turn left on the street before that, Martha Street, we'll come up behind them. Once there, we can see what the landscape is like and adjust our approach from there."

Childs nodded. "Good man."

A bull of a man walked up. "Sir, I suggest we put men in the house and then deploy guards to the east and west."

"See to it, Sergeant. We'll meet in the house in five to go over the approach."

"Yes, Sir." He pivoted and strode away. Childs watched him go. Sergeant Stanton was old-school Army and had served more than twenty years. He was good and Childs trusted him to get whatever the assigned task done. He was also a stone-cold killer, as people had witnessed on several forays into the surrounding areas of the facility. He was of the shoot first and ask their corpses questions later, mindset. A great man to have on your side in a fight but not one to let off the leash unless necessary. He had to make sure Stanton understood they needed some of these people alive. After that, well, Stanton would enjoy this mission.

Four men kicked open the back door of the two-story wood construction farmhouse and cleared the rooms. A minute later, someone called out, "All clear."

Childs went to the stairs and climbed. At the kitchen door, he stopped and sniffed. Though the air was stale from being closed up, no smell of rot or decay was present. That meant the owners had the good sense to die elsewhere. He entered and walked through the kitchen, stopping at the large wooden table in the formal dining room. He tossed down his gear and pulled out the map. He stretched it out and traced a finger across the plastic-coated paper until he found the streets Cash mentioned. Then he circled a two-mile radius, trying to picture what he might find in that area. Judging from what he spotted around him now, he thought there was a good chance they'd encounter farmland. That could be good and bad—the fewer houses around, the less chance of being ambushed or spotted.

Stanton entered with Cash. "I want to send a patrol out moving up this road and coming at the location the tracker shows from behind."

"What size patrol?" Stanton asked.

"Use four men. Once they get close, have them split up and reconnoiter from different directions. They are not to engage. We do not want them to know we are here."

"What if they're spotted?" Stanton asked.

"They are to rabbit. No engagement. Understood."

Stanton's lip twitched, showing his displeasure, but he said, "Yes, Sir."

To Cash, Childs said, "Any change in the location?"

"No, Sir. Holding steady."

Childs didn't care much for Ohtanda, but she was brilliant. Seeing she could lose control of her star patient, she planted a tracking device under the woman's skin.

"Go with the sergeant and show the patrol what you see."

"You want to go with them?"

"No. I want you to do what I just ordered." His tone was sharper than usual, but they were on a mission—an important mission, and he would not have them questioning his orders.

"Yes, Sir." They left.

He walked to the front room and gazed out the frilly window covering the view of the front yard. It had once been a nice house on a productive piece of property. He wondered if anyone would ever call this home again. All things change.

He climbed the stairs to the second floor, found the master bedroom and dropped onto the bed. He wasn't tired, but this position enabled him to use the ceiling to play out how he envisioned the assault would take place. He ran the simulation over a few times before reaching what he considered the best outcome. He smiled. He hoped they put up some form of resistance, or at least made the assault interesting. Judging from the damage these farmers had done while at the facility, he thought they might be capable of entertaining the men for a few minutes at least.

It had been months since their last battle and that had been a rag-tag group of men who thought of themselves as a militia. They had barely been a challenge for his troops. This was going to be fun.

CHAPTER FOUR

Britta had a bad feeling. Since they'd been forced to walk, her imagination had gone crazy. Each subsequent outcome took on a deadlier, more hopeless scenario than the previous version. She saw Mark dying in numerous ways, each more gruesome than the last. It caused her pace to increase to almost a jog.

"Chieftess," Maretha said, "I'm not sure what images are running wild through your head, but if we keep up this pace we'll be of no use to anyone when we arrive. Not to mention we are not taking our usual care when entering a new, unexplored area. You don't want to lead us into an ambush."

Britta had been so lost in her dire thoughts she was unaware of anything surrounding her. She felt the color drain from her face, recognizing the mistake that could prove fatal. She slowed and glanced around.

They were still on the turnpike, perhaps five miles past the city border. She had no idea where they were going. She only had Mark's vague directions to go by. If her accounting of the distance traveled was accurate, they still had about five miles to go. By now, the convoy had long ago passed them, but the nagging question still pestered her. How did they know where to go? It's not like Mark would've told them. They did have Becca, however, and she was drugged. She might have given up the location without realizing it. From what she'd seen of the woman's capabilities, she doubted any amount of torture would've resulted in the directions. But if drugged, who knew what she revealed.

Their pace slowed. They moved in a diamond formation with ten yards separating each side with Mariah on point. Maretha had closed her position to speak with Britta. "I have the nagging feeling we are already too late," Britta said in a low voice.

"Then there's nothing we can do for them. No sense getting us caught or killed because we rushed into a situation unprepared."

"You're right. Thank you for getting me under control."

"You are reacting with emotion rather than acting with sense. This is unlike you. Has this man dug his claws into you so deep you no longer think rationally?"

"God, I hope not."

"Well, if you don't know, I doubt God does," Maretha said. "What do you expect from this reunion? That you are going to fall madly in love and live happily ever after?"

Britta glanced at her friend. "Happily ever after no longer exists, if it ever did. I recognize I'm being driven by some inexplicable force, but I am not so over the moon as to not recognize the danger. Thank you for pointing out my flaws. I'm back now."

Maretha eyed her, then nodded. "Very well. Do you have a plan for when we arrive?"

"That will depend on the situation. We'll scope it out. If we're needed, we'll adopt a plan based on what we see."

"And, if we're not needed?"

"I've been giving that some thought. I think we stay hidden. If we arrive before the convoy, we don't want to be caught inside their compound. We can get word to them of possible trouble, but it will be best if we are outside the attack zone. We can decide what to do then."

"Wouldn't we attack?"

"I'm not making that decision for everyone. Each person has to decide for themselves."

"Forgive my saying so, but that is a mistake. We follow you because you are our leader. Lead."

"That's not right. I don't want to place everyone in danger because I want to help these people. It should be a group decision. I am no longer your chieftess. I'm just a part of the group."

Maretha harumphed and moved back to her position.

Minutes later, a pickup truck barreled toward them. From a distance, it was difficult to see how many were in the truck, but Britta guessed three. "Seek cover," she called, but her team was already moving.

Britta raced for the cover of an abandoned car. The driver's door was open. The interior had been ransacked. She knelt at the rear of the vehicle and aimed her rifle over the trunk. The truck came fast. Too fast. If the people in the truck had seen them, would they be coming so fast? If this was an assault, they were making it easy for her team to fight it off. She couldn't take a chance on her team's safety. She'd let them close another few seconds, but if nothing changed, she'd be forced to give the order to fire.

Her team was too well-trained to fire on their own unless they had no choice, but Maretha eyed her, a strained question displayed on her dark, sweaty face. Britta shook her head and motioned to stay down. Mariah and Alishia looked in her direction. Mariah, being the first point of contact, appeared nervous.

Britta glanced over the trunk. The truck was not slowing down. If anything, it sped up. It reached the forty-yard mark. If the decision was to be made, it should be now. Still, she waited. Twenty yards. Her finger added pressure to the trigger. They blew past Mariah with no gunfire. The truck whizzed past her spot. One of the men in the back shouted something and pointed behind them. She couldn't make out the warning but glanced back. Nothing was there.

After it passed and was down the road, Maretha ran to her side. "How did you know?"

"By the speed."

"The speed? Did it occur to you they were just going to ram us?"

She shrugged.

"Oh, dear God."

"They weren't going to ram us and leave their vehicle incapacitated."

Maretha leaned against the car and shook her head.

"It was obvious they knew we were here. Did you hear what the guy in the back said?"

"Yeah. Run."

Britta looked at her. "Run?"

"Ah, Chieftess," Mariah called.

They turned their heads and both women's jaws fell open. Mariah pointed down the road at a long convoy of vehicles. Four over-sized pickup trucks led the procession. Each had a mounted weapon of some sort that reminded her of the technicals so popular in the middle east where she'd been deployed. Behind them was a semi. After that was a military deuce and a half-troop carrier with a brown canvas top. They were followed by two HMMWMs with mounted guns like the ones they were chasing. Another troop carrier and four more armed pickups brought up the rear.

They turned to each other and said at the same time, "Run."

The four sprinted off the road to the right. The convoy traveled on the left of the divided highway. They climbed the barrier and dashed up a slope to where a wire fence had been erected. Behind them, they heard an engine race. They scampered over the fence as the mounted machine gun opened fire on them. Bullets tore at the ground to their left. They cleared the fence and dove to the elevated flat ground above the roadway as the gunner got on target.

They heard shouting and excited voices. Maretha lifted her head for a glance. "Four men, giving pursuit."

"You two crawl away and make for those trees." Without a word, Mariah and Alishia moved. To Maretha, she said, "The gunner will have us zeroed in. Move a few yards to your right and come up firing. At the very least, we have to slow them down."

Maretha did and Britta went left. The gunner could not track them both. Maretha was up and firing before Britta by two shots. Britta rose with the rifle already up. She acquired a target, a man halfway up the slope, and planted two shots in his chest. He pitched back and rolled down the hill. The machine gun barked in Maretha's direction after she shot her first man.

The remaining two knelt to return fire. The machine gun kept Maretha pinned down, so Britta targeted the gunner and fired. The first shot ricocheted off the protective metal to the sides of the barrel. The second swung the man around but did not put him down.

Bullets ripped through the air around her. No longer pinned down, Maretha aimed at the man targeting Britta and placed a round through the side of his head. Britta returned the favor and took out the man in front of Maretha. As he rolled down the hill, they rose in a crouch and ran. Britta gave a quick look down the road at the sound of revving engines. The next two trucks in line increased speed. The troop carrier vomited six men from the rear under the canvas. All were armed and wore desert-style camos. As soon as they hit the ground, they were in full sprint.

Britta and Maretha ran hard as the remaining machine guns opened fire. They dodged and ducked until they reached the trees. They ran without slowing. Mariah and Alishia fired several times to slow the pursuers, then turned and joined them.

They had no idea where they were going or any plan other than run. They were all in good shape, but if the men following them were military like they appeared to be, they'd have to do something other than run.

CHAPTER FIVE

Britta tried to form a plan as she ran, but without knowing the land or what lay ahead, it was hard to do. They had cover for the moment, but the trees wouldn't last forever. Even as she thought that she could see light ahead. The trees were ending.

A long brown sea of what might have been wheat at some point before nature recaptured the land stretched before them. Beyond were an old farmhouse and several outbuildings. They'd never reach the house before the men broke from the trees. They'd be easy targets.

She slowed to allow Mariah and Alishia to catch up, and then they continued toward the house ahead. "When you hear gunshots drop into the field and keep low." She veered to the right. Maretha followed.

"What's the plan?"

"We'll set up an ambush from the side. Once the men come out and see Mariah and Alishia, they'll follow. We'll take them from here."

"So, you're using them as bait."

Britta blanched at the word. That hadn't been her intent, but in essence, it was just that. "Guess we better not miss then."

"Two against six. No problem."

They went about thirty yards, then ducked. Maretha changed out her magazine and Britta followed suit. Keeping low, they moved another ten yards before separating. The field went perhaps another quarter mile behind them, then wound around a small copse of trees. It was a large farm. If things went wrong, they'd have to make for those trees, but it was a long way to go with bullets chasing you.

She knelt on one knee and peered through the waving wheat and weed combination. She had a clear line of sight on the tree line. She lifted her rifle, targeted one of the trees, and waited. Seconds later, she caught movement. They did not burst from the trees at a full run as she hoped. They appeared too well trained for that. Instead, one man signaled to the others, and the line spread out. One man, an M16 to his eyes, scanned left, while another scanned right. The other four emerged in a staggered formation.

She watched through her scope. One of the men pointed in the distance. Britta didn't look but knew they'd spotted Mariah, and Alishia. Instead of giving pursuit, the man giving commands said something, and two of the men took aim. *Oh God, they're snipers.* She couldn't wait, or Mariah and Alishia were dead. But to do so would give away her position to the man scanning for her. She had to take the risk. The lives of her teammates were at stake. She slid her sights to the right, locked on, breathed out, and broke the trigger. The sniper flew sideways and dropped from sight.

Shots erupted from everywhere. The wheat gave no protection from the steady barrage coming toward her. She found a slight rise in the ground and burrowed into it. The shooter on her side fired a steady, one shot at a time stream. She envisioned him moving forward as he fired to lessen the space between them and force her to move so he could pinpoint the shot.

She had nowhere to turn. If she moved or tried to pop up for a shot, she was dead. Her mind raced to search for a solution. The shots kept coming, spaced every two seconds. It came to her then. He was drawing his shots out to conserve ammo and avoid having to change out magazines. How many shots had he fired? A bullet tore through the wheat a foot from her. The next one was four feet to her right. He hadn't locked her location down yet.

She angled the rifle upward from her prone position and focused her efforts on listening for the magazine exchange. When it came, she would have seconds to find, target, and shoot him. Her muscles tensed, ready to spring. Then doubt crept in. What if there were two of them?

She couldn't think that. Regardless, she'd be dead. This was her best, her only option.

The click came, and she rose on the slap of the new magazine. She heard it seat, heard the bolt drawing back. She saw him twenty feet to her left, just as he saw her. They swung their weapons on target. A true race to the death. Triggers were pulled, and fire exploded in her arm, but her shot was already away. She spun and went down, unsure of her shot's result.

She fought the pain, rolled to her left, and pulled her sidearm free. As she came to her knee, sighting down the barrel, she saw she was alone. Had he ducked, or did she put him down? Another man was on the move in her direction. He hadn't seen her yet but knew she was there. She fired four times in rapid succession. From the red blooms on his chest, she knew at least two rounds struck home.

His legs worked for two more steps before he disappeared into the field. She looked up. Only three men remained, and they were retreating into the cover of the trees. Gunshots to her right told her Maretha was still alive.

Her arm was on fire. She cradled it to her chest as she moved toward the far edge of the trees. No shots followed her, but she could not rush, or the bending growth would make her location obvious. She reached a point where the ground sloped downward. She lowered herself into the open area. No wheat had been planted there, but thicker brush grew. Below the tree level, Britta was able to stand, though she had to crouch as she worked her way along the tree's eastern edge.

Gunshots continued. If the man in charge was smart, he'd send one of his men to flank Maretha. She had to be in position when that happened. She moved fifteen yards down the tree line before climbing up and entering. Behind a thick tree, she waited and took note of where the bulk of the shooting came from. She did not have a line of sight but had the location pinpointed. She stepped out from behind the tree to advance when she heard something moving fast somewhere in front of her. She ducked and leaned toward the tree. It did not give her cover but might help her to blend in.

She caught sight of a body as it moved through the trees. The path would take him directly in front of her and near both the front and side tree line. He was working his way to Maretha's flank. Maretha was a smart and fierce warrior. She would not stay in one place unless she were unable to move. That thought gave Britta pause. She had never considered Maretha might be wounded. She had to take this man out.

She crept closer, staying in a crouch. The man pulled up next to a large oak. He sighted his rifle along the outer side of the tree, waiting for Maretha to show herself. She rose to move faster. The burning in her arm was stealing her focus. She stopped and hid behind a tree until she could gain control of the pain, but the pressure of non-action and the result might mean Maretha's death. Through gritted teeth, she pushed the pain back and stood.

A large tree blocked her view of the assassin. She had to move. Britta went left. The gunfire had ceased. What was going on? The crackle of a radio made her freeze. It was close. A man answered. "Sir." He listened, but Britta could not make out the other side's words. "We have taken some casualties. Two of the targets are down. We're working on the other two now." Static filled noise, "No, Sir. Not at the moment. I'll keep you apprised." Static. "That's fine, Sir. We'll catch up to you down the road."

Two targets down? Who else had fallen? Not Maretha, or they wouldn't be moving to ambush her. She hoped they thought she was one of those down. It would give her an advantage. One she was about to use. She angled away from the tree, and then a man came into view. Her eyes bore into the man's back. A leaf crunched underfoot, causing her to freeze. The man stiffened. He knew she was there.

Britta pulled the trigger as the man dove and rolled. Her shots went high. She tried to track him, but he moved fast. He got off a shot before ducking behind a tree. She was the one exposed now. Two quick steps and she dove out of the trees. She hit hard, driving the wind from her lungs and setting her arm on fire anew. She rolled down a slight slope, worked to get to one knee, then ran down the tree line until she could safely duck into the woods.

She had no idea where her foe was, but if he was as smart as she thought he was, he'd have already changed positions. It was a waiting game at this point. Whoever made the first mistake lost. Next to a tree and behind a fallen trunk, she had a relatively good cover and perspective on what lay in front of her. She kept the gun up and her eyes moving.

Minutes passed, each adding to the strain and stress. Sweat dripped into her eyes. She dared not wipe at them for fear in that second, the end would come. In the end, her vision blurred bad enough to obscure her sight. One eye at a time, she leaned her head to her shoulder and wiped, keeping the other eye trained. The effort didn't help much but did cut the burning.

A twig snapped to the left, and she turned her eyes in that direction. Had it been someone, or was it misdirection? She swung the gun back. Nothing. Another sound to the left, this one a crunch of leaves. She glanced that way but kept her weapon pointed forward. The third time she caught a blur of movement, not ten yards away. She was sure he knew her position.

She swung that way, ready for the attack. When it came, it was from the front. The man raced forward, triggering shot after shot as he approached. She was pinned down with nowhere to go. She fired the gun blindly, hoping to at least slow him if not to score a wound, but the shots kept coming.

Her gun ran empty. A hand grabbed and yanked it away. A gun barrel was pushed into her face. Then a demon took flight over the man's head with a face so distorted it could only have come from hell. It descended on the man, driving a long blade down with so much force it penetrated the skull and emerged out through the eye.

Britta ducked away just as the reflex of the finger pulled the trigger. The shot went high, but only by a fraction. The heat scored her scalp. She landed hard on her back and watched as the man's body was bent over the fallen log. The gun fell from his hand and landed on her chest. She grabbed for it and caught sight of running feet under the trunk. Maretha was in full-blown berserker mode, stabbing the dead man repeatedly. She was unaware of the danger that approached from behind.

Britta rolled on her side, gasped at the pain in her arm, aimed, and fired. She saw the explosion of blood as one round snapped the shin bone. The man fell, releasing a horrible scream. Maretha whirled at the sudden sound.

Though in severe pain, the assailant recognized he was dead if he didn't continue shooting. He lifted his gun, and Britta fired into his face. She pulled the trigger again, but the gun was empty. She only had one round left. She then collapsed, amazed either of them was still alive.

Maretha vaulted the log and landed next to her. "Chieftess, you're wounded."

Britta didn't respond. Now that the shooting had ceased, the pain was overwhelming. In all her battles, both foreign and local, she'd never been wounded. This was excruciating. As Maretha worked, a sudden thought came to mind. "Maretha, there's still one left."

Maretha gave a wicked smile and shook her head. That was good enough for Britta.

"But we must hurry. Others may come."

"I heard them talking. The convoy is moving on. These men were going to join them down the road."

"Ha," Maretha said, "They're gonna be waiting a long time."

"He also said they put two of us down. Did you see either of the other two fall?"

"No, but I was a little preoccupied. Once I get you patched up, we'll go check on them."

Maretha cleaned the wound and bound it, cutting strips of cloth from the dead man's shirt. She tied the dressing tight and helped Britta to her feet. "We should strip them of their weapons. I'm already running low."

"Okay, but let's do it fast. I want to check on Mariah and Alishia."

They each grabbed an M16 and whatever ammo they could find for them, but most of the sidearms were not calibers they carried. "Take the bullets. We can always use them for trade," Britta said. They took water and food, then hurried to the last place they saw the others.

As they approached, they heard soft crying. Closing in with caution, they found Mariah with Alishia's head in her lap. Much of Alishia's forehead was missing. Britta's heart sank. The woman's death was all her fault. How could she live with her decision to send them forward as live bait? It hadn't been her intent, but that didn't matter. Her decision had caused Alishia's death. She'd lost warriors before, but this would haunt her forever. Alishia had put her trust in Britta, choosing to come with her rather than stay in the town's relative safety.

Through her tears, Mariah looked up. "We were running, then suddenly, Alishia was falling. I thought she tripped. I yelled at her to get up, but she didn't. She couldn't."

Britta didn't know what to say. She sat on the ground and felt her tears well up.

Mariah said, "I know we don't have time, but I don't want to leave her for the animals. I want to bury her."

Britta nodded. Maretha groaned and scanned the area. In a quick move, she bent, hauled the body up, and leaned it over her shoulder. "Come," she said and hurried toward the farmhouse.

When they arrived, she set Alishia down under a weeping willow on the banks of a small pond, then jogged off to the barn. She returned five minutes later, carrying two shovels. Without a word, she tossed one to Mariah and dug the blade into the ground. They took turns digging as the sunset began. Once the hole reached a depth of about four feet, Maretha declared it deep enough. Alishia's body was handed down to her, and she set it reverently on the damp earth.

She climbed out and looked at Britta. Britta frowned, knowing it was up to her to say the final words over their lost teammate.

"Alishia was a good warrior, a fine teammate, and a great friend. She will be remembered as someone who always did the right thing and who could be relied on to be there for her friends. We will miss her whole-heartedly." She had no idea what else to say.

Mariah said, her voice cracking. "She was my friend and my love. I will struggle to go on without you. I love you. I wish it were me instead of you." Her sobs prevented her from saying anything more. Maretha placed an arm around her shoulders and held her. Mariah turned her face into Maretha and cried.

"To a great warrior and friend," she said. "You will be forever missed."

With that, Britta picked up a shovel and began covering the body.

CHAPTER SIX

Mark joined the workers as they put up the plywood siding. With nearly forty workers, the job went fast. As the topmost layer of plywood was attached, others climbed to the roof and began closing it in. As one row of plywood was laid, another team followed with an ice and water shield underlayment. Milo and his team had done a great job raiding two lumberyards. While he waited for the cement to cure on the foundation, a small group constructed a two-car garage from a packaged kit they picked up, and it was already stacked to the rafters with extra supplies they might need.

Without the benefit of a hydraulic lift truck, the shingles were carried up ladders one bundle at a time. Two ladders had been set up on both the front and back sides to ensure the roofers did not have to wait long for materials.

The sun was bright, but the air was cool, another reminder the weather was changing. By noon, the frame was complete, and the lower level windows were installed. They took a break for lunch with a cacophony of excited chatter rising over the assembled picnic tables. Four fire pits had been constructed, and each was lit. Kettles of the strange greens and vegetable soup Elijah's people were known for bubbled with a promising aroma.

Caryn and her baking team brought over loaves of bread from the new brick ovens. Lines of people stood at the four kettles, and the soup was ladled into bowls taken from a local Walmart. The food items had long ago been scavenged or perished, but most people entering looked only for food and drink. Mark's community looked for things to be used daily. The various kitchen utensils and equipment had the kitchens stocked enough for more than a hundred people. The way they were growing, though, they might have to search for more.

At lunch, Jin, his wife, and daughter came out of the house with Lincoln and Jenny. It was Jin's first public appearance since the encounter at what they called the facility. His wife had been shot but seemed to be recovering well. The color had returned to her face. Their daughter wore a permanent scowl on her boyish face.

Lincoln was his usual exuberant self, but Jenny still looked pale. She seldom left the house or joined with any of the other groups. The loss of her newborn baby several months back still affected her. It was good to see her out and mingling.

"Man, you got a lot done today," Lincoln said.

"Still lots to be done if you care to lend a hand."

"Man, don't give me that. You know what I've been doing all day. With you gone all the time, the job of organizing hunting parties fell to me. As soon as we're done eating, we're going back out."

"Finding anything?"

"No, not much. We did bag a few rabbits Caryn's making into a stew for dinner, but as far as anything worthwhile in the houses we search, it's all been pretty much picked clean." He leaned over the table and whispered, "I did find something I think you'll want to check out, though." He gave a sly smile and a conspiratorial wink.

Mark laughed. It could only mean he found a bottle of booze of some sort.

"I can help," Jin said.

"Great," said Mark. "We'll be happy to have you. You see the big bald man down there?" he pointed. "I'll introduce you to him, and he'll give you something to do."

Jin wore a confused look. He turned to his wife, who translated. "Ah. Good," he said and went back to slurping his soup.

Before the meal broke up and the workers scattered, Mark climbed up on the bench and got everyone's attention. "A lot has gone on lately, and there are some new things that need to be discussed. I'm calling for a whole community meeting tonight after dinner. If anyone has anything they'd like to discuss or any questions, that will be the time to do so." He went to sit, then had another thought. "This building is a great example of what can be accomplished when we all work together. Milo and your team, you've done great work here. I have to say I'm very proud of what this group of survivors has done. Thank you one and all."

He sat to some applause and cheering, but that was not his intent. He'd been giving a lot of thought to his future with the community and had come to some hard decisions. Now that the events of the past week had settled down, it was time to implement those changes.

As he moved away from the table, Lincoln caught him. "I've got about twenty minutes before it's time to leave. You up for a sample?"

Mark smiled. He knew Lincoln would try to pump him for information about the meeting. "You see how high that building is? I'm gonna walk around up there. I think I'll pass for now. Let's sample it tonight."

Lincoln eyed him but didn't push. "All right. Tonight." He clapped him on the shoulder and walked away. Mark took another look at the building. It *was* a long way up.

Using binoculars, Corporal Diaz scanned the grounds of the farmhouse. He was impressed by the numbers. He estimated twenty-five at the house and more than forty across the street at the construction site. They were gathered for a midday meal. That might prove important, especially dealing with this many targets. If they ate at regular times, they might be able to catch them unprepared and take the bulk of them off the board before sustaining casualties of their own. But he had to locate the Asian family and the test subject. They couldn't risk hosing down the tables if they also took out the people they'd been sent to retrieve.

He did a slow pan across the entire compound. No fence or protection of any sort surrounded either lot. That was a mistake in his military mind. They had no way to defend against an assault. He did note that except for a few individuals, mostly younger kids, everyone carried or wore a weapon of some kind. They were armed, but his men were well trained. He'd take one of his to a hundred of theirs any day.

He stopped his pan as he spotted an Asian man, woman, and child walking with a large black man and a skinny white girl. They crossed the street, had a few words with some of the people, then joined in the chow line. Now he knew part of his package was there. He just wasn't sure who the test subject was or what she looked like. The description he'd been given matched six or seven of the younger women, but he had to identify her before an assault order was given. A mistake could lead to severe punishment for whoever shot her. He was going to make sure it wasn't him.

"Let's backtrack and cut through the corn. I want to see them from a different angle. You two," he pointed to the pair, "cut across to the far street. Get an angle to observe them, but don't get caught. If anyone sees you, bail fast. Understood?"

The men nodded. He motioned for them to go, and they ran.

"What do you have in mind?" Private Rand, his remaining man, said.

"I want to get a better look at the two outbuildings and know their purpose and how many, if any, people are inside."

"That's gonna take us close."

"Problem?"

"Only if we get caught."

"Then don't do something to get us caught."

Rand looked skeptical. He shrugged.

"Let's go."

CHAPTER SEVEN

Bobby stood looking through his binoculars at the gathering in the barn's hayloft, or what passed for the medical facility. It was his turn to stand watch, a task he didn't mind, especially when he got to do it in the loft. The vantage point gave him a long-distance view of the surrounding land. At certain places, through the back loft door, he could see Central Avenue, the main east-west road to the north of the compound. He often found himself sighting down his rifle, wondering if he could make a shot from this distance.

Bobby was a good shot with the rifle, perhaps the best in the community, including his father. He'd made long shots before, important life-saving shots, but this would be a new record. Since it was a road, most likely the target would be moving to add difficulty to the shot.

He also liked the solitude of standing watch. It gave him time to think. The people of the community were great, and he liked being with them, but sometimes he liked to be by himself. He'd grabbed a slice of venison, a warm loaf of bread and filled his canteen with hot coffee, then made the trek to the loft. He sat in the open hayloft door and using his knife to slice the bread in half, made a sandwich. Once finished with his meal, he stood and walked from front to back every few minutes to do his job.

He stopped the glasses on Becca. It was good to see her moving. She was still stiff and a little weak, but after the fear of being paralyzed from the waist down, any movement was good. She laughed at something one of the other girls at the table said.

He slid down the line, this time stopping at his father. His dad had been through a lot lately and was becoming withdrawn. Bobby often caught him staring off into space and wondered what ran through his mind. He was worried about his mental health. He wished Lynn and he could settle whatever their differences were and get back together. That was the best medicine for his father.

He moved the glasses in a slow arc across the grounds, through the trees, and to the left down the road. The corn was browning. They'd picked as much as they could before it began to go bad. Jarrod, their farmer friend who lived a few miles down the road with a small clan, said he wanted the corn for feed for his livestock. He hadn't come to collect it yet, but Bobby knew he'd be there soon.

He began his slow pan to the right, past the new building, the far corner wooded lot, and the three houses across the street. Even at this height, he couldn't see past the trees. He meant to bring that up to his father. It might be a good idea to post someone in the upstairs back room of one of the houses. It would give them a quicker warning should something threatening come from that direction.

Finished with the front, he paced to the rear. The door at the back was smaller, about half that of the front door. They'd cut away three six by twelve-inch ports, big enough to see through with the glasses and spaced far enough apart to allow full coverage of the fields to the north. If anyone approached from the rear, they also served as gun ports.

Again, he took his time sweeping over the fields from left to right and then back. Then he lowered the glasses to repeat the process closer to the farmhouse grounds.

He was on his second pass when something caught his eyes. He stopped and panned back. What had it been? He closed his eyes to recall the moment. The corn moved. Nothing strange about that. It moved when the wind blew. He studied the corn but saw no other movement. Either the wind blew in short bursts, or an animal was moving through the stalks.

He returned to the approximate spot then jumped ahead. There. Movement. He could make out two brown objects. Were those helmets? He let the glasses drop, bouncing against the strap he wore around his neck, and slid the rifle off his shoulder. The high-power scope offered a better, more detailed look.

It appeared to be two men wearing military helmets and carrying assault rifles. Alarms went off in his head. Could this be some sort of drill General West from the Air National Guard base was running? No, not without telling someone. They might be mistaken for intruders, and someone could get shot. They wouldn't take the chance.

He grabbed the walkie talkie from his belt. "Armed intruders in the northern cornfield. Repeat. Armed intruders in the northern cornfield. In the yard, an air horn blared. An instant of silence, then loud chatter. He knew from experience that everyone would be moving fast to get to their assigned defensive station.

Bobby ignored the noise and drew a bead on the back intruder's head. If they did anything threatening toward the community, the man would die. As soon as the horn sounded, the two men stopped and dropped from view.

"Details," the word crackled through the receiver.

Bobby recognized his father's voice. "Two—two that I can see. Armed men in military camos. Left of the garage, forty yards back."

"Do you have a shot?"

"Negative. They dropped from sight once the alarm sounded. Wait. I see stalks moving. They are crawling and moving away from the compound.

"Scan for others."

"Roger. Scanning."

He knew his father would be in action mode, giving orders and taking steps to protect the community.

"Update. Still moving away. Fifty yards. They're up and running now. I have a shot."

"Hold." Silence. Then. "Any chance they're from the base?"

"Unknown but doubtful. West would know better than to send men here without notifying us."

"One would hope."

Outside, Bobby heard two engines start. They'd go down the street to cut them off. Bobby scanned to the right. He stopped. Two more soldiers were crouched in the corn to the right of the barn. They were closer than the other two had been, giving him a good look down at them.

"I have two more behind the barn."

"Repeat."

"Two more armed men, behind and to the right of the barn. Thirty yards out."

"Doing?"

"Nothing."

"Do you . . .?

"Yes. I have a shot."

"If they approach, fire a warning shot. We are moving into position."

In a crouch, the two soldiers moved east.

"They're bugging out."

"Direction?"

"East."

His dad's voice filtered through the hayloft door behind him. He sent two more vehicles to intercept on the east.

The first two men were three-quarters of the way to the far road. The closer two were halfway to the eastern road and he didn't see anyone else. Had this been a group of men thinking of sneaking in, stealing supplies, and retreat, or was this a scouting party sizing up the community and their defenses?

In the distance, Bobby saw the vehicles his father sent out make the turn onto the first road. They slowed as they searched but went out of sight. Below he caught more movement. It was a search party from the community. He spotted his father to the right and about twenty men and women, forming a long line across the corn.

In the distance, automatic gunfire erupted. Bobby didn't need to report, since the sound of the shots carried. He lifted the rifle and focused on the road. He found one of the three spaces that gave him access to the road. Gunshots continued, then ceased. One of the vehicles turned around and sped off. The firepower directed against them was perhaps too much to stand. He did not see the second vehicle and fretted that those inside had met a dire end.

Then the trunk of the car backed into view. Someone was still alive. The vehicle was not moving fast. The scope revealed one body slumped in the back seat. The driver was the only one moving. One of the soldiers stepped into view. He paced the car and angled toward it. A feeling of desperation kindled within his chest. Bobby forced a long breath, locked on the target, and as the soldier raised his AR to finish off the driver, Bobby fired. The man arched back, one hand lifting from the gun, while the other pressed down on the trigger, a reflexive motion as he died.

The second man ran to the first and squatted next to him. He checked for a pulse, then lifted his gaze searching for where the shot came from. It was a huge mistake. Bobby's round entered the left eye. The man slumped next to his partner.

"Two down," he said into the radio. "I repeat. The first two are down. Our people took damage and will need medical attention."

"What about the other two?" his father said.

Bobby swept the rifle right. He did a slow scan, then back. Nothing. He switched to the near port and tried again. The two men had either taken to ground or had managed to get across the street and out of sight.

"Do not see them."

"Continue spotting. We'll check the last sighting."

"Roger."

CHAPTER EIGHT

Corporal Diaz and Private Rand set a fast pace. They reached the main road known as Central Avenue and crouched behind a seasonal farm market shed. Diaz used his scope to look down the road. A group of armed men stood around three bodies. A pickup truck made the turn around a corner and stopped on the grass short of the group. Two men and a woman hopped out. The woman carried what he guessed was a doctor's bag.

Two of the men on the ground wore desert camos like him. He hoped they were still alive and could be saved. Then he thought better of it and preferred they were dead. They couldn't be tortured into revealing their plans if they were dead.

Rand backtracked. "Ten to fifteen men just emerged from the corn."

"We have to get across the road without being seen, or they will hunt us."

He looked around. They had no place to hide, and few places offered cover strong enough to deflect bullets. If they darted across the street and were spotted, they'd send cars and people after them. The best bet was to stay on this side and move further away until they were dots on the horizon. "Let's move. Keep low and try to keep this shed between them and us."

He ran in a crouch. The road ahead remained straight, giving anyone who looked a clear line of sight at them should they try to cross. They went on for twenty minutes before stopping to look. He could still see them using his scope, just not with his eyes alone. He moved another hundred yards to be sure, then crossed. From there, they had plenty of cover and worked their way back to the farmhouse they were using as a base.

Captain Childs was seated at the dining room table with maps and a note pad next to him. Without glancing up, he said, "Report."

Diaz said, "This camp is much larger than anticipated. From the numbers we saw gathered for lunch, I'd put the total at near eighty. Every adult was armed. Two of my team were spotted. They ran as ordered, not wanting to engage, but we heard gunshots. When we got to the road, we saw several bodies and a host of these people all around. I believe both our men were killed."

Childs worked his jaw from side to side. "You think they're dead?"

"Yes, Sir."

"What gives you that assurance?"

"I scoped the bodies. They were covered. Neither man was moving or breathing. I believe they were shot multiple times. Those around them did not have weapons pointed at them as they would do if either man were still alive."

"You'd better pray they're dead. Otherwise, they'll be prepared and ready for us."

"Sir, I think they'll be ready regardless. The mission may be impossible to achieve."

"Oh, it might be more difficult or take additional planning, but it won't be impossible. We just need enough leverage to bend the enemy to our will."

Over the next hour, Childs and Stanton questioned the men, pulling every tiny detail from their memory. They were dismissed after that, and the two men sat in silence, pondering their next moves.

"Ideas?" Childs asked.

"Lots."

"Such as."

"One, consider the whole shock and awe notion. Go in from three different directions with the fifties blasting. Have the men come in through the corn and from the woods behind the new structure. Light them up hard and continue until there's none left but the dead."

"We still have certain people to capture and guinea pigs to collect."

"Second, we bomb the buildings, move in with the fifties—send the men looking for those we need—haul them out and be on our way."

"Same thing. We need to know where the targets are, isolate them, then wreak havoc."

"Okay. Third—stealth approach at night. We take out the guards, gain control of the buildings one at a time, bring all the living to the middle of the yard, and make our demands. Once we have who we need, we have them all in one place, so it will be easy to dispatch them."

"I do like that option. But what if we start by taking hostages first. We may be able to leverage who we want from them if they think they're getting their people back."

"But there's no guarantee those we seek will be willing to give themselves up. They might see it as trading a life for a life, and why shouldn't it be their life that's saved?"

"That's why you up the emotional ante by kidnapping women and children. Especially children."

"How do we get to them? It's not like they'd let the kids wander off the grounds."

"We need full reconnaissance. It may take longer but will be less costly for us in the end. I need a complete record of everyone who leaves the base. I want to know where people go and if it's something done with regularity."

"When do we start?'

"Tonight. We'll rotate four-man teams. Place each member in a direction far enough away, so they are not noticed. We'll do a twenty-four-hour pass, then go from there. If we need more, we'll take the time. If we have a clear winner, we'll go first chance."

"We'll need less recognizable vehicles and I think we need to change our base in case we've been spotted."

"Check the garage. We might get lucky. Otherwise, send the team that is not on duty tonight in search of four vehicles. I'll leave the logistics to you. Make sure they know to take cars that have gas. We don't need them running out of fuel when they're needed."

Stanton stood. He didn't bother with a salute, nor did Childs expect one. He left to see to the details, and Childs leaned over the map. He took a note pad he'd made a crude drawings on depicting the buildings on both sites and tapped a finger on the barn. "We need to take the barn to have control of the yard," he said to himself.

CHAPTER NINE

After dinner, the community was abuzz with the new threat at their doors. Mark did not recognize the uniforms, and they held no insignias other than name and rank, but he had a good idea where they came from. Dr. Ohtanda was loath to give up her prize test subjects, but the nagging question on his mind was how did they find them? Did someone follow? Unlikely. It would've been hard to follow and not be seen. After all, few vehicles were on the road these days.

But if not with a tail, how? The answer hit like a slap to the forehead. Either Jin or Becca had a tracker on them. More like in both. He'd have to check. Maybe ask Doc if there was a way to discover them inside a body.

The noise level reached rock concert level. He glanced around and noted most of the community was gathered. He turned to Lincoln. "We still waiting on people?"

"Yeah. I'm sure there'll be some stragglers, but let's get started anyway."

Mark nodded and stepped up onto one of the picnic tables. He held up his hand for quiet. Several people whistled to get everyone's attention. The sight of so many people coming together still thrilled him. They had come so far in such a short time.

As the crowd quieted, Mark tried to organize his thoughts. He'd been working on that ever since returning from the site of the gun battle. A fight that took one of their group's lives and seriously wounded two others. It was a sad day. Not once since they'd formed this community had anyone died of a typical 'normal' death. They'd all died in one conflict or another. The world might have been cruel before, but it was crazy now.

"Thank you all for coming. We have much to discuss, and I'll need your attention so everyone can hear and everyone understands what's going on.

"First, I'm sure everyone is aware of the attack earlier today. We lost a good man in Charley Applebaum. The wounded, John Matties and Carol Johnson, are in Doc's care. Currently, John is stable and in recovery, and Carol is in surgery.

"We do not know who the attackers were, but at least two got away, so it's essential to remain vigilant. Do not go off alone or unarmed. For those who live off the grounds, be sure you have each other's backs and regularly check in. If anyone wishes to move in here temporarily until we get a handle on what we're facing, let us know, and we'll make accommodations for you.

"I said, I don't know who these men are, but I do believe they are with the government medical facility we visited a few days ago."

"You mean real government, like our government?" a woman asked.

"To be honest, I don't know. If they are government, they no longer care about the people. In fact, the only reason they want them at all is to use as lab rats testing out their so-called vaccines. I believe they have tracked us here because they want some of our people for more tests. The Doctor in charge of the facility is a cold-hearted—well, she's not a nice person. It sounded to me like she was either the creator or on the team that created the virus that killed the population. Whether it was released on purpose or accidentally, as she claims, is nothing more than a guess. The truth is whatever they were working on is deadly."

"Can't we talk to them?" a man said. "You know, negotiate a deal?"

"It's my impression they don't make deals. They take what they want by force, if necessary, and kill anyone who gets in their way. I'm not just telling you this because I don't want them involved here. I'm saying it because I believe they will either take control of our community or wipe it out after they take what they were sent for."

"Which is?" Another man called out.

"They want my daughter, Becca, and our newest members Jin and his family. They may also spare some of us to use as test subjects."

Voices rose, and Mark lifted his hand again for quiet. "We have been in these situations before. As long as we remain calm and look out for each other, we'll be fine. Lincoln will increase patrols and guards. He had some ideas for setting up alarms in the cornfields and perhaps the woods behind the new building. The earlier we get a warning, the better we can be ready to repel an attack. It was the alertness of our guards that prevented any encroachment by these attackers."

"Do you think they'll come back?" Caryn asked.

"Yes. I think they were sent here on a mission and will not stop until they attain their goal.

"I know this is important and weighs heavy on your minds, but before this happened, I had already called for this meeting. There are other things we need to discuss. For one, you see how much progress has been made on the new shelter house. Milo and his team and all the other helpers have done a great job getting the walls up. They started on the interior walls this afternoon. If anyone else can lend a hand, even for a short time, it will be appreciated.

"On that topic, I would like to start a list of possible improvements and construction that you feel we might need. Write the proposals up, and if we think it's something we can do, we'll put it on the list. But please, if you're not willing to help others, don't put in for something to be repaired or built and expect us to rush to your side. We call this a community for a reason. Everyone helping everyone. That's the way this continues to work. If you have a physical situation that prevents you from doing manual labor, add that to your proposal. We will honestly consider it."

He glanced around the group to see expressions that would tell him how any of this was being received. His scan was inconclusive.

"I already have the next project in mind, and it's one that either has benefitted many of us before or will in the future. It's renovating the barn into a real medical facility. It's long overdue. Speaking of medicine, we have a decent stock of medical equipment, but drugs and blood are in short supply. If you have anything lying around that you are not using and may benefit someone else, please bring it to us. Doc can decide if it's something we can use. When you're out hunting, keep medical supplies as one of your priorities.

"Food is becoming scarce. We can no longer count on finding packaged food. If you haven't done so already, you need to plant a garden. It's too late to plant one outside, but one can be grown inside. It may be the only food you have for a while. If you're not sure how to do so, talk to Donna or Jill or anyone from the southern campus, as we've begun calling it. They are experts in living off the land.

"It's also important that you step up and give blood. Our reserves are low. It doesn't cost you anything but time . . ."

"And blood," someone quipped.

"And the life you save may be your own."

Mark paused now. The next part would be difficult. "The last part of this meeting's agenda has to do with something I've been thinking long and hard about over the past month or so. It's time for me to step down from whatever position it is I hold. This is a great community, and it's continually growing. Now's the time to put a council in charge. I'm not around enough to be a leader. You need someone who is here and will guide you through whatever times are ahead. You can discuss how this is to be done, with an election, of course, but decide on how many members and set guidelines for them and the community to follow.

To this point, we've just been winging it, and because we have surrounded ourselves with good people, it's worked so far. Moving forward, I believe it's in the best interest of all for a council to be voted in. I'd like to see that happen within the next two weeks. I know that's rushed, but it's also essential."

"Are you leaving us?" a woman asked.

"No. I'll still be around." He left it at that. "Does anyone else have something they'd like to discuss?"

Shout outs came from all directions. He held up a hand. "Now, if you start doing that, you'll scare off anyone who was thinking of running for a council seat." He got some laughs. The meeting lasted well into the evening before breaking up. Many stayed to discuss the meeting. Before they left, he reminded everyone about being safe.

CHAPTER TEN

When Mark stepped down, he came face to face with Lynn. She wore a look of concerned puzzlement. He had hoped to avoid this discussion for a while. She was about to speak when Lincoln came up and put an arm around his shoulder. "We have a meeting to attend right now. Remember?"

"Oh, hell, yeah. Let's do this." He smiled at Lynn and allowed himself to be led away. They went across the street and into the backyard, where Lincoln produced a key to unlock the padlock on the garage's side door. He entered, struck a match, and lit a kerosene lantern. The dull yellow glow cast just enough light to see within a ten-foot radius.

Lincoln reached beneath a workbench and pulled out an unopened bottle of Evan Williams bourbon. He set two coffee mugs on the bench and cracked the bottle open. The aroma filled their nostrils, and each breathed in with a sigh of satisfaction. Lincoln poured out two fingers for each, capped the bottle, and set it down with reverence. He lifted his glass. "To your retirement."

"Yes. May it come fast."

They took a deep sip. The amber liquid rolled down his throat, leaving a slight burning trace behind. Mark appreciated the taste, but Lincoln smacked his lips. "Ah, the simple pleasures."

"What else do we have?"

"True. So true. But once in a while, something comes along that makes you appreciate it to the max."

They relaxed as they drank.

"So, what's your plan? You leaving or staying?"

"Not sure. I don't really have any plans. It's time for me to step down. I haven't done these people any favors lately with all the dangerous situations I've dragged them into. Lynn is quick to remind me of that."

"Maybe. Maybe not. But I tend to believe your decision has more to do with her than anything else."

"I can't deny it's a consideration, but the burden of being in charge and the person everyone looks to was too much to bear alone. Besides, it's time for others to have a say in how things are done here."

"Heavy is the head that wears the crown, huh?"

"Yeah, something like that."

He sipped again. "Not the best I've ever had, but far from the worst."

"Beggars can't be choosers. Considering what else we've had to drink lately, I think it's grand."

"Oh, it is that." He polished his off and refilled their mugs.

"So, in all seriousness and honesty, what do you plan on doing?"

"I've been thinking a lot about this. You said yourself we're having more difficulty scavenging for things. I think I'm going to go further out. Maybe do some overnights. We need a lot of stuff to take care of a group this size. Doc's hurting for supplies. She needs blood. We have enough people here that we should be able to cover that, but it's the drugs and daily medicines she needs."

"You're doing this alone?"

"Yeah. I think that's for the best." I don't want to drag anyone else along."

"You think your kids are going to be all right with that?"

"Guess I'll just have to explain it to them the right way."

"In other words, sneak off and leave the explaining to me."

Mark laughed. "Look, I'm going to do a pattern. I'll start in one direction and cover it street by street for one day. Then I'll do the same on day two. For day three, I'll come back, stay for a day, then head out."

"You got this all planned out."

"I do. I just hope it works."

"All this just to avoid facing your broken heart."

Mark paused with the mug at his lips.

"Seriously, Mark. I wish you two would get back together, but if not, it's not the end of the world. This sounds like a good way to get yourself killed. Is that what you want?'

"Of course not." Both of their tones had grown harsh. "It's easier, that's all. Plus, it may benefit the community."

"Man."

"Lincoln, don't. It's what I've decided. It'll make things easier for all concerned. Just let it be."

"Yeah. Sure." He took a long swallow and stared up at the rafters.

They remained silent for a time, then Mark asked. "What are you contemplating?"

"Ha, running for council."

"Seriously?"

He shrugged. "Why not?"

"I think you'd be perfect. The people here all respect and look up to you. Yeah, you'd be a shoo-in."

"At least I won't have to worry about the paparazzi stalking me or some lame politician looking into my background."

"That would be bad."

"Yeah. Hey. How do you know?"

"Just a wild guess."

"Yeah. Wild would be the term."

They laughed again, and Lincoln refilled the glasses.

CHAPTER ELEVEN

They spent the night in the farmhouse. The yard had an old-fashioned pump well. They poured water into a pitcher they found in the kitchen cupboard and took turns washing. Maretha found a container of powdered lemonade. She refilled the pitcher and mixed a batch. She also found a bag of egg noodles, but without anything to boil water with, they had to snack on them raw. No one was in a talkative mood. Night had fallen. They had not reached their goal and had lost one of their members. They were not off to a good start.

Maretha offered to stand guard, but Britta knew she wouldn't wake either of them to relieve her, so she said, "I'll stand first watch." Maretha frowned, and Britta pointed to her eyes and then at Maretha. Maretha cracked a smile.

The night passed without incident. She had feared the convoy would come back searching for their lost comrades. But if they came, they did not approach the house.

Maretha spelled her, and Britta fell into a restless and fevered sleep. Sunlight poked through the bedroom window waking her. She felt drained, and her arm throbbed. Maretha and Mariah were already awake and enjoying another pitcher of lemonade.

As she joined them, Maretha said, "What do you have planned for today?"

"I don't know. By now, we're too late to prevent whatever was going to happen at Mark's. I'm thinking we just move on until something strikes our interest."

"You don't want to at least check on them?"

"It's not necessary."

Maretha mulled that over. "You know what is necessary? Seeing that arm tended to properly. Mark has a doctor. It is still the best place to go to."

Britta thought that was sound thinking but turned to Mariah. "What are your thoughts?"

She shrugged. "Whatever."

She was still grieving. Britta did not prod her. "Okay. We leave in five minutes."

They pushed away from the kitchen table and stood. None of them moved. They all looked down or away, avoiding eye contact. Death took its toll on the living as well.

Five minutes later, they exited through the front door and walked north. They still had no idea where they were going, but Britta decided it no longer mattered. If they got there, fine. If not, they were patrolling. It was what they did. The only difference was now whatever they found was theirs and did not have to be brought back to share with the town.

They trudged along, heading in a northwesterly direction. The pain in her arm intensified as the day wore on. By midday, she was dragging and sweating profusely. Maretha noticed and called a halt. She forced Britta to sit, then undid the bandage. The wound looked worse. She cleaned it, made a slit to drain some nasty fluid, then used an alcohol wipe to scrub the skin. It burned. Britta fought hard not to pull her arm away. Maretha coated the puckered skin with anti-bacterial cream, then wrapped it with fresh strips of cloth. Finally, she fumbled through her pack for some antibiotics. They may or may not be designed for that particular use, but something was better than nothing.

They rested for a time and then ate a meager meal. Then with renewed energy, they started their trek again. Hours passed, finding few houses to check over the long miles of farmland. In the fourth house, a small ancient dwelling at least a hundred years old, they found a large cache of food and sodas.

The house was covered by overgrown trees and brush and was not easy to get to, even in the best of times. It had been overlooked by many who passed this way before. The only drawback was dealing with the smell of the rotting corpse.

They ran in, holding their breath, grabbed what they could, and ran out. Five trips later, they had enough food and supplies to last them several weeks if they used it wisely. They found an old duffel bag and filled it, then distributed the remaining items amongst their packs. The collection took more than two hours of daylight but had been well worth the time.

They set out again with only a few hours of sunlight left but with high spirits anticipating a good meal.

"We need to find someplace with a gas grill," Mariah said. "We can heat some of those soups and have a hot meal for a change."

"Sounds good to me," Britta said. "You're on point. Pick one out."

"It's not like there's a ton of choices around here."

"Look," Maretha pointed. "Smoke."

They glanced at each other with high hopes. "You think that's them?" Britta asked.

"Don't know," said Maretha.

"Only one way to find out," Mariah said, heading in that direction.

"Let's approach with caution in case it's not them," Britta said. "We should talk about what to do in either scenario."

"If it's not them, I think we should avoid whoever it is," Maretha said.

"Agreed. But at the same time, if it is, I don't think we should stride right in. We should observe them for a while to make sure we're not getting into a bad situation. Just because Mark said it was a good community doesn't make it so."

'Now you're talking like a leader," said Maretha.

"Oh, hush."

The smoke was farther away than they anticipated. The sun was setting as they drew near. They slowed their pace and had weapons ready. "I smell roasting meat," Mariah said. "It's a cooking fire."

"We need to see whose fire it is," said Britta.

"It's making my mouth water," said Mariah.

"Focus," Maretha cautioned.

They crept closer. The aroma of the meat was intoxicating. "Let's separate," Britta said. Maretha nodded and faded away

The campfire was in a small gathering of trees, which only allowed glimpses of the dancing flames but nothing else. Mariah went right, Britta straight ahead. She entered the trees and waited to listen for any voices. She heard none. Another step and she found an opening. She leaned forward for a better look. A lone figure sat on a fallen log with his back to her. A deer was on a makeshift spit and roasting. Slowly she backed away until she felt the hard barrel pressed to the back of her head. She froze. A voice whispered in her ear, "Welcome, fine lady. I'd like to invite you to dinner, but I think you're more a dessert."

He removed her rifle, dropped it on the ground, and then took her sidearm. He groped her body with intent, pretending to search for other weapons. He took the knife from her sheath and then pushed her into the clearing, using the gun against her head.

"Look what I found, Jed."

The sitting man turned, revealing a face that had been burned and scarred. One eye was closed. Several teeth were missing. "Works every time, Pat."

"Yep. You sure know how to set a trap."

"Looky here," another voice called out. Mariah was pushed through the trees. She stumbled and fell. "I got me one too." Before she got up, he sat on her back like she was a horse. "We're going to have great fun, you and me." He swatted her on the butt. Ride 'em, cowboy.

Britta's blood boiled, but she kept it under control. Maretha was still out there. She focused on something her captor had said. "What do you mean, set a trap?"

"Oh sweetie, we saw you coming a long ways off." With the gun still pressed to her head, he leaned close and licked her cheek. She cringed but otherwise did not react. "The roasting meat gig. That always draws them in. We just lie in wait until you get close enough to smell it, then we've got you."

"Where's Donny?" the man with the melted face said.

"He'll be coming. That's right, little girl. We knows there was three of you."

"Here he comes," said the man seated on Mariah.

Donny staggered into the clearing clutching at his neck. A spray of blood squirted through his fingers.

'What the . . ." Pat said. As Donny fell, Pat reached for him, taking the gun from Britta's head. As he bent to catch his friend, Britta kicked him in the ass, propelling him over the fallen man. She whirled and dove for the man riding Mariah, tackling him before he could get off a shot.

The melted face man stood and whirled, showing the double-barreled shotgun he'd kept below the log. Two gunshots ripped through his face. He toppled backward, landing in the fire. His long coat caught, but he was beyond feeling pain.

Two more shots ended Pat's life.

Britta wrestled with the last man, but he managed to throw her off. He reached for the gun dislodged by the tackle, but it was no longer where it landed.

"Looking for this, sweetie?" Mariah asked. She waited for him to see the gun and allowed time for his jaw to drop before she shot him.

Maretha dragged the burning man from the fire, threw dirt on him until he was only smoldering, then dragged him from the clearing. They stripped the bodies of anything useful, mostly ammunition, and dragged them away as well.

Once done, they stared at the cooking meat. Their eyes met, and their smiles spread.

"Let's eat," Mariah said.

Each had camping utensils. They found four metal plates in one of the dead men's packs. Maretha carved off thick slabs of venison and dropped the hot meat onto their plates. They dove in. The meat was a little stringy, but the flavor and the hot meal made up for having to chew a few extra times.

Twenty minutes later, they were stuffed and wondering how to carry the rest of the meat. "Do we have anything to put it in?" Britta asked. "I don't want to waste all this. Who knows when we'll get another chance to eat this well?"

"I've got a couple of gallon size baggies. I carry my toiletries in one. I can dump those into my pack. I won't be able to find any of them when I need to, but I'd rather have the food."

"That's a good start," said Britta.

While Maretha carved, Britta and Mariah collected the slabs and dropped them in the bags. It didn't take long to fill them. "There's still a lot left. We may have to leave it."

"That's a shame," Mariah said.

Maretha said, "Without refrigeration, it will be bad soon anyway."

"Why don't we stay here for the night and have some more for breakfast. If we can't figure out some way to carry it by then, we'll leave it."

"Sounds good to me," said Mariah.

CHAPTER TWELVE

Mark made a great effort at not waking the household as he crept toward the couch he slept on. His head pounded, and he felt a bit off-kilter—the price he paid for drinking with Lincoln. He sought the comfort of the couch. With each step closer, the anticipation of sleep was euphoric. However, no sooner had he touched his body to the cushions, then the bedroom door opened, and Lynn came out.

The fact that it was dark made her eyes appear angrier. The twin embers glowed and felt like they bore deep into his brain. He wanted desperately to lay down but was afraid to move. She glowered at him, then hissed, "Get your ass in here now." She pivoted and disappeared into the room.

Mark hesitated. Any other time he'd have loved being invited into her room, but he knew this was not going to be as pleasant as those times had been. He lifted with a groan and entered her room. The door shut with a quiet touch though he was sure she'd have preferred to slam it.

She whirled on him and got in his face. "What are you doing?"

He thought the answer was obvious. He was trying to go to sleep. Before he could reply, she was on to the next question. "Are you leaving us? Is that your big plan to avoid facing me and your responsibilities here? Did you even think to discuss this with me? I can't believe how self-centered and selfish you are. I'm sorry things didn't work out for us, but why punish all those who have come to look up to you as their leader? It's not fair to them and sure not fair to me. Who do you think they're going to blame when you're gone?"

She paused, giving him a chance to respond, but he wasn't fast enough.

"Well? Explain yourself."

He tried to organize his thoughts, but she'd asked so many questions in rapid-fire that he could not separate them in his current state of semi-intoxication. He opened his mouth to speak.

"Oh, my God." She stepped back and wafted her hand in front of her face. "You've been drinking. Let me guess. Lincoln found a bottle on one of his patrols. That's just great. The one time I need to have a serious conversation with you and you're too drunk to hold up your end."

She reached back and opened the door. The message was clear. It was time to leave. He started through the door, then stopped. He looked at her, and even though his haze thought she was beautiful. "I love you, Lynn." Then he was out and collapsing on the couch. He wasn't sure if it was a dream or real, but he thought she stood there watching him a few moments afterward.

The next morning, loud banging from the kitchen woke him. His eyes fought to open. One eyelid refused to budge. He pushed up with a groan. Three teenage girls stood in the kitchen, preparing for the morning meal. They glanced over their shoulders and giggled, then leaned close to speak in conspiratorial whispers.

Mark knew something was up. He rubbed his face and swung his legs to the floor. An instant spike of pain erupted behind his eyes. Mental note. No more late-night drinking with Lincoln. He stood and crept into the kitchen and to the girls, then waited for them to turn. "Boo!" he said. As hoped, all three girls jumped and screamed. He gave them a wicked smile.

"Oh my God," Rachel said.

"You scared us," said Ruth.

"You deserved it."

"Hey, don't blame us," Alyssa said. "It was my mom's idea."

"Oh, was it now?" That made sense.

"Yes. Now go away. You smell like a brewery."

He sniffed himself and cringed. He did indeed smell, except like a distillery. He needed a shower, but he wasn't on the schedule yet. He had a better idea. Mark forced his body outside, where the bright morning sun pierced his eyes and seemed to make the pain in his head intensify. He turned his head and almost missed the first stair. He grabbed the handrail in time to keep from falling, which he was sure would give Lynn much satisfaction.

Someone called a "good morning" from the cooking area. It wasn't Lynn. Without a glance, he waved and went to his truck. He kept a duffel bag with his travel toiletries and some clean clothes behind the seats inside the cab. He got in, started the engine, and backed out the driveway. Two blocks away was a house that had a large pond. Mark drove there, got out, and walked down to the pond. A small shed next to the pond housed the usual swimming equipment. They used it for a changing room. He stripped out of his clothes, put on swimming trunks, and padded to the water's edge. A quick toe plunge told him what to expect. The water was going to chill him to the bone.

He set the towel down, took the soap and washcloth with him, and walked boldly into the water. When he reached waist-deep, he did a fast squat to acclimate his entire body and came up gasping for air. In less than three minutes, he had washed, shampooed, and climbed out. The brisk morning air didn't help. He wrapped the towel around himself and dried with vigorous strokes. His body held the gooseflesh long after it was dry.

Mark hurried into the shed and dressed, then took the long-poled net out and skimmed the water's surface to remove the soap scum. Once done, he sat at a picnic table and stared off at the horizon. The cool air now felt good, and his headache had been relegated to a dull throb.

The sound of an engine drew his attention. He craned his neck to see around the shed, thinking someone else had the same idea as him, then flinched back. It was a pickup truck he didn't recognize. It stopped behind some trees, kitty-corner from the house and pond.

Moving fast, he ran to the edge of the shed, only then realizing he was without his guns. He'd been in such a hurry to wash and clear his bourbon-addled brain, he'd left them back at the house. Another good reason not to drink with Lincoln. He still had weapons in the truck, but it was in the open and in clear sight from those in the truck. All he could do now was wait and watch and pray they moved on before he needed a weapon.

One man, an officer by the look, climbed up top and aimed binoculars through the trees. Mark tried to imagine what he saw from that vantage point. Whatever it was, it had to be only a small offering. He had to see through the trees and between the houses, Lincoln's home, to see the farmhouse. That didn't offer much of a view. He tried to picture the sight. He'd only be able to see the driveway, some of the vehicles lined up there, the garage, and the fuel tanker they'd transported home after yet another conflict two months back.

Could it be the tanker? Did they need fuel? Or was he possibly contemplating blowing it up? If Ohtanda sent them, he wouldn't put it past her to seek revenge by destroying those who dared escape from her evil grip.

The officer did a slow pan of the area, causing Mark to duck back as he swung his way. He formed a plan if they came in his direction. The truck was twenty yards away and in plain sight. If he had to run, the ground was open beyond the pond for about a hundred yards. He'd never be fast enough to outrun a bullet. The water could serve, but he'd have to hold his breath for a long time, and the ripples would give him away. He was trapped unless they sent one man to check the shed, and he defeated him quickly and without noise. At least then he'd have a weapon to defend himself with. With no safe options, waiting was all he could do. But if they made a move toward the farmhouse, he'd be forced to break cover and sound a warning.

Mark moved to the other side of the shed, which put him closer to the truck. The officer was finishing his sweep of the area and refocused through the trees. Mark ran through scenarios in his mind estimating the time it might take to reach the truck and recover his weapons. As long as the officer continued looking forward, Mark could reach the truck, providing no one inside was looking his way. How many others were inside? Two more would be the max for the cab.

He crouched to make himself smaller, deciding to go for the truck when the officer climbed down and the engine started. The vehicle backed away and drove south down the road, moving away from the farmhouse, perhaps searching for another hidden vantage point from which to study the community.

As the truck drove, Mark inched around the shed to keep it between him and any prying eyes. Once out of sight, he darted for the truck, hopped in, and gunned the engine. The tires caught with a squeal, and he raced back home. How many troops had Ohtanda sent? What was her goal?

Destruction? Or was she collecting more specimens to experiment on? He guessed Becca and Jin would be important enough to her to spare, but what about the others? He doubted she'd need all of them. That meant death and destruction were on the horizon. Again.

CHAPTER THIRTEEN

He braked at the intersection to peer down the road the truck took. It turned at the corner heading east. He floored the pedal, and the truck lurched forward. He reached the house and raced up the driveway. The truck skidded on the gravel, drawing the attention of all those seated at the tables eating their morning meal.

"Defensive positions. We've got company down the road to the south."

It took a moment to register, but then everyone moved at once. This time the table exodus was more controlled and with less noise and panic. They scattered to their assigned positions, and Mark pulled binoculars and his weapons from the truck. He slung the rifle, belted on the handgun, and walked to the street. He then aimed the glasses south but saw nothing. If he were trying to get a clear line of sight, where would he go? The road south was lined with trees on both sides, leaving the only option to drive down the street, making them easy to spot.

He scanned the trees behind the new building. Would they come through there? No, he didn't think they'd risk being spotted by someone in the woods. Guards had been posted there anyway. As long as they remained alert, an alarm would be given. Unless, of course, the intruders were stealthy enough to take the guards out up close. Possibility.

He turned and shouted to the spotter in the loft. "Watch the back." Caleb waved and disappeared inside.

If they were just scouting, they might be looking for the best approach. He swung the glasses east and moved toward the corner of the street. That position offered a long look in each direction. If he didn't already have a plan, the officer would want to take in every angle of the property. Mark realized he must not have a plan, or he wouldn't have been surveilling them.

So, were the men last night sent to attack or scout? Would they send four men to strike? Doubtful. Mark was sure he had other men. If he'd already scouted them, he'd know a lot of people lived here. No, the man was gathering information to prepare for an assault. Where was the best place to observe without being seen? It came to him in a second. He pivoted and aimed his glasses toward the wooded land kitty-corner from theirs.

He swept the glasses in a slow path along the front of the trees, searching for an anomaly. Anything that didn't fit. The officer had been wearing regular ACUs. He'd blend in with the trees to a point. He reached the far end of the trees and started back, this time stopping at spots with thicker covers.

He found a spot next to a thick-trunked elm that appeared denser than it should be. He placed the strap over his head and removed the rifle. With the powerful scope, he was able to bring in more detail. He caught movement amongst the branches, then spotted a hand holding the glasses. Was it the officer? If so, a single shot might end the situation. Would the others continue whatever their agenda was without leadership? That depended on whether the number two man felt confident enough to take over. It also depended on how big the force was. There might be a junior officer in place.

He set the scope just above the hand and readied to fire. The glasses moved on a path that would land on Mark. When they did, he saw the hands jerk at the shock of seeing a rifle aimed in his direction. Mark squeezed the trigger, and the hand disappeared. However, he wasn't sure if he scored a hit or the man ducked in time. He then had a sudden thought. He'd placed himself in the open, vulnerable to return sniper fire. He ran for the front porch. No shots followed him. He waited on the porch, propping the barrel on the cement wall that enclosed the porch. It was good cover, impenetrable for other long-range shots, though a fifty caliber might punch through, depending on the shooter's skill.

From across the street on Elijah's land, Mark spotted four armed men crossing the road and disappearing into the trees where the soldier had been hiding. He listened for the sounds of engagement, but none came. Twenty minutes later, one of the men emerged from the front tree line and waved an all clear. Mark stood and waved back.

He went through the house. At least one armed person knelt at every window.

"All clear," he announced. "But everyone stay vigilant."

He exited through the rear door and shouted the same thing. Slowly the diners returned to their morning meal. Excited chatter came back moments after the eating resumed but never reaching the relaxed tones previous to the alert. He caught Lynn's intense glare and realized she again was blaming him for bringing death to their doors. He sighed and walked toward the southern camp.

Lincoln joined him. "We're going to have to do something before these guys attack."

"Agreed. Thoughts?"

"I was kinda hoping you'd have some."

"I would, but someone gave me a hangover."

"Oh, that's right. Blame me cause you can't handle your liquor."

Mark grunted. "I want to hear what Milo has to say first."

They met the big man, Elijah, and his daughter, Darlene, in front of the new building. Elijah still looked frail and walked with the use of a staff carved from a tree branch. He'd been shot and almost died in their battle with the sea raiders a few weeks back. If not for Doc's skill and her staff's quick work, Elijah wouldn't be here.

Darlene was feisty and reminded him a lot of Becca. The two had squared off a while back before they'd joined forces. He didn't ever want to find out who was the better fighter. He thought Bobby and Darlene were getting close for a while, but with all that had been going on recently, perhaps budding relationships got cast aside.

"What'd you find out there?" Mark asked.

Milo shook his head. "Nothing. We heard an engine but never saw it or where it went. By the sound, they went west, but they were long gone by the time we got there."

"Any bodies or blood?"

"From your shot? No, none that we saw, and we combed it pretty good to make sure."

"We need to send out larger and farther patrols. We can't have them sneaking up on us. Those woods are going to have to be patrolled, too. I saw them two blocks over, watching us, but don't think they saw much from where they were."

"I agree," said Milo, who seemed to have assumed the leadership role in Elijah's weakened condition. "But we need to do more than that. We need to know where they are and how many."

"Yeah. If you and Lincoln will put your heads together to set up the patrols, I'll take a small group and go hunting."

"Sounds like a plan," Lincoln said. "See, even with a hangover, you can still think."

Mark scowled at him and turned to take care of his part.

All eyes were on him as he pushed through the row of mature pine trees that lined the side of the street, blocking the house from the road. He walked past the tables of people still eating. None dared ask questions. He went to his truck and rummaged through his weapons bag. He didn't have much time to clean his guns or refill magazines once they returned from their last encounter. He wanted that done before he went hunting.

He picked up the duffel bag and walked to the garage. Behind him, he heard running steps and knew without looking it would be Bobby. He opened the door, stepped inside, and walked to the workbench as Bobby entered.

"What's the plan?"

"Going hunting."

"I'll get my things."

Mark was about to say, "No, not this time," but recognized the futility and saved his breath. By the time he returned, Mark had the rifle apart and was dragging a cloth through the barrel.

"You need to clean yours?"

"No," Bobby answered. "Already done."

Mark should've known. Bobby was not only an expert marksman but was professional in all aspects of shooting and maintenance.

"Is it just the two of us?"

Mark looked up from his chore but didn't respond.

"Ah. It was just supposed to be you. Put it out of your head, old man. I'm going with you."

Mark grimaced. "Old man?"

Bobby nodded. "If the age fits." He shrugged. "Old."

"I don't suppose you realize or appreciate the fact that I'm trying to ensure you reach old man status."

"Someone's gotta look after you, and I'm the best suited for the job. Besides, I'm the only one who can put up with you for extended periods of time."

"Is that so?"

"So."

Mark chuckled. "Well, instead of sitting there jawing, make yourself useful and start reloading those mags." Fifteen minutes later, they walked from the garage and headed for the truck. As they slid their equipment into the cab, Jin ran over.

"Where go?"

"Hunting bad guys," Bobby said.

"I go too." He said it more as a statement than a question.

Bobby looked at his father, who looked at Jin. He nodded. "Get your gun."

Jin ran toward the house he shared with Lincoln and Jenny. Mark started the motor and backed down the driveway, across the street, and into Lincoln's driveway. Two minutes later, Jin leaped down the front stairs and opened the passenger door. Bobby moved over to give him room. As Jin settled in, he said, "I bring two." He held up two handguns, a nine-millimeter Beretta and a Smith and Wesson forty caliber.

"You got extra magazines?" Mark asked.

Jin looked at the guns. "No. Why I brought two."

Mark smiled. "Bobby, check the stores and bring an extra box of ammo for the forty."

Bobby ran off, and Jin said, "Big fight?"

"Never know. Better to be prepared."

Jin nodded.

Mark was sure the man had either military or police training from wherever he was from. He still thought Jin might be a spy for his government when they first met. Now, he wasn't sure. If he was a spy, would he have left the area he was assigned to penetrate? He did have his family's safety to think of, but Mark also thought they were part of his cover. Regardless, he was an asset to have in the camp. There was no doubting his skill with weapons or hand-to-hand.

Bobby came back, and Jin slid next to Mark. He handed Jin two extra magazines for each gun and a box of ammo.

Jin grunted his thanks and set about filling the magazines. As he did, Mark hoped they wouldn't have any need for extra magazines.

CHAPTER FOURTEEN

Britta's arm ached continuously. She didn't want to stop but knew the wound had to be checked and treated. In the morning, they ate what they could but were forced to leave a third of the meat behind. While the others readied to leave, she took two aspirin and pocketed two more, so she didn't have to stop later and dig them out, risking questions about what she was doing. Now the pills were wearing off.

They'd been walking since sunrise, about two hours, before reaching a road and turning west. It was faster traveling but more of a risk. If spotted they had to hope they were near something that offered cover. In the distance, an echo brought the sound of a single gunshot from a long distance. Britta was on point and signaled for a stop. Mariah and Maretha joined her.

"What do you think?" Maretha asked.

"Gunshot," Britta said.

Maretha gave her a 'Duh!' look. "I meant what should we do." She jabbed at Britta's arm. I think that bullet wound caused some of your brains to leak out."

Britta tried not to wince or show her discomfort, but she knew she failed by Maretha's expression.

"Let's have a look." She reached for the arm, and Britta pulled away. "Don't be difficult. You know I'm going to get my way, so give up before it becomes painful."

Britta blew out an exasperated breath. "Fine, but let's at least move down the road where we have some cover."

They walked into a cornfield halfway down the next block and unwrapped the bandage. The skin around the wound was an angry red. The arm was swollen and had a slight nose crinkling odor. Maretha examined and probed until Britta said, "Stop."

Maretha shook her head. "We'd better find that doctor soon. She cleaned, creamed, and wrapped the wound, then placed her hand on Britta's forehead. "How do you feel?"

"Like I've been shot."

"Tell me, or I'll shoot you myself."

"Fine. I feel fine."

"Liar. You have a slight fever. By tonight you'll be on fire. Tomorrow we'll have to carry your ass."

"That's not gonna happen."

"Got that right," Maretha said. "We'll just leave you here."

"You probably would."

"Count on it," Maretha said, with such a harsh tone and serious expression, Britta was no longer sure the woman was joking.

"Then I guess we better pick up our pace."

They set out again, keeping off-road and closer to cover. Britta held up a hand and ducked. They huddled together, Mariah facing to the side, Maretha facing the rear, and Britta facing forward. "Down the road, I saw brake lights," she said.

"We're close to whoever was shooting," Maretha said.

"Do we want to venture further?" asked Mariah.

"We need to at least check it out in case it's the soldiers attacking Mark's community," Britta said. "I don't see it anymore. That at least gives us a frame of reference as to where people might be." She stood, taking the lead once more. They spread out and kept deeper off-road.

Mark turned right at the corner heading west. Since that was where he spotted them initially, which was the direction they fled in, he assumed their base was that way. They drove slowly, checking each road and building as they went. A slow process, but they didn't want to pass the base and had no desire to run into them. The fifty caliber gun mounted to the top would chew them up in seconds.

They drove ten miles without encountering or seeing anything. Mark moved south a few miles before turning back east. After more than an hour, he began to think they fled west, but their base might be north or east. How he would set up a team for surveillance? He'd want to see the enemy's base from all angles as they'd done when checking out the medical facility. The vehicle scoping them out might have been on their second or third side by then completing the box around the farmhouse.

He continued east, then swung north, keeping to a ten-mile radius and working inward. He was at the halfway point heading west when a truck blasted out of a thicket to the north and rammed them broadside. It continued plowing them sideways until they tipped over in a drainage ditch, landing on the side. Shattered glass rained down on them. With the passenger side door pinned beneath them, there was only one exit left.

The door was crumpled and would not open. Mark placed his hands on the door frame and pressed down, lifting his body through the broken window. He got a foot on top of the door, ready to jump down when a voice called, "Stay where you are, or I'll air condition your body."

Mark froze and glanced up. The speaker was the gunner behind the fifty caliber machine gun. The vehicle towered over them not more than twenty feet away. He was an easy target. Even if he did manage to jump down and take refuge behind the truck, the others would be trapped inside, and in seconds the fifty cal. would rip through the truck, and he'd be dead anyway. He opted to freeze.

Two soldiers exited the rear door and took up positions to the sides. Each carried an M16 and had them pointed at him—a clear case of overkill. The gunner said, "Now then, why don't you climb down off there, one step at a time."

Mark kept his hands where they were in sight and jumped down. He landed on the slope of the ditch and had to lean forward and grab weeds to keep from falling back. He climbed to the top, where the gunman on that side motioned him to lie down. He did so without hesitation.

"Okay. Next one out. I know there's three of you in there, so don't be trying anything cute."

Bobby climbed out next, leaving his weapons on the inside. He jumped down, and the man on the left grabbed him by the shirt front and flung him to the ground.

"Now, the last one."

No one moved. "I will fire on you."

"He wasn't moving when I was in there," Bobby said, spitting the words out in a hurry to prevent the man from shooting. "He's bleeding. From his head. I think he's unconscious."

The gunner leaned down and spoke to the driver. The driver got out, pulled his sidearm, and approached the overturned truck. He climbed up the chassis until he could peer down through the window. "Hey," he shouted. "Get your ass up here. You better move, or I'm firing." Three seconds later, he did. He jumped down, holstered his gun, and said, "Yeah, he's out all right?"

"Did you kill him?" the gunner said.

"Nah, I shot past his nose. If he were faking, he'd have jumped. What do you want us to do with him? We can't climb down in there to get him."

The gunner said, "Well, we can't leave him either. We don't want him reporting back to their people."

"You sure?" asked the man standing over Mark. "That might work out for the best. The Captain said he wanted prisoners to use as leverage. This way, he'll be able to tell them we've got some of theirs."

"It'll put them on alert," the driver said.

The gunner said, "Man, they're already on alert. They know we're here."

"So, the question remains," the driver said. "What do we do with him?"

The man over Bobby said, "I vote we Swiss cheese his ass."

The gunner turned to the other two. "Two choices. Leave him or frag him?"

"Let him go is my vote," said Mark's gunman.

The driver said, "I don't care one way or the other, but let's get moving before one of their patrols comes along."

"I say we leave a bloody calling card for their patrols to find. They killed our men, so I'm gonna return the favor." He lifted the gun barrel, but before he could trigger a burst, Jin popped up through the window and placed two shots in the gunner's smiling face.

Both guards reacted, swinging their M16s toward Jin. Mark did a leg sweep, taking out his man's feet and sending the rounds into the air. Jin fired again, but Mark was too busy to see who the target was, though he hoped it was at Bobby's man.

As soon as the guard landed, Mark was on him. He twisted the rifle and shoved the barrel under the man's chin but could not get to the trigger. He pressed his entire weight down, but the man was strong and recovered fast. More shots were fired. As the gunfight raged over him, his battle reached a standstill. Neither man could gain an advantage.

The man whipped the gun to one side, altering Mark's balance, then kicked out from under Mark, giving him the top. He twisted the rifle, trying to break Mark's grip. The younger, stronger man was gaining the upper hand. Mark knew he was going to lose the rifle, so he planned for when that happened. He'd have to rely on accurate and devastating punches to keep the man at bay. Punches to the eyes, nose, and throat would take some of the fight out of his opponent, but they had to be quick and on target for maximum results.

As the rifle barrel twisted toward his face, it was time to make his move. He stretched his fingers and wrapped them around the trigger guard. The man might be able to club him, but he couldn't shoot. That bought him time enough to land his punches.

The moment was coming. He was about to lose the battle for the rifle. He released the barrel end, keeping his grip firm over the trigger guard. Without the space to swing his arm, the punch was a short jab. He missed the throat as the man reacted faster than Mark thought possible, but as the rifle was wrenched away from him, he managed an eye gouge that sent the man reeling backward. That gave him enough room, however, to swing the barrel in his direction.

Desperate now, Mark threw another punch into the man's throat. It landed, and the man's head lowered. He made choking sounds, but it wasn't enough to stop him. The man's face went bright red. Mark hoped it meant he was about to explode. Instead, the man reversed his swing and clipped Mark on the side of the head with the rifle stock. The blow stunned him for a moment, but his life was over if he didn't keep striking.

Even as he fought on, he knew his attempts were failing. Without intervention, he was dead. He made one last effort, using his core to do a sit up and driving his forearm under the man's chin, forcing him backward. He almost had the leverage he needed to knock the man off, but his opponent countered with an elbow to the other side of the head, knocking him back down.

The man leaned back to have room to bring the barrel on target. Mark had no other attacks to use. Nothing he could do would prevent the shot. Still, he did not give up. He brought both legs up and kneed the man in the back, pitching him forward. The shot roared in his ear but ricocheted off the street.

The soldier lifted the stock and brought it down into Mark's face. He was only able to turn his head enough to avoid full-on contact, but the stock slid down the side of his head with enough force to daze him.

He tried to clear his thoughts and his vision, but it was too late. The barrel swung to within inches of his face, but he refused to look away. He stared down the barrel, waiting to see the round explode outward. What he saw instead was a blade erupt through the man's throat. Blood sprayed, coating Mark's face. He could no longer see.

The weight was lifted from his body. He rolled and wiped at his face to clear away enough blood to see and be able to defend. He rolled twice more, then came to a crouch, ready to spring.

"Mark. Mark. It's all right."

It was a female voice. One that struck a chord, a distant memory.

"It's over. He's dead."

He used his sleeve to clear his eyes. Before him stood Maretha, nostrils flared, eyes hard, the bloodlust still working at her face. Behind her was Britta. Was he dead? Was this where his thoughts turned afterward? Confusion battled with elation. He didn't know how she came to be here, but he was alive to puzzle that out. His son and Jin came around the truck. Both were bleeding, but both walked under their own power.

Mark tried to say something. Anything. But the world began to spin, and he fell.

CHAPTER FIFTEEN

"We found them," Stanton said. "Or at least their bodies. They'd been stripped of anything useful, and the truck is gone." He wiped his brow with a sleeve. "There's a wrecked pickup in the ditch across from the bodies. From the looks of it, they rammed the pickup, perhaps hoping to take some hostages but lost the fight."

Childs slammed the table and stood. "Dammit! They were supposed to be out looking for vehicles and scouting, not engaging. How the hell did they lose a fight when they had the fifty cal to threaten with?"

Stanton shrugged. "Or use if their lives depended on it."

"My God. We're down to five of us. How did this happen?"

"What's the plan?"

Good question, Childs thought. These farmers were proving a more formidable foe than anticipated. They'd taken out more than half of his team, *and* they lost a truck. A major weapon that he was sure now sat defending the farmhouse. "Send a man back to the facility. Have him take one of the cars we found. Tell him—" what did he tell them? "Tell him to say the force is much larger than expected, and we need additional men and-and one more vehicle. Do not let him say we lost men. Not yet."

"Only one man?"

"We can't afford to send more. I still want to grab hostages. We'll have to take smaller groups. One of the teams followed people to a house off the grounds. We'll start with them. If there's one family out there alone, there's probably more. We'll take them tonight."

Mark woke with a start. He tried to sit up, but a hand pressed to his chest and kept him down. For a moment, he felt panic—that he was still locked in combat, then the voice came through. "It's okay, Dad. You're safe."

He saw Bobby and relaxed. "What's going on?"

"Hey there, stranger," Britta said with a smile, "Long time, no see."

"How-how did you get here?"

"A little walking, a little driving."

"How did you find us?"

Maretha snorted. "Followed the gunshots."

They laughed.

"Why are you here?"

"Evidently, saving your life," said Britta. "You're welcome, by the way."

He sat up. "So, you couldn't reconcile with your council?"

She frowned. "The possibility exists, perhaps in the future. For now, it was best to move on."

"Sorry to hear that."

"It was for the best."

Maretha snorted again. "Yes, or some people might have died." She offered a sinister grin, then winked at Bobby.

"Well, nice timing, and I'm glad you're here."

"We came here to warn you about the attack. We saw them leaving the facility and had an idea they were coming here. Guess we were a little late.

"I'd say you were right on time." His gaze drifted to her arm. "You've been injured."

"Yes, took a bullet from some other soldiers."

"Other soldiers?" Bobby asked.

"Yeah. An entire convoy, perhaps a hundred strong— heading east."

"East," Mark said, contemplating. "You think they're heading to the facility?"

"Reinforcements," Bobby said.

Britta gave that some consideration. "I hadn't thought about it. That would mean they were in communication."

Mark nodded. "That means there are other bases out there. Ohtanda hinted at something like that. There could be a whole network across the country."

Bobby said, "But if that's true, they must have had advance warning of the outbreak. Otherwise, how did so many survive?"

Britta picked up the thread. "Which would also mean they gave no warning to the general public. They only tried to save themselves." She shook her head.

"Does that surprise you?" said Maretha.

"No," Mark and Britta said together.

"That still doesn't answer the question of whether this virus was an accidental release or a purposeful attack," Mark said.

"Nor who set it loose," Bobby said.

Jin was driving. "We here," he said and turned the truck up the driveway.

Mark had a sudden fear. He sat up fast. "I have to get out fast before they open fire. Everyone's tense over the various sightings and intrusions." He stood and moved for the door. "They have to see a familiar face. Jin, stay here. Ladies, stay inside until I call you. I don't want them to shoot because they don't know who you are."

Mark opened the door and put both arms outside where everyone could see he was unarmed. He stepped to the ground and stood still with arms raised above his head. From somewhere in the house, he heard, "Hold fire. Don't shoot. It's Mark."

He walked away from the truck and lowered his arms as Bobby exited. Jin hopped out the driver's door. As people came outside, still carrying weapons, Mark let them approach. When they had relaxed, he motioned for Britta, Maretha, and Mariah to come out.

"Lincoln said, "Nice wheels."

"Yeah," Bobby said, "We traded in the old one for an upgrade."

"I'd say." Lincoln poked his head inside the truck and looked around.

Becca rushed over and embraced Maretha. "Sister. So glad to see you."

"And you also, little one. You look fully recovered."

"Getting there."

Everyone wanted to ask questions at once. Mark lifted a hand for quiet and said. "Some new friends have arrived. They need medical care. Let's meet at the tables in about fifteen minutes, and I'll fill you in." The chatter and questions continued. Mark stopped. "Bobby, why don't you get started, and I'll join you after I take Britta to Doc."

He took Britta by her elbow and guided her through the crowd. Maretha and Mariah followed. The crowd followed Bobby to the tables taking the noise with him.

"I'm impressed," Britta said. "This is quite a large community, and they all responded to a possible enemy incursion."

"Unfortunately, we've had lots of practice. These are good people. You'll see once they get to know you."

Maretha said, "I am surprised to see it's unprotected."

He glanced at her. "You mean no walls or fortifications?"

"Yeah."

"So far, we've had little need for that. Our size alone usually is enough to discourage attacks."

"But what if the military comes in force?"

"At that point, walls won't matter. They'll be able to destroy any barricades."

He opened the barn door and led Britta and the others inside. Doc was sitting at a desk, sipping her morning coffee. "More excitement, I see. Oh! Britta."

"Hi, Doc."

"What? How? Oh, you're injured."

"'Fraid so. Took a bullet."

"Okay. Let's have a look. Mark, would you ask one of my nurses to join me, please."

"Sure, Doc." To Britta: "I'll leave you in her good hands."

"Thanks, Mark." She squeezed his hand as he left.

CHAPTER SIXTEEN

Bobby was already well into the narrative of the recent attack. After tapping two of Doc's nurses and telling them their services were needed, Mark stayed in the back. He didn't want to be front and center. It was time for others to take his place. However, when he finished with the story, Bobby was quickly overwhelmed by questions and panicked voices. He sought Mark out with a 'help me' expression, and Mark lifted his voice as he'd done many times before in times of duress. And as before, the crowd responded by quieting.

"Look, the truth is we don't have answers to your questions yet. We need to gather information. I have an idea who is controlling these soldiers and a fair notion as to why. I've explained that to you before. Regardless, we will stand together and deal with any trouble that comes our way. Lincoln has already spoken to many of you about increased patrols. That should start now. We'll also double the guards around both campuses at night. For those off-campus, make sure your radios have fresh batteries. When we know more, you'll know more. I promise. I'm not keeping anything back. Now, go about your normal routines."

Before anyone could corner him with more questions, he spun and walked toward the new truck. Bobby caught up to him. "Thanks for the save."

"You had it under control. You just need to look more confident when people start questioning or commenting. Don't lose your patience or show anger. They're mostly just afraid and want answers. You did fine."

"It's not something I want to get used to doing."

Mark laughed. "Don't want a future in politics, eh?"

"Oh, hell no."

They entered the truck and looked around. It was fully outfitted with weapons, gear, and ammunition. Mark grabbed his duffel bag and his guns. He needed to find a new ride. *Gas.* The thought jumped to his mind. The truck had half a tank. With supplies limited, he'd have to go back to empty the tank.

"What's our next move?"

Mark had been giving that some thought. "I think I'm going to pay a visit to the General."

Bobby nodded. "Yeah. That makes sense."

"I'm glad to hear you approve of the old man's idea."

"Once in a while, your brain still functions."

Mark found Becca. "Would you introduce our new guests to everyone?"

"Of course."

"Make sure they meet Lynn and Caryn. Show them around and find someplace they can settle until we know what they're doing?"

"No problem. Where you going?"

"I'm going to visit West. See if he knows anything about the recent activity in the area."

"Good idea. I'll take care of everything."

"I know you will." He gave her a quick peck on the forehead. "Oh, and would you mention to Lynn where we're going?"

"You should go talk to her."

"Please. Thank you, sweetie."

"You're a coward."

They borrowed a car from the ten that were parked on the grounds and headed for the Air National Guard base about ten miles west. The base was run by a self-appointed general, who at first had tried to force his then small community of about twenty people to join the guard. He'd even brought his full army to the farmhouse threatening a war if they did not comply. However, Mark and his people did not back down and gained the upper hand over the troops. Many who were not real army had been forced into service themselves.

Then when an invading force entered the area, Mark joined with the guard to repel the attackers. Ever since, they'd been on good terms with both sides offering to help the other should the need arise.

Mark hadn't been to the base in a while. He didn't recognize either of the guards at the front gate. Once he identified himself and a call was made, they were allowed through the winding barricade. The base itself was bustling with activity. To Mark, it appeared the number of uniformed residents had grown significantly. They parked and were escorted into headquarters and the General's office.

"Mark. Bobby. Good to see you." General West was a large, heavyset man in his fifties. His hair was all but gone, and his uniform looked tighter across the chest. Either their food supply was good, or the man had been working out. Mark guessed the first option.

He strode forward and shook each of their hands with a warm vigorous shake. His good mood was unlike the man who was usually stoic and reserved. "To what do we owe the pleasure? Have a seat."

They sat in two leather chairs in front of the desk. West perched on the corner of the desk.

"General, you're in a good mood."

"Me? I'm always in a good mood. More so because we just located a new supply of jet fuel and a lot of spare parts from another base in Indiana. We should be able to get two F-15s in the air now."

"Wow! That is something to celebrate."

"Yes, sir, it is. Of course, we still have to be careful we don't overdo the flights. Wouldn't do us much good to fix them if we didn't have enough fuel to use when we needed to be airborne." He crossed his arms and took on a somber look. "I'm guessing this isn't a social call."

"No. We're here to ask some questions."

He frowned. "Okay. I'll answer if I can."

"Are you aware of any other—let's say secret bases around the country?"

"Secret bases? You mean like underground?"

"Maybe. Or maybe just hidden. The kind that keeps to themselves and don't let others know they exist."

"We talked before about this. I told you we've been in contact with another National Guard base. Two now. One is about our size and the other considerably smaller. One's Air the other's Army."

"I'm talking about bases or maybe more appropriately facilities that are government-run and have a military presence. Has anyone reached out to you?"

West eyed Mark with a somewhat suspicious glare. "Why don't you explain why you're asking."

Mark told them of their encounter with Ohtanda's medical facility. West was unable to keep his jaw from dropping open several times.

"If that wasn't enough, we've encountered troops at the farmhouse in the past two days, which I'm guessing were sent by this Ohtanda."

"Troops? Here? Why did she send them?"

"Maybe because she wants her test subjects back and perhaps a few more to do research on. They've been scouting us, and earlier this morning, one of their patrols attacked us."

"I can honestly say we've not been in contact with any groups like that. What makes you so sure they're government?"

"The way the place was run. The uniforms. The equipment. The well-stocked research labs and food supplies. It has the feel of a government black-site."

"That's incredible. I wonder what their purpose is and why they haven't reached out?"

"Based on what we learned there, it's apparent they had something to do with either the creation or release of the deadly virus. Maybe both. Regardless, Ohtanda is working on some sort of cure or vaccine to halt its progress."

"You're telling me our own government may be responsible for this outbreak?"

"It looks that way. However, it's unclear as to whether it was an accident or deliberate."

"Why would anyone release it deliberately, knowing the result?"

"I have no answer for that, but it is a possibility."

They sat in silence. West dumbfounded, and Mark watched him for signs he knew something about the facility. He didn't get the feeling West knew.

"On top of that," Mark continued, "some of our people spotted a military column moving down the turnpike yesterday. They estimated their number at a hundred."

Again West's jaw dropped. "You mean to tell me that sized force passed right by here, and not one of my men saw or reported it? I can't believe this. A hundred, you say?"

"Well, not me, but yes."

"If they knew we existed, they would have stopped in, don't you think?"

"If they thought you were here, they might have, but if you're not in their loop, even if they did know you are here, they might avoid you anyway. Less explaining and complications."

"I think I'll send an envoy to this facility to introduce us and let them know we're ready to serve."

That bothered Mark. He didn't need an ally swinging to the opposition. He hadn't planned on that. He wanted information from West and perhaps a pledge of support. "If you do, be careful. They may not let your team leave. I seriously think their goals are different from yours. You want to help the survivors. They not only may have caused the death of millions but are capturing survivors and experimenting on them."

"Be that as it may, until I have all the facts, I can't reach any conclusions."

"I'd hate to have them recruit your base and turn you against us."

"Unless you pose some threat to them, I can't see how that would happen."

"You know us. We're not a threat to anyone unless they attack us."

They stared at each other for a moment, and the tension made the room feel smaller. West finally spoke. "I have no intention of being your enemy. We've done too much together for the good of both our communities. But I do want to know what's going on out there. If the government is functioning, we need to be part of the recovery. We are government, at least to some degree."

"I understand your need to know. I hope making contact with them doesn't change the relationship between our two communities." Mark stood. "I'd appreciate knowing what comes out of your initial meeting." He offered his hand.

West shook it, but the good mood was nowhere in sight now. "I'll tell you what I can."

It wasn't the answer Mark hoped for. He had a bad feeling their working relationship might have just come to an abrupt and painful end.

CHAPTER SEVENTEEN

"That didn't go as I'd hoped."

Bobby agreed. "No. Didn't inspire confidence in a long-term working relationship."

"Mark. Bobby. I thought that was you."

Mel jogged over and gave each of them a bear hug. "It's good to see you."

"You too," Mark said. And she did look good. Military life had done well for her. Even though she technically had not agreed to join their ranks, she lived on the base with her girlfriend Tara and went through the same daily regiment as everyone else. Consequently, her one-time stocky frame had firmed up, and some of the extra pounds were gone.

"You look happy," Bobby said.

"I am. Coming here is the best thing I've ever done."

"Good to hear," Mark said. "How's Tara?"

"Geeked. They got a new supply of jet fuel, and they've scheduled a test flight. She's still the only trained pilot, and they don't want to lose a plane to a rookie, so she's got the nod. She's floating so high now she might not need the plane."

"Wow! That's awesome, "said Bobby. "When's the flight?"

"Early either tomorrow morning or the next day. They're doing their final checks now. I think a lot depends on the weather. There's supposed to be a storm coming in tomorrow. Not that the plane or Tara can't handle a storm, but I think they'd rather have clear skies and no complications for the inaugural flight."

"I wonder if General West will let us watch." Bobby was as excited as Mel.

"I don't see why not. But even if the general says no, you can park anywhere around the airfield and be able to see lift-off."

"True."

"Mel," Mark said in a lowered voice. "Has there been any talk about other bases or military convoys around here?"

She gave him a strange look. "I know they've communicated with other bases, but I haven't heard of any around here. Why? What's up?"

"A convoy passed by here yesterday heading east. I thought it curious so came to ask the General about it."

"And?"

"He denied knowledge, which I thought to be strange. Why would another army pass up a base without checking in? Unless they were trying to avoid confusion about whether they were being invaded or not."

"They kept going, though, right? They didn't set up camp?"

"No, not to our knowledge. I just thought you might have heard. I don't want to start gossip or cause a panic. It's just better to know things rather than speculate."

"I'll keep my ears open and let you know."

"Thanks, Mel"

They chatted for a few more minutes before getting into the car and driving off base.

"What do you think?" Bobby asked.

"I didn't get the sense she was lying. Besides, if it was a secret, it's unlikely West would have shared the information with the base."

"What now?"

"Let's do some searching."

"You mean since we were interrupted last time?"

"Let's stay more alert this time."

They drove north from the base and made a five-mile square around the farmhouse. They did see a car moving from afar but lost it before they closed the distance.

"You think that was them?"

"Not sure. But it wasn't a military vehicle."

"Maybe that's because we now have it, and they've been relegated to driving cars."

"You might be right. They were using a pickup truck when they were spying on us before."

"Should we keep searching around here?"

"No, I think we should get back. We need to make plans and set up our defenses before nightfall."

At the farmhouse, they found a group of twelve people gathered around the tables. Lynn and Caryn were talking to Maretha and Mariah. Lincoln stood to the side listening, and Becca sat next to Maretha. Food had been brought out for the guests.

"So, you live in an all-female town?" Caryn asked incredulously.

"Yes," Mariah said, between bites of a sandwich. "Or we did. We were kinda asked to leave."

"Really?" Caryn said.

"Imagine that," said Lincoln. "Drama in the all-girl school."

Maretha shot him a nasty look, and Becca said, "Watch your mouth, Lincoln. If it comes to a fight, my money's on them."

He raised his hands in front of him. "It was just a joke."

Mark set his bag down. "My money's also on them."

"Thanks for the vote of confidence, friend."

"Oh, I have confidence in you. I'm confident you'd get your ass kicked."

Maretha puckered up and shot Lincoln a kiss.

"So, if you don't mind my asking," Caryn said, "Why did they ask you to leave."

Maretha chewed with deliberate slowness. She swallowed and said, "For supporting a man instead of our sisters." She flicked a twinkle-eyed look at Mark. All eyes swung his way.

"Guilty." He slid on the bench next to Becca.

"Leave it to a man to ruin everything," Caryn said. Mariah lifted her hand, and the two high fived.

"You know you're not winning this one, dad."

"Not even going to try. How's Britta?"

Becca said. "In recovery. Doc said it was good she got here when she did. Her arm was infected. It might take a while for her to recover."

"Is she awake?"

"She wasn't when we left. Doc said to give her a good hour before she comes out of sedation."

"How long you staying?" Mark asked Maretha.

"That depends on Britta. She was hot to get here to see you. Now that she's here and saved your life, we'll have to wait and see what she wants to do next."

"She was hot to see Mark?" Lynn spoke for the first time. Her eyes stayed on Maretha but flicked once to Mark.

"Yes. With everything they went through together when we thought the patrol was coming to attack you, she wanted to get here and warn you."

Lynn nodded but, to Mark's relief, didn't pursue it further. Not that they'd done anything to feel guilty about. Since Lynn was no longer interested in him, it wouldn't have mattered if he had done something. But deep in his gut, he didn't want her to have those thoughts. They were distant enough as it was without her thinking he'd already replaced her.

She stood. "Can I get you anything else?"

"No," both women said.

Mariah said, "Thank you. This is great."

Lynn offered a smile, then turned and carried dishes inside the house.

Becca nudged him and motioned with her chin to follow Lynn and talk to her, but Mark couldn't convince his body to make the move. Instead, he stood and picked up his duffel bag. "We're glad you're here. Becca will show you where to stow your gear and get you settled in."

He walked to the garage, thinking he'd rather face another ten soldiers than Lynn at the moment.

CHAPTER EIGHTEEN

Private Joseph Bowden was amazed at how many vehicles were on the facility's grounds. Where had they all come from? He was passed through the rebuilt gate and told to report straight to General Martin.

He parked on the side of the building where repairs to the damage from the recent battle were being performed. A lot more men seemed to be on the grounds than when he left. He also noted the different uniforms they wore.

He entered and was led to a large meeting room. Several officers sat around the long table. More than half were men he'd never seen before. As he was ushered in, whatever the discussion was halted mid-sentence.

General Hilton "Hard Tack" Martin glanced up at the intrusion showing no signs of recognition for his own man. "What's the meaning of this interruption?"

The escorting sergeant said, "Sir, Captain Childs sent this private here with a message."

The General swung his hard grey eyes at the private. "Well, speak up. What's the message?"

His harsh tone was enough to send a quake through Bowden's legs. "Sorry for interrupting, Sir. Captain Childs wanted me to report to you."

"Proceed, Private. We have important things to discuss."

"Yes, Sir," he swallowed hard, then gave his report. "The captain wishes to say the community he was sent to take over is much larger than anticipated. He requests additional men and one more vehicle, sir."

"Excuse me? Did I hear you say he needed more men to do his job? More men to take on some untrained farmers? Clearly, I sent the wrong man to do the job."

Bowden didn't know what else to say. He stood swaying, his eyes locked on a spot on the wall a few inches above the General's head.

"You go back to Captain Childs and tell him I'd better have some progress . . ."

"General, allow me," the newcomer with an equivalent rank as the general said. "Private. How many men do you have?"

Without thinking, he blurted, "Five, counting the captain, Sir."

"Five?" said Martin. "I sent you with ten plus the captain. How did those numbers change?"

"Ah, well . . ."

"Stop stammering, Boy. Give me an answer."

"They were killed, Sir." His voice sounded like a squeak.

"Killed? How so?"

"Not sure, Sir, but it appears they had run-ins with the farmers, Sir."

"They engaged and were beaten, or were they ambushed?"

"Unknown, Sir. We found the bodies of four of our men just today."

"Four casualties in one engagement?"

"Where is this battleground?" the other general asked.

Martin said, "On the far side of the city. We have trackers placed in our two most important targets. I sent ten men to capture them and a few others and eliminate the rest. I guess I sent the wrong man to accomplish the mission."

"That's interesting. We lost a few men as well in that same area. I sent them out to cut down a few wanderers, and they never returned. A search party failed to locate them. Perhaps these farmers are better organized than you give them credit."

"Bah. It shouldn't have been a contest."

"Would you allow me to send some of my spec-ops people?"

"Of course. That would prove helpful, I'm sure."

"I'll have them gather who you want, then leave the rest to me. I want to find out who killed my men before dishing out punishment."

"As you like, General."

He turned to a colonel, his second in command. "Send team one with this private. Give them specific instructions. Send word when they have captured them. I want to be there for the interrogations."

The colonel nodded and left the room.

General Bob "Bulldog" Billings spoke to Martin. "Are these people tied to the battle fought here?"

"Yes. Along with a small town consisting almost entirely of women a few miles down the road."

"Women, you say?"

"Yes. We leave them alone, and they don't bother us. Until recently, that is. When I found out they were harboring our test subjects, we had to take measures."

"And yet those measures failed since I'm sending *my* men to retrieve what you lost."

Martin's face reddened.

"Don't worry, General. We'll deal with the townsfolk as well."

"I'm not sure that's necessary."

"Not necessary? They dared raise arms against you. It's more than necessary. It's mandatory. We'll set an example for all those around to see. No one will bother you again. No one will ever interfere with our mission. Now, I'd like to speak with Doctor Ohtanda. I need to evaluate her progress. According to her last message, she has created a vaccine, but she needs to perform further research on this female test subject before she mass produces the drug. We're here to make that, and everything else on the agenda happen.

He turned to his aide and whispered a few words. The man rose and left.

"Now, take me to her."

Martin paused, his teeth grinding. He noted it was more an order than a request. He rose and led the way. Before they reached the elevators down to the main lab, Billings said, "Give me a moment to confer with my men, General." He walked away without giving Martin a chance to respond.

He walked outside to where his troops were gathered. He spoke to Captain Crandall, the skilled veteran officer in charge of team one. "From this minute forward, *our* agenda is the only one that matters. Go. Make a statement, then bring as many back as you can. We're going to step up the experiments. We're not leaving here without the finalized vaccine. Understood?"

"Yes, Sir."

He moved to the second group comprised of teams two and three. "We are going to lay siege to this town. I don't want them killed, although a few bodies can be motivating. I want to use the town for the men's recreation and to gather extra test subjects. Before we do that, I want reconnaissance done. Send in Corporal Dawson. Have her dress in civies and infiltrate the town. Set up how to send and receive reports. Give her two days. Then we send the boys in."

"Yes, General."

Billings had been sent to take over research facility number six. The reports they sent had shown the most promise of the eight other research labs scattered around the country but judging from recent events, the leadership was in question. General Martin was unaware his position was in jeopardy, but he was a smart man. He'd figure it out soon enough. By then, he wanted his men to be in position to take the building by force if necessary.

CHAPTER NINETEEN

Jarrod, Maggie, and Debbie were on their way to the farmhouse. They hadn't been by in a while, and Jarrod had six new hens to give Mark and Lynn. His farm stood eight miles from the farmhouse. With the addition of twelve female nurses and two male stragglers, his farm had become an overcrowded refuge. Not that he minded. In these trying times, it was nice to have companionship.

Maggie did a wonderful job serving as housemother to the lot and organizing the daily routine. After a few difficult days in the beginning, after her husband had been killed, she took control, and the household had been running smoothly ever since. His farm had done well before the apocalypse, and he was blessed with a lot of livestock. Pigs, cows, chickens as well as three horses filled his pens and stables. With the extra hands, he'd been able to harvest his bean and corn crops. They would be set for the upcoming winter. Well, with one minor exception, which was the reason for this trip.

The hens were a bribe in exchange for some much-needed assistance building a new dormer above the barn and winterizing the other new construction that housed half the women. Jarrod knew the bribe was unnecessary. Mark would always offer to help as Jarrod had done for him. But this way, both sides benefitted. And as much as Mark's community had grown over the past month, they could use the extra eggs.

"I have to say," Maggie said, "I'm excited to see everyone again. It's been what, three months since I've been here?"

"You're not going to recognize many of them," said Jarrod. "They've taken in close to forty people since then."

"The only two people I knew were Mark and Lynn," Debbie said. Jarrod and Mark had rescued Debbie from a hotel where a mob they called the Horde had kept her captive. They set all the captive women free, and many stayed on to have someplace to live. Debbie and Jarrod had become close over the past few months.

"I can't imagine where they're housing them all," Maggie said. Maggie and her husband had also escaped the Horde, but in the battle, Jim had been killed.

"You'll be impressed with what they've done. That's what I'm hoping to have done at our place."

"Do you think they'll help?" Debbie asked.

Jarrod smiled. "They'll help. I think that's one side effect of the apocalypse that was good. People are willing to help each other again."

It was later than Jarrod usually liked to travel. It was easier to see the dangers in the daylight. They had a small problem with a cow giving birth that set them behind. He didn't plan on staying long but wanted to get there before everyone settled in for the night. By his estimation, they should be cleaning up from dinner now.

Jarrod glanced in the rearview mirror, then did a quick double-take. A vehicle had pulled out behind him and appeared to be closing fast. He pulled the shotgun from between the seat and the door where he kept it while driving.

Debbie noticed. "What?"

"Not sure, but we got company."

Maggie and Debbie turned to peer out the rear window. Maggie grabbed her thirty-eight from a belt holster and Debbie, who still carried a purse, took out a nine millimeter.

Jarrod picked up speed. They were still four miles from the farmhouse and any possible help.

Ahead, another vehicle pulled out across the road, blocking much of the way, but not enough. Jarrod judged he had room to pass on the right, however, that might be what the driver was hoping for. If he went right, the blocking vehicle could ram him broadside and force him from the road. Perhaps even roll them, although, in his massive pickup, that might be difficult.

"Get ready. I'm faking right and going left. They'll be on the passenger side."

Debbie leaned in front of Maggie to get a shooting position. Maggie turned, facing outward.

Jarrod closed at ramming speed. The blocking vehicle appeared to be military. It had one of those fifty caliber machine guns mounted to the top. He didn't know much about them other than they could rip through his truck and reduce them to chopped meat in seconds. He couldn't let that happen but knew stopping might be worse.

He angled right, trying to gauge the distance he'd need to make a sharp turn back to the left. Then two quick pops from the side of the road, and the truck was skidding.

"What happened?" Debbie asked, a note of high-pitched panic in her voice.

"They shot out the tire. Prepare for contact."

The truck fishtailed left. Another series of flashes and pops, and the other front tire blew. Jarrod no longer had control of the truck. He braked, but they were sliding sideways. They slowed enough not to make the collision deadly, but the impact with the side of the military truck jarred them. Maggie fell into Debbie, who smacked into Jarrod, who fell halfway through the window. His shotgun clattered to the road.

Before he could right himself, the barrel of the fifty cal was a few feet from his head, and two men had guns pointed at Maggie and Debbie from the passenger side. Maggie's gun was yanked from her hand. Debbie lifted hers, but Jarrod grabbed her arm and brought it down. He took the gun from her hand and, holding it between thumb and forefinger, passed it out the window.

"Smart man," a tall man with sergeant's stripes on his uniform said. "Now exit on the passenger side. Any effort to resist will result in someone's death."

Jarrod had no choice but to slide out and stand with the women. They were spun around, pushed face-first into the truck, and had their hands bound behind them. The following vehicle was an SUV. They were placed in the back seat and driven away.

Ten minutes later, they were ushered from the SUV and escorted inside a house that was less than a mile from his own. Jarrod cursed himself for not being more aware of his surroundings. How had he not noticed activity here? Mark would never have let that happen.

They were placed in kitchen chairs and left there under a soldier's gun. Debbie began to cry. Maggie leaned toward her. "Stop it, child. Don't give these bastards the satisfaction."

A few minutes later, the sergeant entered. He ignored them as he walked through the kitchen and into the living room. A whispered discussion ensued. The sergeant walked through again and out the rear door. Seconds later, an engine came to life and the vehicle left.

"What is going on?" Jarrod wondered. They weren't out to rob them, or they'd be dead. They weren't after the women, or he'd be dead. No, they wanted something, but what? Information? That was most likely. But what did he know that they'd want to know?

He thought about his truck and hoped some of Mark's people discovered it unless they moved it from view. But no one would be actively looking for them since he never let Mark know he was coming. Even if they left the truck in the road, it might not be until morning before it was found.

Jarrod didn't doubt that Mark would search for them, but a lot could happen to them by then. They waited. An hour passed, nothing happened. Whoever was in the front room showed no interest in them, and the only person they saw was the soldier guarding them.

Twenty minutes later, two vehicles pulled up behind the house. A commotion occurred. Loud voices, several smacking sounds, and cries of pain followed. Then the door opened, and two more people were dragged in, a man and a teenage boy. The man was being hauled by the sergeant and another soldier and appeared to be unconscious. The boy was helped by a soldier. He hobbled on one leg with blood dripping from the other. He was placed on the last kitchen chair and then bound to it. The man was dumped on the floor with a thud. He groaned at the contact but did not move. His hands were tied, and he was left there. His face bore the signs of being beaten. A small cut over his eye bled, and dried blood congealed under his nose.

Jarrod recognized them as members of Mark's group but did not recall their names. The boy hung his head and cried softly.

Was it a coincidence that both sets of captives had ties to Mark, or was that the goal? In this area, everyone had a connection to the farmhouse, so it could be just random, but somehow Jarrod doubted that to be the case. Somehow, this had to do with Mark and his people. But Jarrod was in no hurry to find out what.

The sergeant walked through the kitchen again, spoke to the still unseen person in the front room, and then left. Outside, Jarrod could hear the man say, "Let's go get a few more."

CHAPTER TWENTY

"So, what do you think?" Mariah said.

Becca had taken them to a room on the second floor of the house. It was a room she shared with two other girls, but for the night, she got them to agree to let the guests use the room until accommodations could be found elsewhere. The girls did not seem to mind and were gracious about not being ousted.

Becca brought towels and asked them to limit their use of water since so many had to share. Then Becca bid them good night and left them alone.

Britta spoke in a whisper, not wanting what they said to carry through the walls. "I'm impressed. It shows that men and women can live together in a community without endless problems. Everyone seems nice."

"Appearances can be deceiving. I don't believe any community is without problems," said Maretha.

"I agree," Britta said. "But this is certainly better than some places I've been." She pulled the sheet back and sat on the bed. Her arm ached. The doctor had given her three pain pills to take if needed. She also said if she didn't need them to return them to the doctor, as their supply was limited. She pondered taking one but decided to forego unless she couldn't sleep.

"Did you notice how that one lady kept staring at me?" Britta asked.

"You mean Lynn?" Mariah said. "Yeah. I noticed. She looked kinda angry."

Maretha took off her boots and dropped them on the other side of Britta's bed. The room was small and had but one twin bed. A sleeping bag on a foam pad was on the far side of the bed. "I asked Becca about her. Mark and Lynn were the community's founding members and, for a while, were a couple."

"They're not now?" asked Britta.

"No. Guess they had a falling out. Becca likes her and has a lot of respect for her. She says she's responsible for keeping this operation together."

"Huh," said Britta, lost in thought.

"Yeah. Huh." Maretha said sharply. "Don't be getting ideas. You'll get us run out of here. It's obvious by the way Lynn kept staring at you that she still has feelings for Mark and sees you as a threat."

"I have no idea what you're talking about."

Maretha snorted. "Whatever."

"You got the hots for Mark?" Mariah asked. "He's got to be like twenty years older than you."

"I don't know what it is. He intrigues me. And regardless of his age, he's still good looking."

"Oh, Lord, help us," Maretha said.

Mariah laughed.

Britta said, "What?"

"Just keep it in your pants."

"Maretha!" her voice held a shocked tone, but her eyes twinkled. "And what about you?"

"What about me?"

"Don't be playing all wide-eyed innocence with me. I've seen the way you look at Bobby. Judging by his return looks, he feels something for you, too."

Maretha stammered. "I, ah, I, what? There's nothing between him and me."

"Whatever," Britta said. Mariah high-fived her, and they laughed.

"Shh! We're getting too loud," Britta warned.

"And even if there was something," Maretha said defensively, "at least he's my age and not old enough to be my father."

"Maybe I see him as a father figure. Would that be so wrong?"

"As long as you don't try to bang him," Maretha said.

"Maretha! That's not anything I ever thought about."

"Bull!"

"No. Seriously. I like him—am intrigued by him, but I'm not interested in anything beyond that."

Maretha slid her long legs under the covers. "Whatever."

Mariah tucked herself into the sleeping bag, and Britta settled in next to Maretha. "What do you think we should do?"

Maretha said, "About staying or you banging Mark?"

"Stop that. I'm not going to, oh, forget it. About staying."

Maretha said, "I think we should stay until your arm heals enough to travel. We can see how life is here and decide once you're ready to go."

"Sounds good to me," Mariah said amidst a yawn. "I'm out. Night."

"Good night Mariah," said Britta. Maretha rolled on her side, facing away from Britta. So much had happened that Britta stayed awake, staring at the ceiling, trying to sift through the events and her feelings.

Becca had taken the sleeping bag on the right side of the bed. They had crammed five people in the room tonight to make room for her new sisters. The place she laid her head was inches from the heating grate connected to the room Maretha and her friends now shared.

Even in whispered voices, most of the words drifted through the vent. She heard it all. Some of the discourse made her smile, while some made her want to voice a comment through the vent, but one thing bothered her. Did Britta come here to be with her father? Why hadn't she seen that back in Britta's town?

For one, she was recovering from her ordeal with Dr. Ohtanda, and two, she'd been secluded away from everyone else. Did it matter that Britta liked her father? It shouldn't, but her thoughts kept returning to Lynn. She was sure the woman still had feelings for her father. She damn well knew he had them for her. What they didn't need was drama.

She hadn't liked Lynn at first, seeing her as a replacement for her mother. She had even threatened physical harm if she didn't back off her father. Over time she'd developed a grudging acceptance of Lynn—one that had grown into deep respect. She gave her father her approval, and for a while,

Mark and Lynn shared a room. Now, that was over, and the two barely spoke. It was sad to watch them avoid each other when she knew in her heart they desired to embrace and hold each other forever. She could never replace her mother, but if she had to choose someone to be in her father's life, Lynn was a good choice.

But with Britta in the mix, did that hurt or help their chances of reuniting? What if he chose Britta, and it became too uncomfortable here that they moved away? She didn't like that idea at all. She'd have to keep an eye on them and watch Lynn's reaction. Maybe there was a way to use Britta's appearance to bring her father and Lynn back together.

On the other hand, Maretha and Bobby, as a couple, excited her. They would make a great and deadly combo. She wholeheartedly agreed with that match. Oh, sure. Darlene had shown interest, but they'd been so busy since bringing her group to the community that there'd been little time to develop a relationship. It appeared to have cooled. But Maretha and Bobby. Now that was a match.

She rolled over, placing her back to the vent when it became apparent her guests had settled in for the night. Bobby and Maretha. She smiled, seeing all kinds of ways to tease her brother about this situation.

CHAPTER TWENTY-ONE

Mark sat at a picnic table long after everyone turned in for the night. He had no desire to go into the house until he was sure Lynn was deep in sleep. Avoiding her was the best way to get through the day, but it saddened him. He didn't want to be at odds with her. If that was how it had to be, he could accept it, but he'd prefer they remain friends.

"Oh, you're awake."

The voice startled him to the point he stood and whirled, his hand on the butt of his handgun.

"Whoa! It's just me." Lincoln stepped into the fading firelight with his hands up in surrender. "Glad you're up. Saves me from having to creep inside and wake you."

"What's up?"

"One of our guards rousted me with a story that he thought he heard gunshots."

Mark's eyebrows went up. He didn't question the statement. He knew only two things sounded like gunshots—a backfiring engine or gunshots. "Did the guard get a direction?"

"He said it was to the north, but couldn't tell how far."

"Out here, there's not much to interfere with sound. It could be miles away."

"Yeah, but it's still something that needs to be checked out."

"Did you send anyone?"

"Not yet. I wanted your input first."

"You mean you wanted me to check it out."

Lincoln flashed a smile. "You know I keep forgetting you have a functioning brain."

"Oh, that's right. Insult the man you want to put his life on the line for you."

"Hey! I'm going, too."

"Oh. You must not think there's much of a threat."

"Easy now. Come on. Gear up."

Mark went inside and grabbed his duffel bag. Lincoln had his SUV waiting in the street with the motor running. They drove north, keeping to a slow speed.

"It's going to be difficult seeing anything. It's a dark night," Mark said

"Yeah. I got one of those plug-in spotlights on the floor in the back seat. Maybe that'll help."

Mark reached back and found the light and then plugged it into the lighter. They drove for about five minutes before Mark said, "Slow a bit." Lincoln did, and Mark switched on the spotlight, playing it over the side of the road.

"Anything?"

"Nope." He flicked the light off, and Lincoln increased speed. A few minutes later, Mark said, "Hey! Wait."

Lincoln slowed.

"Stop. Did you hear that?"

"Hear what?"

"We ran over something back there. It crunched, like broken glass."

Lincoln backed up.

"Stop here. It wasn't too far back."

Mark got out, taking the spotlight with him. The light had a long cord. He squatted and shone the light along the street. Back another four yards, the light reflected off something. He moved closer but was forced to stop due to the cord. "Back up." Lincoln did. "Stop." Mark swept the light along the road, spotting shattered glass. He picked up a piece. The jagged shard was easy to recognize. It was glass from a car's window. "Someone had an accident here recently."

Lincoln got out, gun in hand, and focused his gaze on the side of the road.

Mark aimed the spotlight on Lincoln's side. There was a drainage ditch and an overgrown field. Not that he could see that far in the dark, beyond the light's cone of illumination, but he'd been down the road often enough to know what was there.

He turned back to his side. A small stand of trees stood thirty feet from the intersection. The ground was flat there with no ditch. Beyond the trees was a series of four houses built out in the middle of nowhere. They'd checked those houses months ago and stripped them. Behind the houses was tilled acreage that had not been planted during the last growing season. It was mostly weeds. Thomas Bedrosian and his son David moved into the third house down.

He was about to move further down the road when something reflected the light. He stopped and focused the beam on that spot. It took several attempts to get the same angle to cause the reflection again. "Over here. There's something in the trees."

"Something or someone?" Lincoln said, coming to his side of the SUV.

"Maybe both. You want to check it?"

"No." Mark gave him a look of surprise.

"Just being honest." Lincoln moved forward with his gun out. Mark noticed the gun wavered a bit. He changed positions to have an angle to protect Lincoln if something happened. Lincoln stumbled, swore, and caught a branch to keep upright. He worked his way into the trees and then was lost from sight, his dark skin hidden by the trees and the night.

"It's a truck," he called out. "A pickup truck." Mark waited for more. "Doesn't appear to have anyone inside."

"That's a good thing. Can you tell anything about what happened?"

"No. Not enough light."

"Hold there." Mark placed the light through the passenger window on the seat, then walked around the SUV. He reversed the vehicle, angled it toward the edge of the road, and then turned the wheel so the headlights pointed at the truck. He got out and walked to where Lincoln stood."

"Looks like a flat tire," he said.

Mark didn't respond. He walked around the truck. "Got another one here and some collision damage. That doesn't explain how it got here, though. If it was on the road when the tires blew, it would've skidded and perhaps hit the trees, but the truck would be on the other side. It looks like it's been driven in here. That's the only way I can see it ending up over here."

"Could it have come from the side street?"

"Doubtful, unless they were running at high speed. The broken glass is on this street."

"Don't it seem odd that two tires blew at the same time?"

"Yeah, I was thinking the same thing." He opened the driver's door and looked inside, but there was nothing there to see. He closed the door and then opened it again quickly. Wait a minute. He knew this truck. The sticker on the back window read, 'Farmer's do it in the dirt.' "Lincoln, this is Jarrod's truck." He climbed into the cab and searched for blood. He didn't see any. He backed out and kicked something on the floorboard. He felt with his hand and found a shotgun shell. It was Jarrod's all right.

He was in a crash, but was it an accident, or had someone caused it? "Let's go down to Bedrosian's house. Maybe they heard something."

"If Jarrod was in an accident, maybe he went there for help."

"Yeah, maybe." But Mark had a sudden bad feeling about what they might find. "Let's walk."

"Okay. Let me turn off the engine and get the keys."

Mark didn't wait for Lincoln. He walked into the field and toward the first house fifty yards ahead. Lincoln caught him as he neared the house. "You check the front. I'll take the back. Check to see if there have been any break-ins. I'm pretty sure we left the doors open in case people did check. That way, they wouldn't have to break down the door to get in."

Lincoln moved to the front, and Mark walked on. He wanted these houses intact in case they got so overcrowded at the farmhouse they needed more space. They were a few miles away but still close enough to be part of the community. Thomas and his son were the first to do so.

He moved to the rear door and tried it. It was locked. Did they not leave all the doors unlocked? He checked the back windows. All were intact. He moved to the second house and repeated the process, finding that the rear door was also locked.

At the third house, he stopped, crouched, and waited to see Lincoln out front. When he arrived, he was but a darker moving shadow within the night. Mark moved to the rear door and tried it. Locked. Here he did expect the door to be locked. Thomas wouldn't want someone wandering in during the night.

A whistle drew his attention. He jogged around the far side of the house and peered around the front corner. Lincoln stood on the small square porch. Mark scanned the area for any signs of danger, but if it was out there, he couldn't see it anyway. He walked to the porch.

Lincoln said, "Doors wide open."

That wasn't good. They'd never leave the house open. "Lead on. I've got your back."

"You know, I never understood that. If I walk in and get shot, you've got my back means you might shoot who shot me, but I'm still dead."

"You want me to go first?"

"No. I was just saying." Lincoln stepped past the threshold. Mark was close behind. Lincoln kicked something. "Looks like someone's tossed the place. Got stuff all over the floor."

"We need to check for bodies."

"Yeah. Great." They walked through the dark house and found no bodies, alive or otherwise.

They exited and stood on the porch. "So, no Thomas and David and no Jarrod."

Lincoln said, "Any chance Thomas and David drove Jarrod home?"

"Suppose there's always a chance. Let's go make sure before we raise an alarm."

CHAPTER TWENTY-TWO

They hurried back to the SUV and drove the remaining distance to Jarrod's farmhouse. The house was about the same age, about a hundred and twenty years, as the one Mark stayed in, only smaller. However, Jarrod had a lot more acreage. Jarrod always planted dual crops and had a substantial garden for his own needs and several dozen various fruit trees. He had been self-sustained long before the apocalypse.

The house and grounds were dark. No sign of life showed anywhere. Mark searched the grounds, but there was nothing to see. They went to the side door and knocked. A second try was louder, and then they could hear footsteps coming from upstairs. The murmur of voices reached them.

Mark shouted, "It's Mark and Lincoln. We're looking for Jarrod."

The house went silent for a moment. Then from the rear corner of the house, a voice called. "Show me your hands. If I see a gun, I'm shooting." It was a male voice. Mark knew only two other males lived here. Duncan and Morris.

"Is that you, Duncan? Or is it Morris? It's Mark and Lincoln. Don't shoot. I'm putting my gun away. Okay, we have no weapons out."

"Why are you here? You said you were checking on Jarrod. Why?"

"We found his truck down the road. It'd been in an accident and was hidden behind some trees."

"Hidden? Like it was done deliberately?"

"Yes. Can you get Maggie for me?"

"Can't do that."

"Look, this may be an emergency. Jarrod might be in trouble. I'd like to find him before something bad happens to him. Now please, get Maggie."

"Can't. She was with Jarrod. Debbie went too. They were going to see you."

"How long ago did they leave?"

"After the calf was born. It was near dark and later than they wanted. He was bringing you some chickens."

"We didn't see any signs of those either."

Lincoln said to Mark in a quieter voice. "You think the chickens might be motivation for the assault?"

"That's sure a possibility." To the other man, "So before dark, but the sun was fading?"

"Yeah." The man moved closer.

"So they've been gone for about two hours."

"I suppose."

"Has anyone been around here in the past few days?"

"Saw one of them military trucks from the base drive down Central a day or two ago."

"A day or two. You can't be more exact than that?" Lincoln asked, with a note of disbelief.

Hey, we was busy with stuff. I can't keep track of everything that happens around here."

"Okay. Okay. Settle down. We have to search for them. You got any flashlights we can borrow?"

"Sure. Gladys," he said.

"Yeah."

The voice came from behind, startling them. They pivoted to see three women holding guns pointed at them.

"Well, that was stealthy," Lincoln said.

The man said, "Can you call into the house for some flashlights, please."

Gladys backed away, keeping her gun aimed at them, then jogged up the stairs and into the house.

The man stepped forward. "I'm Morris, by the way. Duncan's the one got you in his sights from the hayloft."

Gladys came back with four flashlights. Morris took them and handed one to each of them. "Where should we start looking?"

"Which direction did you see the military truck going?"

"It was heading east."

"You see how far it went?"

"No. Like I said. I thought it was one from the National Guard base, so I didn't pay it much attention.

"Let's start in that direction."

"Should we go together?"

"You got a car you can drive?"

"Sure out back."

"Get someone to go with you. Two can search better than one. Keep the others on alert in case they turn up, or someone else does."

They drove back the way they came turning left on Central Avenue. He told Morris to keep back a distance in case the SUV was attacked. Gladys rode with Morris and looked very comfortable riding shotgun with her rifle.

They drove for a while, but if something was out there to find, they couldn't see it in the dark. After nearly two hours of searching, they were forced to return to Jarrod's. By then, the household was up, dressed, and worried.

"Why would anyone take them?" Bev asked.

"You know why," one of the other girls said.

Bev cringed. Though months ago, the memory of their captivity was still fresh and painful in their minds.

One of the other girls said, "But they took three men, too. That doesn't make sense. There has to be more going on here."

"Agreed," Gladys said. "Unless they didn't want the guy's bodies to be discovered."

"Gladys," Bev said. "Don't speak like that. They are not dead."

Gladys shrugged. "No sense sugar-coating it."

"We need a large search party and more light," said Lincoln.

"Let's go back to the farmhouse and get everyone up."

"What should we do?" asked Morris.

"Wait here until we get back. We'll organize the search so we can cover the widest possible area."

"I hate to be sitting here with our thumbs up our asses while they might be getting tortured," Gladys said.

"If you want to keep searching, go ahead. Just make sure someone knows where you are and what areas you're searching, so we don't waste time going over the same ground."

They left and drove home.

"This shit never ends, does it?" Lincoln said.

"Doesn't seem to. It's one ordeal after another."

"Sometimes I think it'd be better to pack up and move, but it's gonna be like this no matter where we go."

"Yep. After all we've done here to make it a home, I'd hate to throw it all away and start over."

"Suppose you're right. It's just frustrating. I wonder if we'll ever know a time in our lives where we have peace."

"Wish I had something to tell you. All we can do is make our existence as peaceful as possible. We've come a long way to that end."

"Yet still so far to go."

CHAPTER TWENTY-THREE

It was after midnight when they reached the house and parked. Sunrise was still a long way off. They were going to have to search in the dark and pray for the best.

"How do you want to do this?" asked Lincoln.

"We either rouse the entire compound or move quietly through the rooms and wake a few."

"Don't we want to put as many people out there looking as we can?"

"If someone is out there kidnapping our people, I think it's best we don't give them too many opportunities to take more. I think we wake only the best people for hunting. We can send back for others as the night wears on, but I'd rather not have to worry about their safety.

"I'll get Jin, then cross to Elijah's camp."

"I'll take the house and the garage."

They separated, then Mark stopped and froze. "Lincoln."

"Yeah."

Mark moved quickly toward him and pulled his gun. Lincoln, seeing the move, copied it. His head turned side to side, trying to see what Mark did. "Did you see the guard stationed to the north?"

"No, but I wasn't really looking."

"Let's do that now."

They separated and moved with stealth toward the northwest guard post. It was set up between a series of large boulders that Mark assumed marked the property line's border. Because of their size and circular positioning, a guard could stay there and be unseen in the dark. It offered cover and protection.

Had the person assigned there wandered off at nature's call?

"Who's scheduled for duty here? It's either Caleb or Ruth."

That disheartened Mark. Both were Lynn's children. If something happened to either of them, she'd go ballistic, starting with him.

They rounded the boulders, peering in the center, but no one was there. Something was wrong. He sensed a presence before the man spoke.

"Easy now."

Lincoln and Mark spun, facing the voice.

"You don't want to shoot your pretty little guard now, do ya?"

The man stepped from the cornfield with Ruth in front of him as a shield, and a gun pressed to her head. She appeared unhurt.

Mark took two steps to his right for a better angle and to ensure if the man started shooting, he could only get one of them. Lincoln squatted behind one of the boulders to make himself a harder, more challenging target.

"We're not here to hurt anyone. Not unless we have to."

"Why are you here?" Mark asked, never taking his aim from a spot inches past Ruth's left ear.

"You may be a good shot, but my man back here has his sights on you, and he's wearing night-vision goggles. He won't miss."

"Again, why are you here?"

"You walked off with something we want back."

"Not happening."

"Then the people we've been collecting all night will die."

"They're dead anyway."

That stopped the man, perhaps not knowing how to respond since it was the truth. "No. Here's the deal. You give us what we want, and we release the others. No one gets hurt."

"Except for those we give up to you."

"I can't pretend to know what the good doctor is going to do with them, but it strikes me that if she's going through all this trouble to get them back, she doesn't want them hurt. It's my understanding they're important to her research. She's not about to sacrifice those who might be the key to a cure."

"I've already had to deal with your good doctor. There's nothing good about her. I don't trust her and am not about to send her anyone she can use as test subjects."

"Then this will go very badly for your people. We have enough troops and firepower to level these buildings and bury everyone inside. I'm doing it this way because I'm trying to save their lives. My way, it's a simple exchange. A half dozen people for all those we hold. Simple. Done. We're gone. Your way, a lot of people die. Maybe instead of being hard-headed and making the decision yourself, you should talk it over with your people. I'll bet whoever is attached to this young lady will want her back."

"Give the word, Mark," Lincoln said.

"Yes, Mark give the word. Diaz, you got him?"

"You bet, Sarge. Right in the middle of his forehead." The voice was somewhere to the sergeant's right.

"Good. I'll take the other one. He won't shoot through the girl, and he's standing in the open. See Mark, we can shoot too. And I dare say with our gear and training, we're better at it. Now, you go and discuss the situation with your people. We'll contact you later."

"Leave the girl," Mark said.

"And give you an open shot at me? I don't think so. She'll be fine. I'll take personal care of her. You have until dawn to decide. Then I'll bring our full firepower down on you, and we won't even have to be in sight to do it."

He backed away toward the corn, keeping Ruth pinned to his body, and the gun pressed to her head. She began to whimper. "Now. Now. No need for tears. I'm gonna take good care of you. Remember, we can see you better than you can see us. If you follow us, I'm going to leave her body in the corn, then kill you."

Two more steps, and he melded into the corn like a ghost.

CHAPTER TWENTY-FOUR

"What do we do?"

Mark didn't hesitate. "Wake everyone."

As Lincoln ran to sound the alarm, Mark took off at an all-out sprint. He reached the street and ran parallel to the field. Going through the field would make him easy to spot, but if they came through it, it was a good bet they had a vehicle waiting on the other side. If he could get there before they came out of the corn, he might be able to ambush them and rescue Ruth. If not that, then perhaps follow them long enough to figure out where they were hiding.

Did he have more hostages than Jarrod, Maggie, Debbie, Thomas, David, and now Ruth? Not that that wasn't enough. He hadn't anticipated this move. Lynn was going to be furious and blame him. Maybe she was right. This could all be traced back to his wanting to go fishing. How many people had died because of that decision? How many more would die?

His rage boiled over, giving him all the adrenaline he needed. He reached the corner and cut through the end rows of stalks to reach the side street. It was too dark to see if a vehicle was parked along the road and he dared not turn on the flashlight.

Across the street from the cornfield was another piece of open land. This one offered little cover, but he raced for it anyway. He needed to reach the next street over to be able to see down both. He hoped he'd arrive before they did. They would have to drag Ruth and trudge through the corn. Mark ran through the open field. Unable to see where he was stepping, he caught something and fell. At the speed he moved, the impact was bone-jarring. He hit, rolled, banged multiple body parts, and finally got to his feet and ran again.

He reached the next street, slowed, and crouched. He cast his gaze down the side of the cornfield. No one was in sight, but at this point, he was relying more on sound than sight. Then he looked down the shorter length of the side street. Nothing yet. He had decisions to make and not much time to make them.

From here, he'd know when they came out of the field but wouldn't be in a position to stop them. If he moved closer and they did have night vision glasses, he'd be seen. He could look for whatever they were driving and perhaps hide behind it to spring his ambush, but if he didn't get there in time, he'd be seen.

No matter. He had to get closer to have any options. Mark crept toward the corner, searching for cover. He thought about his run. He'd come down the side street and crossed into this field about halfway down the block. At that point, he hadn't seen a car. That narrowed his search area to half the shorter block and the long side. He could narrow that distance some as well. He doubted they'd have parked near the southern intersection. That would have placed them too close to the house. If it were him, he'd have parked midway down or more. That would give him a shorter, ninety-degree search grid. He darted across the street and moved into the front rows of stalks near the corner.

There he squatted and focused his hearing. He crawled forward and lay down with his head and torso out of the corn. He decided to take a chance. He aimed the flashlight down the shorter road and flicked it on. The light did not reach far, but it illuminated enough to eliminate the first thirty to forty feet of road from having the escape vehicle. Mark decided to play the odds. He hurried back into the corn and came out on the long street side. Through a process of elimination, he figured the ride would be parked on this side, not across the street.

He waited, angst growing by the second over concerns about making the wrong choice. Then the sounds of movement drifted through the corn, south of him, though he couldn't tell how far.

He heard a voice, "Check with the glasses before you poke your head out there."

Mark ducked back and tried to burrow into the ground.

"It's clear."

He risked creeping forward and peeking. Though he couldn't see them, he did hear the doors open. "Get in there, and don't give me any trouble, or I'll hurt you beyond your scariest dreams."

The engine started. Mark rose. He wouldn't get a chance to stop them if he didn't move now. Row by row, he moved south, but when he saw the car speed off, he knew he was too slow reacting. He exited the corn as the small car passed him. He took off in pursuit, angling across the street and into the field. If he stayed behind them, they might catch a glimpse. If he couldn't stop them, he had to at least get a direction to begin the search.

The taillights glowed brightly in the dark. They continued straight for several blocks. Mark recalled each side street they passed and said it aloud to remember it. Ahead, the brake lights lit, and the car rounded the corner to the right. Central. That was Central Avenue. They went east. Instead of following straight to Central, he cut across the field and ran down the next street. By the time he reached Central, he had to strain to see the receding pinpoints that were the taillights. Sucking in air like it was in short supply, he pulled up and watched for as long as he could. About to give up and admit defeat, the brake lights flashed, and the car turned left.

How far down was that? Keeping his eyes glued to the spot he saw them turn, Mark ran on. His endurance had been weakened from the mad dash, so he could only maintain a jog, but he made steady progress to the spot. It was only guesswork, but he had a direction. They couldn't know he was following, so he doubted they'd do a series of turns to throw pursuit off. At least he hoped that was the case.

By the time he reached the area he mentally marked, he could barely breathe or stand. He bent over with his hands on his knees and fought for air as he stared down the road. Was it this one or the next one? Maybe it was still five blocks away. He couldn't be sure. But if this was all he had, he'd at least give it a look.

This area was more residential. Houses lined Central as well as the side streets connecting with it. They weren't packed together, like a suburban subdivision, but eight to ten houses lined the long roads. He'd have to check each one as he went.

They'd want to park the car either in the backyard or behind the house. He might not be able to check the garages, but he had a better chance of finding them if he walked through the backyards instead of on the street.

The problem with that search pattern meant he had to go up and down each street twice to check both sides of the road. It might take all night, but what else did he have to do. Back at the farmhouse, he'd be sitting around doing nothing but answering questions. At least this way, he was doing something, even if his efforts proved futile.

He finished the first block without finding anything of interest. At this rate, it'd be dawn before he finished three blocks. He had to do this smarter. They'd post a guard, to be sure. That would give him a heads up, providing he saw them before they spotted him. But would the guard be posted inside or out? Outside, a guard had more mobility but might be easier to see. Inside, Mark wouldn't have a chance to see him. It didn't matter, and he increased his pace and jogged through the backyards, keeping his head on a swivel. By the time he finished three blocks, it was going on four in the morning. He estimated he had about an hour and a half before the sun began poking its head above the horizon.

He caught a break on the next block. Not only was it half the length of the first three, but it dead-ended. He finished fast and moved to the next street, working his way back toward Central. He decided if he reached there without finding anything, it was time to head back to the farmhouse. It took longer than expected. The sun was already creeping upward by the time he arrived, again finding nothing. He'd covered two streets, three blocks each. That left two more streets before reaching the next main road running north and south. Mark didn't think they'd gone that far, but if they had, there'd be no way of finding them.

He debated searching now, but if he was wrong and they slid by him, he'd never arrive back in time to make sure the exchange went off without a problem. He stood on the corner about to jog across the street when he heard an engine approaching. Mark darted back to the corner house and dove over the shrubs next to the porch. He landed hard but forced himself to peek through the bottom of the small trunks. A car had stopped at the corner of the next block. Two men sat in the front seat. He was sure the man in the passenger seat was the man from last night, the one the other man called 'sarge.'

The door opened, and Sarge got out. Had Mark been seen? He reached down and drew his gun. But Sarge didn't come toward him. Instead, he walked behind the car. The captured people could not be in the car. It was too small. So what was the play?

Mark crept forward for a better angle. The sarge went to a military truck pulled up behind the car, a Humvee, like the one they now had on their property. He spoke to the driver, then pointed across the street. Mark imagined Sarge was giving directions as to where he wanted them stationed. The truck was big enough to hold all the kidnapped victims. Was that how they were going to do the exchange. Hold them until they got what they wanted?

The side door opened, and an officer got out. With the door open, Mark had a clear line of sight into the truck. No one else was inside that he could see. No hostages. No extra soldiers. So, if the hostages weren't there, where were they?

The officer climbed into the passenger seat of the truck. Sarge got back in the car, and they drove off. The car turned right and traveled down Central while the truck drove straight across.

Mark stood and watched them go. If they were going to make the exchange, the hostages would be with them. Unless they were waiting for word to be sent, the exchange was on. If they were going to attack, wouldn't they send a larger force? Counting the drivers, only two men were in each vehicle. Maybe they didn't have a larger force. Mark's people had killed six of their men. So how many were left behind to guard the hostages?

The enemy had a head start. He'd never make it back in time to negotiate or fight, but he might be able to find the hostages. He turned around and walked back the way he came, focusing on the backyards of houses on the next block. He didn't want to walk that street. He'd be in clear sight of anyone posted inside the house, and he doubted they'd keep any vehicles out front like a sign that announced, 'we are here.'

He reached the end of the block with no sign, then crossed the street. The stress of his decision to search rather than go back home to help defend weighed heavier with each house he passed without finding the hostages. Halfway down the second block, he paused and rethought his choice, then shook it off. He'd come this far, he might as well see it through. He prayed whoever handled the meeting with the sergeant could hold his own and not give in or get taken by surprise. He had a feeling that person would be Lincoln.

He reached the end of the second block, and his body vibrated with nervous energy. He had to hasten his search. A voice kept calling from inside his head to go back. The temptation was great, but he went on, jogging now.

At the end of the road, he stopped. Nothing stretched before him but an open field. He had gambled and lost. He gazed right and suddenly had renewed hope. The next street continued alongside the field. It did not dead end, which both delighted and deflated him. The road ran on at least another three blocks that he could see. No, it was too much to do, and he was already long past time to return.

He gave one long last look, pivoted, and started back to the farmhouse at a run. However, something he'd seen in that prior look nagged at him. He slowed to a walk and replayed the images from memory. Then it came clear, and he made an abrupt halt. Mark whirled around and ran back to the last house. Where was it? He scanned from house to house. There. One. Five. Eight houses down—the front end of another military truck peaked out from behind a shed in the backyard.

CHAPTER TWENTY-FIVE

Hope restored, Mark darted across the field toward the house, keeping the shed between him and anyone looking out the rear windows. He sprinted harder, slowing and stopping as he came to the shed. He moved to the corner and peered around. It was a truck, and no one was guarding it. He studied the house. It was a ranch-style home of yellowish brick construction. He started on the right side closest to him and made a note of the windows and what they most likely illuminated—a bedroom. Then a frosted window for the bathroom followed by another bedroom. After that was the small window usually seen above kitchen sinks. A sliding patio door came next, and two more windows he guessed were for a family or dining room.

Once he had the layout of the back set in his head, he imagined the front would have a living room and another bedroom, and the garage. He ducked and ran to the corner of the house. He crouched next to the first window then slowly rose to peer inside. The room had curtains, but they were parted enough to show the room was empty. He moved on.

He could not see into the bathroom but placed an ear close to the glass. He heard nothing, but that wasn't conclusive. The next bedroom only offered a peek through the gap in the curtain. The bed was unmade and had the look of a recent inhabitant.

The kitchen window had frilly curtains but only enough to decorate the side. Mark had a clear view of the kitchen and a portion of the family room. Seated on the floor with her hands tied behind her was Ruth. He saw an arm and leg of another person next to her but couldn't see who. From the position of the arm, he knew it was another prisoner. He found them. Now what?

He pulled back to think. How many men were inside? Did it matter? He had to get the hostages free no matter what, but he still had to know where the guards were. He ducked beneath the kitchen window and crept toward the patio door. Peering from a low angle, he now had a clear view of the kitchen and family room. All the hostages were lined up along the family room wall to the left, sitting on the floor in front of a stone fireplace. He did not see any guards.

While he tried to decide where to look next, Ruth glanced his way then did a double-take. Her expression brightened, and her body straightened more erect. She was going to give him away. He waved his hand and shook his head, then pressed a finger to his lips. She seemed to understand and allowed her body to shrink back down. She shot a furtive glance to her left then back to Mark. He mouthed, how many? And held up one, then two, then three fingers and shrugged.

She glanced left again, then her eyes widened. She motioned with her head, and Mark understood someone was coming. He quickly ran to the end of the house but had nowhere to hide. The fence prevented him from getting around the corner. He knelt, brought the gun up in a two-handed firing grip, and waited.

The door never opened. He waited a few seconds, then crept forward again. He reached the patio door, and Ruth spotted him. She mouthed something he didn't catch, then studied her mouth. Her lips formed an O. Did she mean one? Or, Oh, no? He held up three fingers to have a starting place. She shook her head in slow moves. He lifted four fingers. Again a shake, but now she motioned with her chin downward. He understood and showed two fingers. She shook and gestured down. One finger. She nodded. There was only one guard? He showed one finger again. This time her nod had more emphasis.

So, there was only one guard to deal with. Now, how did he get inside? Or maybe it was better to get the guard to come to him. He pointed to his eyes and then to her, then made walking motions with his fingers and hoped she understood. Mark glanced around the yard to find something to use as a distraction. His choices were patio chairs, a table, or an umbrella. He chose a chair, picking it up and heaving it at the truck. The lightweight aluminum frame did not cause any damage but did create quite a noise. He looked at Ruth, who widened her eyes and gave an emphatic if not panicked nod. Mark slid back, pressing to the brick wall, and held his gun up in one hand. If the man exited, Mark would get the first shot. The time crept by with no one appearing. Then Mark heard something scrape against the kitchen window above him.

He crouched in slow motion and duck-walked to the patio door. Ruth was watching for him. She used her chin to point his direction, letting him know the guard was still in the kitchen. Then her eyes widened again, and Mark knew he was coming. This time he waited, poised to shoot.

He spotted the M-16 first as it tapped against the glass door. A head came into view next, the forehead in contact with the glass. He looked forward, then angled his head in a slow turn toward Mark, then began a slow swivel to the right. Once the head, still pressed to the glass, reached beyond the halfway point of looking straight out, Mark pushed off the wall, stepped in front of the door, and fired.

The guard must have caught movement in his periphery because he stepped back from the glass and lifted the rifle. The glass punctured with Mark's first shot then shattered with the barrage of subsequent shots by both men. Mark's found the target well before the other man brought his weapon to bear. The impacts on the guard's chest drove him backward in unbalanced steps. By the time Mark shot eight times, the man was falling and bloody.

Voices screamed, then settled, then all spoke at once. Mark ignored them, keeping the gun trained on the downed man. He walked up the two cement steps and kicked out the glass. Then he reached in and unlocked the patio door, and slid the near glassless frame open.

As he stepped into the house, the voices rose in volume until he glared at them. Whatever they saw on his face was enough to quiet them. He stepped up to the body and removed the M-16. Blood covered an arm and the neck of the guard, but there was none on the uniform. This registered in Mark's mind a fraction of a second before the man moved. The vest he wore had taken the brunt of the rounds, leaving him bruised but a long way from dead.

In a flash, the man swiped up with a long knife he'd pulled from his belt. Mark jumped back in time to keep from being gutted. The man lunged at Mark. He jumped back again, but the move put his arms out wide and not on target. The man took advantage of Mark's mistake. He got to his feet and continued the steady movement of the knife.

Mark flung a kitchen chair in front of him. The man knocked it aside and drew his hand back for a stab. Mark tripped over another chair and fell back. The misstep saved his life as the blade shot forward with surprising speed. As Mark fell, the distance between the two combatants grew, allowing him time to reacquire his target. He fired once into the chest to back the man up, then lifted the barrel and placed two rounds into the man's face. This time blood erupted. The man took one more step, then fell face first, bouncing off a chair before hitting the floor. From his downed position, Mark kicked the knife away from the man and stood.

He picked up the knife sliced through Jarrod's bound hands. "'Bout time," he said. Mark was too amped to reply. He handed the knife to Jarrod and slid out his own. With the hostages free, Mark checked the body and found a key. "We have to hurry." He stepped outside without further explanation.

He unlocked the truck and climbed into the driver's seat. Jarrod opened the side door, holding the M-16. Ruth entered, carrying the knife, and Thomas followed, holding the dead guard's sidearm. David came next, followed by Maggie and Debbie. Jarrod closed the door and got in the passenger seat.

"Well," the big man said, "here we go again." Mark started the engine and drove straight out of the backyard onto the field. The vehicle bounced hard over the uneven ground until they reached the next street. As soon as the front wheels hit the cement, Mark pushed the pedal down.

"Got a plan this time?" Jarrod asked.

"In the works," Mark said.

"Well, that's progress. Usually, we ain't got one at all."

CHAPTER TWENTY-SIX

Sergeant Stanton stepped out of the car and straightened his long frame while he took in the reception committee. A man and a woman stood in front of a semi-circle of ten armed people. A smile played at the corner of his mouth. He allowed his eyes to scan the house, and then his smile faltered. At least two guns were pointed out every window. He let his eyes drift toward the barn. The hayloft door was open on the upper level. Although he didn't see anyone, he knew one of the better shooters would be stationed there.

He continued his sweep of the grounds, finding others at the garage windows, both levels. They had the firepower to cause some serious damage. That would change in a moment. Keeping his voice low, he said to his driver, "Radio the captain. Let him know we made contact and keep the line open."

He walked toward the two in front he assumed were the spokespeople. He recognized the tall, well-built black man from the night before and focused on him as he approached. That was a mistake.

The woman went from stoic to a full-blown crazy rage in a heartbeat. She slammed the barrel of a handgun under his chin with such force it snapped his teeth together. "Where's my daughter, asshole."

Stanton let his rage boil before saying, "Dead, if you don't get that gun out of my face."

The two glared at each other from inches away. The black man moved forward and spoke to the woman in a low voice. "Let's hear him out first, Lynn."

"Yeah, Lynn," Stanton said. "Hear me out before you die."

Lynn pushed up on the gun, lifting his head further before stepping back in a huff.

Stanton smiled as she backed away. 'I like feisty women. Maybe we'll have a chance to get to know each other better when we're done."

Lynn stepped forward and raised the gun to slash it into Stanton's face, but Lincoln caught her arm and pushed her back. "One of you needs to come get her before she starts a war," he said to the group behind him. They all had raised weapons, prepared for battle.

"They declared war when they took our people," Lynn yelled.

A man and woman stepped forward and guided her away.

"I like her," Stanton said.

Lincoln whirled on the man. "Say what you have to before someone's finger slips and your worthless life is ended."

"Down to business. Good."

"Where are our people?"

"Safe. For now. Something happens to any of us, and they'll die."

"What do you want?"

"Already told you. We want the girl, Becca, the Asian family, the doctor, that woman there," he pointed to Lynn. "Oh, and our truck back." He glanced around. The Asian male was not in sight, but the girl, Becca, was in the center of the scrimmage line.

"Unless we see that our people are alive and well, there's nothing to talk about."

"We're beyond the talking stage. We leave here with our demands, or the exchange doesn't happen."

"No."

"No?" Stanton snorted. "Then you just said good-bye to your friends."

"They're either already dead or soon will be. We're not giving you anything without making an exchange."

"Guess there's nothing left to discuss then." He turned to walk back to the car. Lincoln hit him from behind, knocking him into the hood of the car. The big man was fast and skilled, and before Lincoln could land another blow, the man snapped a kick, connecting with Lincoln's gut. He doubled over, the air expelled harshly from his lungs. An elbow strike landed on the side of Lincoln's head, and he went down.

Stanton bent to pick up Lincoln's gun. When he stood, eleven guns were aimed at him. In the distance, an engine growled, growing louder. The military truck leaped over the curb and plowed through the branches between two pine trees. The fifty-caliber machine gun rattled, and a line of dust and stone rose from the ground behind the shooters.

Some ran, some turned, a few screamed, but no one fired. Stanton lifted a foot and drove it down hard on Lincoln's ribs. A snapping sound was audible, and Lincoln cried out. He pointed Lincoln's gun at his head. The driver now stood behind the open door, pointing an automatic rifle at the house's windows.

"The negotiations are over," Stanton said. "Anyone of you fires, and the machine gun will cut you all down. It will shoot through the house, the barn, the garage, and will rip in half any bodies it contacts."

"You'll die too," Lynn said. Her rage displayed openly on her face, her gun aimed at Stanton.

"That may be, but a lot more of you will die before this ends. The only thing that saves everyone's lives is for you to give us what we want. The choice is yours. Your friend's lives are in your hands."

Lynn was so enraged her hand shook. Stanton eyed her, unsure whether she'd give in or say fuck it and open fire. He didn't give himself much chance of survival if the shooting started, but he decided he'd break for the captured truck. If he could add the second fifty cal to the fight, it'd be over before it started.

A sound to the side caught his attention, but he dared not alter his line of sight for fear that would give this crazed woman the opening she sought to take him down. Was it just a distraction, or was someone there?

It only took a look at the now smug and steady woman in front of him to know which. "I think we've reached an impasse," she said. "Our machine gun versus yours. Now, put your guns down, or you'll be the first to die."

Stanton weighed his options. If he fired once at her and dove, the gunner would have trouble tracking him. Even trained soldiers had trouble with accuracy on a fifty when the target was moving. He could roll close to the truck and come up behind the shooter. As each second passed, he grew more confident in the success of that move. As long as his gunner kept the front line of shooters occupied, he'd be able to accomplish the action unscathed. Once he had the gun, he wouldn't stop firing until no one moved. He'd strafe the house from window to window.

His plan must have shown on his face as the woman cocked the hammer and narrowed her eyes. She was locked on him. She'd be the only one who could do him damage, but it'd still take skill to hit a moving target. Besides, he had a vest, and she didn't. No matter how well he planned, there was no accounting for lucky shots. He'd have to take her down first.

Stanton readied himself to move, but a new sound intruded on the tense scene. The sound of another vehicle. It sounded like one of their trucks. Had the private they left to cover the hostages took it upon himself to come instead? If so, he'd chew him out for disobeying orders but forgive his crime. Perhaps the captain, seeing things were dicey, had called him in. Regardless, it'd swing the balance in their direction.

He smiled at the woman in front of him, the woman who dared challenge him. He was going to enjoy making her pay. She heard the sound too, and her confidence melted away like sugar in the rain.

The truck came into view as it burst through the trees, slowing behind the first truck. It wasn't the best placement. He'd prefer if the truck moved further from the first one to cover a larger area, but the sight alone was enough to alter the balance and to have an effect on the defenders.

His smile grew. He obscenely licked his lips and said, "You're mine, bitch, and I'm going to enjoy punishing you."

CHAPTER TWENTY-SEVEN

Mark sped down the streets, praying he was in time to make a difference in whatever was happening. He wanted to send someone to check on what was going on but was afraid to take the time.

"Jarrod, I'm going to drive right up to the house. See if anyone can fire the gun up top. It takes some skill and a strong, steady hand to handle."

"That's the plan? Go in, guns a-blazing? Man, I had such high hopes for a real plan this time." He shook his head, his wild black hair swaying in each direction. He got up and slid through the opening to the inner section.

He returned. "Thomas is up top. Why don't you let me out before you go running up there? I can come in from the corn and add an extra gun."

"Good idea. Take Ruth with you. Keep her safe. Have David back up his father."

He stepped inside again, and Mark pulled over half a block from the farmhouse on the cornfield's eastern side. Jarrod yelled back into the cab. "Debbie's coming with me. Maggie's staying here."

"Got it. Good luck."

"Wouldn't need luck if we had a damn plan."

The door shut, and Mark moved to the corner and peered down the length of the block. Behind the house, he could see the backend of the other truck. He couldn't see if the gun was manned but was sure it would be. The fact he didn't hear the rapid chattering of the gun gave him hope. He was going to give Jarrod a chance to get closer to the house but decided he couldn't risk the passing seconds. Not with so many lives at stake. He turned right and bounded over the ground on the inside of the long row of pine trees along the side street. He increased speed and shouted back to David. "Tell your dad not to fire unless the other truck begins shooting. Tell him to target the other gunner first."

He heard David relay the message and focused on the truck ahead. A soldier stood in the well behind the gun, which was aimed at a group of people, his people, standing to the side of the house. The man who kidnapped Ruth was in front of them with a gun pointed at Lynn. Lynn had hers aimed at the man— a stalemate. A steel band tightened across his chest. No matter what happened in the next few seconds, Lynn was dead no matter what.

He stopped to the right and ten yards behind the other truck. Even from this distance, he could see the panicked looks on the faces of his people. He had to let them know he was not the enemy. "Thomas, you got the other gunner lined up?"

"My dad says, yes."

"David, can you drive?"

"Ah, yeah, but I've never driven anything this big."

"That's okay. Come up here."

David appeared, and Mark slid out of the seat. David replaced him but looked anything but confident as he glanced over the dashboard. "Keep your foot on the brake. If you need to move, put your foot on that second pedal and give it some gas. You won't go far or fast, but you'll move with a sudden lurch. If the other gunner shoots at you, ram the truck and duck."

"Ah, okay."

"You'll be fine."

Mark got out the side door with gun in hand. The gunner from the other truck eyed him, then swung the barrel in his direction. Mark said, "Better look behind you, Bud. You'll be dead seconds after I am."

The man glanced sideways, then moved the gun again. Mark advanced toward the waiting group. All eyes were on him. He walked through the line of people, past Lynn and straight at the sergeant. The sergeant could not erase the surprised look on his face. Mark thought he saw the man swallow hard. He had to realize where the third truck came from. He'd understand the game was over but for the king to be toppled.

Mark advanced closer. The sergeant changed targets from Lynn to him, which was what he wanted. He could shoot Mark, but not Lynn. He hoped if he fell, Lynn had the presence of mind to put the sergeant down. He kept going until the sergeant's gun was inches from his face. Mark swatted the gun hand away with a fast and surprising move, then placed his barrel on his opponent's forehead.

"Your guard is dead, and I have the hostages. You have no more leverage. You're down to two choices. Leave your weapons and go or die. Frankly, I'm hoping you're just stupid enough to pick the second." He cocked his head and glared hard at the man. "You brave enough, big man?"

Hatred flared in the sergeant's eyes, but resignation followed. He lowered his gun and dropped it to the ground. Mark kept the gun pressed into his head and fought the rage that screamed for him to fire. He backed away, saw Lincoln writhing on the ground in agony, then whipped around and slammed the gun across the sergeant's face, driving him to his knees. The rage intensified, as did the pressure on the trigger. He was a fraction of force away from breaking the trigger but held back. He backed away and pointed at the driver who stood at the door, his gun switching targets every few seconds.

"You. Drop the gun or die. Three. Two." The gun fell. "Get his weapons," he said to no one in particular.

As he reached Lynn, she rushed to him and pressed against him. "Is it true? Do you have Ruth?"

"Yes. She's with Jarrod. She's safe and unharmed."

He made to move past, but she grabbed hold of his shirt front and buried her face against his chest. "Oh, God. Thank you."

"Guess I still have my uses," he said in a tone that surprised him. The anger and pent up anguish was too much to think about then. He pushed past her and walked toward the first truck. "Get down from there," he said to the gunner. The man hesitated. "Take a good look around. Even if you opened fire, you'd be cut down before you did much damage. You want to live? Get down now."

The man stepped back and lifted his hands. He climbed down from the back and walked to the front.

Mark glared at the driver. "You the man in charge?"

The officer did not respond. "Come out, or I'll come in and get you. One way you come out on your own, the other you come out bloody. I don't much care which."

"You're gonna shoot me."

"If I was gonna do that, I wouldn't have given you a choice. Get out now and join your men."

The officer mulled that over but took too long. Mark moved to the side of the truck and began climbing.

"Okay. I'm coming out."

The door opened, and Mark jumped down. He grabbed the captain and shoved him against the truck, and leaned against him. The man's face reddened, and his breathing quickened. "Information saves your life."

"What-what do you want to know?"

"Did Ohtanda send you?"

"No."

"No? You're not from the facility?"

"Yes, but she didn't send me. The General did. He runs the facility."

"And what were your orders?"

"To collect a few key people and take a few others."

"What about the rest of us?"

"Ah, we were to leave you alone if we got what we wanted."

The hesitation and quick words told Mark he was lying. "Is this all of you?"

"Yes. Your people killed the rest."

"Be thankful you're still alive to return to your base. Move." He pulled the captain by his uniformed shirt and shoved him forward. The gun waved the gunner forward, and he marched them to the car where the sergeant had regained his feet.

Mark yanked the sidearm from the captain's holster and dropped it behind him. "All weapons on the ground now."

The two men with weapons did so. "Get in the car and leave. Take a message to your general. Leave us alone. We won't be taken by surprise again."

"What about our trucks?" The captain asked.

"Consider them the price for allowing you to live."

The captain's jaw worked side to side, clearly not happy with losing the equipment. Mark doubted the man would still be a captain when he returned not only empty-handed but without his prized machinery.

"Go, before I change my mind."

The four men got into the car. The sergeant was the last one to enter. He glared at Mark, sending the message this wasn't over. The rage flared again, and Mark advanced on the man with his gun, ready to strike or end the man's life. He wasn't sure himself which. The sergeant almost jumped into the car, banging his head on the door frame. The car backed down the driveway before the sergeant's door was closed.

He motioned to Bobby, who stood behind the machine gun of the first captured truck. Maretha was in the driver's seat. "Follow them. Make sure they leave."

She gave him a thumb's up and drove after the car.

Only after both vehicles were out of sight did Mark relax.

CHAPTER TWENTY-EIGHT

General West was in the lead car of the four-vehicle convoy. Since Mark's visit to the base, he was determined to discover who this other military was. If it was connected to the government, the American government, he wanted to be a part of it and, to a lesser degree, learn why he hadn't been included in the first place.

Going by what he learned from Mark, he had a good idea of where to look. They rolled down Route Two, heading toward the Davis-Bessie Nuclear power plant. Mark had mentioned the facility was near that without realizing he was giving away the location, which he seemed determined to keep secret.

They had been stopped by a barricade, and a toll was demanded to allow passage. They wanted guns, ammo, and food. The General threatened an attack, which didn't faze the toll collectors until he deployed the two fifty caliber machine guns mounted to two of the vehicles. Evidently, they'd had dealings with the guns before because they were quickly allowed through the barricade with no further demands.

With binoculars to his face, he scanned the landscape. Ahead to the right was a large building surrounded by barbed-wire topped fencing. "I think we're here," he told the driver. He pointed to the gated driveway and had the driver turn in. He radioed the rest of the column to take up positions on either side in case they were turned away by force.

West was determined to at least have a discussion with whoever was in charge. He saw machine guns, and two rocket launchers aimed at them. He had the driver stop but couldn't make his body respond to his command of getting out of the jeep. An officer stood beyond the gate, hands clasped behind his back, waiting. But was he waiting to greet them or give the order to open fire?

West's mouth went dry. He had trouble swallowing. He glanced at his driver and realized the man was staring at him, waiting for an order. West croaked. "Wait here."

He exited, straightened his uniform, and marched with more confidence than he felt toward the gate.

The officer, a captain, said, "This is a private military facility. Please turn your vehicles around, or we will be forced to open fire."

"I'm General West of the hundred and eightieth Air National Guard. I would like to speak to your commanding officer."

"Sir, no one is allowed inside."

West took that in for a moment, then said, "Very well, announce me and ask them to come out here."

The captain began to reply.

"Captain, we play for the same team. I'm not an enemy force. We are not here to fight. We are here to let those in charge know of our existence, in case they didn't already, and ask what we can do to help. That's a reasonable request from a fellow military officer. Please, at least pass on the message and allow them to decide whether to speak with me or not."

The captain mulled that over. "Sir, if you will wait there, I'll call in."

"Thank you, Captain."

West put his hands behind his back and stood at ease, which was nothing that he felt. As the captain entered the guard shack to make his call, West took a moment to survey the grounds.

It was a large building, at least three stories with most likely another level or two below ground. Except for the dark brick exterior, the shape reminded him of a hospital. Engine sounds echoed off the building. Several more combat vehicles came around the corner and took up flanking positions, an obvious show of force designed to discourage any attempt to gain entry without permission.

He stood in front of the gate, motionless for almost five minutes before the captain came back. "Sir, the commander of this facility asks that you wait here until he arrives."

Progress, West thought. "Thank you, Captain."

"He also asks that you back your vehicles up to a position across the street and have your gunners stand down, so they appear less of a threat."

That left him in the open by himself. His men would be unable to defend him. He looked over his shoulder, trying to think of a way to counterbalance the request while still keeping him protected. He could see no way. He was the one asking for a meeting, so it was their right to set the terms. He pivoted and went back to the jeep. He spoke to the driver and had him relay the message.

The jeep made a wide turn and led the column across the street, keeping in front of the gate should the need arise to come for him. It was moot. If shooting started, he'd be dead before getting help. He turned back to face the gate, praying this hadn't been a complete mistake.

Fifteen minutes later, a jeep drove toward the gate. West was getting tired of waiting and recognized the tactic for what it was. It was a deliberate attempt to show him who was boss and that he didn't matter, regardless of who he was, who he represented, and despite his rank.

The jeep stopped broadside of the gate, and two officers exited. Both men were fit, more so than West was by a long way. One wore basic ACU's while the other wore a desert combat uniform. Both, West noted with a sigh, wore the rank of two-star generals. They outranked him. He'd hoped to have an advantage in rank, if only to bluster his way inside. Neither man wore a name badge or any medals. They had nothing on them to identify who they were or what campaigns they'd served in. West found that strange.

They marched in stride to the gate but did not give the order to open it. The slight angered West. The man in the green ACUs spoke. "General, how can we help you?"

The man's tone and arrogant stance riled West further, as did the other man's smirk. He fought for control before speaking. "I'm General West of the hundred and eightieth Air National Guard base west of Toledo."

"So we've heard. Why are you here?"

"I was informed of a column passing through our area and was surprised to hear other military bases were operating. I wanted to introduce myself to let you know there is another base close by and ask how we can help and get involved with whatever is going on."

The two men looked at each other, then back at him.

"General West, we are on a special mission that requires top-secret clearance. Since neither of us knows you and no one in authority knows anything about you or your base, you can understand our reluctance to include you in whatever we are doing."

West bristled. "Though I can understand that, it would be nice to have some basic knowledge and understanding of the national scene."

"Such as—?"

"The fact that a government appears to be in operation. No one other than a base in Indiana has ever responded to our radio calls. Is there a government in charge?"

"There is an organization in charge, and our communications are through satellites and need special access and equipment."

"There must be a way to be involved. We are part of the American government. There has to be a role for us in something."

"What's your bases compliment?" the desert camo general asked.

"About eighty personnel." He was about to add the fact they had operating F-15s but decided to hold off until they began speaking to him with the respect he deserved.

"Eighty. Huh. I'm surprised it's that many."

"General," the first general said, "at the moment, there is nothing you can do to assist us with our mission. If we need you for any special tasks, we shall be in contact. This is a highly classified base. Please do not return unless specifically asked to do so." He pivoted and marched away. The desert camo man stared at him for a moment. Something played through his mind. "Hold on a moment, General." He turned and jogged to the other man. They had a brief discussion, and then both men came back.

"General," the green camo general said. "Did you say your base was west of Toledo?"

"I did."

"Tell me, are you familiar with a community near there run by a man named Mark?"

The question startled West. He was aware he showed recognition, and although he wanted to deny knowledge, he knew they'd see through the lie. "Yes. They're a few miles from the base. Good people. We've worked on several missions together. Why do you ask?"

"Does that mean you're close to him?"

"We have a working relationship."

The second general interrupted. "This man Mark has been named a traitor to this country."

That statement stunned West. "What? That's crazy."

"We have dispatched a team to take him and others into custody and bring them back here. He has killed several of our men so far and has attacked this facility, killing more and making off with valuable, we'll say, equipment. What he took is of the utmost importance to the survival of this country. It is top secret and must be returned at all costs. I cannot tell you any more without breaching protocol, but if you have a connection to this man, we ask that you use your influence to either convince him to return or bring him in."

"I can't believe he'd be involved in any plot against our country. He's as much a patriot as any of us."

"Does that mean you won't help fellow military personnel?"

"Well, no," West groped for the right words. The accusations against Mark stunned him. It couldn't be true.

"General West," green camo man stepped forward closer to the gate and lowered his voice. "General, you asked how you could help, how you could get involved and be a part of the government. This is how. I can't begin to tell you the importance of returning this man and a select few of his people to us. Will you help us?"

West's mind whirled in confusion. Two generals were telling him something he found hard to accept and were asking for his help. It was a way inside the circle he longed to belong to. He found himself nodding before he spoke. "Yes, I can do this. Who else am I supposed to bring in?"

The two generals let a look pass between them that made West wonder if he was being played. He was given the names of the others needed, which also included the doctor of the community. That was a big ask. He'd sent some of his people to her when the base medical staff, which did not have a real doctor, could not help. He was also given a way to contact the team that had already been dispatched. He was assured the team would offer him as much support as needed to accomplish the mission.

West shook his head. "I can't believe Mark is a traitor. We've become good friends."

"General, think of it this way. If you don't want your friend and his associates killed, convince him to come in. My team has orders to kill anyone who stands in the way of their mission. And General, my men are supreme killing machines. A lot of bodies will pile up. You don't want that, do you?"

"No. Definitely not."

"Good. Then we can count on you?"

"Yes, Sir."

"Good man." Green ACU nodded his approval and walked back to the jeep. Desert camo said, "And General West, accomplish this mission, and I'll see what I can do about getting you a spot in the inner circle."

That made West stand up straighter and push out his chest with pride. He nodded his acceptance and saluted without thinking about the action. The other man smiled and gave a quick salute back before turning away. West walked toward the convoy. The jeep moved up to pick him up.

"Where to, General?" the driver asked.

"Back to the base. We have a mission for the United States government."

CHAPTER TWENTY-NINE

Corporal Amy Dawson stood in the second story of a house overlooking the town she was to infiltrate. It was the fourth house she'd been in that day. Each one had been selected to give her a view of the compound, the barricades, and the defensive positions. She had already seen enough to know whoever was in charge was good. The women managing the walls were well trained and efficient. No one slacked off in their duties.

She'd seen several patrols leave and return. She followed one and watched what they did. They were search parties scavenging for food, water, and supplies. They sent out three teams each day that went off in different directions.

She'd gathered as much information as she could from the outside. It was time to make her presence known and get beyond the walls.

Dawson reported back to base and told her captain what she needed. His eyebrows went up, and then he eyed her body in a glance. "You sure about this?"

"Yes, Sir. It's a sisterhood, and what better way to be accepted than fight the same battles they have?"

He set it up for later that day.

Dawson noted the patrols never left in a vehicle, always on foot. She followed one such party and radioed in. If the patrol followed the same pattern, they'd return along the Lake Erie coastline, skirting a neighborhood of small houses. As soon as the first woman exited the trees, she signaled her fellow soldiers, dressed in ragged civilian clothes to begin.

Dawson let out a scream and darted around a house. She was in clear view of the patrol's point person. Private Arnett, dressed in dirty civilian clothes, came flying from the other side of the house. He was fast and too enthusiastic. He tackled her. They rolled along the weeds that had once been a front lawn. Dawson managed to move to the top, and as Arnett copped a feel on her breasts, she punched him square in the nose, got up, and kicked him in the ribs.

She didn't make it five running steps before Private Morton caught her. He wrapped her up from behind, squeezed hard, and lifted her from the ground. Corporal Alonzo appeared in front of her, leering her up and down. He delivered an open-handed slap, then inserted both hands inside her shirt collar and ripped the material away, exposing her breasts. He lunged at her, first mashing them with his hands then biting.

He lifted his head with a sinister smile. "Great plan, Dawson." He moved to her belt.

She'd had enough. With her legs still swinging off the ground, she lifted her knee into his groin in a swift move that took him by surprise. He groaned and doubled over. Then she snapped her head back into Morton's nose. He cried out and released her. She whirled, snapped a kick, and rang the bell, dropping him to his knees.

By then, Arnett was back on his feet and approaching with angry curses. "You're gonna pay for that, Dawson."

She risked a glance and saw the patrol on a full sprint toward them.

"Why don't you stick around for a few minutes, and we'll see who pays." She pulled out her combat knife and crouched, hoping the man wasn't stupid enough to attack her, but half-hoping he would.

He caught her glance and looked for himself. His eyes widened. He reached down and pulled Morton to his feet. Alonso was already rising, and the anger on his face told her she was in for payback when this mission was over. Well, bring it on, asshole. She made a swipe at him with her knife that didn't miss by much. The move encouraged him to get away quicker.

The three assailants disappeared around the house as the women arrived. Four of the seven-member team gave chase. The other three approached her. She whirled, holding the knife in front of her. The short, stocky woman with the red hair who she identified on her stakeouts as the team leader, held up a cautionary hand.

"Whoa! Easy. We're not here to hurt you, Sister. We saw you were in trouble and came to help. Are you all right?"

Breathing hard and trying to look crazed, she grunted at her and backed away. "Leave me alone."

"Okay. We're staying back."

The four chasers returned. One reported, "Chieftess, they got into a car and drove away. Mandy managed to hit one with her slingshot. It knocked him forward, and he hit his head on the door as he tried to get in."

Some of the women laughed. Mandy beamed with pride. Then the same woman leaned forward and whispered something in her ear. The leader flicked a glance at Dawson, then looked away.

Dawson knew it was something about her. Had the men somehow given away who they were? She remained poised to defend but backed away another step.

With the message delivered, the leader took a step forward and examined Dawson. "Someone give her a shirt." Several women moved, and a shirt was offered. "Go ahead. Slip it on. You'll be safe."

Dawson eyed her with suspicion then slipped the t-shirt over her head in one quick motion.

"Where are you from?" the one they called Chieftess asked.

"Nowhere. Just traveling. Searching like everyone for food and water."

The other woman nodded. "Do you have any injuries?"

She did a mental check. She had bruises and scrapes from the encounter, not to mention a hickey on her boob, but otherwise was intact. Though she didn't doubt for a moment that had the patrol not arrived, Alonso would have raped her. She was sure it would have been a gang rape. She shook her head. "No. I'm fine. Just a little pissed off."

"I understand. Believe me. You're not the first to be attacked by men, though much luckier than many. I am Alice, Chieftess of this tribe and part of a community of women not far from here. You are welcome to come with us if you choose. I can promise you food and water and safety for as long as you choose to stay."

"What is this place? Like a commune?"

"No. It's a town made up of like-minded people who came together for safety purposes. We have a doctor, a head cook, and nearly a hundred residents."

"Will I be allowed to leave when I want, or will I be your prisoner?"

"We don't take prisoners. You either come because you want to, or we leave you alone. You will remain free and can stay as long as you wish. But there are rules that need to be followed."

"What kind of rules?"

"The kind that makes sense to people living in an apocalyptic world, designed for the safety of all. Come. Find out for yourself."

Dawson didn't want to appear too eager. She hesitated. "And you say I'll be able to get food and water?"

Alice's eyes narrowed just a bit. "Yes, but you'll not be allowed to take what you want and leave. The meals are portioned out to ensure everyone gets to eat."

"That sounds good." She lowered her knife-hand. "I haven't eaten anything substantial in days."

"And yet you don't look malnourished and appear to be in good condition."

Dawson didn't know what to say. She'd overplayed her position and made Alice suspicious. She had to alter the topic. "And you have a doctor?"

Alice nodded, but something had cooled in her demeanor. Dawson needed to accept the offer before it was rescinded. "Okay. That sounds better than trying to make it out here alone.

"Do you have any gear stowed someplace?"

"Ah, no." She realized that was another red flag. Everyone carried a bag of some sort to keep their findings in. "Those men took it. They caught me, took my things, including my gun, and tossed everything in their car. I broke free and ran. That's when you saw me."

Alice nodded again but gave the impression she didn't believe her story. "Very well. Positions, warriors. Everyone moved to an assigned spot. "Walk with me."

Dawson sheathed her knife and stepped next to Alice. They walked in silence for a while before Alice asked, "What is your name?

"Dawson."

Alice glanced at her. Dawson realized it was another mistake. In the military, she was used to only having a last name. "Where are you from?"

"I told you. All over."

"No, before the apocalypse."

"Oh, a small town in Iowa." She felt safe giving that location. Her cousins lived there in the before, and she'd visited enough to describe the area with confidence."

"So, a country girl, then?"

"Yes, although I wasn't raised on a farm."

"What brings you here so far from home?"

Dawson had prepared for this. "I was driving with friends searching for survivors. We made it halfway across Indiana before we got attacked. My friends were either killed or captured. Me and another girl escaped, but she died a few days later when we stopped to help a young girl. It was a trap, and her family fell on us. We killed them all, but Sara Jean sustained injuries that we could not treat. Infection set in and—"

"That's a shame. We all have similar stories. But if you were looking for survivors, you've found them.

CHAPTER THIRTY

A half-hour later, the town came into view. Dawson pretended to be amazed at what she saw. Upon command, a minivan in the middle of a barricade across the street was driven to the side, exposing the entry into the town.

The town was comprised of four blocks down what had once been Main Street. Whatever the town's name had been before, the sign had been painted over, and various new residents all wrote their version of a new name. Amazonia. New Hope. Women's World. Our Town. Each was apt. Once on Main Street, Dawson turned in a circle with her jaw open, taking in the scene.

She caught Alice eyeing her and felt the color rise to her cheeks. She'd have to be careful around the woman. She was astute and didn't miss much. "Wow!" Dawson said with enough exclamation as to make it believable. "This is amazing. How long have you been here?"

"Several months now. It started with a handful of women and grew to what you see now." She turned to one of the other women. "Would you take my things to my room and ask Head Chieftess Iso for an audience?

"As you wish, Chieftess."

The woman trotted off. Two of the patrol stayed with them, while the remaining members took the bags of whatever they'd collected toward what had once been a diner.

They walked down the middle of the street. "I'm going to introduce you to our leader. She will have some questions for you. Once you're done, it should be near dinner time. We'll eat and get you settled in someplace for the night. Your lodgings will be temporary until you decide if you're staying or going. You'll get no pressure from anyone here to stay. With that being said, do not, under any circumstances, attempt to leave the town without permission. Is that clear?"

"Yes."

"You are not a prisoner, but you must follow our rules. If you try to leave, the guards, who don't know you, will think someone is breaching the wall. They may shoot before identifying you. Even if they don't shoot, an alarm will be sounded, waking the entire town. There is also a curfew in place. We rise early to get a lot done during the day and have time for ourselves at night. It's a simple routine, a structured existence that works well for us, but it's not for everyone."

"Who's Iso?"

"One of our founding members. She serves as our leader, although we also have an elected council to govern our daily affairs."

"A council. You are organized."

"It just makes things easier when things are spelled out and rules are established. We still have minor problems and disputes, but it would be far worse if rules and guidelines weren't in place."

They stopped in front of what might have been an American Legion Post at one time. Do you have any questions or concerns before we're allowed in?"

"Ah, no, not that I can think of. Will this leader decide whether I can stay?"

"No. This is just an introduction. Should you wish to stay, there will be an official vote by the council. That is just a formality. They accept everyone. It's up to you whether you're allowed to stay. If you constantly break rules or cause trouble, you'll be asked to leave."

"Has anyone ever been asked to leave?"

Alice smiled. "Yes." She didn't add details. She entered the building, a long, brick one-story, and walked toward the end of the hall. On the far side was a door bracketed by two guards. A line of chairs sat against one wall. She motioned for Dawson to sit and spoke to the guards. "I have a meeting. Is she prepared to see me?"

'I'll check, Chieftess."

One of the guards stepped through the door. She returned a minute later and nodded at Alice. Alice turned to Dawson. "Stay here. I'll be back for you in a moment."

Dawson had half risen from the chair and sat back down. She didn't know what to make of being excluded. Was it standard, or were they discussing her? She flashed back on their earlier conversation. Had she given Alice reason to have concerns? Maybe. She'd have to work hard to overcome them. She was to make contact with the base in two days. She was beginning to see how difficult that might be.

Five minutes later, a woman exited, smiled at Dawson, and motioned for her to come. "They're ready to see you now."

What did that mean? Her nerves came alive, inching up her tension. She walked through the door and followed the woman. She became aware that she was being followed but tried not to look back. Ahead at the far end of the room, a blond-haired woman sat in a high-backed chair that gave the impression of being a throne. To each side were eight-foot folding tables with four smaller chairs behind each. None of those were occupied. Alice sat to the side of the leader, holding a cup of what Dawson assumed was coffee.

As Dawson approached, Alice set the cup down on a table and stood. "High-Chieftess Iso, I'd like to introduce Dawson."

Dawson thought the titles were ridiculous but was unsure if she was supposed to bow, curtsey or kiss her ring. She stood awkwardly, glancing from Iso to Alice.

"Welcome to our town, Dawson."

"Thank you, ah, High-Cheiftess."

Iso smiled. It was a genuine and warming smile. "I know. The titles are a bit silly, aren't they? Just so you know, I think so, too, but it was what was voted on by our residents, and it's stuck." She eyed Dawson. "You look healthy. What branch did you serve in?"

The question took her by surprise. "Serve?"

"You're obviously ex-military. The way you stand, walk, look. You served somewhere."

"Yes. I was raised a military brat. Joined the army four years ago. It's the way I was raised and the only life I knew until, well, this."

"Good for you. Ex-military personnel do well here with our structure. I served as well. A marine. Six years."

That surprised Dawson but also relaxed her. Military veterans always recognized others of their ilk.

"I'm sorry your introduction to our town comes after an attack. That was the main reason this type of settlement came into existence—to protect those who would otherwise be preyed upon. I don't have much else to say. I like to meet the newcomers to our community even if they only plan to stay temporarily. You are welcome here, but Alice will give you the rules you need to follow if she hasn't already done so. Please follow them and be on time for meals and other scheduled events."

"Yes, ma'am, er, Head Chieftess."

"It was nice meeting you."

With that, Alice gave Iso a slight bow and left the room with Dawson following. Her first impression of the leader was she was warm and friendly and a bit arrogant, what with the title and the throne. Yet, there was something behind the eyes. Something intelligent. Something dangerous. Something feral. For the first time since accepting this mission, Dawson began to have doubts.

CHAPTER THIRTY-ONE

Private Bowden stood in the small house, his mouth agape, staring at the body of his comrade and the strands of the severed cord where the hostages had been.

"Private," Captain Crandall said, "other than catching flies, do you have any insight?"

"The captives were all here. I might have thought an exchange was being made since no one else is here and the trucks are gone, except for Private Rands' body."

"So you have no idea where they are or what transpired here?"

"No, Sir."

"They may be at the farmhouse, either attacking or negotiating."

"We're done negotiating. They killed one of ours. It's time for retribution." He turned and shouted over his shoulder. "Lieutenant. Map."

The lieutenant stepped forward and withdrew a folded map from a pocket. He stretched it out over the kitchen counter. With a pencil, he made a small x. "Sir, we're here."

"Private, have you been to the enemy camp?"

"Yes, Sir."

"Show me."

He stepped forward, took the proffered pencil, and gazed at the map.

"Boy, can you read a map or not," the impatient captain barked.

"Y-yes, Sir," Bowden stammered. He traced a road with his fingertip, found the intersection he wanted, and made an x. "It's right here, sir."

"Break it down for me, boy. What's there?"

"The farmhouse is on this corner." He pointed. "Behind it is a barn and a garage. Here. Across the street, they are building a new structure, which I assume is housing. This corner has three houses, and this one is an open field backed by trees perhaps fifty yards off the road."

"Numbers."

Bowden's confidence grew as he recited facts he knew. "A hundred men, women, and children. All residents capable of doing so carry a gun. About ninety-five percent of the population."

"Cover."

"A cornfield runs to this intersection behind the farmhouse. Trees line the north and east side of the property behind the new building. From the west, it's open ground."

"Lieutenant, take two men to this point," he put a finger on the vacant lot, "and give me a sitrep."

"Yes, Sir." The lieutenant left.

"Anything else you can tell me?"

"They do have guards posted and patrols on the road."

That seemed to take the captain by surprise. "Motorized patrols?"

"Yes, Sir. I'm not sure if that's the norm or just since they discovered we were here, but they take their security seriously."

"But it's my understanding that this is all open ground. They have no fortifications on site."

"Correct, Captain. There is a line of mature pine trees on the southern side of the house that runs almost the full length of the street but nothing solid to keep invaders out."

"For people that take security seriously, that seems like a fatal oversight." He studied the map a moment longer, then turned. "Sergeant, we're moving across the street. I want to be in a position to see if anyone returns here. Set up a perimeter but keep them out of sight. I don't want anyone getting close to this place without us knowing well in advance."

"Yes, Sir." He turned and started for the rear door. "Okay, pack up. We're moving."

With quick efficiency the move took minutes. They set up in a house across the street and down two from the original. With the watch set and patrols dispatched, there was nothing more to do but wait.

An hour later, a car pulled up to the first house. Two soldiers disgorged from the car and sprinted around back. Seconds later, they were back. They spoke to someone in the passenger seat. Crandall stood in the front window with binoculars. He was sure the man in the front seat was Childs. He debated between sending a man out to get him or letting him drive away. He decided the man might have information he needed.

"Sergeant, go out and ask Captain Childs to join us."

"You sure, Sir?"

"No, but do it anyway."

Minutes later, the five men entered the family room. Captain Crandall greeted his counterpart. "Captain Childs, I'm Captain Crandall. We've been sent to handle this situation."

Childs stiffened. He looked around as if searching for a response on the walls, and then looked down, deflated. Crandall knew he had no leg to stand on. He'd failed and lost men. By the looks of it, he'd lost his vehicles, as well. That'd be worse for him than the loss of men.

"Captain, I'm not here to bust balls." He laughed. "I'm sure that will come later and from higher up. I need information from you that might help salvage this situation. The faster we can resolve this, the better for all of us. The brass tends to be more forgiving when missions are successful. So, why don't you fill me in on what's happened so far?"

He motioned for Childs to sit, then joined him at the table. "From the beginning, please."

Childs sighed. "We did some recon, discovered there were more people than first anticipated by a good forty or so. They are well-armed and organized. My men were spotted on our first recon. Two of them were hunted and gunned down.

"We took a slower approach. We watched to determine routines. Then decided to begin capturing their people to use as leverage. We had a handful and made contact. Then, an exchange was set up for our primary objectives. Once we had them in hand, we were going to unleash the fifty cals and take out as many as we could. Afterward, we'd collect survivors and return to base."

"Sounds like a reasonable plan. What went wrong?"

"There were too many people to watch at once, plus while we were there, someone discovered our hiding place and released our leverage."

"Killing another one of your men."

Childs stiffened again, then leaned forward. "I want in."

Crandall frowned. "Why would I want that?"

"It was my men who died. We deserve payback."

"You deserve to be demoted, but that's not my call. Still, there might be a way you can be useful."

Childs sighed. "And that is?"

"I'll let you know as the plan develops. For now, you and your surviving men," he emphasized 'surviving,' "can stay in a house across the street. We'll let you know when you're needed."

Crandall stood to signify the meeting was over. Childs stood, gave him a hard, dissatisfied glare that Crandall ignored, then walked toward the door.

"By the way, what happened to your vehicles?"

"They have them."

"Them? How many is *them*?"

"Three." He exited fast.

Behind him, Crandall shouted through the door. "Three!"

CHAPTER THIRTY-TWO

The military truck drove up the driveway and parked. Maretha and Bobby exited and approached Mark.

Bobby said, "Looks like they were going north. We watched them cross Central and enter a small neighborhood of houses."

"That was their base," Mark said. "They left a man there, though he's dead now. Maybe they're picking up gear, too, though I don't remember any being there."

"Do you think that's the last of them?"

Mark shook his head. "No. I think they have an agenda and will not stop until they achieve it."

Maretha said, "Then we should've killed them all." She walked away.

"They only would've sent more men."

She called back over her shoulder, "But it would've delayed them a few days, giving you a chance to fortify this wide-open complex."

Bobby shrugged, said, "She has a point, dad," and trotted after her.

Mark watched them go. He caught the 'you' reference she gave, letting him know it was his problem, not theirs. But she did have a good point. They needed to take precautions, and he knew where to start.

He found Lincoln sitting on his back porch, drinking a warm beer. The man never seemed to run out of a fresh supply. Being on one of the scout teams helped. He'd be first to discover a new cache.

"I have an idea to upgrade our defenses."

"Sounds like a discussion needed to be held over a beer." He popped the can top and passed one to Mark.

He accepted, glad it wasn't a glass of bourbon.

"Pull up a bar step and awe me with your brilliant idea."

Mark heard the note of sarcasm but didn't comment. He took a long drink of the somewhat chilled can, then said, "What's the problem?"

Lincoln sighed. He shook his head, finished the beer, and opened another. "Does this shit never end?"

Mark understood the frustration. It had been a little more than five months since the outbreak. They had survived, yet all they did was continue to fight for survival. It was hard enough to fight the elements, the endless searching for food, water, medicine, and the regular day-to-day routines in a new harsher reality. But it was the constant defending against outside forces that wore them down. That feeling that they could never truly let their guard down for fear of being overrun by another community.

"I wish I had an answer for you. Maybe someday."

"No matter what we do, we're under attack all the time. It would make no difference if it was before the outbreak or after. People can never get along."

"Not all people. Look what we've built here. This community thrives because everyone is willing to accept one another and work for a common goal. It may not be perfect but then nothing ever really is. We've made the best of a bad situation. There's always going to be trouble or difficult times, but so far, we've faced each one as a community and come out on top."

"So far. Have you given any thought to the power those people can bring down on us if they choose to do so? Sending their team back in defeat will only make them more determined to come after us, and next time they'll send more men and bigger guns."

Mark couldn't argue. It was true. "That's why I want to get out in front of this. We need to plan."

Lincoln drank deeply, wiped his mouth with the back of his hand, and stared at the ground. "Mark, I gotta tell you. Jenny and I been thinking about leaving and finding a place for ourselves. I mean, it's nice to have people to talk to and to rely on and do things with, but it seems the bigger our group gets, the more attention and problems it draws. I'm not sure I can do this much longer."

Mark took a sip. He'd had similar thoughts before, but in the end, the community always won out. "Don't worry. I'm not going to try and talk you out of whatever decision you choose but know this is your home and always will be. You're greatly needed and appreciated here. It won't be any different wherever you go except that whatever dangers or problems you face will be alone."

He stood. "I won't bother you with this stuff. I'll call a meeting of the security group and lay it out for them." He drained his beer, set the can down, and walked away.

"No, man, don't leave. Tell me what you got. I'm not gone yet."

"You sure? I don't want you to feel bogged down by the weight of your position into staying."

"Anyone ever tell you you talk too much? Shut up and sit down." He popped a third beer.

Mark sat.

"Now tell me this grand idea."

Mark smiled. "Counting the one we brought home with us from the town, we now have four armed and armored trucks. They need to be positioned to give us not only additional firepower but advanced time to react in case of an attack."

"Makes sense. You want them down the road a bit but not too far where they become targets."

"Yeah, I hadn't thought of that. That's why I run things by you before talking to anyone else."

"Stop buttering me up. I'm still here. What else?"

"I've never liked the idea of erecting walls, but I think some form of barricade is important. Too many of our enemies have entered through the cornfield. I'd like to find enough fencing to at least create a delay. Also, we've picked so much of that corn it's stupid to keep the stalks up. They should be taken down all the way to the road on the east and at least twenty feet behind the barn."

"That's good. Anything else?"

"Not at the moment, but a few more of these beers, and who knows what I'll come up with?"

"In that case, you're cut off."

Lieutenant Mitchell said, "Sir, we did a thorough scan and evaluation of the two sites."

"You're separating the sites?" Captain Crandall asked.

"Yes, Sir. I think we can take one before the second knows they're gone."

Crandall nodded. He already liked where this plan was heading.

"Once they bed down, they have two sets of two guards stationed in the fringes of the trees, here and here." He showed the positions on his map. "They have two walking patrols that circle the tents and building. About half the members of this site are women. They are housed in four large tents all about twenty feet apart.

The guards can be easily taken, then two tents at a time. We don't have the numbers to take them all at once, but shooters outside the flaps of tents three and four will keep them from exiting until others can join them.

"There will be noise. The second site will be awakened."

"Yes, Sir. We keep as many as we can secure and alive and march them toward the other house. They will have a choice to make. The people in the first camp are expendable. The specific people we've been tasked with procuring are here," he pointed to a house across the from the farmhouse, "and here in the main house. We take this house first. Six people bunk there. Two men. Kill the expendables and secure the Asian family. From there, one man can set up a sniper position while we take down the first camp."

"If we choose to use them, we have five members of the original team stationed across the street."

"Assign them to approach from this direction," he pointed to the cornfield. "Once the alarm is sounded, and the farmhouse comes alive, they can pick them off and keep them pinned down until we accomplish our part.

With their numbers cut in half and us with the superior position, they will cave fast."

"I like it, lieutenant. Nice work."

"I can brief the men and be ready to go tonight, sir?"

"Delay that. I got word from HQ that another player is in the game. A local National Guard post, which sounds more like a militia posing as Guard, paid a visit to the base. They want to be included. They know this group and were tasked with bringing them in and the General instructed me to give them a day. They may be able to handle things without us getting too involved."

"Be a lot less fun, though."

"You may still get your chance, Lieutenant. Brief the men, but we won't go until tomorrow night."

CHAPTER THIRTY-THREE

General West paced his office. He had a mission to do, one of importance, but to believe Mark was a traitor to the country was hard to swallow. He wasn't close to the man though he did call him friend, but how well did he know him? He must have done something bad to be wanted by the military.

The question wasn't so much whether to fulfill the mission but how. Did he march in there and take Mark under the threat of violence? He had no doubt he could drive up without being challenged and aim a gun at him. Mark would be angry, but he'd come fearing others might get caught in any crossfire. How did he get the others requested by the generals?

Maybe the best way to approach the farmhouse was during dinner when they were all together. He could collect Mark, Becca, Doc, and this Asian family, then be gone without a shot fired. Oh, the others would be irate, but what could they do. They wouldn't attack an armed convoy. Would they? He knew the answer. Yes, they would. They'd attacked an army of invaders a few months back. They'd been undermanned, outgunned, and inexperienced, but they didn't hesitate. He called, and they answered, just like Mark promised to do.

No, he couldn't believe it. Not of Mark. He was a good man, dedicated to his community, but there had to be something to the accusations. He was unprepared to handle the decision alone. He opened his office door and spoke to his aide. "Call a staff meeting, would you please?"

"Sure, General. What time?"

"Right now."

Mark called for an emergency meeting, and the people responded. He had nearly ninety-five people in attendance. He raised a hand for quiet and got it faster than usual. Everyone was on edge about the recent attacks.

"Everyone already knows what has happened. I'm not going to rehash that. What I want to talk about is the safety of the entire community. I have spoken in length with some of our construction people. We have a lot of projects in the works, and many of you have been working hard to get them done. Your efforts are greatly appreciated. But we're going to bump some of those projects to the back burner to begin working on fortifying these two locations.

"The attacks of the past few days have made us reconsider building defensible positions. I spoke to Milo, and he will be taking a large team to the lumber yard for supplies. He's going to need a lot of help loading what we'll need. We have two trailers that we'll use to haul materials."

"You can use my flatbed," Jarrod said.

"That will help a lot. Thanks, Jarrod." He let his gaze travel across the group as he spoke. "Here's what we need. Diggers to make a trench across the front of both sites. Someone with the experience to take down the cornfield to the side street. Posthole diggers for fencing. Cement pourers. Wall builders. Just a lot of jobs. It will take time, effort, and sweat, but it's something that's needed and long overdue."

A woman's hand shot up. "Does this mean you don't think the threat's over?"

"In general terms, this is a project that needs to be done regardless. But no, I don't think they're done with us. All the more reason to be proactive and start now."

A man called out. "If you're going to pour that much cement, you're going to use a lot of water. What if it drains the well?"

"In truth, that could happen at any time. However, Milo assures me he has a source that will not touch our supply."

"What about protecting those who live off-campus?" another man asked.

"Good question, and that was another thing I wanted to talk to you about. We can't get to everyone. We'll start here and move out to the various houses. What I'd like you to consider is moving onsite until we finish and can get to your properties."

"So, like always, the big places get the attention, and we're left to protect ourselves."

That started shouting for both positions.

"I'm sorry you feel that way, Joe."

"We're either part of this community, or we're not. There are about twenty of us that have come here to protect you guys, but we get nothing in return. It's wrong."

Several others agreed with Joe. Mark let them yell for a moment. Before he could speak, Lincoln stood and shouted. "Quiet. This gets us nowhere. No one has ever treated you like outsiders. You decided to live off-campus. You knew the risks. It was your choice. But when you had a leaky roof last month, how many of us showed up early the next morning to get it fixed? If any of you had trouble at your houses, didn't someone always come out to help? You've got selective memories. We are a community, and you are a part of it. But use some common sense. If we come out to secure your house, how many people can hide there in safety? Here everyone can have a safe place until we can get to everyone else. This is your choice, but it benefits every one of us." He sat as fast as he stood, leaving a lot of murmuring.

"Joe, if you have concerns, I'll be happy to speak with you. You have my word that your property will get the attention it needs, but we have to take care of this place first. This is where the attacks happen and where the next one will occur."

Joe nodded but offered no more comment. Clearly, he was not yet appeased.

"We want to get started immediately and have materials here to start work today."

"Any other questions."

"Is there room for us?" a woman asked.

"It will be crowded, but there is always room."

Elijah stood. "Our lodge is not finished, but it is buttoned up. We can house quite a few people inside though at the moment we have limited bedding."

Bobby said, "We've got a stockpile of sleeping bags in the garage for emergencies like this."

"So, that's taken care of," Mark said. "Elijah, while you're up, I forgot to apologize. I should have asked you if you wanted a wall before deciding for you."

Elijah cleared his throat. "We would prefer not to have a wall. We like the natural look of the land. We do recognize the need for such a wall, though, and agree to allow it to be constructed."

"Okay. Good. Anything else?"

He answered a few more minor issues. "Look, this isn't easy. We didn't ask for this. But they have attacked our home. They will continue to do so unless we band together in defense of our home," Mark paused. He didn't want this to be a pep talk. They already knew what was at stake. "This is our home we fight for. Stand strong. Stand together." He swept his gaze over the tense faces. "Okay, meet with Milo for jobs. The three things we need right away are trenchers, post hole diggers, and a harvester." As people stood, he added, "I need the security council and the guards up here with me."

As the community cleared out, the security personnel came forward. He gave them a moment to arrive. "We'll be changing our routines, and I need everyone to know what's going on. For the time being, we will be increasing the number of people on guard. The length of the watch will increase by an hour to accommodate the extra bodies and lack of replacements.

"The four military trucks will be deployed. Lincoln can show you where they will be. Maretha, will you show them how to operate the machine guns?"

She nodded.

"But no firing. Our ammo is limited. Make sure they all have about the same number of rounds. We'll need two people for each truck."

"The trucks are great added protection," Caleb said, "but the problem isn't so much the weapons as seeing in the dark."

Mark understood. There wasn't much he could do about it, though.

Maretha ran off without a word. While he discussed other changes, she returned carrying something. She pushed through the group until she reached Mark. She handed him what she held. "I searched the compartments in the truck I was in and found six night-vision goggles. That should help."

"Have you used them before?" She shook her head.

Devin, a former marine, said, "I have. I can teach others how to use them."

"Great. Thanks, Devin. We'll check the other trucks to see if they have any others. The gunners should have them. The other two should go to our oversight watchers in the barn and the new building." He scanned the group. "You have the most important job concerning the safety of our people. If you slip up and the enemy gets past you, people will die. I can't emphasize that point enough. I'm done. Go get trained, then join in the work."

CHAPTER THIRTY-FOUR

Mark moved to the front of the house, where Milo was doing a demonstration. "I need the ground dug out about eight inches from the driveway to the corner. It needs to be as level as possible, but we'll worry about that later. I'm going to fill up the cement truck. It should take an hour or so, depending on how much help I have. I need this to be as complete as possible by the time I get back. It should also be framed. Go to the southern camp. A lot of the frame is still together and off to the side after I poured the floor of the building."

Caleb said. "We only have about a dozen shovels."

Milo frowned. "Do the best you can. We won't be able to build on it for a while anyway. We should wait a couple of days, but I don't think we have that much time. As the trench is dug, others can begin framing."

"You told us how long to make it but not how wide," Alyssa said.

"Good point. Make it two, no three feet wide. If there's nothing else, get started. Those coming with me mount up. We need to attach the trailers. We'll meet Jarrod at the lumberyard."

In minutes the compound was in full motion. Mark snatched up a shovel and began digging in the spot Milo marked. As others joined him, he sent them to dig in different spots. They had a quarter of it dug when Jarrod drove up, pulling one of the trailers with a bobcat on the back.

"Thought this might make it easier for you."

"Bless you."

In minutes Jarrod had the bobcat unloaded and was showing one of the men how to operate it. "I brought a few bags of quick-drying cement that can be mixed by hand and poured into the post holes of the fencing." He motioned for all the diggers to follow, and he went to the garage. There he fired up the tractor, drove it out, and attached the harvester to the back. "Once I clear a few rows," he said to Mark, "show them where you want the fence to go."

The work progressed. Workers came and went doing an assortment of jobs. Lunch was taken in shifts, so someone was working the entire time. As the delivery truck arrived, materials were carted to their locations. The metal posts were sunk into the field as others poured cement into the holes.

In no time, the line was up, and the cement was drying. They'd have to wait before stringing the coils of fencing.

Jarrod made quick work of the cornfield. He didn't take the entire field down but cleared two rows behind the barn, then continued to the eastern road. Everything from there to the southern road was cut down. With the ground open, the property looked much bigger. Eventually, they needed to construct a wall there, too, but the sight of so much land gave Mark an idea about erecting more housing. The way the community was growing and the need for housing was in constant demand. That was another project that would have to wait, though.

Milo poured the first section of the foundation, then moved to the southern camp. A long double row of steel spikes ran the length of the pour. Mark wiped his brow on his sleeve. Things were moving along, but the sun was already on its downward arc. They needed more time and more people. He spied Lincoln and walked toward him.

"We should get the trucks into position now before it gets dark. Does everyone know what they're doing?"

"As best they can without actually operating the guns. Those night vision goggles will come in handy."

"Did you find any others?"

"Yeah, three more. I distributed them to the four trucks, the two watcher positions in the barn, and the one in the new building. Any thoughts as to where the other two should go?"

Mark gave the question some thought. "The only area not covered is the woods behind the new building. Give them to the guards in the woods."

"I'll see to it." He walked away.

The community came together for a late dinner. The sun was already setting when they sat. For the first time that he could remember, the tables were quiet. The usual celebratory time had fallen prey to exhaustion. Everyone would sleep well tonight. Of course, if anyone had been watching, they'd know this was a good time to attack. He'd forego sleep tonight to add his eyes and his gun to the watch.

After everyone had turned in for the night, Mark walked the perimeter. He checked on the four trucks and each guard position twice during the night before turning in to catch a couple of hours' sleep before dawn. He crashed in the hospital, so he didn't wake anyone inside the house. He hadn't seen Lynn most of the day except during dinner. She was too busy to pay him attention, not that she would've anyway. His last thoughts were of her before sleep took him under.

The morning started early before the sun rose. Jarrod and Milo were out checking the cement, and then Mark joined them. "What's the word?"

Milo shrugged. I'd like to have more time for the foundation to harden, but I know we don't have it."

"How much more time?"

"Another day would be great."

"Will it matter if we just put a few rows of blocks on top?"

"The less weight initially the better, but as they say, two things cement is gonna do is harden and crack. It's not gonna make much difference, but it will help." Milo picked up a cinder block and set it in place.

"Set your first row of blocks all the way around with the spikes on the inside for added strength. Then do what needs to be done. If you feel it needs more time, take it."

"The posts in the back are good to go," Jarrod said. "We can start stringing fence as soon as bodies get up."

"Wouldn't you rather have a wall back there, too?" Milo asked.

"Yeah, but we may not have the time. With the stalks gone, we can see a long way. No one is gonna sneak up on us from that direction."

"You know if they bring heavy guns, those walls won't hold," Milo said.

"I know. Our guns will have to keep them back. We'll have to devise a flanking move to get behind enemy positions before they get to us."

"Sounds like a job for you," Jarrod said. "I mean, knowing how well you make plans."

"They always work, don't they?"

"Oh, brother."

Breakfast was rushed, and work started early. It continued for an hour before the western gun position, as they were now referred, called in a sighting. A military column was approaching. Then a new, more frantic type of activity swept the grounds.

CHAPTER THIRTY-FIVE

"Positions, everyone," Lincoln shouted from across the yard. From everywhere, people scrambled for their weapons and to reach their assigned defensive stations. "Hold. Hold everyone. It's just a column from the National Guard base."

Mark approached. "Did you say column?"

"Yes."

"How many vehicles in the column?"

Lincoln repeated the question into the radio. "Six."

"Six? Why such a large group if he's just coming for a visit?"

Lincoln spoke into the radio. "They already let them pass. Is there a problem?"

"I'm not sure. Call the eastern and southern trucks to the intersection. Keep everyone else in position."

While Lincoln spread the word, Mark thought back to his conversation with West a few days ago. Had the man reached out and contacted the other group? But West knew him. He should know better than to believe whatever they told him. This was pure speculation. There had to be another purpose for such a strong show of force. Perhaps another threat was out there they were unaware of yet.

The column came in slow. Two troop-carrying trucks came straight and braked near the side of the house beyond the pine trees. A tactical vehicle with a mounted fifty cal stopped along the front street, its gun swiveled in their direction. Another troop carrier pulled up in the driveway behind West's jeep, which also had a mounted gun, and like the first one was pointed at them.

Lincoln said, "I don't like the looks of this."

"Call in the other two trucks and have them target the troop carriers." Mark walked past Lincoln and plastered on a welcoming smile.

West exited the jeep and walked forward. He too put a smile on but was unable to keep it in place. Mark extended his hand in greeting but noted West kept his at his side near his sidearm.

While still a few strides away, Mark said, "General, to what do we owe the honor of this unexpected visit?"

The general was in the process of pulling his gun when he heard the engine. His smile fell away, and he glanced over his shoulder. One of Mark's trucks stopped ten yards from its counterpart.

West spun back, his face reddening. "What's that?"

Mark stepped forward and stopped inches from West's face. The man backed up. "No, General, what's this?" He swept his hand at the two threatening machine guns. "You come here with a show of force. To do what? Are we enemies now?"

The driver of his jeep hopped out and walked toward the general with glances over his shoulder. He whispered something to the general then backed up a step. West's face was lined with concern.

Mark turned and spoke to Lincoln. "If any of the general's troops get out of their trucks and look threatening at any of our people, tell the gunners to open fire."

"Wh-what?" West stammered. "You can't do that."

"I'm responding to a hostile threat. We've had quite a few of those in recent days. We're getting very good at defending against them. And you know what? They were all wearing uniforms."

"What are you talking about?" West said, his voice full of rage. "We haven't attacked you."

"You haven't, but the people you now work for have."

"We're representatives of the United States doing a job we were assigned."

"And what job is that? Harassing American citizens."

"You've been labeled as traitors to this country."

"Labeled by who? Secretive people in secretive facilities who say they're representing the government? Tell me. If the government exists, has anyone tried to contact you? You'd think they'd at least make the effort to see what assets they have out there. Yet here you are, ready to do battle with the only other group that has supported you. You're willing to take the word of someone you don't know over people you've developed a relationship with all because they sold you on protecting America.

"Did they tell you that they were the ones who released the virus that killed everyone? I'm betting not. They wouldn't want that information to get out. Did they give you any evidence that shows I'm a traitor? Doubtful since none exists."

Mark was in a rage of his own now. His finger jabbed at the air inches from West's chest.

"Do you have any idea why they want me so bad? I'll tell you. I took Becca there for medical help. She had a spinal injury that left her paralyzed from the waist down. Since they were once a medical facility, I hoped they had someone there who could help. And they did at first, right up to the time they infected her with the virus so they could try out a new vaccine. They had no idea if it would work, but they had a guinea pig and used her.

"My daughter was the guinea pig, West. They injected my daughter with the virus. How can anyone justify that? She might've died. Then what? Back to the drawing board.

"When I objected, they issued kill orders for us. We fought our way out of the facility and made our way back home. They should have let it go, but they're determined to get their test subject back, so they sent a squad of men to recapture her, and I guess me for daring to stand against them.

"They kidnapped our people. Tried to exchange them for us, then attempted to kill us. Now they have you to do their bidding. And you swallowed their lies all in the name of patriotism."

Mark stepped back and tried to calm down before he did something he'd regret. It wasn't West's fault he was conned into following orders, but he was to blame for believing he was a traitor.

"Leave here, General. Don't ever come back. All cooperative deals between us are off. If you truly believe we—I'm a threat to this country, you have no place here in our community."

Mark stomped away. West made no move to stop him or to speak. He walked back to the jeep and gave orders for everyone to return to base.

As they drove away, Mark turned. "Make sure our people don't fire by mistake," he said to Lincoln. "Have the trucks return to their positions but make sure the column leaves our area."

Lincoln gave the orders then said, "Man, I can't believe this shit. Has everyone gone mad?"

Mark shook his head. West was an ally he hated to lose, but the man had proven he could no longer be trusted. He looked around at the stern faces of the people who made up their community. They didn't deserve this. He'd shouted at the general loud enough for everyone to hear. Would they blame him? Some would.

"Okay, everyone. Fun's over. Back to work."

CHAPTER THIRTY-SIX

The lethargic effort displayed after West's visit was telling to Mark. He was losing them. The people who had stood by him through so much were pulling back. They'd had enough of being caught in the middle of whatever trouble he got into. He needed to see this through, get the council in place, and leave. He promised he wouldn't, but he saw no other way of relieving the community of the constant stress they were under while he was in charge.

He grabbed a roll of silver steel welded wire fencing, placed it in the bobcat's shovel, and drove it to the back of the property. No one offered to help him, and he didn't ask. Each roll was a hundred feet long and four feet high. It wouldn't stop anyone who wanted in, but it was a barrier. With the ground now open to the next road, he hoped just the sight would deter anyone from approaching from this direction. He went to work and didn't stop until the roll was done. He looked up, wiping his face on his shirt. He was the only one putting up the fence. So be it. He climbed back on the bobcat and rode back for another roll.

His muscles protested as he hefted the roll into the bucket. It should have been a two-person job, but he was too angry to ask for help. He took a moment to recuperate after the lift and glanced around the yard. Everyone was busy. That was good at least. His eyes stopped when he saw Lynn. She was at the rear of the house getting lunch ready. She was looking at him. She looked as if she wanted to say something. He waited a beat, then climbed into the seat and drove back to his task.

Before he finished the second roll, Lincoln arrived to help.

"You sure you want to help me? You might be siding with the enemy. Could hurt your chances of becoming the Big Kahuna."

"Like I care. Like I'd want to lead these ingrates."

"I appreciate the support."

"They're just worried, Mark."

"And I'm not?"

"They'll come around."

"Maybe they shouldn't. They want me when they need protection but blame me for being the reason they need protection. I've had it. I'm done."

"A few did ask when they were voting for the council."

"Can't be soon enough. Can you arrange that?"

"One crisis at a time, huh?"

"No, Lincoln. I'm serious. Someone else needs to deal with running this place. I'm burned out and need a break."

"And then what?"

"What do you mean, 'then what?'"

"Exactly that. What are you going to do? Leave?"

"Undecided."

"Bullshit. It's all over your face. You can't wait to get away from here."

"We all need some time off from each other."

"Man, you're just a male drama queen."

Mark stopped and gaped at his friend.

"You heard me." I'm going back to get another roll." He jumped on the bobcat's seat and drove off, leaving Mark as alone as he felt.

"I don't know, Britta," Maretha said. It was one of the few times she hadn't called her chieftess. "This place has more drama than our town. I mean, look at what's been going on. They're always in the middle of some danger. Yes, they work together as a community, but they all hate the one person trying to keep them together and safe. I would've had to hurt someone by now."

"Which is why you're not the leader."

"Look how they shun him. Even his friend is angry with him. He works alone, ignoring the dirty looks the others shoot his way like bullets from their eyes."

Britta set down the cement block she was carrying. "I'm going to help him. It'll give me a chance to speak with him. Something I've had little chance to do since arriving."

"Just remember. Keep it in your pants."

Britta frowned at her and moved across the grounds. When she arrived, Mark was leaning on one of the metal posts and staring off into the distance.

"What? No friends?"

Mark turned to face her. "You should be careful who you're seen with. You might get nasty looks."

"Please. This is nothing. You should try living in a town with all women."

He smiled.

"And you know what? If that's how they treat people, this isn't a place I'd want to stay anyway."

"Was that a consideration?"

"Maybe. We hadn't decided. It's a lot more exciting here than in town." She looked around. "You do have a nice group here. They work hard and seem to get along."

"Yeah, usually they do. Stress brings out the worst in people."

"Always has always will." They stood silent for a few moments. "What are you thinking?"

He shrugged.

"Oh, don't give me that. Something's running through your brain. I can hear the squirrels running."

"I'm thinking about going back and settling things."

"You mean back to the facility?"

He nodded.

"That's crazy."

"I can't keep having them harassing us."

"Us."

"Huh."

"Even after the way they're treating you, you still think of them as us. Will that make you more acceptable to them?"

"That no longer matters. This has to end."

"And how do you plan to accomplish that all by yourself?"

"Haven't figured that part out yet."

Lincoln returned with the next load.

"Well, good luck with that," she said and walked back toward the house.

"Did I interrupt something?" Lincoln said.

"Not hardly."

"Too bad."

"Why's that?"

"Ha. If you think things are stirred up now, you go ahead and take up with that young lady and see where that leads you."

"Stop."

"Hey, I'm just saying. You'd better be able to outrun bullets."

CHAPTER THIRTY-SEVEN

Early the next morning, West was back to pacing his office. He was angry. He wasn't used to being spoken to in that manner. If one of his soldiers had tried that, he'd have cut him off and had him jailed. The fact that he was under a literal gun at the time didn't help his mood. But much of what Mark said bore replaying in his mind. West was confused. Mark was not one for emotional tirades. If what he said was true, something was wrong. Someone was lying to him. But who to trust? Who did he believe? A government that until yesterday he didn't know was still functioning or a man he'd stood side-by-side with during a battle and had come to his rescue? It was hard to know who was telling the truth.

If the people from the base he visited had done what Mark said, what was their reasoning? Surely there had to be a purpose for such behavior. But to actually infect a woman with the virus that killed so many just to discover if an untested vaccine worked was criminal.

If Mark was indeed a traitor to this country, would he have let them go? He'd already accumulated military vehicles from his accusers. He easily could have taken West's trucks and equipment. For that matter, he could have had them open fire. Then he wouldn't have to worry about the National Guard as a threat to him and his cohorts.

No. he couldn't see it. Didn't believe it. Mark was no traitor. But could he let the insult to his men—to him, stand? Mark made him look bad in front of his troops. He was at a loss for what to do. The entire ordeal gave him a headache.

Someone rapped on the door. "Come."

His aide entered. "There's a Captain Crandall to see you, Sir."

He ran the name over in his head. He had no idea who the man was, but perhaps it was someone who had answers. "Send him in."

West stood behind his desk as the tall, lean man entered. He moved with confidence, and though his uniform bore no medals, campaign bars, or identifiers, he had the look of a man with years of combat experience. He stopped and offered a half-hearted, almost mocking salute. West nodded his acceptance. "Captain, what can I do for you?"

"I've been informed that you were given an assignment by my general. I'm here to get a briefing as to how that went."

The man took a seat without being offered. His manner was arrogant as if he saw West as less than him. He felt the anger rising, but for the moment, held it in check.

"Excuse me, Captain, but who are you with?"

"I'm sorry, General, but there's a reason we don't wear identifying patches. What we do is classified, and for the benefit of the country must stay that way." His smile said he was anything but sorry.

He thought about his response. "To know who I'm speaking with, who is your general?"

"In that same vein, if you don't know, I shouldn't be throwing his name around. Suffice it to say, I was told you traveled to meet him, and he gave you an assignment. I'm here to find out whether you've completed that assignment and, if not, why." He straightened in the seat, and his expression grew serious. "Have you even met with the targets yet?"

"I don't like your tone, nor appreciate your implications, Captain."

"Well, sir, I don't give a damn." He shot from the chair and slammed his palms down on the desk. The move startled West. He jumped back, bumping into the wall. A sneer crept across the man's hardened features. "We are on a time-sensitive mission. You were given a chance to contribute to this country's rebirth. The question is, did you achieve your mission goal? If so, you should have a bundle of people for me to take control of. If so, you have done your country a great service. If not, then you are nothing more than I expected from a National Guard commander."

He swept his arm toward the window. "This was a Guard base at one time. What did you do, gather a few people, house them here, and call yourself a guard unit? Now, answer my question."

A red veil of anger covered West's vision. "You're not military. You're a thug in a uniform."

"Better that than a fake general playing at soldier. I'll inform the general of your mission failure."

"You insubordinate . . ."

"Careful what you say next, General. You might make me angry." He gave a wicked smile. "We'll take it from here. Stay out of our way before you get hurt."

The man gave a left-handed salute and let his wrist flop, signifying West's weakness. He pivoted and strode out of the room. West stood almost hyperventilating in equal parts of anger and embarrassment. He had never in all his years in the military been talked to or treated with such contempt. True, he might not have the combat experience, training, or confidence that man did, but he had attained his rank, well, most of it, by hard work and determination. He'd been a lieutenant when the virus spread, but he remained on duty, and when it came time to rebuild the Guard, he took on the rank of general to do the job right. And he had. The base and personnel were proof of his achievements and leadership abilities. He would not allow that street punk to put him down. If that man was a representative of the new America, which he now doubted, then maybe it was a government he didn't want to serve.

But what to do? He needed information. He darted across the room and opened the door. "That man who just left," he said to his aide. "I want him followed. I want to know where his base is."

"Yes, Sir."

He went back into his office, closed the door, and sat at his desk. He had to plan. One way or another, he'd prove his worth.

Sergeant William Bradford sat in the jeep, with the seat fully back, his legs propped on the door extended outside, eyes closed. He had enjoyed his encounter with the actor portraying a general and pretending to be the captain. The situation at the base was as he expected. The base was nothing more than a hangout for wannabe soldiers. "Hey, Sarge?"

"Yeah."

"Looks like we got some company."

He opened his eyes. "Seriously?"

"It's kinda tough to blend in when there's no other traffic."

"What kind of vehicle?"

"Jeep."

He shook his head. West was dumber than he thought. "How far back?"

"He's keeping his distance, but we're on a straight road. He's got nowhere to hide."

"Okay. See that next corner? Take the turn to the right. Get beyond his line of sight and stop. Then pull down about a half a block."

"You got it."

His driver made the turn and braked. Bradford stepped out and walked off the road and hid behind a small tree. It didn't offer much cover, but he wouldn't have to hide for long. While he waited, he thought about which weapon to use. The M-16 would do the job in a hurry but might make too much noise. He kept it slung and drew his sidearm.

The wait wasn't long. The other jeep crept to the corner then made the turn. The driver was quick, noticing the stopped jeep ahead. He shifted into reverse, but Bradford was up and ten feet from the jeep by the time he moved. He fired twice. The driver cried out. His first reaction was to take his foot off the pedal, but just as fast, he stomped down. The jeep leaped backward as Bradford continued to fire. Several shots missed from the side, but as he stepped into the road and had a straight-on shot through the windshield, red blooms appeared in the man's chest. The jeep swerved off-road and crashed into a tree.

Bradford approached, with the gun still aimed. He had fired more times than expected. The shots would carry a long way here in the open. He thought about that and came up with a plan. Motioning the driver to come, he pushed the body to the passenger side and got out. As the other jeep neared, he said, "Follow me."

He drove the jeep as close to the farmhouse as he dared, then left it on the side of the road. He grabbed the body and dragged it into the driver's seat, stripped the body of its weapons, and climbed back into the jeep.

As they drove away, he propped his feet back up and smiled. He hadn't thought the day could get any better. He'd been wrong.

CHAPTER THIRTY-EIGHT

"Hey, Mark," Lincoln said.

Mark wiped his brow and looked up from his task of setting cinder blocks on the second row of the wall. "What's up?"

"Something you should see."

"It's not something that comes in a bottle or a can, is it?"

"No. I wish it were, though you may need either of those after I show you what it is."

More trouble? Maybe it never did end. He straightened his aching back, using his palms to rub out the kinks. Lincoln led him to the road and down to a waiting car. He climbed into the back seat. Caleb was driving.

"Caleb," Lincoln said, "Tell Mark what you found."

"We were out collecting and thought we heard shots. We hid for a while, thinking it might be one of the military groups. When nothing more happened, we packed what little we found and started back to the camp." He made a left turn and drove one block. "That's when we found that jeep."

Caleb stopped alongside, and Lincoln and Mark exited. A soldier was lying across the front seat. Several bullet wounds were evident in his chest. He was well beyond help.

Mark said, "You didn't see anyone or hear another vehicle drive away?"

"No. Just this. His body's been stripped, though, so it could've been a scavenger."

"What do you think?" he asked Lincoln.

"No way a scavenger did this. They would've taken a lot more, including the jeep."

"He's got the one eighty-seconds patch. Why was he out here alone? West would never dispatch a vehicle without at least two people."

Lincoln had no answer. "This is gonna look bad, especially after our confrontation."

"You think he's gonna blame this on us?"

Mark nodded. "Yeah." He turned and looked down the road to the north. "I wonder if it was meant to look that way."

"You think one group is trying to set us up with the other?"

He shrugged. "Just a thought."

"How do you want to handle this?"

"If we leave him here, we create suspicion. Best if we take him back ourselves and get in front of this."

"That might be dangerous."

"Maybe, but I'd rather give my explanation in person rather than on the other side of exchanged shots."

Mark drove the jeep while Caleb and Lincoln followed. Mark had nixed the idea of returning to the farmhouse to gather more people. "A show of force might start bullets flying."

"Yeah, but it might be all that saves your ass," Lincoln said.

He drove to the main gate and advanced slowly with one hand on the wheel and the other in the air showing it empty. Caleb stopped on the road.

As soon as the body was seen, a lot of shouting and gun pointing occurred. Mark tried to remain calm, repeating. "I need to see the general."

He was dragged roughly from the jeep and shoved forward by a gun barrel. Soldiers ran past them toward the gate. West stood outside the headquarters watching. As he spotted Mark, his eyes narrowed, and his face reddened.

"You killed one of my men!"

"No," Mark said in a strong, loud voice.

West turned to the guards. "Lock him up."

"We did not kill your man." Mark was grabbed and yanked. "We found him already dead."

"A likely story."

"But true." He had to shout louder as he was manhandled away. "Why would I bring him here if we killed him. It would've been easier to hide the body and the jeep."

West glared after him but did not respond.

"Someone is trying to make it look like we killed him. You're being used to start a war between us."

West's expression altered. One of the guards, frustrated with Mark's progress, rammed the stock of his rifle into Mark's gut. He doubled over from the unexpected blow. He was then lifted off the ground by his arms and dragged.

"Hold," West commanded. The men turned, waiting.

"Bring him back here. And Paulsen, don't hit him again."

He was brought into HQ and led to West's office. There he was dropped into a chair. The two guards backed against the wall on either side of the door. West sat at his desk. "Where did you find him?"

"A few blocks from the farmhouse. His weapons were taken, but from what we could tell, nothing else."

"So it wasn't some random scavenger."

"No. Why was he out there alone?"

West hesitated then said, "He was on a special mission."

"But alone? Was that mission to spy on us."

West's mouth opened, then he shut it and tried again. "No. It had nothing to do with you or any of your people."

The silence extended before Mark said, "I know we're at odds right now, but unless you or your men attack us, I'd never take action against you, especially not this kind of action. I don't know if his death was random or has to do with his mission. Whatever the cause, it wasn't any of my people that killed him."

West expelled a long breath and looked out the window. "I got a visit today from a man representing this other military group. He wanted to know if I accomplished the mission I'd been given to bring you and certain members of your group in. He was angry when I said I hadn't and became threatening and insulting."

"If I may ask, who gave you this mission?"

"I took a column out to the facility you talked about on Route Two."

Mark nodded. "Did you speak with Ohtanda?"

"Not sure who that is. I wasn't given any names. The whole encounter was strange, as if their lives depended on ultra secrecy. They wore no identifying insignias, patches, or medals, but if they weren't regular military, then this is a boy scout camp."

"You didn't speak to a tall black woman?"

"No. No woman. Two generals."

"Two?"

"They have a lot of firepower there. Like they're preparing for an invasion."

"They told you to take my family and me into custody?"

"Yes. And a family of Asians."

"They want their test subjects back."

West rubbed his face with meaty hands. "I didn't know who to believe. On the one hand, I had supposed representatives of the government I serve telling me one thing, and on the other, I had what I believed to be a correct assessment of you and your people. Since I was given an order, I was required to fulfill it." He stopped and focused his eyes on Mark. "I was wrong. I apologize. As soon as that man left here today, I knew I'd been played."

"Man? What man?"

"He must be with the advance team. He knew all about my mission. When he left, I had my man follow him. I wanted to know where their base was in case it became important to find them. It cost his life. I won't be able to forget that." A new, more urgent look filled West's eyes. "Mark, they're coming for you, and I get the feeling they're going to hit hard and fast."

"Did he say when?"

"No, but he did say I had a day to accomplish my mission before they took over. I failed. My gut says it will happen tonight."

Mark stood, and the two guards reacted, even though they could hear everything being said. West waved them back.

"I need to get back and prepare."

"Yes. Good luck. And again, I apologize for my actions."

"You didn't fail your mission. You had too much integrity to follow something you knew was wrong."

Mark left, and the guards followed. Paulsen said, "Sir, I'm sorry for striking you."

Mark looked at the man and nodded his acceptance. He rejoined Lincoln and Caleb.

Lincoln said, "Man, I'm so glad to see you. I was afraid I'd have to go in there and rescue you."

"Caleb, go fast. We're about to be attacked."

CHAPTER THIRTY-NINE

Lincoln was on his radio calling for a meeting before they arrived. As they pulled into the driveway, people were already rushing around the grounds. They wasted no time running to the tables where about twenty people were already gathered.

Many of Elijah's people were still working. Mark scanned the crowd, stopping on Bobby. "Go get Elijah's people." Bobby ran. In three minutes, with still only half the community joined, Mark started. "I have been told there's a good chance we'll be attacked today." That brought murmurs and chatter. He didn't wait for them to quiet but explained what they found and subsequently learned from West.

"I believe this assault will take place tonight, so we have time to prepare. I do have a plan. Part of that plan involves sending all noncombatants to the Guard base for safety. After dinner, I want anyone incapable of fighting, for whatever reason, especially the children, to meet by the garage. You'll be transported to the base and stay until you're sent for."

"Will they take us in?" a woman asked. "They didn't seem to like us much yesterday."

"General West and I talked today. He apologized for his actions yesterday. Although I didn't bring up housing us, I don't think there'll be a problem. If so, at least you're away from here."

He paused to gather his thoughts.

"We have a lot to do in about six hours, so get going." He shouted over the dispersing crowd. "I need to meet with the leaders." He waited until the crowd thinned before addressing the ten people before him. "Make sure everyone who wasn't here knows what's going on. We need to recall our collection teams now. I don't want them out there when the action starts. We have a good defense established, but this will be against experienced soldiers. They will have the best gear and will have a plan. With their night-vision goggles, they'll know where we are. They'll be wearing body armor and have superior weapons, but we have numbers and the advantage of knowing they're coming. I want to send ten to twelve people off base but within radio distance. Once the fighting starts, you'll come in from behind on the east and the west. Find a place to hide, preferably in a house. No one should be outside."

"What if they use explosives?" one of Elijah's people asked.

Mark hadn't thought about that.

"I mean, what good is all our defenses if they just bomb us."

"I don't think that'll be an option only because they're looking for certain people, people they want. With that in mind, we need to hide Becca and Jin's family. If they don't know where they are, they will have to be more careful with their shots.

"Let them try and take me," Becca said, her eyes aflame.

Maretha, who was standing next to her, said, "I got your back, sister."

Mark caught Britta's eye. She nodded at him. For whatever reason, it bolstered him, knowing she was with them. "We need spotters up high, and they should have the goggles. We need to devise something to keep them safe, though. They'll be the first targets. I'm sure they'll have shooters skilled enough to take them down. Milo, do we have anything that can stop a bullet?"

"I've got some sheet metal, but I don't think it's thick enough to stop a bullet."

"Anything you can think of. We'll need four of them. Your best shooters should be used as snipers. Bobby, you and—" he scanned the faces.

"Maretha," Maretha said.

Mark looked at her and nodded. "Okay, Maretha, will have the barn, front, and back."

"Anything I'm forgetting?"

Jarrod said, "Should we keep working on the wall? We're only one course around and just starting the second. One row doesn't cover much. Two is better."

"Okay, get as much done as you can. Maybe for the first hour, set the blocks. After that, just lay them on top. We'll worry about setting them afterward."

"Providing we're still here," someone said."

"There'll be no talk like that. We're going to survive this as long as we don't panic and give in."

"Are you sure we should be fighting our own troops?"

"If they are our own troops, I'd be concerned, but the way these men act, I have serious doubts they represent any part of the United States armed forces. Someone is controlling them—giving them orders, but whatever their plan is, they view us as nothing more than test subjects. Now, is there anything else?" No one spoke. "Okay, let's get ready. If anyone has a question later, find and ask me. I'd rather you be sure than to guess."

He stepped down from the table, and Bobby, Britta, Maretha, Becca, Lynn, and Lincoln closed in. Britta slid between him and Maretha to stand next to him. Mark glanced around the small group and found Lynn casting a hard eye toward Britta. Britta appeared unaware.

"Bobby, you and Maretha find something to use as a shield while you're in the barn. Becca, I need at least four vehicles ready to go to transport people to the base. Lincoln, let's move the other vehicles across the driveway."

"I was thinking about taking a few of them to the fence we just built so we can place shooters there with some cover."

"Good idea."

"Lynn," the sound of her name startled her. She swung her gaze toward him. "Whatever the meal is you have planned, make it simple and something they can take with them if they're leaving the grounds."

She nodded and turned toward the house. He watched her for a second distracted from his thoughts. "Dad," Bobby's voice brought him back in focus. "Yeah, ah, I'll need two cars of four to five people to leave and find a place to lay low until things heat up. Can you organize that, Lincoln? Maybe you should go with them."

Lincoln eyed him as if searching for an ulterior motive. "I'll get them set up, but I'm staying here."

Mark knew better than to argue. "Okay, but whoever you send needs to be reliable. Getting the attackers in a crossfire may be our best hope." He dug deep into his mind looking for an edge or something he forgot.

"You got any gut reactions as to when they'll strike?" asked Britta.

"They're military, so my guess is between midnight and two. They'll want us settled in and bedded down for the night. Plus, they'll have night vision goggles, which will give them the advantage. Those not on active patrol should be prone as if lying in bed. Too much movement will make them suspicious. We'll only use the trucks for guard duty today. All foot patrols should be inside the perimeter."

He scanned the anxious faces. "If there's nothing else, let's move." As they broke up, Mark called. "Make sure you have fresh batteries for the radios."

Lincoln stayed behind. "You trying to send me away cause it's safer?"

"No, I wanted someone in charge who would know when to attack from behind. Someone who can keep everyone in place and not get caught."

"I'll find someone to handle that, but I'm staying here. You can only be in one place at a time. Where's it gonna be?"

Mark looked around. Where would the bulk of the attack occur? How would he do it? He'd probe with a few shooters in the three directions he wasn't assaulting just to keep them occupied, then, as the battle was engaged, the real target would be attacked. They didn't have a good route of attack coming from the front. Unless they came in from behind the three houses across the road, some would come through the cornfields. Bobby would see them. He didn't think they'd cross the open field behind the farmhouse where they'd taken down the stalks.

To the south, they'd have to pass Elijah's people to get to him. That didn't seem likely. They could attack from long range, pinning them down and creating a siege but he was sure that Ohtanda wanted her test subjects back ASAP.

He turned back to the woods behind Elijah's building. He pointed. "I think it will come from there.

"Why?" Lincoln asked.

"It offers cover, little resistance, and allows them to capture one at a time. Once they have Elijah's people under control, they'll be able to concentrate on us better. That's where I'll be."

CHAPTER FORTY

Mark drove the bobcat across the road to the southern camp. He found Elijah, Milo, Darlene, and two other men behind the construction site. They stopped whatever they'd been discussing as he approached.

"What's up?" Milo said.

"I think the attack will come from one of three places. The woods across the street, though, once they come out of the trees, they're in wide-open ground, the corn behind the barn, which can be seen from the loft, and these trees behind you. To me, that's the weakest point. They allow the opposition to get close before being spotted."

Milo said, "Makes sense. You have an idea of how to protect us?"

"Not protect as much as warn." He pointed to the bobcat's shovel where he'd placed a roll of fencing.

"You want us to string fencing," Darlene said in surprise.

"No. We don't have time for that. Besides, they'd see the fence and cut through it. I want to lay it flat on the ground about midway through the trees and cover it as best we can with leaves. They may see it and step over it, but put twigs or metal on the near side, so if they jump, they land on something that makes noise. One of them will step on something and alert you.

"Okay," Milo said, though, by the tone of his voice, it was clear he had little confidence in the plan."

"If you can think of anything else, I'm all ears."

Elijah spoke. "Wouldn't it be easier to string rope from tree to tree?"

"No, they can easily step over that. And if you hang something, it will be easily seen. This way, the fence is dark and covered, and their focus will be forward with glances downward to ensure their footing. Hey, it's just an idea."

"It's better than nothing," Milo said.

"Gather some people, and let's get started."

Mark drove into the eastern section of the woods. Though some areas were thick, for the most part, a lot of open ground filled the area. He and Milo uncoiled the fence. It was laid on the ground, cut into sections, and flattened with their feet. Once the coil was out, Mark went back for another roll while everyone else gathered leaves, twigs, and branches to cover it.

By the time they finished the southern section, it was getting late. The community was already gathering for dinner, mostly comprised of venison sandwiches and hot vegetable soup. Mark encouraged everyone to eat the soup and take their sandwiches with them.

As dinner ended, faster than at any time he could remember, those leaving filed toward the waiting vehicles Becca had lined up. Loved ones said their good-byes, and a half-hour before dusk, the caravan rolled out. The two carloads of shooters going off-campus escorted them.

Mark went back to the tables, poured himself a last cup of coffee, and sat down. Caryn was wiping down the tables and stopped across from him. "The fun never ends here, huh?"

"I could sure think of better ways of having fun."

"Speaking of fun. What's the deal with you and that woman?"

The question confused him. "What woman?" It hit him as 'woman' left his mouth. He was sure Caryn had seen the sudden change. Was she asking out of curiosity, or had Lynn put her up to it? No. that wasn't Lynn's way. She might have discussed it with Caryn, but she never would've asked Caryn to speak for her. "There is no deal. They," he emphasized 'they' to express that more than one woman arrived, "are people we met a few days ago. They were instrumental in helping us rescue Becca and Doc."

"Sure looks like more than that."

"Does it? I don't know what you're talking about."

"Hmm." She went back to wiping. "That's good because she looks awfully young."

"Hmm," he copied. "Does she? I hadn't noticed."

Caryn gave him a skeptical look, then walked toward the house. In his mind, he pictured her going right to Lynn to make a report. So, what if she did? What if he did like Britta? Lynn had made her position on the two of them clear. He shoved the thought aside. He had more pressing things on his mind.

Lincoln came over and sat opposite him. He slid a beer can across the table. "Didn't think it would hurt to have one."

Mark chuckled. "Just one, eh?"

"Yep. Just the one." He popped the top and held the can up. "To those about to—ah, never mind."

"Yeah, best you don't finish that one."

They touched cans and drank. They sat in a long silence until their beers were gone. "Well, still got things to do," Mark said and stood. Lincoln held out his hand.

"Good luck to us all."

Mark took it, and without another word, the two men went their ways. Mark entered the house. Lynn and Caryn were sitting at the kitchen table, having a cup of coffee and rolling balls of dough for the next morning's breakfast. They stopped and looked at him. He stopped, said, "Ladies," then continued to where he'd placed his duffel bag containing clothes. He dug out a dark long sleeve base shirt, then added two layers of t-shirts. He grabbed a waterproof jacket and left.

As he passed the table, Lynn said, "Mark?"

He looked back.

"Be safe."

"Thanks. You both too."

He picked up his weapons and equipment and walked across the road and into the woods. He didn't expect any activity for another three to four hours, but he needed to be in place when they did come.

Mark stopped to let Milo know he'd be in the woods. "I'll be your early warning in case they somehow bypass the fence."

"Are you going to come back out this way? I'm concerned a nervous finger may cause you a painful problem."

"No, once the shooting starts, I'll make my way toward the street."

Milo nodded. Mark glanced around at the grounds. "I like the new additions." Milo's people had set cement blocks in stacks at various places. In each stack several blocks had been turned so the holes faced out creating shooting ports. That prevented those behind the barricades from having to raise their heads to shoot.

"They should at least offer some cover."

Mark turned to go, but Milo said, "Mark, be careful out there."

Mark nodded and disappeared into the darkening woods. He found a location behind a tree and used a trenching tool to dig out a small cove for his body. That would help hide his heat signature from the invaders. He piled up leaves and found a large broken branch that he placed to the side of the trunk. Then he covered his face, hands, and jacket with mud. He sat on the branch for the first two hours until complete darkness claimed the world around him, then slid his body into his trench and waited.

It was well after midnight when, fighting sleep, he heard the first sound.

CHAPTER FORTY-ONE

"Captain," the voice came through Crandall's coms.

"Go."

"Things have changed a lot since yesterday."

"How so?"

"They took down a long section of the corn and put up a four-foot fence, and they've got one of our trucks on the road doing guard duty."

"And none of this was in sight yesterday when you scouted?"

"No, Sir."

Another voice came through. "Sir, on top of what he said, they've constructed a bit of a cement block wall in front of the place. Cars have been driven across the driveway. They have a Humvee here, too. It's as if they're expecting us."

"Anything else?"

"No, but something about this is making my skin crawl."

"Get a grip, soldier. You've faced worse than these country hicks before. Are you in position?"

"Yes, Sir."

"I need a call from everyone."

"Two in position."

"Three. Good."

He waited for the one other team to respond. He was part of team one, so he knew they were in position. Irritated, Crandall called out, "Childs, you and your team in position?"

"Yeah, we're here."

His tone made him sound like he was bored. Crandall vowed then, that the man was not returning to base. He'd be a casualty, whether by the enemy or friendly fire.

Crandall motioned for the leader to head out and the six-man assault team, including him, moved into the woods. A three-man group was coming through the southern section of the woods. Bradford and two men were moving through the corn as a diversionary force. Childs' four men were charged with assaulting the house where the Asians were housed.

It was a good plan, even if they did suspect an attack was imminent. Once they had the people they were taking back with them, he'd give the 'hose them down' order, and everyone would unload their automatic weapons on full. But the first part of the attack had to be done with stealth.

They entered the woods from the east. Each man was experienced. Each had body armor, helmets, and NVGs along with their M-16s. They moved with confidence and skill. Several minutes later, his visual display showed they were less than fifty yards from the target. They should be seeing the first line of guards any second.

Ten yards more and still nothing. The absence made him more concerned than their presence would have. His foot hit something, and he froze. It sank an inch or two and rustled a lot of leaves. He stopped and squatted, keeping his head up and eyes scanning through the scope. With his left hand, he reached down and touched the ground. It took a moment for him to recognize the feel of fencing.

All along the line, he heard the same thing. They created a line of noise. Not great bell sounding alarm, but enough to make their approach noticed. "Hold," he whispered into the com unit. "Check the ground. They've placed fencing. Careful where you step."

Was the fencing strictly for an alarm, or did it cover a trap? No way of knowing. He inched his foot forward, careful of the placement. It took several steps to clear the fence. To his surprise, nothing happened. No explosions, no screaming, no gunshots. No trap at all. He was reminded of the old saying if a tree fell in the woods and no one was there to hear, did it make a sound? The fence on the ground didn't work if no one was paying attention.

Something cracked to his left, like a snapping branch. He froze. He waited in a crouch several seconds before moving again. That was when the first shot came.

Mark was in the process of redoing the mud pack on his face when the first rustling sound of leaves reached him. He froze to the point of barely breathing and lowered his head to the branch. The sound had come from his right. He shifted the rifle in that direction and waited. More sound of leaves crunching both to the right and left had him sweeping his gaze from side to side. Then there was the snap of a branch to his right, and he zeroed in on a dark moving shadow.

He lined up his shot. He had to make the first one count, or they'd be on him before he had a chance to move. He waited as the invader crept ever closer, moving past trees that blocked his view and had him reacquiring the target. As the man stepped out from behind the next tree, Mark broke the trigger. The target went down, and the forest grew still save for the echo of the shot.

He had thought about this moment most of the night. This was his one chance to move while the invaders were still surprised, to make a run toward the street. With everyone alerted and nervous, if he broke from the woods now, there'd be a good chance of getting cut down by friendly fire. He chose to stay.

A short burst of silenced rounds tore through his general direction. Had someone seen his muzzle flash, or did they have a reading in their night vision goggles? If that was the case, he'd be dead in seconds. He kept his head down and attempted to burrow lower in his trench. Though his back was level with the ground, he wished he'd tried to cover his legs with dirt.

More shots came. He'd taken out the closest shooter, but how many others were spread out through the trees? That was the one bad part of the plan—not knowing the size of the opposing force.

Footsteps were close. They were no longer moving with stealth. One moved past him to the right. He turned his head a fraction and opened his right eye. The shadow was too far away to see. Mark forced slow breaths, expecting a bullet to the back of the head at any second.

Unsilenced shots came from the camp. It was easy to hear the difference. But was it early firing by anxious inexperienced shooters, or were they engaged? He waited but no longer heard movement close to him. That didn't seem possible unless they had a lot fewer men than he anticipated. Did they send a small team to do damage? Possible, but they had to know the size of the force they were attacking. Why so few men? Perhaps the larger force was holding back or even attacking from another direction. The sound of distant fire had not reached him.

Then it came. A rifle. He pictured Bobby in the loft and prayed he was all right. Mark waited another two minutes, and as the gun battle picked up intensity, he slowly rose from his hiding place and advanced toward the enemy from behind.

Bobby was alert. Since the first gunshot, he caught brief green sparks in the night vision goggles but had little experience with them. Something was out there, but he expected to see a lot more green images if it was an attack.

"You see something, don't you?" Maretha said. "Your body stiffened."

"Not sure. I see something, but I'm not sure it's a person or a deer."

She crawled next to him. They found an old yield sign in the garage and propped it up for protection. "Look at the shape. Is it more upright or horizontal?"

"Upright."

"Then it is a man. Kill him."

Bobby took a second to ready the shot before firing. The green image went down. He scanned right while Maretha went left. "I have one," she said. But before she could shoot, a barrage of gunfire ripped through the barn. They rolled away from the opening as the shots punched holes through the metal sign and tore up large splinters of wood.

Fearing the rounds were tracking him, Bobby rolled to the edge of the loft. If not for the wooden railing, he might have plummeted to the floor. Across the street, at the other camp, the gunfire had increased. He crawled in that direction and poked his head out the other door.

He scanned the grounds. A lot of images appeared but deciding which was friend and which foe made him hesitate. Behind him, Maretha fired. She was a good shot, perhaps as good as him. Bobby hadn't seen many forms in the corn, so maybe the main attack was coming from the woods, as his dad said.

He aimed toward the trees figuring none of Elijah's people would be there. He found the flash of an image. A green blur followed by a yellowish red flare he took to be gunshots. He set the scope on that spot and waited. As soon as he saw the image again, he fired. He saw nothing. Did he hit his target, or had he rushed the shot? Regardless, no more shots came from that spot.

"This is very strange," Maretha said. "There are no other targets. That can't be right. Only two?"

Then shots ripped through the floorboards. Maretha scrambled for a safe place. Bobby turned to see one lift Maretha from the floor and drop her hard. The shooter was inside the barn and firing from below.

Bobby moved as slow as possible to the edge of the loft door. He wasn't quiet enough, as another burst plowed holes not a foot from him. He stepped on the edge of the frame and lifted his weight from the floor. No more shots followed him. He looked across the loft at Maretha. She did not move, and he feared she was dead, although his glasses showed her as green. Her body still had heat. He had to get to her fast before that changed.

Bobby cleared his thoughts and focused on hearing anything out of the ordinary. The only way for the shooter to know for sure the loft was clear was to come up. The only way up was the wooden ladder at the far end of the loft, where Maretha's motionless body lay not four feet from where an enemy may be climbing.

Bobby knelt and aimed his rifle at the spot. Nothing moved. No sound came. He glanced outside. If the man left the building, Bobby'd be an easy target in the open doorway. The waiting game had his nerves on end. Sweat trickled, so far missing his eyes. He wanted to wipe his brow but dared not alter his line of sight. Each passing second made the wait more difficult and amped up the angst within his chest.

Something thudded to the floor and rolled. His first thought was a grenade. Without hesitation, Bobby stepped outside the loft and reached for the top of the loft door. He found a foothold on the bottom crossbar of the frame and stepped outside as the flashbang detonated. Though not in its direct path, the concussion had a jolting effect, almost knocking him from his tenuous perch. The door swung, bouncing once off the outer wall and pinning his fingers. He hung in the open outside the loft, an easy target for anyone looking.

The pain in his fingers helped clear his mind. If the shooter climbed up the ladder now, he'd see Maretha. Not knowing that she was shot, he'd assume she was stunned and shoot her. If she wasn't dead already, she soon would be. He had to do something.

With the rifle in one hand and the other holding the door, he had no way to push off and let the door swing him back to the loft. His only recourse was to hope his body generated enough pull to swing the door. He leaned back with some force. His fingers barely held, but the release of pressure across them was evident. He moved, but the door returned to the wall.

This time he pressed his body against the door, lifted his elbow until it hung over the top, and released his hold. Using his bruised fingers, he gave a hard push off the wall, and the door swung. As it closed, he held the rifle waist-high. A figure, more a half figure, stood above the floorboards on the ladder. He brought the gun up to finish off Maretha but heard the creaking of the door. He swung his weapon toward the sound, and Bobby fired. He pulled the trigger repeatedly on his shots, walking them toward the shooter. He found the target on his last shot. His next pull gave no report. The man pitched backward, going airborne off the ladder. However, his last shot found Bobby, too. Using the swinging door's momentum, Bobby dove for the floor. He landed hard and rolled.

Once he stopped moving, he found breathing difficult. His fingers crawled across his chest, discovering a slickness. He tried to remain calm. He didn't want to panic, but the tears came. He thought about his dad and how disappointed he'd be that he got shot. Then he envisioned his sister and how she would tease him.

His vision clouded. He had to move. He had to do something, but he had trouble focusing. That was bad. He fought to stay awake, but his vision narrowed. The glasses saw no images of any color. They appeared to be broken since the images darkened.

He thought he heard movement below. The shooter was still alive. That gave him a moment of clarity, but it didn't last. Then a sharp pain filled his eyes, and everything was brighter. A voice called from somewhere. A woman's voice. His first thought and last word was, "Mom?" Then there she was. A green image, standing above him, never looking more beautiful. Then she was gone.

CHAPTER FORTY-TWO

"Hey Crandall," the voice came through the coms. Crandall had to think who the voice belonged to. Then it came to him. Childs. "Go."

"There's nobody in this house. It's empty. What do you want us to do now?"

He swallowed his first thought. "Attack the compound from the front of the house."

"Okay, but there's a lot of people out there."

"Listen, you chicken shit," but a sudden increase in the volume and direction of the shooting drew his attention. Down the line, one of his men grunted and went down. What had changed?

"Hey, a carload of people just arrived from behind us. They're trying to trap us between the two groups."

Could that be what happened here? Were others coming up behind them? They hadn't made much headway from the trees. A lot of firepower was directed their way. True, most shots missed, but his men were unable to advance. Crandall didn't bother responding to Childs. Instead, he called to his men, "Light 'em up and hose 'em down."

In seconds, explosions rocked the ground before them as grenades were tossed from all angles. He did note it was fewer explosions than he expected. Had some of the men not heard, or were they unable to execute?

More shots filled the woods. He had no doubt the enemy was behind them, now cutting off any retreat. As the machine guns chattered, spreading death and destruction across the grounds, Crandall thought it might be time to retreat.

A bullet whizzed past his head. He ducked on instinct, then moved left. He ran about twenty feet before tripping over something. He stumbled, caught his balance on a tree, and swung his weapon behind him. On the ground was another one of his men. Dead. It was time to bug out. "Retreat south. Repeat. Retreat south."

He didn't wait for responses. Crandall moved fast, keeping his attention focused on the woods to his left. None of the enemy would risk attacking from the camp. His only concern was from behind. This had been a cluster-fuck. And the soldier who made the comment was right. They had been expecting them and were better prepared.

Mark waited for his chance. He moved toward the road wanting to begin at the end of the enemy line. He found a target thirty feet ahead. In the dark, approaching with any stealth was all but impossible. His only cover was the man's shooting. Mark had already slung the rifle and extracted his handgun. He moved to get closer, but his step cracked something beneath it. The man whirled and ducked, firing a burst in Mark's direction. The only thing that saved him was that the man guessed where Mark was and fired just wide. Mark managed to get behind a tree before the shooter adjusted, hitting the trunk.

Mark was pinned down. The man had NVGs and would see him move into the open. He would also be moving at this very second to close the gap to get a shooting angle. Mark had one chance. Run, keeping the tree between them as long as possible. He found another tree ten feet away and dashed for it. The move must have taken the shooter by surprise. The shots came late and missed.

As soon as he made it to one tree, he located the next and moved. He did the same move three times before pausing. If he got into a rhythm, the shooter would be ready. He bent and scraped his hand against the ground, finding a small, dry rotted branch and a small stone. He picked them up and, staying low, tossed them right. He whirled left as the shooter fired. His bullet hit the trunk on the left side, and Mark pulled the trigger in rapid succession, moving his hand an inch to the left with each depression.

His opponent had the same idea. His shots came faster from the M-16 and stitched a line across the trunk toward Mark. Mark went prone, still firing. His bullet struck and knocked the man back a step, but he did not go down. Now on target, Mark fired again, this time raising his hand. Though stunned by the impact to his vest, the soldier continued to fire, though with less accuracy. Still, the rounds flew dangerously close to Mark's head. Mark fired again, this time staggering the man to the side. However, his slide locked back. He rolled behind the tree, fumbled for another magazine, then got to his feet. He ran as he seated the magazine, hoping the shooter was too off-balance to target him. He made it fifteen feet before shots tracked him again.

Mark was forced to dive for the cover of the next tree trunk, smacking his shoulder into an exposed root. Pain fired through his body, and his gun arm went numb. He switched the gun to his left hand. He had little proficiency with the offhand, a flaw he hoped to be alive to correct. It was essential to keep firing, so his opponent didn't know he had a momentary advantage.

He loosed three rounds and halted, listening for movement. There was none. His foe was smart, doing the same thing. Or had he hurt the man more than he thought? That might be the man's play. Lure Mark out, thinking he'd put the man down only to walk right into a bullet.

In the distance, Mark thought by the southern woods, one of the fifty cals opened up. The gunner wouldn't be able to see much, but it was still a good move. Keep the enemy pinned down, making it harder for them to attack the camp. The one drawback to the heavy gun was it masked any small noise made in his battle.

He couldn't wait. The shooter might be closing on him right then. He stood and tested his right arm. It hurt, but feeling was returning. He used both hands on the gun and did a quick peek around the trunk. He didn't see anything but didn't expect to. If the man was smart, he'd be hidden and ready for Mark to move.

He located his next safety spot but couldn't make his body react. The idea was stupid, but he had to draw fire to know where the shooter was hiding. He peeked to the opposite side of the tree, then faked a step away from cover. No shot. No sound. He faked again, then darted in the other direction. To his surprise, he made it without taking a bullet. Even more surprising was none had been fired.

Something had happened. Was the man drawing him out for the easy kill? He focused all efforts on listening. There. Running steps but off to his left, receding. Was it the same man? Mark backed away from the tree, then ran east. No one followed, and no bullets were fired. He noticed the cadence of the gunfight back at the camp had altered. Fewer shots were being fired. The fifty cal had ceased as well. Had the camp been overrun, or had the invaders fled?

Mark veered south, the direction the running footsteps were heading. He moved on a parallel course listening for others in the woods. From the east, he heard the heavy tramping of multiple people. The soldiers were too well-trained to make that much noise. He hid behind a tree and waited. The sound grew louder.

He took a chance and called out, "It's Mark. Who's there.?"

A series of shots ripped through the branches, but none were close. He was even more convinced now that these shooters were friends. He ducked and tried again louder this time. "Don't shoot. It's Mark."

A voice responded. "Mark? Is that you?"

Giving his name would help him be recognized by one of his people, but it could also be used by a foe. Before he stepped out, he needed confirmation. "Identify yourself."

"Yeah, Sure. It's, ah,"

Mark readied to shoot. If the guy didn't know what name to call out, he was not a friend.

"You dumbass," a female voice said. "You're about to get shot. Tell him your name. Oh, never mind. Mark, It's Britta. It's okay. No one will shoot." In a lower voice, he heard, "I hope."

He slid bit by bit away from the tree. Before him stood three people. Thomas and David and Britta. He was glad to see them but more so to see Britta. She moved closer and embraced him. "I'm glad you're still alive."

"That makes two of us."

"We joined the group coming in from behind. There wasn't much action in your camp."

"So you went in search of action?"

"It's what we do."

"I'm glad." Then he turned. "They were moving south. Let's go find some action." He took off at a run and heard the footfalls behind.

CHAPTER FORTY-THREE

Becca hated that all the action was happening across the road. She wanted to join them but didn't want to abandon her post. She was behind the new front wall with six others, including Lincoln. She crept toward him.

"What's up, little girl?" Lincoln said.

She always bristled when he called her that but knew he meant nothing negative or insulting. It was just his way. "I can't stand this waiting."

"I hear you, but we have a job to do, and the camp has not been breached. We stay."

That was not the answer she hoped for.

"Hey Lincoln," someone called from down the line. "I think there's someone in your house."

"What the?" he peered hard through the dark. "Where? Are you sure?"

"No, but I thought I saw a face peek between the curtains in that right side upstairs window."

Becca saw her chance. "We should check it out."

"Nice try. Stay put."

"But Lincoln," her mind worked fast to find anything to back up her argument. "Wh-what if there is someone up there? That gives them a superior position. They'll be able to shoot into the grounds and keep us pinned down. We can't let them get established."

Lincoln eyed her. "Are you that anxious to get into the fight that you'd run across the road in the open to do so?"

"Absolutely. You coming?"

"Becca right," Jin said, from the other side of Lincoln. "Must go." With that, Jin vaulted the wall and darted for the house.

Becca shrugged. "Can't let him go alone." She jumped up and was over the wall before Lincoln could speak. "Between you and your father, it's a tossup to see who gets me killed first." He jumped the wall and followed. "Everyone, stay here and keep alert."

Jin disappeared around the back. Becca took the front and slowed to go up the stairs. Lincoln stayed on the ground, watching her back. From around the house came a car. Lincoln ducked and swung his handgun toward it. The car stopped, and four community people exited. One spied Lincoln. "You need help?"

He waved them over. "You two stay with Becca. You other two come with me. Jin's around back, so don't get trigger happy. Make sure of who it is before you start yanking the trigger."

They clung to the outer wall until they reached the fence around the backyard. Lincoln poked his head around the corner and found Jin on the back porch trying the rear door. Before he got it open, his body stiffened. He put a hand on the black wrought iron fence around the porch and swung his body over. He landed lightly on the ground near Lincoln and stood with a finger to his lips. "They come."

They duck-walked next to the stairs and waited. The door creaked open. "It's clear," someone said. "What are you waiting for? Since the Asian's aren't here, there's no need to stick around to get killed. Let's go."

Footsteps bounded on the weathered wood of the porch. It was hard to tell how many. Lincoln stood, aimed his gun, and shouted, "Freeze." Three men were on the porch with at least one other in the doorway.

One man didn't. He whirled, and Jin shot him before Lincoln even reacted.

"Drop the guns," Lincoln said.

The man in the doorway tried to duck inside but ran his face into the barrel of Becca's gun. "Unh-uh," she tapped him lightly on the forehead, though hard enough to cut the skin and draw blood.

The other two dropped their weapons and raised their hands. Lincoln recognized one as the officer that kidnapped Ruth. Becca forced them down the stairs where the three men were searched and pushed to the ground.

"You got anything inside to tie them up with?" Becca asked.

Lincoln nodded. "In the garage." He left, unlocked the garage side door with a key from his pocket, and entered. A minute later, he returned carrying three long strands of cotton rope. They tied the three prisoner's hands behind their back and sat them up against the porch.

Lincoln squatted in front of the officer. "Not so cocky now, are you? I wonder if Ohtanda and company will even want you back since you've failed so often. Hey, maybe we can exchange you for a bag of potatoes or something."

He stood and moved to Becca. "This enough action for you?"

"Not even close."

"Don't even think about it. Your dad will skin me alive."

"I have no idea what you're talking about." She took three running steps and bounded over the fence.

"Like I didn't see that one coming," Lincoln said to himself.

Becca ran across the road and hurdled the wall. She plotted her course of action as she moved. *Cross the street, enter the woods from the side and proceed with caution until you find a target.* Ahead she spied three people running into the barn. Must be casualties. She glanced up at the open door of the hayloft and thought about her brother. Strange. She should see Bobby or Maretha up there. Or both.

Someone shone a light on the floor of the loft. Neither Bobby nor Maretha would do something like that and draw attention to themselves. So, if they didn't turn the light on, who did? A chill swept through her. She stopped and stared at the loft. She felt more than knew something was wrong. Her course changed, and she ran into the barn.

As she entered, someone was being lowered from the loft. The body was on a stretcher attached to ropes. As the stretcher got lower, she saw the dark skin and, with a gasp, knew it was Maretha. She rushed forward to be by her sister's side. She drew up short, stunned by the sight. She did not look well. Blood soaked her entire front. Her eyes were closed, and she strained to see movement of the chest. Did it? She covered her face with splayed fingers.

As they untied the stretcher, two women carted Maretha toward the operating room. Becca forced her eyes from Maretha and stared upward at the loft. She called her brother's name but the word caught in her throat. She cleared it and tried again, but a voice behind her got her attention.

"Becca. Good," Doc said. Her usually concerned look had deeper furrows on her face. "You're here. Suit up. We're going to need all hands for these surgeries."

She nodded absently and went to don a garb and wash. It was while she was at the sink scrubbing her hands that she realized Doc said surgeries. She whirled, frightened at what she might find in the operating room. "Oh please, God, don't let it be Bobby."

CHAPTER FORTY-FOUR

Amy Dawson had to move with more caution than she'd ever had to before in her life. Guards were at each end of the town, and others stood on the roofs of the buildings. She stayed in the shadows. Having done a complete walkthrough of the town earlier in the day, she thought she'd found the one gap in the defenses beyond any guard's view.

At the corner building, she stopped and did a sweep of the street. No one was in sight. She had no idea what business was run out of the storefront but didn't care. It was dark, and as far as she knew, had no one inside. She passed the front door and rounded the corner. A short walkway led to a side door. This spot was beyond the guard's line of sight.

She worked the door, using her combat knife to pry back the frame and popped the deadbolt. It made noise, but she ducked inside and closed the door before anyone came to explore. She relocked the door and moved to the back of the building. The back wall had two windows that led outside the town. How no one noticed the flaw was amazing, especially with how tight the security was everywhere else.

She unlocked the first window and tried to raise it, but it didn't budge. She checked the frame but found nothing holding it in place. Her conclusion was the window had been painted shut. That was still bad security. With her knife, she inserted the tip and dragged it along the length of the upper seam, then did the same along each side. She tried the window again and it rose slightly. She repeated the process with the knife and, by the third try, had the window lifted enough to squeeze out.

Once outside, she pressed her back against the brick wall and waited. No one came. The next step was the tricky one. She had to cross an alley and scale a fence into the backyard of a house. The backyard was twenty yards long and offered no cover. It had to be done in one quick dash.

She crept away from the wall keeping her eyes up until she had a view of the guard above. The woman held binoculars and had them directed outward, but a long way off. The guard lowered her glasses, rubbed her eyes and the bridge of her nose, then walked about ten steps to the left. Dawson waited. The guard repeated the ritual two minutes later. As soon as she turned her back to move to the next position, Dawson broke cover. She swung over the fence and ran toward the far corner of the house. There she stopped and peered back. The guard was in her normal position and didn't appear anxious or concerned. She hadn't been seen.

Breathing easier, she trotted off to make her meeting. Three blocks east, then two blocks south. Headlights blinked on, then off. She moved to a Dodge Charger. Two men got out. Her lieutenant and a Colonel.

"Dawson, what have you got for us?" the colonel asked. "Is it doable?"

"Yes, Sir. It depends on how many survivors you want. They're good, well-trained, and organized. If you attack, they'll see you coming. Weaponry is good but not heavy. Defenses are nil other than the cars blocking the roads. We can bust through those using the trucks. After that, it's just a matter of how much damage you want to do."

"What are the chances of getting inside?"

"I may have a way. The same way I exited. Depending on how many you want inside, it will require me taking out a guard or two, but I don't see that as a problem, as long as entry can be done with stealth."

"Show me."

He reached in a shirt pocket and withdrew a pencil and notepad. Dawson took it, drew a map, and added commentary. "Do you have a time frame in mind?"

"Tomorrow night."

She thought about it. "I'll have to find a way up to the roof and check out the guards. I'll use a flashlight to signal. Up and down is a go. Side to side is abort."

"Dawson, if you signal abort, that will only stop the stealth entry. We're coming no matter what. Getting inside might save a few more lives, mostly on their side, that's all. The general wants this, as does the scientist." He flashed a leering smile. "And the men are looking forward to it as well."

Dawson couldn't help herself from blanching at the thought of all those women being repeatedly raped. When she first joined the army before the apocalypse, she'd been harassed but never abused. However, after the chaos, things had changed. The general himself had given her a choice: Be passed amongst the men or be consensual with him. She chose the easy route as he knew she would, and her skin crawled every time she was reminded of those long, loathed nights.

"Problem, Dawson?" The colonel smiled. "Don't worry. Once we have control of the town, you can return to base, though you'll miss out on all the fun."

"Is there anything else, sir?" She tried to hide the revulsion that rose in the back of her throat.

He chuckled, glanced at the lieutenant, then back to her. "No, Dawson. We'll see you on the inside tomorrow night."

The return wasn't as easy. She had to wait a long while before approaching the building. Once through the window, she closed it, made sure nothing was disturbed then sat for a long time thinking about what was to befall this mostly peaceful community.

She reached the floor of the building she was housed in as a woman exited the room next door. "What's the matter? Couldn't you sleep?" she was asked.

Dawson shook her head. "It's almost too comfortable and too peaceful. I'm used to sleeping outside and having to keep one eye open."

"I understand. Before coming to this piece of heaven, I was the same way."

"Looks like you're still having trouble sleeping."

"No. It's my shift. I've got guard duty. If you stick around long enough, you'll understand. It's just something you get used to. It's worth it, though, to have that feeling of safety. It was truly the best decision I made during these crazy times. Well, I can't be late. Hope you can sleep."

"Yeah, thanks. And I hope your night passes uneventfully."

She entered her room and collapsed on the bed. At one time, the building had been an old hotel, although she couldn't understand how the four-story building survived in this remote area. Was there anything in the old hotel or around here worth spending the night to see?

She lay awake, deep in thought, for a long time before ever trying to sleep.

CHAPTER FORTY-FIVE

Mark reached the end of the forest and paused. He didn't want to burst out if the enemy was waiting. The area beyond the woods was open. The street running east and west was deserted.

"There," Britta said, pointing to the left. The shadow of a lone man moved along the road. His gate was uneven and unsteady, as if he had an injured leg.

"I'm going to follow. You all go back and help Elijah's people. Those guys unloaded on them."

The men from the car moved, but Britta said, "I'm going with you."

Mark started to respond but changed his mind. His words would do no good, so he jogged toward the road.

Once there, he kept to the left, hoping to stay out of sight from anyone ahead of the wounded man looking back. They quickly gained on the man. They saw no one else, but they were out there somewhere unless his comrades had left him behind. That would tell Mark a lot about the professionalism of the men.

Ahead, the man stumbled and was forced to stop or fall. He looked back and spied them. His wound forgotten, he whirled and opened fire. Britta and Mark dove for whatever cover they could find, which wasn't much.

Britta shot back before Mark got up. The man lurched backward, fell, but rose to one knee. "Body armor," Mark said.

He lined up a shot with his rifle and fired. The man pitched backward and stayed down.

"Nice shot," Britta said. She reached a hand down to help him up. He looked from the hand to her and thought, she must think I'm old.

As if reading his thoughts, she said, "Come one, old man. Let me help you up."

He took the hand, surprised at the strength of her grip. They stood face to face before the awkward moment was broken by the sound of an engine firing up. They looked down the road. Brake lights flashed for a second then the car moved away.

"It's not a military truck," Britta said.

"No, they wouldn't want to draw attention to themselves or the truck."

"Does it strike you as odd that there's only one car?"

"Yes. I thought the attack would have a lot more combatants."

"Perhaps it was a probe to test the defenses."

"Maybe. Or maybe they underestimated us and didn't send enough."

Britta cocked her head then turned it. "Seems the shooting has stopped."

Mark hadn't noticed, but she was right. "Come on. Let's go see the damage."

They walked back along the roads, fearing that someone might mistake them for the enemy if they exited from the woods. They spotted the truck in the middle of the road and approached with hands up and empty. The gunner recognized them and offered a lift, which they accepted.

The southern camp was a disaster. Much of the rear of the building was destroyed, either from bullet holes or explosions. Several people were being treated for minor injuries. Some were being carted across the road for the doctor. The worst was the line of bodies, six, set along the back of the building. They'd paid a heavy price. The toll of Mark's fishing trip was still climbing. How many had it been so far? The conflict wasn't over yet. He'd never be able to forget. The deaths were his fault.

"Dad," a voice shouted over the crowd. "Dad."

It was Becca. Panic was in her voice. His mind went into hyperdrive. It had to be bad. Bobby? Lynn? He broke into a run. "Becca. I'm here."

He spotted her, and she ran into his arms. "Oh, Daddy, it's bad. Real bad."

"What is?"

"Bobby. Daddy, he's been shot. It doesn't look good."

Becca caught sight of Britta over his shoulder. "You need to come, too. Maretha is just as bad."

They sprinted across the road to the barn. Mark burst through the outer door and went to the operating room. The door had no window, so he opened it and stepped inside. Bobby was on the table. Six people worked around him. Without lifting her eyes, Doc said. "Get out. Now."

Mark tried to speak. In a more forceful voice, Doc repeated. "Get. Out. Now!"

Mark backed from the room.

"Becca, I asked you to gown up. You're needed in the other room."

Becca exited and went to get dressed and washed again. Once she discovered the severity of Bobby's wound, she tossed everything on the floor and ran to find her father. Mark staggered away and paced what passed for a lobby.

Britta stayed out of his way, her own shock evident.

After a while, Mark could no longer remain in the confined space. He went outside to get some fresh, rejuvenating air. Britta came out a few minutes later. They looked at each other then fell into the other's arms. Britta wept. Mark held her tight, his tears falling freely.

He couldn't lose his son. He'd already lost so much in Sandra, his wife, and Ben, his youngest son. Not Bobby, too. They broke apart and, without a word, began walking. People came up to him, wanting to report, to talk, but Mark was no longer capable of listening.

A man ran up and grabbed him by the arm. He spun him around and went to punch him in the face. Mark made no effort to block the punch, but Britta caught the man's arm and shoved him away.

"My wife's dead. All because of you and your stupid wars. It should've been you instead." Mark turned away after muttering, "I'm sorry."

Behind him, Britta said, "And his son is dying. You don't have a monopoly on grief."

Mark stopped at the wall and sat. He had so much to atone for. So much blood on his hands. Was this to be the ultimate price for his folly?

Lincoln walked up and put a hand on Mark's shoulders. "I'm praying for him. He's a strong boy. He'll pull through."

Mark couldn't speak. He just nodded.

"I know this is a bad time, but we do have some things to talk about."

"Whatever it is, can you handle it?"

"I can, but I thought you'd like to know we took three prisoners, and one of them is that officer who kidnapped Ruth and Jarrod and the others."

That brought Mark into focus. "Yeah, that might prove a nice distraction."

"Thought it might."

CHAPTER FORTY-SIX

They walked around Lincoln's house and found Jin standing guard over the three men. Their hands were bound behind them, and they were propped up against the back porch. Jin nodded to Mark and backed away.

Mark approached and stared down at the officer who had taken Ruth at gunpoint. He wanted to question the man—to berate him for how the wheel had turned, but his mind focused on beating the shit out of him. His fist closed and opened, and his breathing became quick and shallow.

Lincoln stepped in front of him. "If this were a fair fight, I wouldn't stand in your way, but these men are captives and can't defend themselves. As angry as you are, I can't let you do this. You think you feel bad now, wait to see how you feel after beating a defenseless man to death."

Mark backed away, now angry with himself for having to be talked down from doing something he'd have stopped someone else from doing.

He took a step forward and squatted in front of Childs. The man pulled back, fearing he was about to be beaten, and smacked his head into the porch bricks.

"How many men were involved in the assault?"

"Ah, just four of mine."

"That's not what I asked."

"We-we were kept separate from the other group. This hotshot captain, Crandall is his name, was sent here to take things over. I don't know how many men he had, but I don't think it was more than ten, twelve tops."

"What things did he take over?"

"Ah, you know, capturing some of your people and bringing them back to the base."

"Which people specifically?"

"I think his list was different from mine. I was supposed to get you, your daughter, and the Asian, ah, his," he motioned with his chin, "family."

"That was all?"

"Yeah."

"What about the rest of the people?"

"As long as they didn't stand in our way, we were to leave them alone."

Mark studied the man's face and thought that part of the story was a lie. He couldn't maintain eye contact, and his words were quick, like it was important to get the sentences out fast.

"Where did this other group come from?"

"I don't know. They arrived after I left the base."

"Their uniforms look like those of the column I told you about," Britta said. "They were aggressive and hunted us. All we did was be seen."

Mark said, "Is there a government in existence?"

Childs shrugged. "Who knows? It's what we've been told, but it sounds more like the military is running things than any politicians."

"Who's in charge of the facility. Dr. Ohtanda or the general?"

"Ohtanda runs the lab, but the general has the final say."

"Who supplies you?"

"I assume the government. Once a week, supplies are brought in. We don't question where it comes from, but there's always more than enough to feed more than a hundred personnel."

"Must be nice," Lincoln said.

"What are you going to do with us?" asked the man next to Childs.

"What should we do with you? You attacked and killed our people. That doesn't look like it's going to end. There's no level you won't stoop to accomplish your mission. I have every right to execute you right now."

"You can't do that," the man said, agitated. "We have rights."

"Excuse me," Lincoln said, his anger at an instant boil. "What about our rights? We should have a say in whether we live or die, but I don't see you giving us any choice." He pulled his gun from behind his back and held it down at his side. His hand twitched as if he had trouble controlling its desire to put a bullet in the man's face. "I should shoot you right now. One bullet for every one of our people you killed."

"I didn't kill no one," the man said on the verge of tears. "Honest."

"You came to kill. Last I looked, we're still American citizens. You're supposed to serve and protect us. We're not attacking you. We're defending against you. How wrong is that?" His arm lifted to the point that if he fired, he'd hit a leg. The arm dropped and swung as if trying to gain enough momentum to rise higher.

He turned to Mark. "I can't stand here and listen to this fool. I want to shoot him."

"I don't blame you. But perhaps you should step away."

Lincoln nodded. "You know what, asshole? We should turn you over to the families of those who died because of you and let them decide your fate. Now that would be true justice." He walked away and went into the garage.

"He has a point. I'm not going to make that decision. I'll bring you in front of our community."

"Why can't you just let us go?" the man sobbed. "I swear I'll keep going. You'll never see me again."

Childs lashed out with his foot. "Stop whining, you gutless bastard."

"If I let you go, you'll just come back with the next assault team."

"No, I won't. I swear. I won't even go back."

Britta said, "And give up all that abundance of food? I doubt that."

Jin stepped forward, lifted his gun, and shot the man in the forehead. He turned to Mark. "For my family. An example for others." He walked away, leaving them stunned and the two remaining prisoners screaming.

As Jin walked calmly into the house, Lincoln ran from the garage, gun up and ready for battle. He looked at the scene then at Mark. "Jin."

"Sure. Let the new guy have all the fun." His body relaxed, and he went around the house toward the front.

CHAPTER FORTY-SEVEN

Early the next morning, Dawson was awakened by a knock on the door. She rose and, out of habit, picked up her knife. "Who's there?"

"Chieftess Alice sent me to fetch you for the morning meal."

Morning meal? Was the sun even up yet? "Ah, okay, just give me a second to get dressed." She'd slept in her clothes minus her boots, so getting ready didn't take long. She gathered her belongings and opened the door. A tall, dark-skinned woman stood in front of the door. She offered a smile, and a nod as a greeting, then turned for the stairs.

"Is this the normal time that you eat?"

"For those going out on patrol, yes."

That made sense. "What about everyone else?"

"Thirty minutes later."

She gave an inward groan wishing she had that extra thirty minutes. Sleep hadn't come easy. They exited the hotel. It was still dark. No one had awakened the sun yet. "No sun. It is early."

"Though we have electricity, it is designated for specific things. We try to utilize as much daylight as possible. By the time we're done eating and ready to leave, the sun will be rising."

Her guide brought her to a long building with tables placed end to end. Perhaps forty women were already seated and eating. Dawson was led to the rear of the building, where a buffet was set up. Following her guide's example, Dawson picked up a plate and silverware and proceeded down the line. They had scrambled eggs that looked real, not powdered, thin slices of some meat that wasn't a pork product, fried potatoes with green pepper and onion, toast, and coffee. She looked at her plate and felt it was a proper meal. Perhaps not as abundant or as diverse as at the base, but more than adequate.

The guide nodded to a seat and walked to the other side. Dawson sat. Alice and her team sat around her. Most offered a "good morning" or a smile. A few ignored her. Alice sat at the end of the table, holding a cup of coffee between her hands.

"How did you sleep, Amy?"

She wasn't used to being called by her first name. "Fine," she said, with a mouthful of eggs.

"We're going on patrol this morning. Thought you'd like to join us."

Dawson paused with another forkful of eggs and potatoes near her mouth. That surprised her. She expected to use the day to study the town and the guard positions. "Ah, is that allowed? I mean, since I'm new here."

Alice smiled. "It's allowed. It'll give you a chance to see what we do. To begin forming a bond." She smiled again, but something changed in her eyes—something almost feral. "It'll give us a chance to get to know you."

Dawson had trouble swallowing her next bite. Was there an implied threat in there somewhere? "Sounds good," she said through her eggs.

"Good. And child, slow down. You have plenty of time to eat. We can't have you getting sick out there. It'll be a long way to get back to town."

Dawson kept her eyes down on her plate the rest of the meal, only glancing up when the conversation was directed toward her. She did slow her eating pace. Again, at the base, she was used to eating fast and being ready for duty. She was also used to protecting her plate against those who thought her too weak to stop them from enjoying her meal as well as theirs.

Alice stood a while later, the signal that the meal was over. Everyone else stood and bussed the table, placing the dirty dishes in a bin at the back of the room. She followed the group outside, where they joined in a huddle in the middle of the road.

Alice unfolded a map, found the proper location, and folded the map into a square showing that area. "We left off here last time. There's not much between that location and the next one. We'll be traveling about three miles past the last area. This will be our longest journey so far. It's clear not much is left to be found, but we still have to check. Questions?"

Dawson hesitated before raising a hand.

"This isn't school," the woman next to her said. "You don't have to raise your hand."

"I wasn't sure and didn't want to interrupt."

"What's your question, Amy?" Alice asked.

"Do I need to bring anything?"

"A pack if you have one and your weapons."

"Oh. I don't have a pack, and my only weapon is the knife. The gun was taken from me when I entered the town."

"We'll get you a pack and your handgun. One of you take her to the armory. See to it she gets a rifle too. We'll be waiting at the eastern gate."

Dawson followed one of the women. Behind her, she heard, "Run." She did, hearing the others laugh.

They were back in under three minutes. Her new team was gathered by the wall of cars that served as the eastern gate. As she joined them, she was handed a Hello Kitty backpack. A joke by the looks on the other's faces. She accepted it, and as she slid her arms through the straps, she said, "Ooo, my favorite." That brought more laughter.

As they climbed over the cars to get outside the town, she thought they were just like the military. She'd be teased and tested. She had to learn not to take it personally and respond in kind, like one of the team. At least with this team, she wouldn't have to put up with the constant sexual innuendos, harassment, and supposed accidental contact. Or at least she thought she wouldn't.

She was placed in the middle of the pack. Alice was always one person behind or in front of her. She had the feeling of being watched by her. Was she suspicious? Was there an ulterior purpose of being asked out on patrol? She tried not to think about it and stay relaxed.

They were on the road for more than an hour when Alice stepped up next to her. "You seem to be handling the hike well."

"What else is there to do when you're out here by yourself except walk. I'm used to traveling miles each day."

"Have you ever been to this area before?"

She had to be wary of how she answered, giving each question the time it needed to be thought out before spoken. "No. I only arrived on the day we met."

Alice seemed to be calculating her questions before they were asked. "Where did you serve?"

"I was Army, based out of Fort Campbell."

"I thought you were Army."

"I understand how you might think I was military, but what made you pick Army?"

"Well, for one, your condition. You appear fit. Also, the way you move in the group like you've been trained and done this many times before. Your boots look fairly new. How long have you had them?"

"Long enough to break them in and make them comfortable."

"Where'd you get them?"

"I found them at an abandoned base somewhere in Indiana." Anticipating the next question, she said, "All the guns and ammo had been cleaned out along with the food and MREs. Most of the clothes had been picked over. This was the only pair of boots in my size, so I took them."

"Lucky you."

"Yeah. Been luckier if I got there soon enough to score the good stuff."

"Never underestimate the advantage a good boot can make."

They walked on in silence. Dawson became aware they were about a mile north of the facility. She didn't glance in that direction.

"Have you been to the base here?"

The question caught her off guard. Her body reacted. Now she knew she was being tested. She went with the closest truth. "Yes, once. I recognized the types of vehicles stationed around the perimeter, so I walked up to the gate. I had a lot of guns pointed at me. I explained I was former military looking for a new home. I was turned away and encouraged never to return."

Alice didn't respond. Dawson wondered where this line of questioning was coming from. She thought her answer was good and delivered with a natural tone. They walked another hour, this one passing much slower. She fought to maintain a relaxed posture but, judging by the stiffening shoulder muscles, lost the fight. With each passing step, she expected another barrage of questions. Her mind whirled with possibilities as she worked to practice responses to potential pitfall questions.

Dawson wanted to alter and hijack the conversation? "Why don't you use cars?"

"They draw too much attention. We used cars early on but kept getting attacked. Some of our patrols never made it back. We found a team of four, dead and tossed to the side of the road. Their car and whatever they carried had been stripped away, as were their clothes. Whoever caught them raped and brutalized them. They died in pain. It's what all men want and do. It was the last time we used any vehicle when out on patrol. Since then, only one patrol has been attacked, and it was the men who died that time.

"It might take longer, but we're able to stay hidden this way. On foot, we can react to a dangerous situation better than being trapped in a car."

That made sense. She thought about the fate of those women. It would be the same for everyone in the town, only they might not be killed. At least not right away. Guilt became a heavy burden. She'd be the one responsible for the fate of everyone in the town. The screams and pleas would be a nightly event she'd have to block out. And in the end, what was to stop any of those soldiers from doing the same to her? Only two other women were in the battalion. One, she knew didn't mind the attention and bragged about how many of the men she'd done. The other one made a deal with one of the officers that he'd be the only one. So far, that had worked out for her, at least until he found a replacement.

These women might be termed enemies, but they were women—human beings, not pieces of meat to be used and passed on. They were like her with the same fears and concerns as she had daily. Oh sure, the army had treated her reasonably well. They'd provided for her. She had good food, equipment, medical attention, and supplies should she need them and usually a warm bed to sleep in each night. But the price was creeping up to a point she felt she could no longer afford to pay.

But which side of the battle did she want to be on? The battalion had greater numbers, superior firepower, and more and better equipment. They'd win and, most likely, easily. If she sided with the women, she'd either be killed or added to their ranks. The thought of the men in her squad using her night after night sent a shiver down her spine.

"You all right, Amy?" Alice asked. "You're white as a ghost. Something troubling you?"

"No, just a bad memory from the past."

Alice didn't respond, but Dawson could feel the woman's eyes on her, boring deep into her soul.

They were three hours out before Alice called a halt. Everyone found someplace to sit. A few broke out canteens or water bottles. Others took out snack foods like nuts and granola bars.

Dawson walked toward Lake Erie and peered out over its rolling, grey water. Would she be back in time to see to her part of the invasion? To her surprise, she found she hoped not. Why? What had changed? She had orders. These people, for whatever reason, had been deemed hostile, though she didn't see that as believable. It was her duty to see the mission through regardless of the result.

There it was, she realized. The result. She had no desire to aid in the killing, rape, and torture of these women. They'd built a new and peaceful life. How were they a threat? They weren't her friends. She didn't want to get close to any of them. But they were still humans, and she did belong to that team. It was wrong to take these hard-working people and force them into servitude just to act as test subjects or to get her fellow soldiers' rocks off. She knew she'd do her job, that's how she'd been trained, but hoped she didn't have to.

CHAPTER FORTY-EIGHT

It was deep into the afternoon before Doc emerged from the operating room. She looked exhausted. She spotted Mark, and he rose to his feet. She held up a finger and ducked into the recovery room. Several agonizingly long minutes later, she reappeared.

He tried to speak, but she stopped him. "I need a cup of coffee and to sit. Walk with me."

They left the barn and walked to the tables. Britta had been seated at the table, her head down on her arms. Upon seeing them, she rose and hastened over.

"Both of them needed extensive surgery," Doc began. "Both nearly died. Maretha coded once, but thanks to some quick work, she was resuscitated. They are both resting and will be out for a long time. I placed both into medically induced comas to aid in the recovery. I am cautiously optimistic about their full recoveries, but there was so much damage to both that anything could happen to alter that outlook. We are drastically low on so many antibiotics that when an infection occurs—I say when instead of if because it's a very strong probability, we might not be able to fight it with what we have left."

They reached the tables. The midday meal had finished, and the cleaning almost concluded. A pot of coffee sat over the fading cookfire embers. Mark poured a cup of coffee for each of them, and Doc sat. Mark was too nervous to sit. Britta sat across from Doc.

"They were not the only ones injured. The other two doctors are working on Elijah's people. The more serious wounds have already been treated. Now they are on flesh wounds and grazes. Minor things. We lost one on the table. Nothing we could do. She'd lost too much blood by the time we got to her. We're extremely low on all types of blood."

She sipped her coffee and closed her eyes. Mere seconds later, her head bobbed, and the motion startled her back awake. She shook her head and rubbed her eyes.

"Anyway, I don't know what else to tell you."

"What were the injuries?" Mark asked.

"Bobby took a bullet to the upper right chest. It did internal damage to bone, tissue, and lung. His overall surgery wasn't as complex as Maretha's, though. She took a round from underneath. It entered her abdomen and traveled upward before lodging under her scapula. She has organ damage that may result in more surgeries, the loss of body functions, and possible death. Quite frankly, considering the amount of damage, I'm surprised she survived at all. She will need long term care if she lives. I don't have any of the drugs she needs to recover quicker, so she will have to rely on her body's recuperative powers. Regardless, healing for her will be lengthy."

"What if I could get her the drugs she needs?" Britta said.

One of Doc's eyebrows went up. She thought for a moment. "You mean from your town?"

"Yes."

"Well, obviously that will help, but will they be agreeable to parting with the amount I need?"

"All I can do is ask. Can you give me a list?"

"Absolutely. Mark, would you go inside and get me a pen and paper, please?"

Without a word, he stood and hurried up the stairs. Inside he was so focused on where to find the needed items he never saw Lynn. He went into the front room and rummaged through an old desk. When he turned, Lynn was there. He stopped short and wavered on his feet.

"How is he?"

He felt his face crumble, then forced it back in place. His first words were choked. "He's still alive, but Doc says just barely. He needs drugs that we no longer have."

She stepped forward. For a moment, he thought she might embrace him, but she stopped short and placed a hand on his arm. "Oh, Mark, I'm so sorry."

He sucked in air to steady his voice. "Thank you. I have to take this to Doc. Britta thinks we might be able to convince her people to let us have some of their drugs."

Lynn stiffened for a moment at the mention of Britta's name. Her hand dropped away. "You'll be going with her, of course."

"Yes."

"I'll pray for Bobby and also for your quick and safe return."

Not knowing how to respond, he said, "Thank you." She stepped to the side and let him pass.

Mark placed the pen and paper in front of Doc. She wrote down a must-have list and a wish list. She set the pen down and picked up the mug, her mind still deep in thought as she drank. After a moment, she picked the pen up and added two more things. Finished, she slid the paper to Britta.

Britta looked the list over and spoke each word. Then she folded the paper and slipped it into her back pants pocket. "I'll leave now."

"The faster, the better," Doc said.

Britta stood. Mark did too. "I'm going with you."

She nodded. The two gathered what they needed and met at an SUV. Mariah joined them as Mark went to find who had the key. It turned out to be Becca who had moved the vehicles across the driveway. She decided she was going too. "I can't sit around here all day worrying about Bobby. This way, I'm at least doing something."

Mariah joined them and, with Britta at the wheel, headed back to the town that had shunned Britta just days before.

Britta cared little for caution, pushing the SUV to speeds up near a hundred. Under Mark's direction, she took the turnpike driving on the opposite side of the road. Mark guided her to the path they'd taken a little more than a week ago when escaping the sea raiders. The SUV bounced off-road and down the slope leading to a side road. From there, she raced to Route Two, by-passing the barricade a mile back down the road.

They made the usual hour and a half trip in an hour, fortunate not to encounter anything or anyone intent on delaying them. They arrived early evening, with still several hours of daylight remaining. If they could conclude their business in a short time, they might be on the road and nearly home by dark.

Britta maneuvered down the roads leading to her former residence, stopping three blocks away. The same location where Mark had stopped days before when negotiating for his daughter's medical treatment.

They got out.

"Mark, I think it's best if you and Becca stay here. They may not take kindly to having you show up again so soon after everything that went down."

"What about me?" Becca asked. "I thought I was an honorary sister."

Britta nodded. "You don't want to stay here and protect your father?"

"As much as I know he needs protecting, no."

"All right. Let's go. But please, don't speak unless directly spoken to."

Mark said a prayer as the three women walked away side by side like something out of a western movie.

CHAPTER FORTY-NINE

Captain Crandall took a circuitous route back to the house they were using as a base. They were the first to arrive. Four of them, one with a wound to the upper arm, were all who survived from the eastern team. Fifteen minutes later, another car arrived with two soldiers, the survivors of the southern assault team. An hour later, it was apparent anyone who could make it back had.

"You think Childs and his team were killed?" one of his men asked.

Crandall believed they fled as soon as the shooting started. "If they're lucky."

He waited another hour before calling in. It was not a call he looked forward to. He had never had to report a failed mission before. He wasn't even sure how to begin. He thought about spinning the story to make it appear Childs had screwed up, but in the end, it would still fall on him as the mission leader.

"Sir, it's Crandall. I report the mission failed. Yes, Sir. No, Sir. No excuses. Counting me, we have six men. Yes, Sir. We'll wait for you."

His men, who were scattered around the floor, looked up at him. "The general is not happy with the outcome. They have an assault planned on the town for tonight. Then he's bringing the entire column out here to wipe the farmers, as he calls them, off the planet."

"Farmers, my ass," one man said. "They don't fight like no farmers I ever saw. And I was raised on a farm."

"Where the hell did they get all those fifty cals?" another asked.

Where indeed, wondered Crandall. He thought about Childs. They had to come from him and his lack of training, experience, and basic common sense. How had the man ever become an officer? The man's failure had led to his own. That was the excuse that settled in his mind. The way he rationalized his loss. It was all Child's fault. If he ever saw the man again, he'd put a bullet in his face.

The trip back was long. After a full day of collecting, which according to the others was only a medium, successful day, Dawson had to admit she was tired. The lack of sleep hadn't helped. The girls joked and bantered with each other. They whooped with joy when they discovered anything useful. In one house, they found a modestly stocked, hidden wine cellar with more than a dozen expensive bottles of wine.

Although Alice refused to allow them to open one, they anticipated dinner back at town with a glass of wine.

Dawson laughed along with them and had to admit a glass of wine did sound good. She had little other than some prescription medicine and two full unopened tubes of toothpaste in her backpack. Her load was considerably lighter than the others. She wondered if that was by design.

They walked toward the setting sun, making it easy to witness the passing of time. She wondered if they'd arrive before dark. She estimated there was still an hour of daylight left when they entered the neighborhood where the town stood.

One of the girls gave an owl hoot sound, and everyone scattered to the side of the road but her. Her delay made the other hiss at her. She ran to the side and ducked behind a woman name Dottie, a short, squat southern girl with a deep accent. Alice crept toward the woman on point. They had a brief discussion then Alice came back and motioned for everyone to join her.

"Up ahead is a man. He's just sitting on a front porch. He appears to be alone, but it might be a trap."

"I can sneak up behind him and slit his throat," one woman offered.

"No. I want to know why he's here and why he is so casual. He must know the town is here and that he's an outsider, but his demeanor is so relaxed it's like he doesn't care."

"What do you want us to do?" another woman asked.

"You two," she pointed to the ones she wanted, "Go around the block and cut through the yards about midway down. Cross the street without being noticed and come up behind him. When you see us in the street, gauge his reaction. If it's hostile, take him down. Try to take him alive though, so I can question him."

She motioned with her hand for them to go. The two were around the corner and out of sight in seconds. They watched as the two climbed fences of the houses about ten down from the corner. They waited as the women vanished behind the house. Several minutes later, the woman on point made a motion to Alice.

"Okay. We're going to spread out on the street and advance like nothing's the matter. Watch what he does. Nobody shoots unless we have no choice. Allow our sisters to do their job from behind."

They moved out. Dottie motioned for Dawson to stay near the back. She did. She wanted to see these women warriors in action. As they came into view of the man still sitting on the porch, one of the women dropped back to Alice.

"Isn't that the man who," Dawson heard before the woman leaned too close to Alice's ear to hear more.

Alice slowed and studied the man. He noticed them, raised both arms over his head, and stood.

Alice moved straight for him as her two appointees came from between the two houses and pointed weapons at his back. As the group closed on him, Alice motioned for them to spread out. "Eyes open," she said.

Curious about who the man was, Dawson followed Alice until someone pressed a gun into her back and said, "Far enough, sister."

Dawson was taken by surprise. She began to turn, but the insistent pressure of the barrel kept her looking forward. "Don't turn around. Keep your weapon down, pointed at the ground. If I think this is a trap and you're a part of it, you'll die first."

Dawson's blood chilled. She stopped and didn't move. Here she was, thinking she was fitting in—becoming part of this team when all along she was being played. She was the outsider and, as such, fell into suspicion at the first sign of trouble. That made her angry. All the doubts she'd had during the trip faded from her mind.

"Hi," the man said, "My name's Mark. You might remember me. I was here a few days ago."

"I remember," Alice said. "I also remember you were instructed never to return."

"Yeah, sorry about that. There was a medical emergency."

Alice cut him off. "I don't care. You should not be here. You have disobeyed and now are considered a threat to our community.

He spoke rapidly. "I'm here with Britta and Mariah."

The mention of those names sent a murmur through the team. Alice turned and issued a harsh, "Shh!"

He continued. "Maretha has been seriously hurt and needs help. Britta is here asking for that help."

Alice approached. The man did not move. "I will check that your story is true. If you lied to me, I will order your death. Stay here. Do not move from this spot."

"No problem."

Alice spoke to the two behind Mark. "Take his weapons. Stay with him. If he tries to leave or does anything remotely threatening, kill him."

"With pleasure," one of the women said.

Alice gave him one final glare then proceeded down the street to the barricade. Dawson eyed him as she walked. The gun was no longer pressed to her spine. That did little to appease her. Though the woman backed off, she knew the gun was still aimed at her. Mark. Wasn't that the name of the man Team One was sent to capture? Man, were they looking in the wrong place. She'd be sure to mention the sighting when the town fell tonight.

That thought hit her like a slap. Gone were all the concerns about what was in store for the inhabitants. All because the woman had treated her like the enemy. Now she was determined to complete her mission. Now she thought she might enjoy the cries that would fill the night.

They climbed the barricade. She was asked for her backpack and the rifle and gave them up. She was surprised they didn't ask for the handgun. Now she was sure it had all been an act. Perhaps they didn't think she was much of a threat inside the town. Well, they'd soon learn their mistake. The others dispersed without a word. The day's companionship forgotten.

CHAPTER FIFTY

"Britta, it is good to see you again and so soon," Iso said. She stood and embraced her. "I hear you have some sort of emergency and wish my assistance."

"Yes, High Chieftess . . ."

"Come now, my old friend. Let's dispense with the formalities. Sit. Tell me what has happened."

Britta sat at a table, and Iso moved to sit across from her. She noticed how slow and stiff Iso moved, the result of a gunshot wound received in the attack on the town by the men from the facility.

"You're in pain, High, er Iso. Is the wound still giving you trouble?"

"It's been less than a week since the attack. I don't heal as fast as I once did in my youth."

Britta scoffed. "Youth. You're only two years older than me, and I just turned thirty."

"Being shot ages you. As does being in charge." She reached a hand across the table and covered one of Britta's. "So tell me. What brings you begging at my doorstep?"

"It's Maretha. She's been badly wounded. She may not survive without the proper drugs."

Iso nodded. "So you came for our drugs. I take it you found whatever or whoever you were searching for."

"We did to a point."

"Please tell me it wasn't that man."

"Not entirely. At least not at first."

"Oh, Britta. I thought you were smarter than to chase after a man. At least not one you're not trying to kill. And he's so much older than you. Why?"

"We didn't start out looking for him. We spotted a column from the facility heading west and followed. I had a feeling they were looking for Mark and, uh, Becca. I wanted to do nothing more than warn them.

Along the way, we discovered a large military convoy heading this way. From what we've learned, they have reinforced the facility, except these troops are much more aggressive. They sent a team to attack Mark's community too. It was during that fight that Maretha was shot. She almost died. That's why I'm here. To beg for the drugs the doctor needs to help her survive."

Iso gazed into Britta's eyes, then sighed and withdrew her hand. "You understand what you're asking of me? I can't very well hand over vital drugs that may save the lives of our sisters. Not to strangers and definitely not to men."

"I'm not asking for them. I'm asking for Maretha. A true and loyal sister. Who served you well since the beginning."

"A sister who chose to give up all she had here to go traipsing after you. I'd argue she had more loyalty to you than to us."

"Please, Iso. I only need a little of your abundant stock. The doctor made me a list." She took the paper out, unfolded it, and set it on the table.

Iso never so much as glanced at the paper. Britta felt her heart sink. Not just for the life of Maretha but the obvious loss of her once close friend, Iso.

"I'm sorry, Britta. As much as I respect both you and Maretha, I cannot give you what belongs to the town. Not for an outsider. And before you object, that is how the council will see her. As an outsider, which you are as well."

"I'm only an outsider because you banished me."

"Technically, I did not banish you. You opted to leave on your own accord."

"Only because you made it clear that was the best option— for me and the town."

"It was. If it went to a council vote and you lost, you would've been banished, and that would be permanent. Leaving on your own allows you to return at some future time when the memory of all that occurred has faded."

Britta shook her head. "So, you'll just let Maretha die."

"No, Britta, you'll let her die. It was your choice to let her join you. She'd be safe and unhurt if she'd stayed here."

Britta felt her blood begin to heat. She rose before she said something she'd regret.

"Please, Britta, stay a day or two. Allow me to work my magic with the council. Perhaps we can come to some accommodation."

"Maretha doesn't have a day or two."

"I do have an idea. Let me run it past a few people and see what they think. I don't want to disappoint you and send you away mad, but you have to understand my obligation is to those currently residing in the town."

Britta was too angry to trust her voice."

"Please, Britta. You still have supporters here, and I have ways of getting what I want. It won't be a popular choice, but there may be a way."

Britta nodded and started for the door.

Iso followed, but slower. "How are Mariah and Alishia?"

"Mariah is here with me, along with Mark's daughter, Becca."

"I remember her." Iso brightened.

"Alishia is dead."

Her face fell. "Oh, I'm so sorry to hear that. She was a good kid."

"She was killed by the same convoy of soldiers that now resides at the facility. You may want to take note of their presence. They may not be as acceptable to sharing the area."

"I can't believe they'd suddenly become aggressive with us."

"Iso," Britta spun on her. "They sent men after us when all we did was be seen crossing a road. How could they see us as a threat? They hunted us and killed Alishia. This is a different breed than what we have now. Trust me. Be very careful and don't assume they won't attack."

"Okay, Britta. Please stay for dinner. I will try to have a decision for you by then."

Iso stepped closer and hugged Britta. "I miss you, my friend. I miss your counsel and support."

"I miss you, as well."

They parted, and Britta wondered whether any of those last words were true anymore.

CHAPTER FIFTY-ONE

She walked out onto the street and was met by Alice, her replacement on the collection team. "Britta," she said in a cold tone. She had never been a fan of Britta's. It was hard to accept that she took over for her.

"Alice." She matched the other woman's tone and impassive gaze.

"We found a man outside the gate who says he's with you. Is that true?"

"Yes." She offered no other explanation.

"Still breaking rules."

"Whatever, Alice. Have a good evening."

She started past her. Alice grabbed her arm. "Don't you dare disrespect me. You don't belong here. You never did."

"That may be true. But I never disrespected you. I just never had any respect for you."

She snapped her arm from her grasp and walked away, feeling the daggers shoot from Alice's eyes.

She walked toward the dining hall, where Mariah had taken Becca. She found them at a table by themselves, ignored by the rest of the residents. As Britta entered, silence descended, followed by whispering that spread throughout the hall. Some ignored her or averted their eyes, while others smiled warmly and nodded or greeted her.

Two members of her old team came up and hugged her. They exchanged pleasantries, then let Britta grab some food. She set her plate down, and as she sat, she heard a voice from the table behind her. "What right does she have eating our food? She doesn't belong here."

It took all her effort to keep from getting up and confronting the woman. Causing a scene now might hurt whatever chances she had of getting the drugs Maretha needed.

"We've had a very mixed reception," Mariah said. "Some are happy to see us and wonder if we're coming back. Others would like to see us run out of town."

Becca said, "I don't understand. I thought this was a sisterhood. Everyone should be accepted and made welcome."

"You forget," Britta said. "A sisterhood is made up of women. There's always drama when too many of that kind get together."

Mariah laughed. Becca was still confused.

"Don't let them bother you. It's not you who they're upset with. Some are angry because of what I did. Others are pissed because they feel I abandoned them. Sometimes no matter what you do, you can't win."

"What did you find out?"

Iso asked me to wait until after dinner. She was going to try to work her magic, as she calls it. It'll have to go to a council vote."

"Seriously? No one would have to vote in our community. You show up injured, and we'll do the best we can to help you. This is bullshit. Maretha's one of their own. They should want to help her any way they can."

"That's not how it is here. I'm not saying it's a bad way of doing things because it's worked for a while now, but this is one of those times when it'd be nice to have the leeway to make an out of the norm decision."

One of Iso's guards entered and came to the table. "The High Chieftess has a message. She is meeting with the council in thirty minutes and requests that you join her afterward for their decision."

"Thank you. I'll be there."

The guard nodded and left.

"So, we wait?" Becca said.

"Yes. In the meantime, I'm going to go let your father know what's going on, so he's not wondering. Mariah, stay with Becca. Don't let her out of your sight in case some old enemies want to get even with me through her."

"I'd like to see them try," Becca said. "I'll fight them for the drugs we need."

"And my money would be on you," Britta said and left.

Because of the hour, Britta had to get special permission to go outside the barricade. The sky was an assortment of vibrant red, yellow, and orange hues as the sunset began. She walked down the middle of the road, not wanting to spook Mark. She found him sitting in the same place they first met: The front porch of the corner house three blocks down the street from the eastern gate.

"Ah, I was beginning to worry."

"No need. We're all right." She sat next to him.

"Does that mean you got the drugs?"

"No, that's being debated as we speak. I have to go back for their decision."

"Any guesses as to the outcome?"

"Fifty-fifty at best. I think Iso has something up her sleeve, though. She'll ask something of me, make it a requirement of the deal. That's just a guess, but I know how she thinks."

"Will she ask something that you can accept, or will it be a massive burden?"

"Oh, it will be servitude of some type. Perhaps coming back into the fold as a grunt."

"Is that something you're willing to do? Give up your newfound freedom?"

"I don't know. If it means the difference between Maretha living or dying, I'd do whatever she asks."

Mark sighed.

"Does that bother you?"

Mark didn't answer at first. "Yeah, I think it does."

She turned to face him. "Why?"

"I'm not sure I have a good answer for you."

"Try."

He ran his thoughts through his mind, surprised they were bundled up with his feelings. He started to speak, but two guards arrived. "Your presence is requested."

Britta noted the lack of respectful greeting and hoped it didn't bode well for the decision. "Well, we should know something soon." She got up. "There's a chance we might be required to stay until the morning. Don't go storming the gates if we don't come right out."

"Okay. I'll wait until the morning before I come calling."

"We can continue this discussion then."

He smiled. "Sure."

She left, and he went to the SUV. It was getting chilly outside. It was time to get warm.

CHAPTER FIFTY-TWO

Iso stood as she entered, but Britta wasn't sure if that meant a good outcome or bad. A few of the council members nodded toward her. One reached out a hand as she passed and gave her hand a quick squeeze.

She was not a council member, so was not offered a place to sit. She stood by Iso, as the leader of their town took her place at the head of the table.

"I have put a proposal to the council considering your request." Iso gazed around the table as if looking for a challenge. "I won't lie to you and say it was a popular decision, but I think we came up with a solution we can all live with as it benefits the community." She looked up at Britta with a broad smile but a strange look in her eyes. Was it a warning?

"First, as to your request. We sent word to the doctor as to the abundance of the products you requested. He says all but one are in sufficient quantities to give a small portion. Since that is the case, we have decided to grant your request."

She let those words settle for a moment, but Britta knew her friend well. There would be a catch.

"However—"

And there it was.

"The decision comes with conditions. One, the doctor has a shortlist of items he has in limited supply. He'd like a trade."

"I will take the list back, and if the doctor has those items, I'm sure she will be willing to send them."

"Fair enough. We will rely on your integrity to ensure that happens."

Britta waited. There would be more. Iso didn't deal unless she could gain an advantage.

"Second, once Maretha is strong enough to travel, the doctor wishes to treat her here."

Britta started to speak, then withdrew her words to give the request more thought. What was she really asking?

"I know, that sounds strange, but what we want is Maretha back with us. We also want you and Mariah to return as well."

So that was what the strange look had been for. Iso manipulated the council in some way to allow her to return. But is that what she wanted?

"You will have to start at the bottom and work your way up the ranks, but you will be home again."

Britta didn't so much as bob her head for fear it might signal acceptance.

"And lastly, we wish for Becca to join us as well." She paused.

Britta was unable to hide the display of shock. To ask an outsider to join by council request was unheard of unless the candidate had spent enough time in town to be judged on how they fit in and added to the community. But to make her admittance a condition of the agreement was wrong. Becca had her own life to live, and she had a family. She'd never go for this. Now Britta understood the condition for Becca to join was added because the council, or perhaps Iso herself, knew she'd never go for it. Then they'd be able to turn the request down officially, as they wanted to do in the first place. Britta guessed Iso had made a strong, forceful case but had to give ground to get to this point.

All eyes were on her now. Britta kept her gaze focused on the back wall above the council's heads. She didn't want to make eye contact for fear they'd see the anger.

"Well, sister," Iso used the term purposefully, "do you have anything to say?"

Britta struggled to find the words. If she chose against the proposal, she was dooming Maretha. If it were just her they wanted, she'd do it in a heartbeat. She was almost certain Mariah would agree as well. But Becca? She might agree, knowing the medicines would benefit her brother as well. The trade was one-sided, to say the least. If the doctor from Mark's community had the drugs to trade, the deal should be even and done. The added extras were the council's clear decision to overweigh their end. If agreed, fine. If not, they didn't want to make the trade in the first place.

"I can offer no decision at this moment. Since these conditions concern more than just me, I will have to consult with the other people involved. If I might be allowed to speak with them, I can return shortly with the answer."

"Is that acceptable to the council?" Iso asked.

One member said, "Since it's getting late, take the evening to decide and give us your answer in the morning."

Britta knew it wasn't a request. They were forcing her to stay. Was something else going on here that she had yet to discover? "Very well. Thank you, council members, for your time and consideration."

She exited, keeping her eyes straight ahead. Once on the street, she hurried away from the building in case anyone was

watching her. She didn't want them to see her when the
façade fell away, and she embraced the anger welling inside.

She found Mariah and Becca sitting outside the dining hall.
As was the norm when a stranger was in the town, a guard for
each of them stood nearby. One followed her at a distance as
well.

Mariah and Becca looked up as she approached.

Mariah said, "Uh-oh, I know that look. They said no, didn't
they?"

Britta said, "Oh, they said yes, but in typical fashion,
attached conditions." She explained. When she got to the part
about Becca, she exploded to her feet with such force and
aggression the two guards reached for their weapons.

"What? Are you kidding me? They're already getting a fair
trade with the medicine. To make us a stipulation of the deal
is ludicrous."

"You'll get no argument from me," said Britta. "It's how Iso
operates. She's going to get the best part of the deal."

"And what, if we say no, that's it? Deal's off?"

"Yes."

"I'd do it if it means saving Maretha," Mariah said.

"I know you would," Britta replied. "I would, too. But we
shouldn't have to, let alone feel forced."

"Now what?" asked Becca.

"It's up to us. We have to give our decision by the morning."

Becca exploded again. "The morning. So we have to stay
here overnight? Don't they understand their delay means both

Maretha and Bobby might die while we sit here playing stupid games? This is insane. If Bobby dies because they delayed . . ."

Britta stepped close and grabbed her arm with a firm grip. "Careful what you say. The guards will report that you made a threat against the town. You could be arrested and imprisoned, and the choice of staying or going will no longer be yours."

Becca fumed. Britta felt the hardness of her tensed muscles. She released her arm. Becca paced a few times before saying. "I forgot about my dad. He has to know we're staying the night."

"I told him that might be a possibility."

"You went out and spoke to him?"

"Yes, while waiting for the council's decision. I wanted him to know what was happening."

"I need to speak to him, too. And I want to go alone."

"That will take special permission since it's dark."

"Then get it for me, or I'm going anyway."

Britta took no offense at the harsh tone. Becca was angry but not at her. She was just the closest outlet to vent on. Britta turned and approached the guard watching her. The guard backed away at first. "Sister, you know me. I'm not going to attack you." She put her arms out to the side, palms forward to show she was unarmed. "Will you take a message to the High Chieftess. Tell her Becca has a request to speak with her father outside the gate."

"I cannot do that. I am tasked with watching you."

"I understand and applaud your commitment to your duty, but there are two other guards here, and you have my word I will not move from this spot. Please, sister. This is important, and Iso will see it that way."

The guard paused, unsure of what to do. Britta reached for her knife and withdrew it with deliberation. The guard backed away and drew her gun.

"Easy now, sister. This is the knife Iso herself awarded me for my service. I wouldn't go anywhere without it. I am setting it down, and I will walk away. Take it with you to ensure I will do as I promised."

She placed the knife on the street and walked back to Mariah and Becca. Decision made, the guard scooped up the knife, turned, and ran toward the council building. She was back in two minutes. "High Chieftess Iso says she has permission to go, but only her, and she must be accompanied by a guard."

"Agreed. Thank you, Sister."

The guard advanced closer and handed her the knife. Britta nodded, and the guard backed away to resume her duty.

"Okay. It's set. You can go, but a guard will follow."

They walked toward the gate. The streets were almost deserted save for guards and few stragglers. A line of dim yellow lights had been strung along the sidewalks, casting an eerie illumination over the street. The light did little to overpower the shadows, but they weren't walking blindly into walls either.

They reached the gate, and the guard repeated Iso's permission. Becca's guard climbed over first to prevent Becca from running away. Becca began to scale the wall of cars. Britta said, "Don't stay long. We need to find a room for the night and have a discussion."

"No problem."

She leaped to the ground on the other side and was quickly engulfed by darkness.

CHAPTER FIFTY-THREE

Corporal Amy Dawson was accomplishing her mission. Earlier, she snuck out without her tail and made it safely to the far building, entered, and opened the window. She then left to take out the roaming guard on the roof.

It had taken a while to find the rooftop access. It was in a closet on the top floor. While she'd been wandering the street after dinner, she spotted a guard watching her. She wasn't sure, but there might have been two of them. They were on to her. She had to be careful. She entered the hotel and climbed the stairs to her room. Once behind the relative safety of the closed door, she made her final plan, which now also had to include dodging the guards.

She went to the window and pulled the heavy curtain aside far enough to see the street. One of the guards was leaning against the wall of a building across the street. She didn't see the other one but assumed she was close, perhaps in the hotel's lobby.

She peered out her door in case the guard was stationed in the hall. The hall was empty and quiet. At each end of the hall was a window. She left the room and went right. From what she could see in the darkness and the faint glow of the yellowish streetlights, the window looked out over a line of buildings in the direction she needed to go.

The building next door was only one story which made the drop from there too dangerous to attempt. From a lower level window, however, she might be able to make the fall without injury. Dawson followed a projected route. She'd have to cross two buildings of the same height before coming to the tall one where the guard was posted.

That building had windows on the side as well. She might have to break one to gain entry. In this quiet town, any loud noise would carry and be heard, and the guard below watching her might look up. If seen, her mission would be blown. Still, she had no other option. She had to check it out.

She pushed through the fire door leading to the stairwell and descended with stealth. She reached the second floor and entered the hall. The large old-style wood frame window was to the right. The drop to the roof was maybe six feet, unless she hung and dropped. She pulled her knife, expecting the window to be painted shut, but to her surprise, it slid open without protest. She poked her head through the opening, an easy drop.

Sheathing the knife, Dawson slid a leg out and sat half in, half out. She sized up her move then shifted her weight to slip both legs out. In an awkward position, she pivoted her torso while balancing her weight on the narrow ledge. Using one hand pressed to the glass, she lowered the window as far as she could. After all her efforts, it wouldn't do to have someone wander by and notice the open window.

She then turned with the intent of pressing her hands to the sill and lowering, but her body weight and gravity took over, and she dropped faster than intended. Her grip broke, and she fell, making too much noise. If anyone were inside the one-story building, they'd be aware someone was on the roof.

Rising fast, she crept across the roof in a crouch. She reached the edge and stepped over a small sidewall to the next building. She squatted and paused. High above, the guard was on the near end, scanning the surrounding landscape. Dawson wondered how much she could see. Did the glasses have night vision capability? If so, she had to hurry. By now, the men were deploying.

Moving faster than she would have liked, she reached the wall of the taller building. She glanced down on the street. Her watcher was still back in the shadows, barely in sight but not showing concern. Dawson pressed against the wall and stretched her frame as high as it would reach. She was a good six inches short of the sill. She jumped, missed, and landed lightly on her toes. Doing a deeper squat for more power, she pushed off again but was still well short. She cursed under her breath.

She studied the problem for a moment, then backed away from the wall and took a running start. Lifting a foot, she hit the wall and pushed down, giving her added height. Her fingers cleared the sill, and her hands splayed open. Using all her strength, she pressed down, lifting her body. Her face was at the window, but how to maneuver into a position where she could open it? For that matter, would the window even open?

Running her feet up the wall gave her more height. As she rose, Dawson twisted her body and planted her butt on the ledge. She took a few moments to catch her breath and examined the window. This one was more modern. It was an aluminum frame with a storm and screen insert. The screen was up out of the way, but the storm window was in place and locked. Dawson called to mind the windows she had in her house growing up. They were similar. The twin catches were either on the top or on each side. She tested the glass. It bowed a bit in the frame on the sides, telling her the locks were on the top. She put more force into her lift, hoping to snap the usually plastic catches, but they held.

She took out her knife and wedged it into the space between the top frame and bottom. It took longer than she wanted, but eventually, she widened the gap far enough to force the window up. She swung her legs inside and shut the window, leaving it unlocked.

On the top floor, Dawson entered the closet where she'd discovered the roof access. A cubby with an attached metal ladder. She hadn't tested it earlier, so she wasn't sure if it opened, but how would the guard get back down if it didn't?

With a light push on the edges to keep the cover from banging, the panel rose. Cool night air seeped in from around the edges. Once the cover cleared the roof level, she shoved it to the side and climbed up. Crouched next to the opening, she scoured the roof for her target. Chimneys, air conditioning units, exhaust pipes, and a few other things she did not recognize sprouted from the tarred roof, giving her cover for her approach. The guard was out of view from her position. She moved.

Hiding behind an air conditioning unit, she waited until the guard walked past, heading to her next viewpoint. The guard stopped at the far end to the right, the spot where she'd have the best line of sight at the approaching troops.

Dawson rose and advanced. She planned on taking the woman using her knife but didn't want to take it out too soon. If the woman turned and saw her, a knife in hand would indicate her purpose. She'd have to time it right and pull the weapon when only a step or two from her prey.

She stepped out, and the woman lowered the glasses. She rubbed her eyes. Was she moving already? The guard put the glasses back to her face and leaned forward as if to get a closer look. Something had caught her eye. Dawson had seconds to act before the alarm sounded. With the guard intent on whatever she'd seen, Dawson rose and made her move.

That was when the gunshot sounded, and she froze in place.

CHAPTER FIFTY-FOUR

Mark was dozing when Becca rapped on the window. Startled, he gripped his gun before he saw it was his daughter. He blew out a breath of relief, opened the door, and got out. As soon as his feet touched the street, Becca was hugging him. "Oh, Dad, this place is such a cluster, er, ah, is so screwed up."

"How so? Did they deny our request?"

"Not exactly. They agreed, but with conditions."

"Such as—?"

"They want drugs they're short on in return. They want us to transport Maretha here for treatment. And, they want Britta, Mariah, and me to stay here."

"To stay? For what purpose and how long?"

"They want us to become permanent residents."

Mark didn't know how to respond to that. "Are they nuts? Why would that be a part of any deal? Like being pressed into the navy. You're servants. No, there has to be another way."

"Britta thinks they're doing this so they don't have to tell us no. If we get the drugs or not depends on us. They don't want to give them up, but they will if we give them drugs and us in return."

"They can't expect you to give up your freedom."

"But, Dad, if it means saving Bobby's and Maretha's lives, it'd be worth it."

"What are you saying? You'd be willing to move here?"

"It can't be that bad. I'll be with others in a community. It's as safe as our home."

"Oh, Becca. This is so wrong."

"I know, Dad, but it's for Bobby."

They stood in prolonged silence. What else could he say? "Tell Britta I want to address the council."

"I doubt they'll allow that."

"We won't know until we ask. When are you supposed to give your answer?"

"Tomorrow morning."

"So, they're forcing us to stay the night too, even though two lives depend on how fast we get the drugs back."

Neither knew what else to say. Mark was about to break the silence when something else did. He cocked his head, trying to hear the sound again. What had it been? It certainly wasn't a normal sound of the night or its nocturnal residents.

"Did you hear that?"

"Hear what?" Becca asked.

"It was like a—" a what? He played the sound over again in his mind. It came from a distance. Not close. It might have been an echo of the original sound. How did it go? Like a putt-putt and a hiss and rattle. It didn't come again, so he shoved it aside.

"Go back and ask. If they force us to stay the night, let me know as early as possible. I'll approach the gate and wait for the answer." His stomach rumbled, reminding him he'd missed dinner. "Did you eat?"

"Yeah."

"Was it good?"

"Yeah. Not as good as what Caryn and Lynn make, but good enough."

As if to comment, his stomach growled again. "Sorry. I should have brought you some."

"It's all right. I'll survive."

She hugged him and kissed his cheek. "Love you, Daddy. Be safe out here."

"Love you, too. See you in the morning."

He watched as she and her escort walked away. He stood for a moment, leaning against the SUV. Then, movement down the road to the left caught his attention. Considering the darkness, all he could see were shadows, but when the shadows moved, it was either the wind or something living.

He focused hard. Yes, there it was again. A steady rhythm of moving shadows. Putt-putt, hiss rattle. It was the sound of an engine in need of a tune-up being turned off. Someone was out there. A lot of someones. It clicked in an instant, and he was running to catch Becca.

His footsteps echoed off the corner houses. In the dim light at the gate, he spotted two silhouettes. He wanted to call to Becca, but if his footsteps echoed, his voice would carry far.

The guards at the gate came to life. A spotlight was illuminated and aimed at him. "Halt," was shouted, and Mark threw up his hands and stopped. He was still a short block from Becca. "Becca," he called in a loud whisper.

"Dad? What's the matter?"

"Get inside fast and tell them they're being attacked."

The guard's eyes widened, and she lifted her rifle.

"What?"

"Trust me. Just do it. To the south one block. Hurry."

Becca whirled and sprinted for the gate. Mark backed away and ran for the SUV where he'd left his rifle. He ran on the balls of his feet to lessen the impact on the street and muffle the echoes. He reached the SUV, eyes scanning the streets. He was about to open the door when the shadows moved down the next block ahead of him. A stream of darker shadows came right for him.

Mark ducked and peered through the windows. The assault team, at least he assumed that's what they were, halted across the street. They melded so completely with the darkness he was no longer sure he saw what he did.

He slid to the rear passenger door and opened it with a slow and steady hand. The dome light had long ago been removed. In newer models, the dashboard lit up when the door was opened. That was one of the reasons he preferred older models, which this was. If the key wasn't inserted, the dashboard didn't light.

He reached in and slid the rifle out. The magnification of the scope, even without night vision, would help solve the question of whether he saw things or not. He didn't bother closing the door, afraid the click would be heard. He crawled to the rear tire and aimed the rifle under the chassis. The scope showed the dark silhouettes of at least a dozen men— all armed, armored, and black-faced. They wore helmets, and each carried an assault rifle.

The town had to be warned, and there was only one way to ensure everyone woke up fast. He sighted on the first man, aimed for the center of the dark shape, and fired. A rifle has a distinctive report compared to a handgun. If it were a musical instrument, it would have a deeper, more refined tone. On a still night in mostly open ground, the shot could be heard for miles. He only needed it to be heard a hundred yards.

Mark didn't bother to see if the man fell. He ran toward the front of the SUV and used it as cover, angling toward the second house on the block. Return fire came for him but appeared targeted at where they'd seen the muzzle flash. He ducked around the corner and ran between the houses.

Above, on one of the buildings, an air horn went off. If the shots hadn't done the trick, the horn certainly did. Lights came on in town, all aimed outward. Gunfire erupted up and down the line of the town. Whoever was attacking was doing so on multiple fronts.

Mark kept moving, hopping over the rear fence and circling to his right. An engine started and grew closer. He stopped at the fence overlooking the side street. One of the military Humvees, similar to those they now had at the farmhouse, drove by at high speed. This one did not have a mounted gun but did have an enhanced bumper. They were going to ram the barricade. Mark knew the glass was bulletproof, so he didn't bother trying to take out the driver. He waited for the troops that ran behind the truck and picked off the first man.

The heavy chatter of a fifty cal fired somewhere close by was followed closely by a crash. From his position, he couldn't see what collided into what. He pulled the trigger and dropped another man. This time, however, someone had seen where the shot came from. He ran for a wooden shed at the rear of the yard as automatic fire tracked him. The rounds thudded into the wood siding, some passing through like it was paper.

Mark didn't slow. He put a hand on the crossbar of a low fence and hurdled it. He dodged between the first two houses near the corner. He was one block away from town. The fifty cal continued a non-stop barrage. He peeked around the corner of the house and saw the ramming truck had crashed into the corner house across the street. The fifty was being fired from the town. Mark forgot they had acquired two of the vehicles after the battle at the facility and subsequent attack on the town just days before.

He moved to the rear of the house and used the scope to check the advancing line. They were in full retreat, unable to stand before the deadly machine gun. There was nothing for him to do but try not to become a target.

CHAPTER FIFTY-FIVE

Becca and the guard hustled over the barricade. "You have to sound the alarm. You're about to be attacked." The guard at the gate looked at the guard accompanying Becca. She shrugged. "You're about—oh, never mind." She leaped down from the cars and looked for Britta. "Britta, you're being attacked. Sound the alarm."

A voice behind her shouted, "Hey, don't do that."

Then the gunshot came, and everyone was screaming and sounding alarms.

Becca ran to Britta and Mariah and the befuddled guards watching them. "I need my gun."

"We all do," Britta said. "Follow me." The three took off running. Britta went to the council building. Armed guards blocked the doorway.

"Sisters," Britta called out as guns were pointed at them. "Our weapons are inside the armory. We have no way of defending the town without them."

No one moved. "Our job is to guard this door and not let anyone pass," one said.

Yes, I have done this job many times myself. I commend you, but please send someone inside for weapons so we can help fight. I have not been gone that long that you forgot who I am."

One of the other guards said, "You come with me. The other two stay here."

"Sister!" the other woman said.

"Oh, use some common sense."

They went inside. Minutes later, Britta was back with three rifles, three handguns, and an extra magazine for each of the rifles. "It's not much but better than nothing."

"Where should we go?" Mariah said.

Britta motioned up. "The roof. I want to see what's going on." They raced for the tallest building in town and ran up the stairs. Five flights later, breathing hard and legs leaden, they reached the access. It only offered enough room for one at a time. Britta led the way. Becca climbed last.

Ten women were in various positions firing down at whatever targets they could see. Only one, the leader, had night vision goggles. For the others acquiring targets was guesswork.

Britta approached the leader who was calling out targets. She walked back and forth with the glasses pressed to her face.

"Amanda," Britta called. "What can we do to help?"

"Britta? Good to see you and just in time. I've lost two warriors down at that end. There's a sniper somewhere targeting them, but for whatever reason only on that side."

Becca jumped in. "They must be trying to breach in that location. What's there?"

"Nothing unless they tear down the wall," Amanda said.

They started to move. "Britta, wait. Before the shooting started, there was a stranger up here. I haven't seen her before. By her reaction, I got the feeling she was up to something."

"You think she's part of this."

"I don't know, but something was off about her. Not to mention if she was new, why was she up here? How did she even discover the access unless she was looking for it?"

"Okay. We'll check it out later."

They made it to the end of the roof and lay down to be smaller targets. Each rifle had a scope, and they used them now to scan the ground five stories below. Nothing appeared out of the ordinary.

A shot pinged off the edge, inches from Mariah's face. They scooted back. "We're the highest building in the area," Britta said. "A sniper has to be shooting from an inferior position. Out there, the tallest house is two stories, so unless we get right on the edge, he has no shot. Scan the second story windows of the houses."

"There," Mariah called out. "Second street, first house, third window."

"Are you sure?" Becca said. "I can't see a thing."

"He's there. The window is open."

"Let's target him then," said Britta.

They each sent two rounds through the window but had no idea if any of the shots connected. Becca wished she had Bobby's skill with a rifle. That thought ignited a memory of Booby's current condition. Angered, she placed two more rounds through the window. The lack of return fire was encouraging.

"Hey," isn't that your father?" Britta said.

"What? Where?" She shifted the sights to where Britta was pointing. She caught a flash of movement and had to track faster to see him. It did resemble her father, but in the dark, it was difficult to be sure. The rooftop had four spotlights aimed at the ground, but two of them had been shot out, and the other two were on the far end.

Again that seemed strange to Becca. They had a sniper on this side and had taken out the lights on this side. Now, her father was running toward something on this side. She turned to Britta. "They found a way in down there someplace."

"How do you know?"

"It all fits. What if the stranger was up here to take out the guards?"

Britta gave her a skeptical look.

"Look, I'm not sure about anything. It's all guesswork, but if they found an unprotected space that they can get people through, this fight will be over fast. Maybe my dad saw it too, and that's why he's moving in that direction."

"All right. Let's go."

As they ran for the ladder, Britta detoured and explained to the guard in charge what they thought was happening. The guard immediately sent two of her remaining team to protect the far side. As Britta reached the cubby hole to climb down, she heard another long-range shot. She looked up in time to see one of the guards fall, bounce, and roll. They either had two snipers, or they shot at the wrong window.

Determined to stop whatever was about to occur, Britta hurried down the ladder. The best way to stop them was to handle it herself.

Dawson was almost caught. The guard spun on her as the first shot was fired and reached for the air horn. If she was closer, she might have been able to stop her. Instead, she turned and ran. As she descended the ladder, she wondered who had fired. None of the troops would've done so. It took away whatever element of surprise they had. Now she had to hurry to get to the building and mark the entryway.

She ran down the stairs, almost losing her balance and falling twice. She burst through the outer door and collided with another woman. Dawson kept going, but the other woman went sprawling.

Dawson fought for control of her thoughts and emotions. She had to slow down and not draw attention to herself. She slowed to a fast walk. As she reached the building she'd broken into, Dawson did a slow turn to make sure no one was watching before disappearing around the corner. With a good kick, she crashed the door open and went inside. She ran to the back window, took out her small pocket flashlight, and blinked the beam twice.

She counted to fifteen seconds and did it again. On the third try, she got the flashing call back. They were on the way. Soon the town would be theirs. Her elation faded, replaced by guilt. She wished there was a way to stop the butchery and debauchery that was about to occur. It was too late now and what happened afterward was on her shoulders.

CHAPTER FIFTY-SIX

Down the line of backyards, someone flicked a light on and off twice. It wasn't for long or had much brightness, but it revealed several bodies moving with stealth toward the rear of the town buildings. Surely someone must see them. He scanned the roofline. All the gunners up there were aiming in other areas. The lights on that end had been shot out. If a secret way in had been found, it was doing a good job of remaining hidden. Where were the troops heading in such clandestine fashion?

He had to find out and stop them if he could. The troops were only one block from the town. Perhaps they were going to scale the brick wall. Or maybe even blow a hole in the wall. The first would be quieter, and if they gained the roof, they'd have the high ground and be able to rain death down inside the town.

Mark moved through the yards, stopping at each fence and checking through the scope before hopping into the next yard. By the time he reached the spot where he thought he'd seen the light, no one was there.

He moved to the front of the house then crossed the street. This row of houses backed up to the town. The yards backed to an alley that ended at the walls of the businesses that lined the main street. Down four houses to his left, a line of men crouched in a back yard. Two at a time, they climbed the fence, crossed the alley, then slid through a window into one of the buildings.

Mark felt panicked. There had to be forty men waiting for their turn. Once inside, they'd control the street, be able to divide the defenders, and do a building by building clearance.

If he couldn't figure out a way to stop them or at least alert the defense, the town was lost, and with them, his daughter.

With little time for planning, Mark decided his first best option was to prevent anyone else from entering the window. The action would make him an instant target. He wouldn't be able to stay for long. The men at the back of the line would swarm toward him. He'd be pinned down and trapped.

If he fired and ran, he might get away, but he'd only delay them for maybe a minute. Plus, if he were running near the building, he'd be a target from the defenders. They'd have no way of telling him apart from the soldiers, and even if they could, they might not care. He was just another invading man.

He darted to a garage that backed to the alley. The location gave him a clear shot at the men as they hopped the fence and climbed through the window. How many had entered already? They'd wait until they had sufficient numbers before attacking, but that was coming fast.

He lined up his shot and waited. As the next two men scaled the fence and dropped to the paved alley, he targeted the second man that came over and fired. The man went down. The first man was unaware of his partner's demise until someone shouted. As he turned, Mark punctured his forehead.

No one else dared climb until the threat was dealt with. Whoever was in charge had to be searching for him. The garage blocked their night vision goggles from seeing him, but it also prevented him from seeing them or if anyone was coming for him.

Someone poked a head over the fence to look down the alley. There was a better chance of him being spotted than making the shot to take him out, so he ducked back. He moved toward the front of the garage, knelt, and took a quick peek. He heard, rather than saw the approaching men. He rolled from cover and fired four quick shots in the area of the sound. He could hear the impacts but had no way of knowing if they were kill shots or merely absorbed by the body armor. But the steps did cease.

Shots peppered the ground around him. They now knew where he was. He had to risk moving even though it put him in the open. He ran to the side fence, keeping behind the garage. After a hurried look back down the alley, he hopped the fence, putting him in plain view, and ran. The next yard had no garage to hide behind, making him run farther than he wanted to with no cover.

As soon as he passed the next garage, he placed a hand on the fence and vaulted, but his back foot caught the crossbar, and he tumbled to the ground. Pain lanced his knee. He hit something hard and sharp but to allow it to slow him meant sure death. He scrambled to the side wall of the garage then hobbled toward the front.

Men were in the yard he left searching for him. They didn't appear to know where he was. He went back to the alley side. Dark shapes moved. They had resumed their entry. Two men with laser sights stood aiming down the alley in his direction. He'd only get one shot off before the other man zeroed in on him. It was a chance he had to take to slow the advance.

He steeled himself for whatever was to come, stuck the rifle around the corner, then his head. He acquired the target and fired as one of them said, "There." The laser sight shot skyward. He squeezed the trigger until the magazine was empty, unsure if he made any other contact, then ran past the garage toward the side of the house in view of the advancing men hunting him.

The move was his only one. He hoped his sudden appearance might cause a delay in shooting or at least leave their targeting behind him. He almost made it. As he reached the fence, two rounds impacted him, one on the right shoulder, the other along his back. Mark was about to vault the fence when the bullets struck. His body slammed into the crossbar, driving the air from his lungs. The rifle went flying to the other side. Pain surrounded him and clouded his mind. Yet somehow, the drive to survive fought through. He leaned over the crossbar, grabbed the fencing, and flipped over, landing hard on his back. He struggled to rise but found he was unable.

They would surround him now. His body would be riddled with bullets. He rolled toward the house and kicked something metal. His legs fell. Unable to control his body, he fell into a tight metal frame. It took a moment to understand what happened and where he was. It was a basement window well.

He snagged the rifle and ducked. Cramped as he was, he slid the wounded arm down his leg and lifted the handgun from the holster. He switched it to his left hand, forced his body as low as possible in the tight space, and waited.

Men rushed to the fence. "Where'd he go? I know I hit him."

Mark knew his heat signature would be apparent if they looked in the right place.

Men came around the front of the house. "Where?"

The man in the yard said, "Gone. Must be around the front. He's wounded. He can't get far."

Mark could hear the men in the front moving away but had no idea where the men in the yard were. Then he heard someone climbing the fence. He aimed the gun upward, knowing if they discovered him, any defense was futile. Still, he'd never give up without a fight. The wait grew unbearable, as did the pain. Even if they didn't find him, he doubted he'd have the strength to pull himself out of his hiding space. He might die right there. No one would ever discover him until long after the rodents and scavengers devoured his corpse.

What was keeping them from finishing him? He was right in front of them. Were they waiting, rifles aimed, for him to poke his head out like a real-life whack-a-mole? Well, he had news for them. He was too exhausted and too much in agony to move. If they wanted him, they'd have to come to get him.

Mark fought to keep his mind clear, to not focus on the pain, but the effort was a losing battle. In the few focused moments, he noticed the lack of sound around him. He still heard the battle being waged, but it was in the distance. Or was that because he was slowly losing consciousness from blood loss?

He had done the best he could to warn and help the townspeople. He may never know if it was enough or if they were successful. He thought of his daughter, the warrior. He prayed she was alive, that she made her escape. But if not, he prayed she died in this fitting place for her, rather than at the hands of Doctor Ohtanda.

CHAPTER FIFTY-SEVEN

They ran down the street, desperate to reach the southern gate before an all-out assault took place. An assault that might overwhelm the defenders and signal the doom of the town.

Britta came to an abrupt stop. When Becca noticed four strides later, she turned to find the woman looking back the other way.

"What is it?" Becca asked.

"The machine gun has been moved. It should be here protecting this gate."

"Maybe whoever's in charge moved the gun thinking the main attack was at the eastern gate."

"Yes, and that's what worries me. What if you're right, and that was a fake to draw our attention that way while the main assault happens here?"

"We're going to need that gun."

Britta took a step back then stopped. "I can't move it unless we know for sure."

"Then let's make sure." Becca turned and followed Mariah, who was already at the far gate ducking behind a bullet-ridden minivan.

Becca joined her, and Britta arrived seconds later. "I don't see any actual attack here. If anything, it's kind of weak here. They're only taking long-range shots."

"Which fits into what I was saying," Becca said. "The rest is to draw us away from here. The real attack is happening here."

"But from where?" Becca said.

They both looked at the end building and down the short walkway to the side door."

"There," they said at the same time.

"Mariah, go get that truck down here."

"What if they won't listen to me?"

"Convince them, or the town is lost."

Becca and Britta advanced toward the building with their weapons at fire ready positions. They reached the side door, and Britta slid her hand down the frame. "It's been jimmied." With as much care as she could, she turned the knob and pushed the door open. She paused a moment for an ambush then turned her head to listen for any sound coming from what should be an empty building.

When nothing happened, she leaned forward to peek through the doorway. Bullets ripped into the door and frame, whizzing past her face. Heavy footsteps thudded toward them. They backed away, in their excitement and momentary panic, firing through the doorway before anyone was there.

With no available cover, shooting was their only defense. "We have to cover the front door too," Becca said, changing out her magazine.

"I'll try to hold them in the building until you get us some help."

"I'm not leaving you to face this alone."

"If we don't get help fast, we're both dead. Go."

Becca hesitated, then set the rifle down. "Just changed out the mag. It's ready to go." She pulled her handgun and ran to the southern gate thirty yards away. She got a woman's attention, pointed, and shouted, "They're inside the town. Britta's alone holding them off."

Then she turned to look down the street. Both trucks were still at the eastern gate. She sprinted. The nearest truck was nearly two blocks away. She prayed Britta could hold out that long.

As she arrived, she noticed Mariah was in the street arguing with a woman. She shouted and pointed but appeared to be losing the argument. Becca wasted no time getting involved. She knew what had to be done and was determined to make it happen.

She ran around the truck, ripped the driver's door open, reached in, and yanked the driver from the seat. She flung her to the ground, hopped in, and put the truck into reverse. The truck lurched backward, knocking the gunner down.

Becca swung the wheel hard, shifted, and headed down the road. The woman arguing with Mariah jumped in her path but soon saw Becca wasn't going to stop. She fired twice into the windshield then dove to the side.

Becca increased speed, worried about Britta. A glance in the side mirror showed Mariah running behind the truck. Becca scanned the street but didn't see Britta. A swarm of soldiers exited the front door of the building. Some were along the side, firing at the few remaining defenders of the southern gate. Panic rose, burning up her throat. She was too late to save Britta. These bastards were going to pay.

She slowed and called to the gunner. "Shoot those bastards." Nothing happened. She rose from her seat but did not see the gunner. Had she abandoned the truck? Bullets put divots into the windshield, but for the moment, it held. Becca stood and climbed through the small passage leading to the outer body and the gun. She found the woman on the floor bed with a bullet wound in her head.

She leaped the body and took the gun as men closed on the truck. She grabbed the weapon and aimed, but men were already at the truck. Gunshots from behind knocked two of them down. Becca freed her handgun and fired on all sides of the truck to clear the enemy away.

Mariah arrived and climbed aboard, allowing Becca to use the machine gun. She swept left to right close to the truck, then aimed higher and swung back the other way. Bodies fell. They were so many and so close together she could hardly miss.

They scattered, and shots began to rain down on her. Behind her, Becca heard a grunt and a thud. She recognized both sounds for what they were and knew she was now fighting alone.

A loud crash exploded the vehicles of the southern gate inward, creating a wide opening. A truck with a heavy round steel bar attached to the front plowed through and aimed for her. Becca turned her fire on the truck. The massive fifty caliber rounds punched through the windshield. The driver did a death dance, but the truck continued forward smacking into the front quarter panel.

The contact, though not major, was enough to jar her from the gun. She tripped over a body and fell. Her hand touched a rifle. She picked it up and stood, realizing the weapon belonged to Mariah, though she no longer needed it. She had no time to allow the sadness to enter. She knelt at the sidewall and sniped at anything that moved.

Something struck the inside of the bed. A glance back showed the grenade resting on Mariah's chest. Becca's eyes widened. Decision time. Go for it or abandon the truck. Either way was sure death.

Then she saw Mariah's hand move. She gripped the grenade and tossed it over the side, one last bit of heroics. Then her hand collapsed, and her head lolled. Anger exploded behind Becca's eyes, turning everything red. The world around her slowed down as she stood and once more took up a position at the machine gun. If this was where she died, she'd go out taking as many of them with her as possible.

Becca screamed at the top of her lungs as she fired. Bullets flew. Men were torn apart. Pain lanced at her body, but she didn't stop. She was only barely aware of the gunshot behind her until the body fell on her.

She turned then ready to strike, but the man slid down her body and was still, a bloody mess at the back of his head. She glanced up, breathing so hard the air felt like a wound all to itself. Standing in the street not twenty feet away was the blood-soaked figure of her father.

She sobbed at the sight until he turned his handgun and fired at something along the side of the truck. She turned back to the gun and hosed down the street. Not long after, the gun ran dry. Still, she kept the bar pressed down, and the sound of discharge rounds continued. In her mind, she assumed it was all in her head, but noticed men were still falling, so she kept firing imaginary rounds.

Then she noted the second truck pull up next to her and slumped as emotionally spent as the gun. She felt an arm around her and looked through tears and blood-filled blurry eyes to see her father. With the last of her strength, she hugged him tight and cried.

"It's all right, baby girl. I've got you."

CHAPTER FIFTY-EIGHT

Dawson exited the building last to leave, her sidearm ready for use. She watched as the lone woman fought off the men. She was amazed at the woman's fury, her determination, the lack of concern for her safety. This was the warrior she'd always wanted to be—wished she could be. How ironic she was responsible for the woman's death.

Others joined her. They fell one by one under the superior firepower and training of the men. Her weapon empty, the warrior bent and snatched up a second. Her only cover was a fire hydrant. The berserker rage she wore on her face told of her fearlessness. How did she do it?

Then the inevitable happened. She was hit and went down only to rise again, firing her rifle on automatic with one hand. She was hit again. On her back, she drew out a handgun and attempted to rise once more. As the other men moved into the street, one man walked toward the fallen warrior. It was Arnett. No, she wouldn't allow him this pleasure. She stalked behind him.

As the woman tried to rise, he placed a foot on her chest and shoved her down. Pinned beneath the large combat boot, the dying woman no longer had the strength to rise. Dawson hastened her pace, closing enough to hear, "It's too bad you'll be dead by the time we're done. I'd have enjoyed a few rounds with you." He pointed the rifle at her head.

As the bullet struck the back of his head, his body twisted, giving him a last look at his assassin. She thought she saw a look of surprise pass through his eyes as the life faded from them. He fell. Dawson was almost as surprised by her actions as he'd been.

She checked quickly for anyone who might have seen, then rushed to the woman's side. She was bleeding badly from several places. She'd die without immediate medical help. "I'm sorry. I'm so sorry."

"Help me," the weakened voice pleaded.

"I wish I could. I'm not a doctor. I don't even have any medical supplies."

A bloody arm rose and pointed down the street. "Doc—tor."

"You have a doctor here?" she glanced down the street. Could she get her there without being shot? She studied the woman. How much longer did she have? Guilt-ridden over her decision to help these butchers, she made up her mind. Holstering her gun, she bent and lifted the almost dead weight. Once upright, the woman had strength enough left to support most of her weight.

They stumbled across the street. Shooters on both sides ignored them, concentrating on those who were firing back. One of the trucks arrived and kept the invaders occupied, allowing them to make it to the sidewalk on the opposite side of the street.

It felt like an eternity before they arrived at what passed for a hospital. She pushed her way through the door, all but dragging the now weakened body. The outer room was filled with bloody bodies and activity. A woman, Dawson guessed was a nurse, saw them, and came over.

"My God, Britta." She wrapped an arm around the other side. "Help me get her to the back." They pushed through an interior swinging door. The lights were brighter on that side. The nurse led to an examination room. They lifted Britta and laid her down on a white paper-covered exam table. "Get her clothes off. Hurry."

They undressed her, cutting away the clothes and letting them fall in bloody piles on the floor. The nurse examined her body. Under her breath, Dawson heard the nurse count. "Two. Three. And a few grazes. Stay with her." She left the room. Less than a minute later, she was back with another woman who was clad in surgery scrubs and wheeling a gurney. The three of them transferred Britta to the gurney, and she was wheeled out.

The first woman called over her shoulder. "Clean that up for me, would you."

Dawson guessed she meant the bloody clothes. She picked them up, deposited them in the biohazard container, then looked at her hands. How appropriate, she thought. She had the woman's blood on her hands both figuratively and literally.

She exited the room then the building. The battle had intensified in the short time she'd been inside. She withdrew her gun and studied the street. Battles raged at three sites. She tried to decide where to go, then which side she was going to help. In the end, she sat down against the hospital's outer wall, buried her face in her hands, and cried.

Several minutes later, she heard shouting and the changing gears of a truck. The second truck that the defenders owned was moving to the far gate where she had aided in breaching the grounds and allowing the horde of killers inside. She wiped her eyes, stood, and marched down the street to aide in the defense.

She lifted her handgun, moved behind the truck, and followed it down the street. A soldier moved up to the side of the truck to get a close shot at the gunner. Dawson stepped out and fired two rounds into the side of the man's head. For the first time since she'd arrived in town, for that matter since she joined this battalion, she felt right with herself.

She put down two more men, one she knew from her unit, before running out of bullets. She dropped the mag and slid another in. As she stood to take down another man, a heavy thud hit her in the chest. It knocked her off her feet. Her head snapped back and cracked against the street. To her surprise, she didn't feel pain. Instead, as the darkness swallowed her vision, she realized she finally felt at peace.

CHAPTER FIFTY-NINE

As the sounds of the battle lessened, Mark held his daughter in the back of the truck and waited. The attack at the southern gate had been repelled. Sporadic gunshots were all that remained. A handful of grenades were tossed, creating more chaos than any real damage. Mark assumed it was to allow the attackers to retreat.

The two trucks had made the difference, which made him wonder why the attackers hadn't used their own. They used trucks to open the gates but not as weapons. He thought that a tactical mistake. One he was grateful for.

Mark was challenged under four rifles when he attempted to climb down from the truck. He tried to speak but was outshouted. He raised one arm, unable to lift the other. His daughter jumped from the vehicle in front of him. She roared at them, then threatened to gut them all if they didn't put down their weapons.

A blood-smeared Iso stepped through the crowd, recognized Becca, then her father, and gave the order to lower the weapons and help the wounded.

"Have you seen Britta?" Iso asked, a note of concern in her voice.

"No. I left her there," she pointed, "to get the truck. I never saw her again. Mariah's on the truck."

Iso stepped to the backend and peered in. Mariah's body was on top of several others.

"She saved my life," Becca said. "Twice. If not for her, we might have been overrun."

Iso nodded, then used her arm to wipe the blood from her face. "You both need the doctor." She turned to her guards. "See that they get to the hospital. If anyone questions their right to be there, you have them come and see me."

With the help of the two guards, Becca and Mark were taken to the hospital, where they were seated in the waiting room with nearly twenty others. A nurse made the rounds checking on the various wounds and injuries and assigning them a number based on priority. Becca and Mark were both twos. Serious but not immediately dangerous wounds.

Mark slumped next to Becca. At first, she thought he was asleep, but as his weight grew heavier on her shoulder and she didn't see the rise and fall of his chest, she called for assistance. The nurse upgraded him to a one, but he still had four people ahead of him. They took him to the back and placed him in a room with a woman with a gunshot to the shoulder who was already hooked to an IV. They prepped Mark and started an IV drip for him. Then they were left alone. Thirty minutes later, they came for the woman.

Becca dozed. By the time she woke, her father was gone. Panicked, she jumped to her feet and prowled the hallway until the nurse came out of one of the operating rooms and told her they were working on her father and she should go back to the waiting room. There she noted the room still held the same amount of injured bodies. Some of the faces were different, but the number never changed.

The invading force dragged back to base. Of the hundred men he'd arrived with, he sent sixty on the mission. Of those sixty, thirty-four returned. Counting the men lost on the other front and the team he sent out to hunt down the women that never returned, General Billings force was down forty percent.

His counterpart stood and watched the supposed superior invading force return. The satisfied smirk on Martin's face had grown each passing minute. Immediately behind the column came one of Martin's troop carriers. It was filled with civilians.

"What's going on here, general? Who are these people?"

Martin said, "The test subjects Doctor Ohtanda requested."

"How did you . . ."

"I sent an envoy to the barricade down the road a few miles, the one you threatened to destroy if they didn't let you pass. Before you arrived, we had an arrangement with all the local groups. If they stayed away from us and didn't interfere with our work, we'd leave them alone. You threw off that balance. I sent someone to make amends. We offered food and free medical services for twenty of their people. They volunteered to come, and no one died."

"They volunteered to be test subjects?"

"Of course not. The food will be injected with the virus. Once the subjects show signs of it taking effect, we'll introduce the cure. Others will get the vaccine first during their routine physicals, then given the disease. In a few days, if all goes well, they'll be released, and we'll have the next level of data for the final cure."

Billings eyed him. The man had outmaneuvered him. "Good. Very good. I'll report that to the leadership council. When we leave here, we'll take the vaccine with us for our teams to study and disperse."

"No, General. You won't. We've already spoken to the council. Both Ohtanda and I made a report. Needless to say, the council is not thrilled about the carnage you have introduced to the region. You're to return to the capital tomorrow, well before the vaccine will have its final test."

Billings stammered. "What do you mean? You spoke to them?"

"Yes. They are not happy with you. They'll be even less pleased when they learn how many men and how much equipment you've lost. It appears you overstepped your mission and went rogue with an agenda of your own. It's just a guess, but I don't think anyone will be referring to you as general for much longer."

The color drained from Billings's face. Of all the things Martin thought he'd remember about this entire failed campaign, the look on Billing's face right then was by far the top.

Becca had to be wakened to take her turn. She was prepped, drugged, and out by the time she was wheeled into the operating room. She woke in a dark room with only the low glow of monitor lights showing. Soft snoring came from across the space. She wasn't alone. After listening for a while, she was sure at least three others shared the room with her. She felt no pain but was sure that was because of whatever drug she was on.

She wondered how her father was doing. Then she thought about her brother and Maretha. Had they both survived? After such a devastating and bloody battle, did the doctor still think he had enough spare drugs to send back? Judging from the amount of wounded in the waiting room, she didn't see how that was possible.

Her thoughts flitted around with no goal until she came to one of her attending some sorority ball back in college. How strange that life seemed now. At the start of the pandemic, she never imagined she'd be who she was now. She'd been through so many deadly situations the images of her before were difficult to recall. From snobby society girl to bad-ass warrior in a few short months. She much preferred who she was now over that stranger who occupied her body back then. Still, it'd be nice to have some extended downtime when this was over.

Her eyes grew heavy. She slept through the night.

CHAPTER SIXTY

In the morning, she woke as a nurse she hadn't seen before made the rounds. She'd been wrong about the number unless more were added after she fell back asleep. Seven other women were crammed into the small room. She was told it was one of four rooms in the building. Those with lesser injuries had been transported across the street to the council hall.

She asked about her father and was told he was in recovery in another room. Then she asked about Britta. The nurse's lips thinned, and she averted her eyes. Without another word, she left, leaving Becca saddened by the loss of her friend.

Later that afternoon, Iso made a tour of the wardrooms. She made a point of stopping at Becca's bed. She placed a hand on her arm and smiled. "I hear you are once again to thank for saving the town."

"I just did what any of your people would have."

"But you reacted faster. Your actions saved a lot of lives. We might have lost the town. Thank you."

"Can you tell me what happened to Britta?"

Whatever façade Iso had been wearing crumbled before Becca's eyes. The sight drove a spike of fear for her friend through her heart. "Is-is she dead?"

"No, but the doctor doesn't hold much hope for recovery. She took four bullets and lost a lot of blood before getting medical attention."

"She's strong. She'll make it."

"I pray you're right. You rest and get well. I need to visit others. Far too many others. We'll talk again."

She left. Minutes later, the tears streamed.

Mark was awake and attempting to get out of bed under the watchful eyes of three other patients. Wearing nothing more than a hospital gown and a sling on his repaired arm, his efforts were amusing to his roommates. After a low whistle of approval, he gave up trying to be modest and just stood.

A search of the room showed no clothes. He was bent over, ass high when the door opened, and Iso and her guards entered.

Mark whirled around, flinging the gown open even wider. "Oh my, that's the most interesting greeting I've ever had," Iso said amidst the snickers and laughter.

He stood and pressed the gown down, his face burning. "Ah, I, ah, I apologize, High Chieftess."

"Don't worry about it. It helped brighten a sad day. I see you are ready to move."

"I was, ah, just looking for my clothes."

"Have you been released by the doctor yet?"

"No. I, ah—I haven't seen him yet."

"After such a long night, he's catching some well-deserved sleep." She turned to one of her guards. See if we have anything for Mark to wear and find someone who can check him out."

"Thank you."

"Before you send some of these ladies into swoons, why don't you get back in bed. I'm sure someone will be with you soon."

"Can you tell me anything about my daughter?"

"I just spoke with her. She should be fine. The staff will arrange for you to see her."

"And what about Britta and Mariah?"

She frowned. "Mariah is dead. Britta is in recovery. Her chances are low."

A lump formed in his throat. He tried to swallow it but was incapable of speech.

"She needs all of our prayers now."

She moved around the room, speaking with the other wounded. Mark climbed back in bed and wrestled with his emotions.

General Billings climbed into his jeep. He was not only embarrassed by his failure, but fumed over how he was being treated. He had half a mind to take down this facility and control the vaccine himself. The leaders would have to give him the respect he deserved if they wanted the cure. The problem with that course of action was his lack of men and equipment. He had no doubts about the men's loyalty. He'd handpicked his men and rewarded them for their continued service. Of the one hundred men he'd brought, he was leaving with sixty.

The lack of equipment was also a concern. The men were crammed into fewer vehicles. Martin refused to lend him any of his supplies. That added to the anger—an anger that grew with each mile they traveled. Once the storm reached rage level, he was ready to take action, if only to make him feel back in charge.

"Corporal," he said into the back seat of the jeep. "Are you still able to reach Captain Crandall?"

"Yes, Sir."

"Do it."

The corporal made the connection and handed the headset to the general. "Crandall, what's your situation?"

"Waiting for your orders, Sir."

"Status?"

"Six men. Two vehicles. Low on ammo."

"We're coming your way. Meet us on the same road we came in on. As we get closer, I'll radio the exact location."

"Plans?"

"We're destroying that farm and everyone there. I'm unleashing everything. We're going to have our victory before returning home."

"Excellent. We'll be there."

Billings handed the headset back and began planning. It had been a tactical mistake on his part to eschew the use of the fifty cals opting instead for stealth. Once his men were inside the town, he should have had the fifties rip the town to shreds. In truth, he never thought he'd need them. He wouldn't make that mistake again.

Those people at the farm would pay for how he'd been treated. Then he'd decide whether to return to home base or go freelance. His men would follow. They might do much better on their own than taking orders from a bunch of narrow-minded, desk sitting, fake officers who were nothing more than bureaucrats.

Lincoln drove the pickup truck to the base gate. He was met by armed guards, all with weapons pointed at him and the other occupants.

"I've got a present for the general."

"Who are the men in uniform?" the lieutenant in charge asked.

"Those are the gift. Members of the invading force and perhaps the ones who killed your man."

The lieutenant stiffened, his eyes narrowed, and a fire lit in his eyes. "I'll accompany you." He stepped to the back and climbed over the side wall. He squatted inches from the supposed captain's face and glared at him. "The man you killed was a friend of mine."

Childs stammered. "It wasn't us. It wasn't us. I swear. It was the other group. They're crazy. They kill everyone." The words flew from his mouth as if in one long sentence. The lieutenant didn't blink. He continued his hard stare. "We'll soon know for sure.

Lincoln was let through, and he drove toward the base HQ. The lieutenant jumped down and went inside. Minutes later, he returned with General West and several other officers. "Get them down from there," he said, and the men didn't hesitate. Nor were they gentile with the removal process.

After they'd been taken inside amidst some cries of pain, West approached Lincoln. "Where'd you find them?"

"They were part of an attack on the farmhouse. Those men you were so quick to believe about how we were traitors struck hard last night. They killed a lot of us, but we managed to repel them."

West looked away. "I'm sorry. I can't apologize enough for, well, just my poor judgment. We've been in contact with the other base in Indiana. They told us that column passed by them and used their authority and strong-armed a lot of their limited supplies. The general there has his doubts as to whether they're even attached to any government entity since they refused to give him a way to contact them. I have my doubts, too. We may never know. I'd like to return to the way we were before if that's possible. If you need us for anything, we'll be there. You have my word." He extended his hand.

Lincoln looked at it, tempted to ignore it, but changed his mind. No sense in creating anymore animosity than already existed. He took the hand and shook it with a firm grip. He climbed back in the truck and was about to drive off when the lieutenant called to him. "Hold up." He ran to the driver's window and handed a large radio to him. "This is a satellite radio. It's set to the frequency to reach us. If these bastards show up again, give a call. We'll be there fast."

"We appreciate that, lieutenant. I'll let the community know."

Perhaps things could return to the way they were, but he wasn't about to forget how quickly the general turned his back on them, willing to believe strangers over what he should have known all along.

CHAPTER SIXTY-ONE

Thomas and David Bedrosian sat in a car down the road from where Mark had told them the attacker's base was located. Even as he gave the location, he added his doubt they'd be stupid enough to return there, but it was worth a look.

David kept the binoculars trained on the house. Since taking up his position, he'd seen nothing to indicate the soldiers were there. This was a waste of time, but his father insisted they stick it out, at least until the sun began setting.

For the hundredth time, David lowered the glasses and blew out an annoyed and disapproving breath. For his part, his father ignored it for the ninety-ninth time.

"Dad, how much . . ."

The hand went up again, cutting him off. "Already gave my answer. We've got a few hours to go before I'll think about leaving. You want to be responsible for quitting too soon and have those murderous," he fought back the word bastards, even after all this time unwilling to curse in front of his son. "If they were here and we didn't let everyone know, and they came back and killed someone else, that would be on us. Is that what you want?"

David sighed. "No. But it's obvious no one's there."

"We've waited this long. A few more hours won't make a difference."

Resigned to the boredom, David lifted the glasses again. To his shock, he saw movement. "Dad. Dad, I see something."

Thomas leaned forward, trying to catch sight of whatever it was, but the distance was too great. "What?"

"It's one of those military trucks, like the ones we got. It came around from the back and stopped on the front lawn. There's a second. Men are coming out and climbing in. They're soldiers. They're dressed like the ones who kidnapped us, except the color is brown instead of green."

"That's them."

"Should we go and tell the others?"

Thomas thought about that before saying, "No. Let's see where they go. If they leave the area, we're done with them. But if they stay, we have to get back fast."

They waited. The trucks reached Central Avenue and turned east, away from them. Thomas edged the car forward to allow for a better look down the street. The two trucks drove for nearly a mile before turning south. Once out of view, Thomas drove onto Central and followed.

"You got the street they turned on marked?"

"Yeah, I haven't taken my eyes off it."

Fearing he may lose them, Thomas increased the speed, then slowed as he approached the turn. The trucks were five blocks down the road. They sat and watched until the trucks turned east again before pulling onto the road.

"Where do you think they're going?" David asked, his eyes still focused through the glasses.

"I don't know. Maybe back to that medical facility everyone keeps mentioning. Don't much care as long as they don't come back."

Thomas raced down the road until he reached Airport Highway. The trucks were nowhere to be seen. "Shit," Thomas said, then shot a glance at his son. Oh well, the boy had heard much worse, probably used worse as well.

"We gonna search for them?" David asked, a nervous note in his voice.

Thomas wasn't sure. Had they turned off, or were they waiting in ambush for them? In the end, his need to know where they were won out. He turned but drove with extreme caution. They reached the overpass of US-23, and David aimed the glasses down the long straightaway. "There they are. On the expressway. They're driving up a ramp. Looks like they're turning left."

How much further did he want to take this? If they were driving away, it was best just to let them go. He waited until they cleared the expressway and were out of sight before deciding a little further shouldn't hurt. He hoped.

Thomas reversed and drove down the ramp. An exit later, he drove up the ramp the trucks had taken and turned left on Dussel Road. The road wound quite a bit, never offering a complete long-distance view of what lay ahead. That alone was enough to cause him to go slower. What was down this way? Dussel didn't go that much farther before coming to a residential neighborhood. Maybe that's where they were going to hide.

He kept driving, his angst growing by the mile. At any second, he expected the two trucks to converge on him. They'd be trapped and gunned down, all because he didn't know when to stop. Still, he continued. Dussel Road was coming to the junction with Conant Street. Then their possible destination hit him just as his son said, "Stop, Dad. Stop."

Thomas did, the abruptness throwing them forward in their seats and against the seat belts. "There they are," David pointed. "In that car lot. But they're not alone. There's a bunch of other trucks with them."

Thomas looked where his son pointed. On the left was a new car lot. In the middle was a group of brown trucks.

David gasped. "Oh shit! One of them is pointing at us. Get us out of here, Dad. Go."

Thomas needed no encouragement. He spun the wheel around, bumped over the median, and sped away. An explosion, not more than ten feet behind and to the left, rocked the car, almost tipping it on its side. Both father and son screamed.

The car righted, and Thomas drove as fast as he could. Another explosion struck to the side but in front of them. Thomas swerved the car taking the next intersection and driving down the opposite side of the road.

David spun in his seat and pointed the binoculars down the road. "One of them is coming." Panic restricted his throat, causing the words to come out at a higher pitch.

Thomas drove with the pedal to the floor. He'd never been one for speed. It scared him, but the thought of being caught by these crazed killers frightened him more. The speedometer reached a hundred. He blew past the on-ramp for US-23, moving too fast to make the turn and not willing to slow to do so. He kept driving until he reached a street he recognized and knew it to cut through to Airport Highway. He had to use his advantage of knowing the area better than these invaders to make their escape.

"I-I don't see them anymore. You think they gave up?"

Thomas wanted to reassure his son, but doubted they'd quit. If they did stop pursuing them, that meant they didn't care if they'd been spotted and were moving on anyway. But if they still chased them, it was because they had plans and didn't want their presence known. In that case, they might chase them until they reached safety or until they caught and killed them.

He took the turn too fast and hit the opposite side curb going near eighty. The car lifted from the ground, crashing down on a sidewalk and sideswiping the building. Metal crunched and was torn back from the tire area. If they hadn't hit the building, the car would've flipped. Thomas fought the wheel to keep the car moving. They bounced down the curb and drove back onto the road. He pushed the pedal down, but a loud scraping sound was now evident. That did not bode well for the long-term or their escape. It was only a matter of time before the tire blew.

"We've got to ditch the car."

David responded with fear. "What? No."

"We don't have a choice. I don't want the tire to blow out with them in pursuit. We should get out now and hide before they spot us."

"But they're not behind us anymore."

"I'm not taking that chance." Thomas scanned the road for the best place to hide the car. He found it a short distance later. A series of industrial businesses where other vehicles were still parked. He aimed the car up the driveway and around the rear of the building. He braked hard, keeping the car as close to the rear wall as possible to keep it hidden from the street.

"Let's go. Hurry."

David was out the door before his father, grabbing their equipment and a small bag containing snacks and water. They ran for an open field that someone had planted a while ago with new saplings, their narrow trunks inside plastic piping for protection. Cords had been attached and sunk into the ground with pegs to keep the trees from being blown over until their roots had taken hold enough to do the job on their own.

In the distance, the heavy engine could be heard approaching fast.

"Down," Thomas yelled and gave his son a shove. Thomas dropped while his son fell and rolled. "Don't move."

The truck raced past without hesitating. Thomas felt the air rush from his lungs, only then realizing he'd been holding his breath as if the men in the truck might hear the expulsion. They waited until the truck moved in front of the next long building before crawling further away from the road.

"Dad, the brake lights came on. I think they're stopping."

"Stay low and keep moving. Maybe we can lose them in the trees."

A long narrow band of trees stood a hundred yards away.

"They're moving on, Dad. I think we're safe."

Thomas looked back. They were moving but not at the same speed. Whoever was in the truck knew they'd gone off-road. It was only a matter of time before they doubled back and found the car. Then they'd know his son and him were on foot. Before that happened, Thomas had to get them as far away as possible. Surviving was paramount. If they managed that task, they might find a way to get back to the farmhouse and warn them the enemy was still in the neighborhood and perhaps planning another attack.

CHAPTER SIXTY-TWO

Mark got his release an hour later. He wanted to leave but had to wait for Becca to get her release. That took longer than his patience tolerated. The doctor was hesitant to release her but saw their determination to get home.

"Before you go, Iso would like a private word. She's waiting in my office."

"Before we go," Becca said, "can you give us an update of Britta's condition."

"She's alive. Other than that, all we can do is hope she stays that way."

"There's nothing more you can do?"

He shook his head. "Just pray she's strong enough to pull through."

He led them to his office and opened the door. Iso sat behind her desk alone, her feet propped up and a cup of tea in her hands.

"Ah, thank you for coming. I understand your need to get back home, but I have a request."

"And that is?"

"I'd like to bring Maretha back here to either be treated or buried."

Becca and Mark exchanged looks. "You want us to drive all the way home, put her in a vehicle despite her condition, and drive back?" Mark said.

"No way," Becca said.

"Look, I understand your concern. I'll send a transport vehicle with you, so you won't have to make the trip back."

"She's injured," Becca said. "And she's my sister. She left here for a reason."

"A reason that should have never existed."

"And who's fault is that?"

Iso's face reddened. She glanced away, steeled herself, and said, "Mine. I was wrong. It should have never come to that. But Maretha is one of us. Britta is here and won't be able to travel for a long time if she survives. Maretha will be alone. We can and will look after her." She set the cup down and lowered her feet. "She's my friend, and this is her home. At least let her make the decision. If she refuses and tells my people so, I'll not pursue it."

"And what if she's already dead?"

"Then I'll want her body so she can be laid to rest with the rest of her sisters. Is that really so hard to understand?"

Mark said, "No." But Becca wasn't willing to give it up yet.

"She should be laid to rest where she felt she belonged, and that's with us."

"Becca," Mark said. She glowered at him and wiped at a tear. "This is the right thing to do. Let's hope she's still alive to decide for herself."

"I'll sweeten the deal. I'll give you the list of drugs you asked for, providing there's still enough after this recent attack."

"As long as it's her decision and she's not coerced to make it," Becca said.

"You have my word. Besides, you should know Maretha could never be coerced into doing anything she didn't want to."

Becca nodded.

"Good. I'll have my envoys join you. You can go together."

They had a final consult with the doctor about care for their various wounds, then were allowed to look in on Britta. Her body was sunken as though being drawn into the bed. Lines were attached, and monitors blinked and beeped. She was not awake, but she was alive.

After leaving the hospital, they walked toward the recently rebuilt eastern gate. This time two rows of vehicles had been set across the road. They were escorted to the SUV still parked three blocks away and met there by three women in a larger SUV. Mark slid gingerly into the seat. His back was bandaged where the bullet had cut a path and burned. Becca lowered her seat, and by the time they were five miles down Route Two, she was into a gentle snoring rhythm.

"Has anyone heard from or seen Thomas and his boy?" Lincoln asked at the midday meal.

No one had.

"Problem?" Lynn asked.

"I had them watching the house the attackers used as their base. Since then, I haven't heard from them."

"You think they were discovered?"

"It's a good possibility. I told them to stay out of sight, but it's amateurs versus trained military. They might have been spotted."

Lynn shook her head. "It truly just never ends."

"I don't know what to tell you. It's not like we go looking for trouble. It's all around us."

"Well, *we* might not . . ."

"Hey, stop that. You can blame Mark all you want, but the truth is trouble *is* out there. It'll come for us in one form or another, one way or another. If you think for one moment, Mark would bring this stuff down on us because he's into danger, then your wrong, and I'm disappointed in you. He's a good man who cares about the people in this community. And even though you're no longer interested in him doesn't mean he still doesn't care about you. I might be just an old football player who's taken one too many helmet to helmet collisions, but I think you still care about him, too. I saw the way you bristled when that pretty young thing showed interest in him." She started to comment, but he cut her off. "Your hair all standing on end, claws sticking out like some feline." He smiled. "I half expected to hear hissing."

Lynn blushed then smiled herself as Lincoln laughed loud. "Ha! I knew it."

"Whatever, but we were talking about Thomas and David."

"Yeah. I'm going to take a car and drive over there."

"Is that smart?"

"Never been accused of being smart. I have to know. I'm the one who sent them. They're my responsibility. Damn! Now I know why Mark wants to be free of this job."

"At least take someone with you. And take one of the radios."

He nodded and left. He went to a Chevy Malibu and pretended to look through the back seat until Lynn was no longer watching him. He intended to drive away alone, not wanting to risk or be responsible for anyone else's life. He glanced up over the front seat to see she was still watching him. She didn't trust him to take someone.

He closed the back door. She was calling to someone at the table. Now was his chance. He hopped into the car, started the engine, and had it backing down the gravel driveway in seconds. By the time he shifted into drive, Jin was standing in front of the car. Lincoln braked hard, surprised to see the man.

Jin walked to the passenger's side and rapped on the window. Still in shock, Lincoln pushed the unlock button, and Jin slid in. "Lynn say you need help."

Lincoln looked from him to the window, where he saw Lynn wearing a superior smirk. She gave him a little finger wave, and he drove away.

"What do?" Jin said.

"Checking on some people I sent to scout."

Jin pulled his gun and checked the magazine before seating it again. "I good scout. We find your people."

They came to the area Mark had described. Since he hadn't been there before, he was guessing which house was the enemy base.

"What do?"

"I'm searching for the house the enemy hid in."

"You don't know."

"No."

Jin was out the door before Lincoln could speak. "I find." He darted between two houses and out of sight.

CHAPTER SIXTY-THREE

Unsure of what to do, Lincoln waited in the car and swept the houses with his binoculars. Twenty minutes later, Jin was back. "Find base. All gone."

"No soldiers?"

"No."

"None of our people?"

"No."

Lincoln had no idea what to do next. He decided to drive and search. If he found anything, he hoped he saw them before they saw him. Now he was glad Jin came along, though he wouldn't admit that to Lynn.

He made a circuitous path up and down some of the roads intersecting with Central Avenue, the main east-west through the area. They found no sign of Thomas and David or the enemy. After making a pass of Thomas's house, Lincoln stopped in an old soft-serve ice cream store's parking lot on the corner of King and Airport. He was out of ideas and feared the worst for Thomas and David. They would've reported in if they were still alive.

Jin said, "What do?"

Lincoln shook his head. "I don't know. Any suggestions?"

"Yes. Return home. Your friends gone."

Gone? What did he mean, 'gone?' He wanted to ask him, but the radio crackled. He picked it up and worked the knob to clear the voice. "Co...in...incoln. Mas. Ouble. Help."

What? He pressed the button. "This is Lincoln. Who's this."

The voice on the other end grew excited and louder. "Tho...need..."

"What say?"

"Not sure. I think it's Thomas, and he sounds like he's in trouble. Either he's someplace where the reception is blocked, or he's out of range."

"Drive. I check radio."

Jin snatched the radio from Lincoln's hand. Lincoln stared at the man. Jin motioned with his hand for him to go, and Lincoln did—but which way? He chose left and drove slowly. He pulled his handgun and set it on the console.

"Hello. Hello." Jin said. He held the receiver to his ear and listened. They weren't getting anything now.

"I think we're moving away from him. I'm going to turn around." Before he could make the maneuver, Thomas came through with more clarity. "Lincoln. Being chased. On foot."

"Where?" Lincoln said as if he held the unit. "Ask him."

"Where?" Jin said.

"Be..chased. ...foot. North of Air..."

North of Air? Airport? Did he mean the highway or the actual airport? Lincoln braked. The airport was back the other direction by the Air National Guard base. But if chased there, he'd just go to the base for help.

"Near …clova."

Jin gave him a confused look, which Lincoln returned. Then a loud noise came through clear. The two men looked at each other with wide eyes. "Gunshot," Jin said.

"Yeah, but which way do I go."

"Woods. Monclova Road. Shoot…"

Monclova Road. He knew where that was. He sped up and took the next right at high speed. He lowered the window, listening for gunshots. If they were being fired, they were too far away to hear.

"Hello. Hello. Anyone."

The voice was younger and more panicked.

"David?" Lincoln said again, forgetting he wasn't on speakerphone. He nodded at Jin to speak.

"David."

"Yes. Yes. We need help."

The voice was clearer. They were getting close.

"Where?"

"I-I don't know. My dad's busy shooting at the men chasing us. He told me to keep running and try to connect with someone."

Lincoln was about to speak, but it was a waste of time talking through Jin. He grabbed the radio. "We're coming, but you have to stay calm and tell us where you are."

"Oh, there's a lot of shots now. My dad—please, you have to help my dad."

"We will if you tell me where you are."

"I'm in some woods. We crashed the car and stopped behind these big like warehouses or factories."

"Do you remember any of their names?"

"No. We just ran into these woods behind the buildings. We thought we got away, but they found us and have been hunting us. Please help."

Frustrated at not being able to pinpoint the boy's location, Lincoln sped toward Monclova Road.

"Find some sort of landmark that will guide us to you."

"Ah, okay, but there's nothing but trees."

Lincoln roared. "Look, can you see any roads from where you are?"

Jin smacked his arm and placed a finger to his lips. He leaned his head out the window, then pointed to the right. Lincoln did not know what the man heard but made the turn at the next cross street, one major intersection before Monclova.

He leaned out further to a point Lincoln worried about him falling, then he slinked back in and almost dove across Lincoln's lap. This time Lincoln heard it too. A gunshot. Jin pointed. Ahead to the left.

"David, which way are you facing?'

"Facing? I don't know."

"Look up. Where's the sun?"

"Over my head but a little in front of me."

"West. You're facing west. I want you to go to your right and keep walking until you reach a road. Check that, don't walk— run."

Lincoln kept moving while Jin had his head out the driver's side window. He grunted and motioned with his hand to keep going. They were getting close, but how much time did Thomas have before being overrun and gunned down?

Jin motioned for him to slow, then grabbed the window frame and in one slick move, flung his body out the window. Lincoln braked. Jin used his grip on the frame to twist in midair, land on his feet, and take off running.

Lincoln shifted into park, about to follow when he saw a figure emerge from the trees a quarter mile ahead. He put the car back in drive and sped down the road. He braked hard next to David. The boy ran to the window. "They've got my dad pinned down back there. He needs help."

Lincoln got out. "Get in and back the car up. Then wait in the street for us to come back. Keep the engine running." Lincoln took off running, wondering if David knew how to drive.

As he entered the woods, the gunfire escalated. He guessed that meant Jin had joined the fight. Lincoln didn't want to crash through the woods and announce his presence, so he forced himself to slow.

Ahead he saw motion and ducked. He watched, wondering if it had been his imagination, then he saw it again. A lone man dressed in ACUs was stalking through the woods with great care. The weapon was up and at his eye, ready to fire once he had the target. The target had to be Thomas. The fact the soldier was still trying to flank him meant Thomas might still be alive.

Lincoln dared not move for fear of making a sound and becoming a target. He waited. More gunshots. Some not far away, though Lincoln did not see who was firing. The soldier moved closer, still fifteen yards away. His path took him in and out of Lincoln's line of sight. Then the man froze. He straightened a bit. He'd acquired his target. Noise or not, Lincoln had to move now. He stepped from behind a tree, walked forward, closing the gap, and fired. The first two shots did not score, but the soldier jumped enough to fire his assassin's bullet high.

He dove for the ground, rolled, and returned fire, causing Lincoln to seek the cover of another tree. Before the man could zero in on his location, Lincoln moved. He made noise, but that couldn't be helped. Bullets followed him, but he stopped and ducked before they caught up. However, it had been close. His opponent was good.

Once again, trouble had come, and he'd stepped in its path. Lynn was right about that much. There was no end to the violence. Hiding in the woods trading shots with trained soldiers was not his idea of survival. He was getting too distracted. Time to refocus and end this standoff. He scanned the area looking for his next hiding spot. Finding a fallen elm, he was about to move when a thought occurred to him. His opponent had neither moved nor fired for several seconds. Not a long time, but in a gunfight an eternity. He tried to cipher the reason. The man left. Doubtful. He was injured. Possible. He was so well trained he was waiting for Lincoln to poke his head out so he could remove it from his shoulders. Hmm.

Lincoln removed his light-weight jacket, placed it over a broken branch lying a few inches away, and poked it out from the trunk. Seconds later, gunshots tore through the jacket, snapping the branch and sending both flying from his hand. Ding! Ding! Ding! We have a winner. He was trapped.

While he searched his brain for an idea designed to keep him alive, he became aware of the sudden stillness in the woods.

There hadn't been any other shots fired except those by his opponent. Who won? Who was left alive? He had to know what was going on. The enemy might be sneaking up on him at that moment. The thought made him more nervous than he'd been. A glance at the now air-conditioned jacket was all the reminder he needed of the other man's skill.

He had to know where the shooter was. Lowering his body and steeling his nerves with the thought if the bullet came, he'd never feel it, he did a fast peek. He caught movement but was already ducking back when he realized it and never got off a shot. He swung the other way, gun up. Before he acquired a target, a shot was fired. Too slow. He ducked back and found his entire body was shaking. How was he still alive?

A voice called, "Lincoln."

He knows my name?

"Lincoln. Come."

It was Jin. He peeked around the tree and spotted Jin, motioning for him to come. Fearing it was a trick to draw him out, he ducked back and looked from the other side. Jin was watching him as if curious about what he was doing. He motioned again, and Lincoln stepped reluctantly away from cover. He approached, keeping the gun up.

A body clad in desert camos lay near Jin's feet. He smiled and gave Lincoln a thumbs up. "You make very good, ah, good, ah," he made a throwing motion with both arms then a winding motion with one. It took a moment for Lincoln to understand what Jin was doing. Mimicking Fishing. "I'm good at fishing?"

"Yes. No."

He curled his finger and performed a charade of putting something on his finger. A hook. He was baiting a hook.

"Hook?"

"No."

"Bait?"

"Yes." He pointed at Lincoln. "You make good bait." He pointed a finger at the dead man. "Blam! Blam!"

"Yeah. Great. Thanks."

CHAPTER SIXTY-FOUR

They found Thomas leaning back against a tree. His eyes were closed. Blood covered his shirt and ran in streams down the side of his head. Lincoln was sure he was dead and was already trying to figure out how to tell David when his eyes fluttered open.

"Lincoln." His voice was weak.

Lincoln dropped next to him and examined the damage. He had a bullet wound in the left shoulder and a long gouge the length of his head that bled a lot. Lincoln had nothing to stop the bleeding with, so he took off his shirt and pressed it hard against the wound.

"Where's David?"

"He's fine. Waiting in the car. Let's get you up to back to the farmhouse."

Jin helped him. As they rose, Lincoln caught sight of two other bodies. "They put an arm over each of their shoulders and walked Thomas out of the woods. "How many men were there?"

Jin said, "Four."

"You killed all four?"

Jin shook his head. "Three. He kill one."

"Wow!"

"Not 'wow.' Skill."

"I hear that."

"You no hear?"

"No, I mean—never mind."

They got Thomas back to the car and guided him into the back seat. Upon seeing his father's condition, David screamed, "Dad," and hopped out of the car.

"He's fine. Get in on the other side and keep the shirt pressed to his head."

David hesitated.

Jin said, "Go. Now." His voice left no room for hesitation. David got in and laid his father's head on his lap.

As they drove away, Lincoln scanned the road behind them to ensure they weren't being followed. "What were you guys doing so far away from where I sent you?"

David said, his eyes full of tears ready to spill, "We saw them leave. Dad wanted to see where they went."

"And you got spotted."

"Yeah. But we did see where they went first."

Lincoln looked in the mirror at David's now tear-streaked face. "Where?"

"I'm not sure of where. It was in a car lot. But they met up with an entire army."

"Army?"

"Yeah, there was a ton of them."

Lincoln inhaled and breathed out. "David, this is important. Think. How many vehicles did you see?"

"Ah."

"Close your eyes and pull up the image from your memory."

He did so. "I see, one, two, three, ah, I 'd say eight."

"Okay. Good." He was relieved there were only eight. "Can you guess how many men you saw?"

Again he closed his eyes. "No. Most stayed in the trucks."

"What kind of trucks?"

"They had four like the ones we have. Two big ones with the canvas covers, like tents over the back and two jeeps."

If he figured six per gun-truck that made twenty-four. The troop carriers might have twenty men in each for sixty-four. The jeeps might only have two as they were usually reserved for the officers, but he wanted to figure high, so he made it four per jeep. Seventy-two men. Hopefully, he was off by a good fifty or sixty, but he doubted it.

"Did you see or hear anything else?"

"No." He was crying now. "Is my dad going to be all right?"

"I think so. We'll get him to the doctor and let her do her magic."

They turned up the driveway, and Lincoln honked the horn. It drew several people running toward them. They got out, and he sent one of the boys for a stretcher. They carried Thomas into the hospital where Doc was finishing up her rounds. The look on her face was a clear, *You've got to be kidding me.* They left him in her capable hands.

Lincoln offered a hand to Jin, who looked at it quizzically before accepting it. "Thank you, Jin."

He nodded and walked away. Jin wasn't much for talking, but if you needed someone killed, he was your man.

Lynn came over. "You found him."

"Yeah. He'd run into a bit of trouble." Lincoln looked at her. "You were right. Trouble is never-ending."

"I don't want to be right. Not about that."

"The world was always a violent place to live. With the laws no longer enforced, it's become ten times worse. Still, good people do exist. I have to believe we'll win out in the end."

They stood in silence. Then Lynn said, "Have you had any word from Mark?"

"No, but I haven't been listening either." He had been wondering, however. It had been more than a day since he left. He expected them back last night. He prayed his friend hadn't fallen into another dangerous and deadly situation. He couldn't handle much more. He, no, they all needed a break. With the invading army at their doorstep, it didn't appear a break was in the schedule anytime soon. He knew in his heart, though, that if Mark needed him, he'd be first in the car to go to his aid.

Thinking of the army gave him an idea. He crossed the street, entered the house, and went up to his room. He came back down carrying the satellite radio West had given him. He needed to keep this with him from now on. He exited, stood on the porch, and made the call.

When it was answered, he had no idea of the exchange protocol, so he just said, "Tell the general an army has come into our territory. Last seen north of Airport Highway coming from the east. Ah, out."

"This is a restricted channel . . ."

"Oh, for God's sake. This is Lincoln from the farmhouse community. Give the general the message. He'll want to know.

Over and out." He turned the volume down and crossed back to the farmhouse. If a damn army was coming, he needed to get everyone prepared.

CHAPTER SIXTY-FIVE

Mark drove up the gravel driveway and parked. The vehicle following stopped behind them. Six different guns were aimed at the new SUV until Mark waved them off. Becca was still asleep. He left her and motioned for the women to join him and they walked toward the barn.

The trip had been uneventful. The only bothersome part was the unattended barricade across Route Two. The path was open, and no one was in sight. What had happened to them?

They found Doc and four others inside the operating room, working on a new patient. He strained to get a view at the man's face, praying it wasn't Bobby. Whoever they worked on was shorter than Bobby by almost a whole foot. He was relieved, then swamped by guilt for being happy it was someone other than his son.

He turned to the women. "I'm sorry, but Doc's occupied. Let's go outside and wait 'til she finishes."

"Where is Maretha?" one asked.

"She's in recovery, but we can't go there until we get Doc's permission."

The other woman was more hostile. "We don't need your permission to see one of our sisters." She turned with the obvious intent of searching for her.

Mark raised his voice. "Hey. Our place, our rules. You will wait."

She squared up on Mark. "Or else . . .?"

"I didn't give an or else. I'm asking you to respect our rules and ways like we did when at your place."

He held her gaze another second, then, rather than make it more confrontational than it was, walked away. He wanted to go into recovery and check on Bobby, but if he did, they might get the idea to do the same. If they saw Maretha, confrontation may spur action. Instead, Mark went outside toward the tables where dinner was being prepared. Lincoln and Jin sat at a table with David Bedrosian. He moved toward them.

Lynn and Caryn came out of the farmhouse carrying bowls of prepped veggies. He wanted to talk to Lynn, to explain what was going on, but Lincoln called to him, "Mark, we need to talk."

Those words, spoken in that tone, made Mark want to turn and walk away. He'd rather deal with the female warriors than hear whatever Lincoln was about to tell him. His step faltered, but he kept moving. "Now what?"

"Well, you just came from the hospital, so you know about Thomas."

"That's Thomas they're working on?"

"They shot my dad," David blurted out, and tears fell.

"Who shot your dad?"

"That's what I was about to tell you before you copped that attitude."

"Lincoln, I'm sorry. I, it's—it's just been a long couple of days."

"Ain't been no parade of roses here either."

"Okay. I'm sorry. What's going on?"

"I had Thomas and David watch the house you told me about in case they showed up again. They saw two trucks leave and they followed. They got seen and chased, but before they did, the trucks met up with a much larger group. It sounds like we may be in for another attack."

"Those soldiers followed us and shot my dad," David said.

He wanted to ask Lincoln how bad Thomas was but didn't want to do it in front of his son. "Did you send the scouts out?"

"Of course. I've spread the word to all our people and called West out at the base."

"That's good. He's a little pissed at these guys."

"Yeah. I dropped our prisoners off with him. I think those two are in for a bad time."

"They deserve whatever they get."

"No argument here."

Mark looked around. "I didn't see any of the trucks out."

"No. I've got them off-road for now. I was afraid if they were sitting in the open, the army might have a way to nullify them. They made a huge difference in the previous defense."

"I need to check the number of rounds each has left. We keep going through them like this, and we'll have nothing to use for the next time."

"If we don't use them now, there may not be a next time."

Lynn said, "It'd be nice if next time never came."

They looked her way.

"Agreed," Mark said.

"I hear that," said Lincoln.

"How're Elijah's people doing?"

"Not good. They're a little pissed about being targets. They buried six people earlier today. You see that section of freshly dug ground back by the corner of the woods? That's now a cemetery. Sections of the building have to come down and be rebuilt. They took a lot of damage."

"I'm glad we were able to fight them off. I don't think they anticipated such an organized defense. They didn't send the numbers they could have."

"You think that's what's coming next?"

Mark nodded.

"Another night attack?"

"That'd be my guess, but who knows. Maybe if they feel they have the numbers, they can attack whenever they want. Although I'm not sure how many men they have left. They assaulted the town we went to last night. They almost took it but lost a lot of men in the attempt."

"I wondered where you got the new wounds from," Lincoln said.

"They attacked a town?" Lynn said.

"Yes. A well-fortified town. You see, it's not just us. Insanity is rampant."

"And these men purport to be from the United States Government. Where do they get off assaulting their own people?" Lynn asked.

"If they are a government entity, they have an agenda apart from the people. I have my doubts about who they work for."

"I spoke to West. He feels the same way."

"I can't believe this," Lynn said. "We might as well declare ourselves an independent country as long as we have to fight our own government." She went back inside the house.

"Wouldn't that be something? Our own country. I can see it now, Lincolnland."

"Oh, dear God," Mark said.

"Or maybe New Lincoln."

Mark walked away.

"Wait. I got it. Lincolnia."

"Man, your ego—"

"Ego nothing. I'm a sovereign nation. I'll be a God. Worshiped by all my people. My Lincolniaites. Hey, where you going?"

"To see if you have any more beer."

"Cool. Wait. What? Where're my royal guards. He's robbing the kingdom's treasure."

CHAPTER SIXTY-SIX

While they waited, Mark, Lincoln, Milo, Elijah, and Lynn made plans. The hospital was emptied, and everyone was transported to Jarrod's home. After meeting with Doc and Maretha's transport team, they loaded her up, and Mark drew alternate directions on a map back to the town that kept them from the army's path. After loading Maretha in the car, the team leader handed a bag of medication to Mark. "I was instructed to give this to you only after Maretha was in the vehicle."

Mark accepted the bag but, not trusting his anger, did not comment.

Because of the new threat, the community gathered as before and fed in three seatings. They didn't want to get caught with a majority in one place.

While they ate, Mark filled a canteen with water from the pump, swallowed three pain pills, and removed the sling. The arm's mobility was limited but not enough to prevent him from shooting. He took up his son's position in the hayloft. A distant thrumming sound drew his attention skyward. He aimed the binoculars and spotted a helicopter. That was a good sign. General West was scouting the area. Hopefully, under the new spirit of cooperation, he'd share any sightings with the community.

Word came as the third group was sitting down to eat. Lincoln answered the satellite phone. He listened, asked a question, listened again, and finally signed off. "They're coming. Lots of them. From the east and north. This time they're bringing the big guns."

"Okay, everyone vacate," Mark shouted. "You all have your new assignments and know what to do."

The community responded with quick efficiency, moving to the line of evacuation vehicles along the road. In less than ten minutes, the entire community was gone, as decided by an almost unanimous vote on the suggestion by Elijah. "It's better to lose the buildings rather than lives."

As the caravan began to move, Lynn rolled down her window. "Why aren't you in a car?"

Mark smiled. "I'll be along. I just want to make sure everyone gets away safely."

Her eyes narrowed. She leaned out the window and stared at him as the car picked up speed. "You're not coming, are you?"

He waved as her car moved, she called to him, "Mark, I . . ." Whatever she wanted to say was lost. Once the last car was out of sight, he went into the house to kit up. Jin was there already. The four trucks were the only other defenders left. Mark placed one in the eastern and northern roads, then one off-road to ambush the attack. Once they had caused damage, they were to turn and flee.

Mark and Jin planned to snipe from a distance and keep moving. The intent was to annoy and frustrate before escaping. They may not be able to win the battle, but they sure could even the odds.

As they left the house for their assigned positions, Mark offered a hand. "Good luck, my friend. Hope to see you again."

"Yes. Friend." They shook hands and ran in opposite directions.

Mark climbed into the loft and closed the outer door leaving enough space to shoot through. He tied off a rope and flung it out the rear loft door. He wouldn't have much time once he began shooting before they returned fire. The fifty cals would tear through the wood with little loss of speed. Mark had to make his shots count, then get out to continue the fight from the ground.

The engines announced the approach. Mark focused down the road. Two trucks with the fifties on them came roaring down the road from the east. A troop carrier stopped and unloaded behind them. He swung the glasses north and spotted the same formation there.

The community fifties opened up. Neither opposing gunners gained an advantage. As the first truck passed the ambush spot, the second community vehicle fired, taking out the gunner of the army's second truck. The battle was fierce and loud.

As the soldiers closed in, it became increasingly difficult for the gunners to stay safe. Mark's two trucks gave a last salvo and retreated.

The northern side went much the same. No damage was done until the ambush was sprung, but Mark's team was less experienced and retreated within the first minute of the battle.

Mark aimed and fired, wanting to score as many hits as possible while the fifty cals were still firing. Their distinctive sound helped cover his single shots. He scored two hits before missing. By then, some of the men were returning fire. He targeted one more, dropped him, then bolted for his escape route.

An explosion caused him to stop. He pivoted and went back to the loft door. The farmhouse had taken a hit. A second explosion crumbled the back side. He used the scope to scan the ground, searching for whoever was launching what he assumed were RPGs. He found two men. He lined up a quick shot and missed. Both men launched their grenades, both struck and did damage.

A red veil of rage lowered over his eyes. He sighted and drove a bullet through one man's forehead. The second shooter hesitated as he saw his partner go down. That hesitation was enough for Mark to put him down before he launched his next grenade.

He looked at the farmhouse, and his heart sank. All the months they lived there. All the hard work to make it feel like home. It was all gone in a flash. All for nothing. He turned and ran for the rope, determined to make these men pay.

Climbing was difficult with his wounded shoulder. Unable to hold the rope through the pain he fell the last eight feet. As soon as his feet touched the ground, he was running. He across the newly exposed ground until he entered the cornfield behind the barn and ran east. He intended to come up behind the advancing soldiers. He prayed that once they saw the place was deserted, they'd stop the bombing.

Another explosion went off. He didn't dare take the time to look. He let the sound play over and over in his mind allowing it to fuel the rage within him. Whatever control he wanted to keep was lost. The man he never wanted to be—the man Lynn now thought he was, came out fully exposed and ready not just to kill, but to destroy.

He ran harder until he reached the edge of the stalks. There, he poked his head out. At the intersection, seventy-five yards away, was a jeep. In that jeep, he knew the officers would be watching the battle. The cowards allowed their men to get killed in the name of whatever agenda or master they served, but they'd stay safely away from the conflict, moving their men like pieces on a chessboard.

Mark squared off to the cross street and aimed his gun. Before he got off the shot, the jeep moved forward, stealing his line of sight. With no other targets in sight, he sprinted across the street and over the open ground until he was far enough down the next block to turn south. He came out on the cross street, giving him a straight-on view down to what remained of the house. The jeep was last in line. He gave himself a second to control his breathing, then lined up the shot.

The officer in the passenger seat stood for a better view. He had to be so proud of his plan and his men. They finally won a victory. Of course, it's easy to win when the other team doesn't show up. He squeezed the trigger. The officer pitched forward, hanging over the windshield. The gunner in the back turned his head and whipped the machine gun around. Mark shot him in the face before he got off a shot.

The driver gunned the engine and raced around the trees to the left. The officer's body was tossed to the ground. Mark shot twice more, taking down two soldiers who never saw where their deaths came from. As others began looking around for the sniper, Mark ducked away and reloaded. Once done, he moved again.

At the next intersection, he darted across the street to the south side. Now more than two hundred yards away. He lay down in the grass and took his time. Men were wandering around the street, realizing they had no one to fight. It was time to give them someone.

He lined up his first shot then created a firing sequence. After the first shot, that most likely would change, but it was worth a try. He broke the trigger and sent a red mist into the air as the round bore through the back of a head and out the front. The scope was already moving as the first round was on the way. He managed to score a hit on the second of his three targets but didn't think it was a kill shot. The third man dodged behind a pine tree before Mark ever got aligned on him.

Some of the men located him and fired back. The fifty-caliber machine gun was turned and aimed his way. He chastised himself for not taking the gunner out first. That may yet prove to be a fatal mistake. Now he had no shot. The truck moved forward, and men scrambled to get to safety behind it. Smart. Things would get harder from here out.

He rolled across the road to be as small a target as possible, then got to his feet and ran. Out of sight from the enemy, he had choices to make. He could either go right farther away from the approaching men and set up down the road or run all-out north and try to get around them.

One way would be less work but still may not offer him a shot. The other took longer to accomplish but might allow him to get behind the soldiers and take out a few more before being chased again.

Mark chose straight and hoped he could reach the end of the block before the soldiers reached this road. Two-thirds of the way down, he decided to create a path across leaping roots, large rocks, and discarded trash. As he came to the next road, he slowed. Three soldiers were moving north directly in front of him. Two stopped and looked in his direction. He had approached too fast, making too much noise. They knew he was there somewhere but hadn't pinpointed his location. He had light cover but nothing substantial enough to stop bullets. Before they decided to hose the area down, he pulled the handgun and fired two rounds at each, ignoring the third man who kept moving.

The rounds struck, knocking one down but only staggering the other. The body armor absorbed the impact. He fired again, elevating the barrel with each shot until the last round punched through the man's eye.

The third man loosed a barrage about chest high. Mark was already diving to the ground. The rounds tracked him. He hugged the ground as bullets ripped through the tall grass and weeds inches over his head. Then he heard, click, click, click. The magazine was empty.

He got to one knee, aimed as the man expertly grabbed another mag as the first hit the ground. Mark's shots hit the shoulder, chest, and neck. The man went down. The first man was rising again. Mark ejected his magazine and sprinted across the road as a host of other soldiers sprinted toward him from the south.

CHAPTER SIXTY-SEVEN

___

With little cover, he raced on an angle toward the few trees on the northwest corner of the block. He exchanged the magazine on the run and slid it back into the holster. Shots chased him. Heat on his cheek told him how close a round came to finding him.

He tripped, went down, and tried to roll to his feet only to have his legs bang into something solid. Pain ignited in his shins. He feared a broken bone but forced himself up. The pain stole some of his speed, but he hobbled on.

Behind him, he could hear increased shooting, then excited voices. To his amazement, he reached the trees and collapsed against the biggest trunk. He could barely collect his breath but lifted the rifle and sighted. No one followed. The sight should have brought a breath of relief. Instead, it created more panic. Where were they? He whipped the barrel to the right, then back to the left. Nothing. Then, as if expecting a bullet from behind, he dropped to his knee and whirled around. No one behind him either.

There had to be at least six men in pursuit. Where—there. He spotted movement forty yards south of him. They were trying to flank him. He lined up the shot waiting until they broke into the clear. As the figure emerged, he pressured the trigger then lifted the barrel as Jin came into view.

The near-fatal mistake drove the wind from his lungs. He sank to the ground, drained of strength, energy, and thoughts. He wasn't sure how long he sat, or where his mind went, but shooting brought him back to the moment. Mark rose, scanned for threats, then moved west again.

He reached the northern edge of the cornfield that ran behind the barn. Four rows in he slowed. He now had cover and used it to catch his breath and do a quick reload of the rifle. How much longer could he keep avoiding that final bullet? He'd been lucky so far. If not for Jin, he might have already been put down. That thought had no place in his head. He shook it off and continued to the end of the stalks.

Across the street was the broken and rundown remains of two old wood plank sheds once used to house farm equipment. A long look down the road showed the way clear. He darted across the street and moved behind the sheds. He stayed there for a minute and took a deep drink from the canteen before moving on. He wanted to hit them from the west this time, hoping most of the force had gone east in search of him.

It took nearly fifteen minutes to reach the block behind Lincoln's house. He was in the open but had no line of sight at any target. He lay prone, and alligator crawled, stopping at a short tree stump four feet from the road. From there, he did have a shot. A lot of shots. With the barrel on top of the stump, Mark scanned, searching for a specific target.

He found the man standing halfway down the next block, hands on hips, and gazing up at the new structure on the south side of the street. An officer. He adjusted the focus, trying to see the man's rank. He didn't want to give away his position by shooting a lieutenant or even a captain. He wanted the head honcho, who he figured had to be at least a colonel. A glint off something medal on the collar had Mark straining for clarity. Were they bars or stars? He took his eyes away from the scope, rubbed them gently, wiped them with his sleeve, and tried again.

Mark wondered what the man was looking at, then a stream of white smoke rose into the air giving him the answer. With no one to kill, they had resorted to destroying the new building. Again a feeling of sadness filled him. So much work had gone into the building was all lost because of this asshole.

The anger flooded back, rekindling his energy level and his need to make the man pay. He almost didn't care about his rank, but he took one more look. Stars. By God, he was a general. He lined up the shot, released his breath, but before he could let the round loose, someone yelled and pointed. Gunshots followed, and by the closeness, he knew he'd been seen.

He tried to reacquire the target, but he was no longer in sight. One of the fifty caliber machine guns opened up on him, tearing chunks of bark and wood from the stump. He didn't have much time before the cover was reduced to kindling or a soldier gained an angle at his position. But with the constant stream of rounds being poured into the trunk, moving had little chance of success.

Mark drew his legs in, trying to stay as small a target as possible. The engine sound grew louder, indicating the truck was on the move. He had little chance of surviving the next minute, so he prepared himself for death and to go out, taking at least one more enemy down first. He drew in short rapid breaths preparing to rise and fire.

A bullet hit near his leg. Someone was in position to hit him. Mark was out of time.

A distant roaring sound tickled a faint memory. It grew stronger and sounded like thunder, yet only white clouds filled the sky. Then he spotted a black dot high on the horizon. Recognition bloomed, hope rekindled, and he smiled as the first bullet tore into his leg.

Though the pain was intense, it could not wipe the smile from his face. The F-15 fighter jet dove and unleashed a deadly storm of 20 mm rounds from the internal M61 Vulcan

Gatling gun in the right wing. The rounds chewed up the concrete road marching toward the enemy.

Mark could not help but peek over the stump to witness the destructive force as it tore through bodies, ripped through the first deuce and a half truck, exploding it, and advanced down the road. It reached the end of its run and rose with such beauty as to cause tears of joy to mingle with those of pain. It soared high, banked, and came around for a second run.

Mark was all but forgotten with the more dangerous threat overhead and descending again. He glanced down the street. Two of the remaining trucks advanced, their machine guns already barking at the fighter jet.

Mark had to help the pilot. Neither General West nor Mark could afford to have that plane downed. He didn't have a shot at the first gunner, but the driver of the second truck had the intelligence to move, so both vehicles could not be taken out at the same time. However, that caused the gunner to swivel positions exposing him to a side shot. Mark took it and one less gunner fired at the jet.

The fighter's second pass took out the remaining truck and a jeep, scattering the men in all directions. However, a thin black trail of smoke rose from one of the wings. As it shot skyward and banked, Mark knew that was the last pass. However, it gave him the chance to run for cover.

While everyone was distracted, Mark hobbled for the backyard of Lincoln's house. He didn't want to get trapped inside, but it offered the best cover and possibly some additional targets. Stopping behind the garage, he worked his way to the side and peered around. The backyard was clear, and he saw no one between the houses. He hopped the fence and tried the side door. Locked. Of course, it'd be locked. That's where Lincoln hid his booze.

The lack of gunfire allowed the screams of the wounded and dying to fill the air. He moved toward the house and up the back stairs. He could hear approaching engines. It sounded like several, but he couldn't pinpoint the direction.

The back door was locked, too. He thought about kicking it in, but his leg wouldn't cooperate and the noise would alert the enemy of his location. He hopped off the porch and walked to the corner of the house. From there, he could see more of the destruction of the farmhouse. The entire rear was gone.

Two men came into view. He ducked.

"General, a convoy of trucks is coming."

"Are they General Martin's men?"

"I don't think so, sir."

"We need to retreat. Tell the men."

"Sir, what about the wounded?"

"Leave them."

"But sir..."

"That's an order, Lieutenant. You want to be here when that other army arrives? Let them care for the wounded."

Mark watched as the general walked away. No way was he allowing this man to escape. He hopped the fence landing on his good leg and hopped one footed along the side of the house. Once he reached the front, he scanned the area. Bodies and body parts littered the blood-stained road. It was a sickening sight.

CHAPTER SIXTY-EIGHT

The general walked along the side of the farmhouse and around the back. Mark glanced right. The lieutenant was squatted next to a wounded man whose arm was hanging by skin and tendons. The man was clinging to the lieutenant's arm, begging for help. Then he gulped air, stiffened, and fell back. The lieutenant's body racked with a sob.

Mark looked around. No one else was near. He walked across the road keeping his eyes on the lieutenant. He didn't want to kill the man if it could be avoided. He reached the side of the house and skip-ran to the rear. The general was walking toward the line of pine trees. As he pushed through the overlapping branches, Mark broke into a hobbled run. He reached the same spot and pushed through after him. On the other side, the general was climbing into a jeep.

The carnage on the road was beyond horror movie bloody. Men were walking, hobbling, or jogging eastward. There weren't many of them in view. The driver had blood on one sleeve and a furrow along the side of his head. The general didn't seem to notice. "Get us out of here," he said. The driver started the engine.

Mark dropped his rifle and hustled toward the jeep. As the vehicle started forward, Mark snagged the general by the shirt collar and ripped him from the seat. Shocked, the driver braked and gaped at the sudden appearance of Mark. He held a gun to the general's head. "Drive away, son. You don't have to pay the price for this man's stupidity."

The soldier looked at the general, then at Mark. His tongue flicked across his lips.

"Help me, Soldier. Do your duty."

"Do you want to die for this man?"

That made the decision easy. He shook his head and pushed the pedal down.

"Come back here, you coward."

Mark clubbed him on the head, producing a cry of pain and a bleeding slice in the scalp. The sound of engines grew louder. He feared the general's men might reach him before Mark got his revenge. He slammed the barrel into the general's head and cocked the hammer.

"Mark," a voice shouted. "Don't shoot him, Mark."

He looked up to see General West standing on the front seat of an approaching jeep, holding on to the windshield. He waved his hand sideways as a signal to stop. He said something to the driver, and the jeep sped up. Behind him was a line of trucks filled with men from the base. The trucks stopped, and the men offloaded, spreading out to cover the area.

Mark looked back at his prey. No, this man had to die.

"Mark, I need him alive."

Alive? He looked up as the jeep braked ten feet away. West leaned forward. "Mark, listen to me. I promise he will pay for what he's done, but I need him alive."

"You see what he's done? Do you know the misery and the lives that he's cost?"

"Yes. I do. But this is a military matter. He'll be court marshaled and punished, but it has to be done our way. On top of that, he has valuable information I need. That information may be important to all of us. I may be able to get the answers we all want. To know what's going on and to understand our place in the rebirth and growth of the country.

He stepped down from the jeep and approached with hands up. "Mark, I know you're angry. I don't blame you. But just this once, let me deal with him."

"Is that an order, General?" Mark barked.

"No. Not an order. It's a request. Please. We came to your aid as you have done for us. Let me take him as a thank you."

An internal battle raged within his core. Revenge or mercy. That's what it came down to. He wanted revenge in the worst way. He wanted to make this man pay for the damage he did. For the lives he stole. He had to pay for all of it.

West came closer, his voice softened. "Will one more life make a difference? Think about what we might learn."

"What if he refuses to talk?"

"Oh, he'll talk. I promise I will deal with him."

As much as he wanted to hold on to the fury, he felt it ebbing away. He shoved the man down and backed away. West said, "General, you're under arrest." He motioned, and several of his men hoisted the man to his feet and marched him to a truck.

Mark dropped to the ground and sat with his head down. Jin emerged from somewhere and sat next to him. Blood dripped from several places. His face was smeared with blood and dirt. Mark wondered if the blood was his or one of his prey's. The man turned his face skyward as if soaking in the sun. He smiled. "Good fun, huh?"

While West's men rounded up stragglers and carted off the wounded to the base, Mark and Jin moved to the tables. Surprisingly none of them were damaged in the assault. West joined them. "Hell of a thing to witness. I'm not sure which revolts me more, American fighting American or soldiers in service to the same country killing each other."

"It's all sick," Mark said.

"Yes. I'm glad you evacuated everyone else."

Mark nodded. "I'll wait until the bodies are removed before sending for them. They've seen enough carnage to last a lifetime."

"I'm having my men load the bodies." A lieutenant approached, leaned forward, and whispered into West's ear. He nodded. "Thank you." He mulled over whatever he'd been told. "Do you have any idea how many men attacked?"

"No. Fifty to sixty." He shrugged. "They came from different directions, so no way of knowing."

"We found twenty-seven bodies. Since none of your people were here, it must be all theirs. Most of them were on the road on the other side of the pine trees."

"That must be because of the strafing run your F-15 made. Thanks for that, by the way. It made a huge difference."

"It was a tough decision—risking the plane and using the fuel, but it was to save lives, so it was worth the flight. Besides, we've been planning on a test flight for weeks. This served multiple purposes."

"Well, I'm glad I could arrange this little war so you could run your test."

West ignored the sarcasm.

"Who was the pilot?"

"Tara. We don't have anyone else with any experience."

"Thank you for riding to the rescue, General."

"No problem. You'd have done the same for us." They shook hands, and a few minutes later, he was driving away.

Mark walked to the road to survey the damage. The new building was nothing more than a few blackened uprights. The kitchen and rear bedrooms of the house were ruins. It was lucky more damage hadn't been done or that it wasn't set ablaze.

The bodies had been removed, but so too was anything of use. Mark should have paid attention to what West's men were taking. With all the rounds spent to defend this property, they could use a restock. Maybe he could ask for some of it back.

So, what did they do now? Move to a new location or rebuild? It was no longer his decision. It was time for others to step up and decide what was best for the community. His only concern was making sure they stayed together. Buildings could be replaced, but people, especially these people, were too valuable to lose.

CHAPTER SIXTY-NINE

Two days later

General Martin sat in the passenger seat of the second jeep. The first jeep had a large white sheet attached to a pole strapped to the windshield. The sheet flapped and snapped as the jeep moved. Bringing up the rear was a troop carrier with six men. Martin waved the flag of truce but wasn't sure how well he'd be received considering recent events, so the men were just in case.

He couldn't fault the women if they refused to speak with him, but he wanted the air cleared and the situation explained, so his men didn't have to be looking over their shoulders every time they left the base. Not that he feared the women or any outcome that may result from this debacle, but he wanted their leaders to know his men weren't to blame. He hoped to negotiate another peaceful arrangement where neither party bothered the other on their daily rounds and routines.

They may not forgive what happened to their home, but peace was best for both of them. And if not, well, he had more confidence in his men putting down an insurrection than Billings men. After all, they were just women.

They slowed as they came within shooting range of the town. Martin hadn't been here in several months when they were first scouting up the base and wanted to know the lay of the land and who resided here. He spoke to the tall, good-looking blonde woman then, though her unusual name escaped him. They came to an easy agreement. One he hoped to be able to expand on by visiting the lovely leader from time to time for other more intimate negotiations. But that had never happened. He regretted that now. Was she still in charge? Hell, was she still alive?

The driver said, "Sir, we have a lot of guns pointed at us."

"Keep calm. We don't want to spook or provoke them."

A warning shot was fired ten feet in front of the first jeep. It came to a sudden stop, as did Martin's jeep.

The corporal in the passenger seat of the first truck stood to deliver his message. Martin thought it prudent to have someone else initiate contact in case bullets started flying.

"We-we come in peace," the man's voice cracked. Martin couldn't blame him, but better the corporal than Martin. "Under a flag of truce. We'd like to speak to your leader about, about the stuff that happened."

"You mean like attacking us?"

"That wasn't us."

"It wasn't? They were all wearing uniforms like yours. They came from your base."

"But they weren't us. I mean, they're in the same army, but they're outsiders. We didn't know what they were going to do. Anyway, we'd like a chance to explain to your leader or leaders whatever the case."

"Wait there. If we see anyone get out of their vehicles, we will shoot."

"Understood." The man sat down.

Martin waited impatiently. He was doing them a favor by being here to bury the hatchet. How dare they make him wait.

He wouldn't be there at all if he hadn't been ordered to do so by his leaders. After reporting the mixed results of Ohtanda's vaccine to his boss, who resided somewhere in Colorado, he was ordered to make peace with the women. More than half of the people they brought into the facility almost a week ago were either sick or dying. Ohtanda insisted she was close to having the formula perfect but said she needed more test subjects. She made her plea to leadership, who in turn ordered him to collect those test subjects, and here he was, making nice with the locals.

The other interesting part of that conference was learning General Billings never showed up at the Colorado facility. Had he gone rogue or been waylaid by a superior force somewhere along the road? Or perhaps his men killed the prick and went out on their own. Not that he cared what happened to the man, but if he was dead, that left an opening at the main base. If he procured the test subjects and Ohtanda got her damn vaccine perfected, he might be able to use that success to his advantage.

The wait stretched on, and Martin was about to give the order to turn around when a blonde-haired woman stepped up onto the barricade. He looked closer, then snapped his fingers at the driver who handed him binoculars. He scanned the woman from head to toe. Yes. It was her. He tossed the glasses back at the driver without looking.

"Who speaks for you?"

Without hesitation, Martin stood and waved. The sight of the woman was encouraging. "May I approach?"

The woman mulled the request over. Under his breath, Martin said, "Come on, you bitch. Stop making me wait. Stop treating me like someone of no importance, like you."

"What is your name?"

"I'm General Martin."

"Well, General Martin, you may enter, but just the two jeeps and you. The truck stays where it is."

Martin didn't care for that. He might be trapped inside with no support. Sure, it would be nice to have a team outside to break him out if the situation called for it, but he could be dead by the time the issue was resolved.

An SUV was slid back from the barricade exposing the town's interior. Did he take a chance they wouldn't capture and use him as a hostage? The idea bothered him but not as much as leaving his fate to Dr. Ohtanda. Would the bitch even bother negotiating for him? He doubted it.

The woman called out. "Come on, General. I promise you'll be safe." She flashed a beautiful smile and waved him forward.

It was the smile that cinched it. Like a siren's call, he sat and ordered the driver forward. His eyes never left the woman's face. The jeep passed through the barricade of vehicles, and the SUV was driven back in place.

The woman walked to the side of the jeep. The smile widened as she approached. This might go better than expected.

"Are you the man in charge?" He slid out of the jeep and raised his arm to accept her proffered hand.

He liked how she said that. "Yes. I am."

As soon as their skin touched, he felt a rush of adrenaline, but as the smile vanished into an evil sneer, he realized the sensation was of his blood dripping from the knifepoint that pricked his neck.

"Not anymore, you're not."

Forty minutes later, the jeeps drove back out. Martin sat in the passenger seat as before but this time, less happy than when he arrived. A grenade had been secured to his shirt collar at the back of his neck. Attached to the pin was a string, and holding the string was a woman on the floor of the rear seat.

The woman driver now wore the previous driver's uniform. She'd had her hair buzzed and wore black-rimmed sunglasses to help hide her face. Iso and one of her guards rode in the back seat playing the part of guests.

Two women in uniforms rode in the first jeep with two more honored guests in the back. They drove past the truck, now with three women in the front seat and more than twenty warriors crammed under the canvas top. Behind them rode one of the two armored vehicles with the big machine gun they confiscated during a previous assault. Though no one stood at the gun to make it less threatening, two women waited to spring to action, and six more were inside.

They drove slowly as if out for a joy ride with not a care in the world. Iso leaned her head back and stared at the sky. This was an extreme gamble on her part. The council had already been planning a retaliatory strike on the facility when the pompous general showed up at the gate. It had been a while since the entire town council had been unified in anything. To her surprise, when she first brought up the notion, it was members of the council who began the discussion and subsequent plans. This was her plan. It needed to work. Too many lives depended on her success.

Only a handful of guards remained in town, both protecting their homes as well as keeping the soldiers under guard. The hospital was still full of wounded, some who might not recover. It was there the idea for the assault was given birth.

With the return of Maretha and the slow but steady recovery of Britta, Iso went for a visit to hear them discussing how to deal with the attack. They hushed when Iso entered, but she encouraged them to continue. Over the next hour, the idea took root, and she brought it to the council. Her one regret was that neither co-founders of the attack were in a condition to join.

The fenced compound came into view on the right. They passed by a guard jeep sitting inside the fence near the corner of the grounds. "Wave at the man, general," Iso said.

He did so. The guard nodded back. Iso noticed only one man sat in the jeep where two used to be. One of her scouts reported seeing a convoy leave the facility the day after the attack. Were they short on men?

The lead jeep pulled to the side to allow the general's jeep to enter first. The general winced as the woman on the floor not only pulled the string tight but stuck the point of her knife into his side.

"Stay calm, and no one has to die," Iso said. "What do you think you can accomplish here. You'll be trapped inside with nowhere to go."

"Let me worry about that. If all goes well, we'll be gone before you know it. See to it we get inside, or you'll be the first to die."

They neared the gate. Four armed men stood inside. In front of them was an officer who watched them approach. To either side of the gate were jeeps with mounted machine guns. Counting drivers, nine men stood between them and entry.

The gate rolled back, and for an instant, Iso thought entry was going to be easy, then the gate stopped moving, leaving enough space for the officer to exit and approach.

"Why is he coming out alone?" Iso asked.

"It's protocol. No one is allowed free entry without being checked first. Not even me. It protects against exactly what you're attempting to pull off."

The officer halted ten feet away and saluted. "General, is everything all right?"

Martin hesitated. The officer's eyes flicked to the two women seated in the back. "Yes, Captain. Let us in."

"Who are the people in the back seat, sir?"

"Ah, my guests."

"Yes, we're the general's special guests," Iso said, using air quotes and laughing. She smiled and blew the captain a kiss. "Maybe you can join us, captain." He backed away, blushing, and motioned for the gate to be opened. The two jeeps entered, then the truck, but the armored truck stopped midway through the gate, preventing it from closing, and turned the gun on one of the jeeps.

Iso hopped from the jeep and, as the captain walked toward the guard hut, wrapped an arm around his neck and placed a gun to his head.

Women hopped down from the truck and aimed weapons at the guards. Iso's driver got out and walked behind the driver of the second jeep, placing her gun in his ear. "Step away from the gun, or your driver dies."

No one knew what to do. The nervous soldiers looked from the captain to the general for orders. A tug on the grenade pin had the general ordering his men to stand down.

In seconds her team had control of the gate. Iso stood, "No one has to die here. I need you to get into the truck and sit down. One man resisted, throwing a punch that caught the woman nearest him in the side of the head. The warrior on the other side jammed her knife into his throat. Other's started to move until they saw the body of their comrade fall.

"No one has to die," Iso repeated, "but if you choose death, we'll be happy to oblige."

Through eyes that ranged from hateful to frightened, the men watched as their weapons were collected. They were marched to the truck and loaded in. Iso motioned to the now vacant guard jeeps, and two of her warriors clad in army uniforms climbed in and drove toward the front two corners of the compound.

The left side went smoothly, and the guard was taken and bound. The right side ended in a fight. The guard dove out of the jeep, landing on top of the warrior. His fist could be seen lifting and pounding down, once, twice, and on the third punch, the second warrior drove her knife into the back of the man repeatedly.

His body was lifted and deposited in the back seat, and the two jeeps drove back.

With the front of the facility now under her control, Iso had the gate closed and left two women to guard it. They drove around the building to the right and down the ramp leading to the loading dock. According to Britta and Maretha, it was the only way inside.

They entered the massive dock area and unloaded. Iso sent warriors to the entry doors to keep them clear, then ordered the captured men out of the truck. They were told to sit and take off their boots. Two women collected them and tossed them in a dumpster. The men were then told to lay down on their stomachs. That command met with resistance until Iso whistled for their attention.

"If I was going to kill you, I would have done so out there and saved all of this trouble. We're not like you. We don't kill for enjoyment. So either lay down with your hands interlocked behind your head, or I'll instruct my warriors to start slashing throats."

Once they complied, Iso told three of her team to watch them and led the remaining force into the building. She took the general along with her.

"You realize there are cameras all over this building and men watching the monitors. By now, they are sending an army of men to intercept you."

"They will need an army to do so, but I have a feeling you no longer have an army here to deal with us."

The general stammered a reply that convinced Iso further that she was correct. Following maps drawn from memory by Britta and Maretha, they marched through the bright white corridors without meeting any resistance. Both the front and rear guard posts, which had once been information desks when it was a hospital, were vacant.

They found a half dozen workers in white coats but no military and no upper-level administrators, either military or medical. When the main level had been swept, Iso smiled. The first phase of their plan was done. She knew about the lower levels but was not going to worry about them. She knew one of the places they could come up from but to do so, they'd have to pass by her guards. Eventually, as food and water ran out, they'd come up.

"Ladies, welcome to our new home."

The remainder of the day was used to pack and move the town. Once that was accomplished, she had the soldiers questioned, and all but two of them released. The two men agreed to stay on doing general maintenance work. The general and the remaining men were released, their boots tossed over the fence. They were given a day's worth of provisions and knives but no other weapons. In all, twenty-two men walked away, none of them stayed with the general.

CHAPTER SEVENTY

On the same night the community voted to stay and rebuild, they also voted in a council. Six of Elijah's people decided they'd had enough and set out on their own. Though the vote to rebuild had not been unanimous, those who lost agreed to stay and do their part, though it was more of a wait and see decision.

The new council consisted of Elijah, Caryn, Lynn, Milo, Maggie, Caleb, and Lincoln. Lincoln grumbled about his stupidity for taking on the job, but it was apparent to Mark, it was what he wanted to do.

The first order of business was to establish a committee to plan the rebuild. With the loss of the new building and the use of most of the house, the plan was ambitious. It also meant a lot of people would be crammed together for the time being.

Milo took charge, and by early morning of the second day after the attack, work commenced. They were pushing into mid-October. Time was not on their side. But with full community support, the work showed fast progress.

Mark and Jarrod took on the job of collecting building materials. It took many trips and several lumberyards and construction sites to find the amount of materials needed. The days were long and the work hard, but after five days of non-stop effort, both buildings took shape.

Each morning at breakfast, Milo reported on the progress and assigned jobs. He poured a brick edge around both the new building and the addition to the house. "Brick will give added support to the structures," he said. "Sure, it'll be more work, but it'll be worth it. Besides, what else you going to do?"

He was booed for adding work, but no one refused to do it. Once both the new building and the addition to the house were buttoned up, Milo set about pouring cement. His first job was the hospital floors. Once the floors hardened, a team went to work constructing real walls doing away with the hanging sheets.

Milo's next project was to pour a new foundation on the ground the corn was cleared from. It was a little smaller than the first new building but should serve to house another twenty people. That project would only be started once everything else was completed. If the weather turned bad, it would wait until spring.

His last task was to pour a foundation for a wall around both camps. The council voted, if they were staying and putting the time into rebuilding, the camps needed to be fortified.

Mark stared out the side window as Jarrod drove. They had stripped most of the materials from two lumber yards and were now returning from one an hour away. It was their last trip of the day. Mark was tired. His body still ached from the assortment of bruises, and his shoulder still gave him pain, especially on the colder days.

It was more than two weeks since the attack. A cautious sense of normalcy had returned. The daily routines and community goals had done a lot to restore the community. Mark was glad to be out of the hot seat and enjoyed his role as worker bee. Yet, the events of the past month left him unsettled. He was more withdrawn and spent a lot of time alone.

When he did converse with others or join in after work activities, he spent time with Lynn. Though they weren't back together, at least they were speaking.

Movement to the right caught his attention. He stiffened, then a smile crossed his face. "Jarrod, look."

Jarrod, who had been humming the same country song for almost as long as they'd been driving, said, "Huh! What?" Then his eyes widened, and his face wrinkled with delight. Off the road, in an open field, was a small herd of deer.

"Everyone's been working hard. I think it's time for a celebration."

"Oh, hell yeah."

He pulled the flatbed to the side of the road. Mark jumped down, rifle in hand, and targeted. Jarrod held his shotgun, but from this distance, it had little chance of hitting anything. Mark fired. A large doe fell. It tried to rise but was unable to. As the echo of the report reached the deer, their heads lifted, and they bolted. Mark fired again, taking down another doe. A third shot missed as the deer reached the woods at the back end of the field.

"Nice shooting," Jarrod said.

They hiked down a slope and across the field. The first deer was still alive. Mark hated that the animal was in pain. He pulled his knife to end the misery, but Jarrod said, "I'll take this one. You go get the other."

Mark approached the second deer. It did not move. He squatted. It was dead. He set the knife to its neck, but before he could begin field dressing the animal, a sound from the woods drew his attention. He looked up to see a man with a hunting rifle aimed at him.

"I'll be taking that meat."

Mark began to speak, but the shot hit him in the chest, lifted him off his feet, and dropped him to the ground. Shock took hold, followed by pain. He tried to rise, but, like the deer, he was unable. In the distance, as if in a dream, he heard a shotgun fire. Was that one shot with an echo, or had it shot multiple times. He didn't know. No longer cared.

Facial images danced before him. Bobby, who had just started to walk after the long recovery. Becca, who had been through so much and always came out stronger. Lincoln, his hand extending toward him with yet another warm can of beer. Britta, he prayed she was alive. Lynn, they had just started talking again, and he had cautious hope for the future.

The images dimmed. Then a brighter light appeared and haloed within it was his wife, Sandra, and his son, Ben. They looked so happy. It brought joy and warmth to him. He walked toward them. Sandra had tears of happiness streaming down her face. Ben jumped up and down, clapping with excitement.

Then the light faded, no not faded. It was blocked by a large dark shape. "Mark. Oh, God. Mark. Stay with me, brother. Stay with me."

Jarrod hovered over him. Mark wanted to tell him it was all right. That he was fine and for once felt at peace. He tried to peer around the man, to see Sandra and Ben, but his bulk prevented it.

He had a sudden feeling of weightlessness, like he was floating. A sharp pain made him gasp. Sandra and Ben were gone. Jarrod was carrying him. He tried to speak—to tell Jarrod to let him go, but blood came out instead. The pain was too intense. He was tired of the pain. He wanted to feel the peace he'd felt moments before. To be with Sandra and Ben.

Something firm pressed against his back. Loud bangs followed, then movement. After a few moments, the pain began to subside, and the bright light returned. As Sandra and Ben came back into view, he smiled. It was time.

ABOUT THE AUTHOR

Ray Wenck taught elementary school for 35 years. He was also the chef/owner of DeSimone's Italian restaurant for more than 25 years. After retiring, he became a lead cook for Hollywood Casinos and then the kitchen manager for the Toledo Mud Hens AAA baseball team. Now he spends most of his time writing, doing book tours, and meeting old and new fans and friends around the country.

Ray is the author of thirty-eight novels, including the Top 20 post-apocalyptic, Random Survival series, the paranormal thriller, Ghost of a Chance, the mystery/suspense Danny Roth series, and the ever-popular choose your own adventure, Pick-A-Path: Apocalypse. A list of his other novels can be viewed at raywenck.com.

His hobbies include reading, hiking, cooking, baseball, and playing the harmonica with any band brave enough to allow him to sit in.

You can find his books on all of your other favorite online booksellers.

You can reach Ray or sign up for his newsletter at

raywenck.com or authorraywenck on Facebook

Other Titles

Random Survival Series

Random Survival

The Long Search For Home

The Endless Struggle

A Journey to Normal

Then There'll Be None

In Defense of Home

Danny Roth Series

Teammates

Teamwork

Home Team

Stealing Home

Group Therapy

Double Play

Playing Through Errors

The Dead Series

Tower of the Dead

Island of the Dead

Escaping the Dead

Pick-A-Path Series

Pick-A-Path: Apocalypse 1

Pick-A-Path: Apocalypse 2

Pick-A-Path: Apocalypse 3

Stand Alone Titles

Warriors of the Court

Live to Die Again

The Eliminator

Twins in Time

Ghost of a Chance

Mischief Magic

Reclamation

Short Stories

The Con   Short Stop-A Danny Roth short   Super Me

Super Me, Too

Co-authored with Jason J. Nugent

Escape: The Seam Travelers Book 1

Capture: The Seam Travelers Book 2

Conquest: The Seam Travelers Book 3

The Historian Series

The Historian: Life Before and After

The Historian: The Wilds

The Historian: Invasion

Bridgett Conroy Series

A Second Chance at Death

Traveling Trouble

Ray Wenck

Made in the USA
Coppell, TX
01 July 2022

79466609R00227